BIG SWAMP

Kelly Dean Jolley

OYSTERVILLE, WA

BIG SWAMP

ISBN: 978-1-68131-068-8

This is a work of fiction. Names, characters, places, and incidents are products of the author's imagination or are used fictitiously. Any resemblance to actual events or persons, living or dead, is entirely coincidental.

Cover design by Janet B. Taylor
Front cover image: *Southern Discomfort*, a drawing by Syd Edwards © 2022
Edited by Dee Gott and Ellen Pickels
Book layout and design by Ellen Pickels

Published in the United States of America.

For Tilly, with thanks

CONTENTS

Chapter 1: New Client 7

Chapter 2: Soft Boiled 14

Chapter 3: Coffee, Tea, and Decency 24

Chapter 4: Noble Hall 36

Chapter 5: Clubbable 52

Chapter 6: Courthouse 64

Chapter 7: Pyne Park 76

Chapter 8: Confessional 86

Chapter 9: Hymn, Her, and Fireflies 97

Chapter 10: Risk 108

Chapter 11: Far from the Wicked 119

Chapter 12: Baby, Banana Bread, and a Briefcase 130

Chapter 13: Windfalling 148

Chapter 14: Entrances and Exits 160

Chapter 15: Surrounded 170

Chapter 16: Warnings, Jokes, and Considerations 181

Chapter 17: Wave 192

Chapter 18: Dust 205

Chapter 19: Disinter 217

Chapter 20: Disburden 227

Chapter 21: Inextricable Difficulties 237

Chapter 22: Slow Show 249

Chapter 23: Twine Backward 258

Chapter 24: Trophies 268

Chapter 25: Con Games 279

Chapter 26: Intercession 289

About the Author 297

A good man, struggling in his darkness,
will always be aware of the true course.

— Goethe, *Faust*

CHAPTER 1: *New Client*

Not all detectives are the same—some play bad cop, some are awkward, some are funny.

— Juliette Lewis

The sun—overseer.

I melt into my car, start it, and twist the AC knob so eagerly that I worry it will wrench off in my hand.

It doesn't.

Instead, cooling air fans out of the vents. It's not enough. Not enough cold. The black dashboard of my car has soaked leisurely, parked, sunbathing in the infernal Alabama midday. The dashboard's now hot enough to be the scene of eternal punishment.

I reach cautiously for the steering wheel, knowing from painful experience how hot it might be. I'm right. More *searing* wheel than steering wheel. I steer as if the wheel's a stovetop red eye, the fingers of each hand barely touching it—never lingering.

I'm in a shitty mood, and not just because of the beating sun.

I'd been eating my lunch in Ed's Diner, a place I go for three reasons. One, the AC chills the place like a morgue, and there are days in the Alabama summer when you would rather die than sweat. Two, because the food is tasty and a country mile from *haute cuisine*—call it *low* cuisine—kinda like the contrast between high church and low church. Three, the waitress, Ruth, is one of those women you find now and then in Alabama—small of frame but large of heart with enough figure to reveal she's a woman but not so much as to insist on it.

When I'm at Ed's, I do my best to study my food and not Ruth, even though she's made it clear she likes to be studied by me. I should do something about that, I know, but I can't seem to bring myself to action, and so, partly because I'm a gentleman and partly because I'm a coward and partly *just because,* I keep my eyes to myself. Mostly. Speaking of eyes, Ruth's are entrancing—slightly tilted and exotic (think Middle-Earth, not just another country)—and deep. You know how some people, women especially, have eyes that you just bounce off of? Not Ruth. Although I should say, I get it. About some women's eyes, too many men are asshats. I'd shut myself off too.

Sorry, I was in the middle of a list, wasn't I? I spiral sometimes: follow thoughts further than I should, forget where I'm going. So anyway, Ruth's the third reason. The fourth reason is that Ed's Diner is near my sister's office. Helen's a doctor—general practice—and she gets so lost in work that she forgets to eat. I sometimes drag her from the office to a booth in Ed's and feed her. Another thing I like about Ruth is that she likes my sister and my sister likes her.

So, as I was saying, I'd been eating my lunch without Helen—she had patients—when my phone buzzed. I answered, still chewing on a French fry.

"Ford?"

"Yeah," I mumbled in French-fried near-English, "It'sh me."

I don't normally answer the phone with my mouth full. But I saw that it was my assistant, Talbot Norton, calling and...well...let's just say we don't always bring out the best in each other.

"You're at Ed's," Talbot concluded from the sound of my answer.

"Listen, we just got a case. And when I say a case, I mean a *case*. Real Chandler stuff. A tall blonde slinked—*slank? slunk?*—into the office a few minutes ago... No, not *a* tall blonde—*the* tall blonde. And maybe *slinked* isn't the right word. Anyway, she's the tall blonde to end all tall blondes—*end* 'em—one of the shock troops in some mighty Amazonian army, and I mean *shock*—"

"Talbot!" I said in a tone that capped him mid-gush. Talbot's enthusiasm for women is matched only by his failure with them. The failure's no mystery. I said I was part gentleman, part coward. Talbot's not even part gentleman.

"Sorry, Ford, but this woman—" He stopped himself this time and inhaled. "This woman"—his tone was then as businesslike as he could make it—"she's waiting in your office. Says she needs help but that she'll only talk to you. She's just sitting in there, quiet, and...well, you need to come right away. Not just because she wants you, but because... well, because she scares the hell out of me. I don't think I can go back in there and sit in silence with her. She *radiates*...something. I'll end up like a Spinal Tap drummer; I'll spontaneously combust."

"Talbot"—I said his name again because hearing it focused him—"Talbot, what have I told you about clients? What's the first rule?"

"No ogling the clients."

"Good, and what's the second rule?"

He took a minute to think. Lists with more than one item challenged him. Not a disciplined mind. "Um, don't invite waiting clients to play video games?"

"That's right. So, just go back to the front room and sit quietly. Do not stare at the client. Do not speak to the client unless spoken to? Got it?"

"Got it. Will do, boss."

Talbot is my oldest friend. Long story. Not the best idea to hire a friend, but he needed work, and my files were a brush pile, and so I hired him to disentangle them. It was meant to be temp work, but I couldn't get him to leave, to find another job.

I don't pay him much, but he doesn't mind. He lives with his mother in an aging house a few blocks from my office. He pays no rent and bikes to work. I guess he can live on what I pay him—he does—and he seems to like the work though there isn't much of it.

Given all that, you might think I'd have been glad for his call, but I wasn't. I'd hoped to have lunch with Helen; it'd been a few days since I visited with her. That was one thing: I was disappointed. But I was also due at St. Dunstan's where I sing in the choir.

I know, I know. Not many PIs are choirboys. It kinda jolts the whole *voice-over, roman noirish* thing I've got going here, huh? But I like to sing, and though my relationship to the church is…um…complicated, I keep returning for the music. For the music and because I've become friends, I guess you'd say, with the priest, John Halsey, who doubles as the choir director.

We don't have much in common. He's not a talker, and I am. Funny thing: a priest not being a talker. He grunts. I asked him one day if grunting was him speaking in tongues. He didn't grunt at me for a few days after that, but he forgave me—priest and all. He started grunting again but quieter. I sometimes say things I should only think. And maybe *not* think.

So, Ruth was swamped by the lunch rush, and I was disappointed about Helen and looking forward to choir practice and trying to eat the remains of my lunch, and I got this call, so I had Ruth box my fries, and I went to my car.

That's how I ended up driving to the office in a shitty mood—in a sweltering car that would only cool down by the time I got out at the office. I called St. Dunstan's and told Father Halsey's church secretary, Diana, I would not make it to practice, and when I finished, I pulled into my parking space. As I expected, my car had only just become comfortable.

I sit for a moment, enjoying the coolness, and then I sigh and open the door.

My office is in the back half of an old house, one that was built shortly after the Civil War, low and long. The front half is a law office, the office of Miller Solomon. I rent the back from him. He's a good guy once you get to know him. He's intimidating until you do. Come to think of it, he's intimidating afterward too. But still, a good guy. He's a tall black man with a baleful stare and a rare smile. Folks who come to see him park on the street out front. Folks who come to see me park around back in the irregular gravel parking lot behind the house.

That parking lot is now empty except for my car, a dusty white Camry; Talbot's gray bike, an old Trek; and a shiny, navy Porsche that has no business in any such lot. I stare at the car, the California plates. The car seems to stand gingerly on the loose gravel, a little girl lifting her fancy skirt to her ankles when she realizes she's standing in a puddle. I imagine it's in a hurry for its owner—the blonde, undoubtedly—to rescue it from its sojourn among the unwashed like my Camry.

I take a breath and then climb the wide back stairs leading to the narrow door of my office. I can't afford any fancy front sign, so I make do with a reflective brass sign affixed to the door:

Ford R. Merrick, PI
Closed Fridays

I like long weekends. Unfortunately, it's Tuesday, and I have a client.

I delay, considering the sign. My name is a harvest of *r*'s. I can see myself in the reflective surface as I focus past my name. I'm tall, certainly not fat but not skinny—a swimmer's build, my sister says. (Actually, she says *Michael Phelps without the definition.*) My curly, reddish-blond hair is never ruly, particularly on days as humid as this, days so humid a swimmer's build counts as a blessing since walking is a vertical Australian crawl. I offer my reflection a grin, but his gray eyes don't seem impressed.

As I open the office door, I glance back over my shoulder at the shiny Porsche. I feel sorry for it. I vow to return its owner to it ASAP.

The refrigerated air of the office I notice first. Just the few strides from my car to the door have me sweating again. Second, I notice *her*. And then the AC is no help.

The arctic would have been no help; I'd melt glaciers.

She's sitting in a chair, and her posture is so perfect that I realize it's possible not only to stand at attention but also to sit that way. She's blonde and tall and so much more. Despite her beauty—vast and formidable—it's her eyes that seize me.

She looks at me with a cool, velvety blue gaze; her eyes are not deep like Ruth's, but they aren't the kind you bounce off either. I don't know what to make of them. I have no word. But they grip me like strong hands and hold me. It takes me a moment to find my way to her full lips, to her smile, half-amused, half-doubtful. She stands up. She stands as perfectly as she sits, a plumb line.

I am tall, and I am taller than her. But she is *tall*. The black pantsuit she wears fits her so exactly that it clearly has never been on a store hanger. It has been made for her, bespoke. She has on low black heels, and their toes come to sharp points. A bit of blue ruffled silk shows above the jacket. She wears no jewelry except a small, gold, woman's chronograph. Her hair is pulled back in a simple, refined ponytail. I didn't know ponytails could be refined.

She's all Talbot said and so much more. I've said that haven't I: the *so much more* thing? But she really is so much more than so much more. That I manage to extend my hand and audibly say my name is, I declare, the single greatest accomplishment of my life.

"Ford Merrick."

She takes my hand. Hers is as cool as her gaze, but she shakes my hand with surprising strength. I have the sudden, disconcerting suspicion that she is probably stronger than I am. Oh, well, Helen's always telling me to join a gym. No definition.

The woman smiles at me. The smile's not mechanical; it's real, but it also seems practiced, too ready. A whiff of artifice.

"Hello, Ford—is that *really* your name?"

It takes me a minute to hear words because all I hear is the music of her voice when she says "Ford." It takes me a minute to catch up to the rest of her words.

"Oh yeah, um…yes, it is. Ford, like the car, although my sister says I should just use my initials, F. R. Who ever heard of a serious detective named *Ford*? But I am—a serious detective that is. And called Ford. Who wants to be called F. R.? Which really is my name—Ford—really."

I make myself stop talking, or whatever it is I'm doing.

Her smile becomes less practiced, and I warm to it more. She laughs softly. "Okay—'Ford' it is."

She reclaims her hand, and I realize I had kept it until then as if she'd surrendered it to me.

"May we talk in your office? I've come on a confidential matter. I hope to hire you." She glances at Talbot then back at me.

It's not often a guy like me, a detective in a small town in Alabama—a town named Opelika, which, I'm told, means *big swamp*—feels like a detective in Raymond Chandler's 1950s Los Angeles, but I do just now. I do. The most beautiful woman I have ever seen has blue-Porsched wearing black to my begrimed, back-half office, and she hopes to hire me.

Hope. That word strikes me funny. Disbelief, boredom, and vague loathing are commonly involved in cases for a detective like me—not hope. But seeing her causes me to hope. I'm not sure for what, when, or why, but I am sure for whom. I'll probably regret the hope, but my shitty mood vanishes, and I lead her into my office.

"Sure, come with me, please. Talbot, hold my calls."

"But Ford—" Talbot starts.

I cut him off. "*Hold* my calls." Of course, I usually answer my own phone; I don't trust Talbot to do it. So, my order confuses him. But the woman doesn't need to know all that.

CHAPTER 2: *Soft Boiled*

I open the door that leads from the front room—the room Talbot and I call the waiting room, although almost no one ever waits in it; mostly, Talbot and I play video games there or watch movies on the TV—and into my office.

I admit I read too many roman noirs, detective novels: Chandler, Davis, MacDonald, Thompson, Ellison, Ellroy. That not only affects my thinking and speaking—my patterns and sometimes, to my regret, my sentiments—but that affects my taste in office decor.

Mainly, it means I have little—décor, not taste.

Well, maybe taste too. Maybe.

My office is a small room with a tall desk. The massive metal desk is olive drab. I found it deployed at an Army/Navy surplus store; I reckon it is a re-purposed Sherman tank. Behind it is my old, heavy, wooden desk chair. In front of it are two straight-backed wooden chairs, which always strike me as infantry support for the desk.

A filing cabinet huddles in one corner—khaki-colored, a lone enemy armored car—an old, metal fan atop it like a turret, always on, and making a barely audible, metallic, whirring sound. A bare battle scene.

No knick-knacks. No flowers. No singing birds. Lots of dust.

A large, black-and-white *Blade Runner* poster hangs on the wall behind my desk. As I said to the woman: I am a serious detective.

I gesture to one of the chairs as I hurry around the desk, and I am standing in front of my desk chair as she sits. I didn't want to miss that. I could have watched her sit down a second time and a third and given each sitting a standing ovation. The grace of her movements, the economy, that bewitching black pantsuit, those pointy heels. She crosses her legs, and it might as well be the Apocalypse; the world could end, and I'd end happily.

Again, she sits at attention. She glances at her gold watch.

"Am I on the clock?" I ask without really thinking. I'm still replaying her seating herself in my head. (That doesn't sound right, does it?)

"Am I?" she replies, one eyebrow shaking free of gravity.

"On the clock? No, no. I do get paid by the day, but I'm not working for you, not yet…"

She does not respond but looks around the office, taking it in. She seems marooned between curiosity and…*what*? Contempt, maybe?

She turns to me and gives me a frank, assessing stare. It unmans me enough to make me sit.

"So," she says at last, just when I feel like a specimen beetle in a box, "I'm Rachel Gunner. R-a-c-h-e-l. Are you one of those *hard-boiled* detectives?"

I can't tell whether she's joking with me, or serious, or what. Like before, there's something artificial about her tone, about her—not fake. No, that's not the right term. There's a deliberateness in what she does, what she is. It's connected to what I called *contempt*, but I'm not sure that's the right word. I don't know how to say it any better. If she weren't here, I'd exhume the *Webster's* from my desk and try to divine a better word.

"Um…uh…no, Miss Gunner," I stammer. "I suppose I'm more a *soft-boiled* one, a few minutes short of hard."

She blinks at me for a moment; now she's unsure. She's unsure about being unsure. A few more blinks, then she smiles that better smile, the natural one, but even better than before. I caught her by surprise, it seems. Her voice changes. "'Rachel,' please. Few detectives, few men, would admit to that."

Again, I can't quite make out her tone. This feels like banter, but I can't tell. She's not dressed to banter; she's dressed to kill. She's killing me.

I look at her and shrug. "Honest to a fault."

She gives me a long, speculative look, her head tilting slightly as she does, that better smile still playing on her lips. "So, how does an honest, soft-boiled detective make a living in Opelika, Alabama?"

She doesn't say the town name quite like a native, but she's close.

I *am* a soft-boiled detective, so that's a hard question. The truth is I don't strictly make a *living* as a detective. I do okay, but not well enough to pay all the bills. Luckily, I have other sources of funds. When our parents died, they left Helen and me a nice house in town and a tidy sum. We're not rich, not close to it—remember, I drive a six-year-old Camry and rent the back half of an old house as an office—but we have enough not to have to worry about making ends meet.

And of course, Helen—the doctor—makes plenty of money, but she donates a lot of it to charities. I'm also a writer. Yep, believe it or not, words are my side hustle. You see, I don't read all those detective novels just for fun; I read them for profit. I write detective novels on the side and under a pseudonym. No one knows that but Helen. And Talbot.

She's waiting. "It's not easy," I answer misleadingly. Rachel continues to look at me, her head still tilted as if she's trying to get me into focus. She has a faint spray of freckles across her nose, so faint as to be almost invisible. If they were more visible, they'd clash with her pantsuit.

"Can you do it, Ford?" She says my name again, and it's the way little bells ring on trees. "Can you *do* your job and be honest?"

"It's not easy," I say again but with a different meaning, no longer misleading.

It isn't easy. I could make a living if I were willing to skulk around town, taking photos of unfaithful spouses, say, but I haven't the tele-photo lens—or the tin stomach—for that. I leave shit like that to the other PI in town, Doug Certaine. Certaine's not choosy.

She finally stops giving me that speculative look, but as she does, I'm surprised to realize that the look was also reflexive. She wasn't just speculating about me but about herself. That's the last thing I need: a client this beautiful with haunted depths. Too much like the beginning of one of my novels.

Besides, I'm part coward when it comes to women. Just ask Ruth.

Rachel drops her eyes, puts her hands—one on top of the other—on her knee, and then sighs, sitting at ease. "No, I'm sure it's not. As I said in the other room, I hope to hire you. What I want you to do may not seem like a job for a detective, but I need help, and I don't know anyone in town. You see, I'm staying out at Noble Hall..."

"Oh, out toward Auburn?"

I know the place: a big, beautiful antebellum home, a petrifaction of the Old South.

She nods. "Yes, I'm staying there with my uncle"—she glances up at me, and I am almost certain he's not her uncle—"and I want to hire you to...get to know him."

"Get to know him?"

I must have made a face because she immediately begins to explain. "Yes...no...I don't mean... You see—"

I hold up my hand, and she stops. "Wait—your uncle is Wylie Stroud?"

I have seen Stroud around town a few times in recent months and been introduced to him once or twice, though we've never really had a conversation.

He is a fit man in his fifties, sporting a full head of non-gray hair and a mouthful of non-dull teeth. Annoyingly attractive. Each time I've seen him, he looks like he is dressed for a haberdashery window, with emphasis on -*dashery*.

Stroud bought Noble Hall recently after the death of its longtime owner, an elderly woman named Jane Pimberly. She sometimes walked the grounds at night with a swinging lantern for reasons no one understood, and she sometimes stood on the upstairs balcony, singing in the nude. The South's a hotbed for eccentricity.

The sale of the hall had been all the gossip in Ed's for a couple of weeks, especially with the widows and divorced women, each hearing *Gone with the Wind* theme music in her head and seeing visions of herself presiding handsomely with Stroud over her own plantation, her own Tara. Did I say I didn't take to Stroud the times I saw him, the times I met him?

"Yes," she said, "I'm his niece. I came out to visit him a couple of weeks ago."

Again, I don't believe the niece bit. But I play along. It's her business, but it does make my shitty mood begin to collect again like morning fog in a valley.

"I see. But I still don't understand why you want to hire me."

She nods. "I want to hire you to get to know my uncle. He's always been *difficult* with me, kept things from me. I worry he's up to something."

"Up to something?" I am beginning to sound like an oversized parrot. So, I add another repetition, but this time in my own words. Better to parrot yourself. Or is it? "I still don't understand."

She smiles at me, a smile with a weight of weariness in it. "My uncle sometimes crosses the double yellow line between criminal practice and *sharp* practice. He's made his money mostly legally—if mostly unpleasantly." She fidgets and seems angry with herself for doing so, but the anger's the barest flash; it might have been my imagination. "But I worry that he's taking the plunge into something big, something criminal—something that could get him into serious, irrevocable trouble either with the law or…with the lawless."

"So, you think he's up to something shady?"

She nods. "I do—shady, or worse. And I can't get him to tell me what it is. That's why I need you. I need you to get to know him, befriend him, see if he'll tell you what he's up to."

"But why would he tell me?"

She twists her lips to the side. The expression's so adorable. I want to thank her aloud for doing it, mail her a fan letter. "He's always been more willing to talk around men. Maybe it's just his way of showing off, trying to be the *alpha*, but it's true. And I think he's lonely for a friend here. You may not know it, but the South's reputation for hospitality is…um…inflated."

I nod. "I do know it. All the superficial 'honey,' and 'how do you do,' and 'bless your heart' in that unsulphured molasses accent can obscure the deep clannishness of the South, its mistrust of strangers. You can live here a long time and remain an outsider."

She gives me the speculative look again, her blue eyes instinct with intelligence. "You talk like a writer; you know that?"

I shift uneasily in my chair. I'm not about to give up my pseudonym. And no one has ever said that to me before—the writer thing.

"My sister, the doctor, just says I talk too much. That I'm prone to logorrhea."

She winces a bit at my word but then responds, "Is that a medical diagnosis? Logorrhea…like in the other room?" She grins.

I had mercifully forgotten my display of fractured English, but now it comes cruelly back to me. "Yeah, I fear that folks tend to remember my spirals better than my flourishes."

She laughs softly. "Aren't you a cradle Southerner?"

"No, *not*, actually. My parents moved here when I was young, but I wasn't born here. Dad taught at Auburn. Mom was a doctor, like my sister. They met out East. Mom was an undergrad at Harvard, and Dad was a grad student at Boston College. They met on the T."

Rachel leans forward. "I know Boston—the T. People on the T don't normally interact much."

"No," I agree, laughing, "but I guess Dad stepped on Mom's foot. He was reading some fat book, struggling to balance it and himself as the T moved, and at some point, he over-balanced, and, trying to keep from falling, he stomped on Mom. She was reading too. He apologized. She asked about his book. He asked about hers. Four years later, Helen was born."

"So, I guess he failed," Rachel says with a smile.

"Failed?" I do it again—the parroting thing.

"Yes, failed to keep himself from falling."

"Oh! Right." I laugh, and her smile brightens. She seems pleased to have made me laugh. I like her far, far more than ten minutes should allow. Too much.

"So," she asks with an interest that surprises me, "your mom was at Harvard?"

"Yeah, a legacy. Her dad and her dad's dad graduated from Harvard."

"Huh." She nods. "And you?"

"Nope. I didn't. I disappointed my grandfather, seriously disappointed him. I didn't even apply. I went to Oberlin."

"In Ohio?"

"Yes, I wanted a small college, small town. I graduated and came back here to be with my sister."

"What's her name? Oh, Helen, you said."

"Helen, yes. She's a doctor in town."

"Oh."

She offers me nothing about her past, her un-avuncular family. We both realize that we've wandered off-topic.

Rachel clears her throat and pulls us back. "So, about my uncle..."

"Right, right. Wylie. So, you want me to...befriend him and see if I can find out what he's up to. Is that it?"

"Yes."

"But won't he be suspicious? This is still a small town; it's hard to keep secrets. People know me, know what I do."

She leans back as if she is one of the people who knows me. "That's fine. I don't want to keep what you do a secret, just that you're doing it for me. I assume you and Talbot can keep my visit today confidential, our business confidential?"

I'm not entirely sure Talbot can, given the phone call this morning, but I hope for the best and nod my head. "We can. So, if I do this, how do I get into your uncle's circle? I don't exactly move among the social elite hereabouts. I'm more Ed's Diner than Lee County Country Club."

"That's okay. My uncle's less fussy about that sort of thing than he looks. I'm convinced now that you're the man for the job—that he'll like you. He'll abuse you, probably, a little, but that will mean he likes you."

Great, that's what I need: abusive liking. "So, if I take the job, do I just wait to run into your uncle somewhere?"

She shakes her head. Her face betrays a moment of nervousness. "No, we're having a party Friday night, and I was hoping you would attend."

"By myself?"

"No, you should come—as my date."

I laugh out loud. I suppose a man ought to have more self-respect, but the image of that woman on my arm strikes me as the very image of *unequally yoked*. But I also laugh because that image complicates my understanding of what is happening between Rachel and her...*uncle* Wylie. Maybe he is her uncle after all. But that still seems unlikely to me—though I can't say why.

When I look at her, I'm baffled to see a trace of hurt in her eyes. I stop laughing.

She makes herself smile—loads of artifice this time. "You don't want to?" She tries to make the question light, mocking, but it sounds disappointed.

I wave both hands in the air in front of me, apologetic little circles. "No, no, I'd be pleased to be your date. Pleased. I just—" I pause and change directions. "Will your uncle mind?"

She stares, puzzled. "Wylie? Why would he mind? It's his party, but I can invite anyone I want."

"Do you think he'll buy it, that I would be the person you would invite?"

She tilts her head again and continues with her puzzled stare. "Of course. Why wouldn't he?"

I do have enough self-respect to answer that evasively. "I don't know…" I make a vague gesture. "As I was saying, different social circles."

She brushes the comment aside. "Let the Old South go, Ford. Live a little. *Northern up.*"

I bark a laugh and sit forward. I take a moment to gather myself. "By 'date,' what do you mean?"

"Why, Mr. Merrick," she says in a remarkably accurate Alabama accent, "what is on your mind?"

She makes "on" a two-syllable word and inserts a "y" somewhere in the middle of "mind." It makes me wonder about her mispronunciation of "Opelika."

"Oh, nothing like that!" I now wave my hands more wildly. "I meant logistics, times, cars, that sort of thing."

She laughs at my exaggerated reaction. "How about I pick you up at your place? Seven p.m.?"

"Won't we need some sort of backstory, some cover, if we're going to con your uncle?"

Her reaction to that surprises me. Her face slackens for a second. Then she gathers it back into a smile. "Right, right—how about I call you this week and we construct one together, make plans? You can give me your address then." Her tone is unexpectedly eager.

I feel an upsurge in my chest. I know it's a job, work, a client, not a real date, but her eagerness warms me head to toe. "Okay."

A moment of silence passes.

"So, I've hired you?" she asks, and as she does, some of the warmth drains back out of me. She seems to sink a little too.

"We should talk rates."

Another moment of silence as she stands. "That's not a problem," she says as she straightens her jacket. "I'm happy to pay whatever rate you charge."

I don't want to talk about money; I regret mentioning it. It changed the temperature of the room. The last of the warmth drains out of me. Her eyes are velvety cool again, her face impassive.

I suddenly wonder about a black pantsuit on an infernal Alabama summer day. I'll never forget the suit, but she must be preternaturally cool.

"So, I'll hear from you before Friday."

"Yes, you will," she says simply, her tone ending things.

I start around the desk to open the door, but she is out of it before I manage to get there.

I'm standing at my office door when she goes out the waiting room door and down the steps. Sunlight and heat pour in as she goes. Framed by the door, dark against the light and dark in her black suit, she glances over her shoulder as she steps into the parking lot.

I then remember the poor Porsche standing just so in the gravel, and I wish them both well.

CHAPTER 3:
Coffee, Tea, and Decency

I nurse a cup of coffee through two refills, but I'm about to abandon it to live or die on its own.

Ruth hasn't talked to me much, but that's the morning rush. During the rush, Ed's unfurls in its full glory, and Ruth perches atop it like one of the golden eagles atop a flagpole, wings out.

I watch her seat customers, take orders, balance trays, and fend off overly familiar comments without ever losing a step or her balance.

She's admirable, and I wish I were more like her.

I stumble and overbalance as a rule, not as an exception. My dad's son, I guess, despite losing him long ago.

When Mom and Dad were coming home from a party in LaGrange, Georgia, a truck driver fell asleep at the wheel on I-85 and ran them off the road. It wasn't anyone's fault. The truck driver still sends Helen and me a card every year at Christmas. He never writes anything but his name below the printed sentiment. We've never displayed the cards, but we've also never thrown any away. A shoebox in a cupboard keeps them all for us. I'm not sure what we plan to do with them.

When I see them, they make me sad, not only for Dad and Mom, and me and Helen, but the truck driver too. We live without something we should have; he lives with something he shouldn't.

"Ruth," I hear Doug Certaine shout above the plate-and-fork, chit-chat hubbub, "*sway* this way and *warm* my coffee." A crowd of wannabe Certaines huddles around him at the central, circular table, and all guffaw at their idol's gift with women.

Others in the restaurant look up, hearing his shout.

Ruth slides a plate of steaming scrambled eggs in front of Thelma Cruett, who eats the same breakfast in Ed's six days a week—like God, Thelma sleeps late on Sunday—and lances Certaine with a jousting stare, almost unseating him.

"You've never made a woman *sway* in your life, Doug Certaine. I doubt you've ever witnessed it; I know you never caused it."

In unison, the circular table stops guffawing.

The other customers suppress smiles and return to their food or coffee. I look down, trying not to grin, but I notice Certaine catch my reaction and frown a pissy frown.

Have I said we don't like each other?

It's not just that we are rivals as detectives. We were rivals in high school too, although odd rivals.

Certaine was, predictably, the star athlete: a guard on the basketball team, a running back on the football team. Despite being tall enough for basketball, I was not on either team. I was class valedictorian, president of a bunch of clubs, and lead guitar player in a popular high school band.

Certaine was the absolute monarch of the jocks; I was the constitutional monarch of the non-jocks. We both ran for class president each year, and I won each time. He never forgave me when I beat him in the election for president of the student council our senior year.

I went on to Oberlin—like Rachel Gunner said, *in Ohio*. Certaine went to Troy—in Troy, Alabama. Scholarships, both—mine academic, his athletic. His freshman year, he blew out a knee in the first practice in pads and never recovered enough to play. They let him keep the scholarship, and he managed to graduate, but barely.

The knee injury left him with a gimpy leg and a chippy shoulder.

A year ago, maybe a little more, he started asking Helen out. She was not interested; she turned him down each time: kindly at first, with attitude later. He blamed me for Helen's refusal and her attitude. While I hoped she would refuse and didn't blame her for her attitude, I never interfered or talked to Helen about it.

Helen knows her own mind. I stay out of her way except when she forgets to eat.

Ruth circles to me with the coffee pot, ignoring Certaine's now-lifted cup, lifted above his head like a distress signal.

"More coffee, Ford?" She speaks louder than usual.

I know this was for Certaine's benefit, and I cringe inwardly. She cocks her hips as she warms my coffee and treats me to her best smile: slow, lazy, and wide. "Have you heard about the big party out at Noble Hall?"

I nod. "Yes, surprisingly, I have." I immediately regret saying anything but especially regret the "surprisingly." It invites questions, and I am supposed to keep Rachel Gunner's visit to my office confidential.

Luckily, Ruth's more interested in tweaking Certaine, who *still* has his empty cup in the air, than in carefully considering my words.

"Are you planning to go?"

I see the head-on collision coming but have nowhere to swerve. I drive on, dreading sudden impact. "Yes, I'm going."

"I got invited too," Ruth notes chirpily, "why don't we go together?" *Crash!*

I look at the tabletop—drop my voice almost to a whisper. "I can't."

"You can't?" Ruth asks, her surprise causing her to ask louder than she means to. I see Certaine's cup sink to the circular table and hear the guffaws rise.

26

"No," I continue in a whisper. "I've already made plans. Sorry."

She uncocks her hip and swirls coffee in the pot, almost as if she's tempted to dump it on me.

"I was hoping you would go with me—my *plus one*," she says more quietly, her unhappiness checkering her expression.

Ruth's father, Big Jim Sutton, runs the Briggs and Stratton plant on the edge of Auburn. The Suttons are one of the oldest families in town. It figures he and his wife and Ruth would be invited and that those invitations had gone out earlier. I never saw an invitation for Helen or for me.

"Merrick would be *plus zero*," Certaine quips, just loud enough to be heard.

The circular table finds this high comedy. I ignore it, more concerned about Ruth's reaction to my refusal.

"I didn't know you were hoping that," I say weakly, and I know it was the wrong response because the checkering gets worse.

"How could you not, Ford Merrick? For a detective, you haven't got *a damn clue*." She marches away from me and straight to Certaine. She sways as she does, glancing back at me before facing Certaine.

"What do you say, Doug Certaine? The party at Noble Hall Friday? Will you go with me?"

Certaine gives her a crowing look. "You think I want Merrick's *throw-backs*?"

He makes Ruth stand in the silence following his remark for just long enough to humiliate her a little more, but her annoyance with me carries her through it.

"Sure," he says finally, smiling his Certaine smile, a dental trick of self-congratulation, "I'll take you. Wear something that shows those legs. Merrick needs to know what he's missing."

I am about to slide out of my booth, to try to save Ruth any further comments from Certaine since I'm his target too when a wide gray suit blocks my escape. I peer up into the doleful face of Father John Halsey.

If he weren't a priest, he could make a living posing for gargoyles.

Father Halsey is a big man, thickly muscled. Were it not for the suit and the collar, no one would imagine him a priest. He doesn't have the expected priestly backstory.

One night we were sitting together—a fifth between the two of us in his office—and he became, for him, chatty. He told me he'd been a Marine for a time. He didn't tell me more, but that brought him into better focus. You know that hymn the Salvation Army likes, "Onward Christian Soldiers"? That's the processional music I hear whenever I see Father Halsey walking around town. Like that passage, Second Timothy 2:3—"Thou, therefore, endure hardness, as a good soldier of Jesus Christ." Father Halsey is an *endure-hardness* priest, a soldier of Christ.

"Hey, Father," I say quietly, greeting him and gesturing to the other side of the booth. He glances narrowly over at the circular table, at Ruth talking to Certaine, and slides heavily into the seat. "I see Certaine's spreading peace and goodwill as always. I heard some of that when I came in."

I shrug. "I didn't anticipate Ruth hoping I'd go with her to the party. I only knew about it yesterday."

He gives me a long, long look. "Merrick, you are a holy innocent. Ever since that girl came back to town a couple of years ago, she's been waiting on you to take her to one event or another—for anything! Get your head out of your ass and decide. Leaving her to pine away isn't right."

"Telling me to get my head out of my ass isn't exactly priestly communication, Father."

"Oh hell, Merrick, we're not talking about *me*. Don't start your double-talk. We're talking about you and that heartsick girl. I believe the only reason she came back here was for you."

I don't want to meet Halsey's eyes, so I tinker with a creamer from the small bowl on the table.

"I know," I finally sigh, "but I just don't feel like she's the one, you know. She's great, and I like her so much, and I admire her, but I'm not sure I'll ever feel anything else, and I don't want to lead her on."

Halsey grunts, and the table shakes. "But you don't want to let her go either, do you? To tell her it's hopeless?"

I become completely engrossed in the creamer, praying he'll leave before I must answer that. But I guess his prayers trump mine—priest and all. I glance up. Halsey waits for my answer with a face that would sink a thousand ships.

"Honestly?" I ask.

"Let's try that. I have a vocational preference for it." Halsey's mouth moves, but somehow his face never changes.

"No, all right? No. I don't know that she's the one, and I don't know that she's not the one, so I—"

"Just keep dicking her around."

"Language, Father!"

"Decency, Merrick!"

I guess this is what it's like to be a soft-boiled detective in Opelika, Alabama. You end up friends with a boy-man who begs you to play video games and with a martial Episcopal priest who demands you be decent. I nod and feel myself blush.

"You're right, Father. I am not being fair to Ruth." I steal a look at her as she talks to Certaine. "We went to senior prom together; did you know that?"

He shook his head. "An item in high school?"

"No, not really. We found each other kind of late, and we dated a few times that summer, but I was in Boston for most of it with my grandfather, my mom's dad. I worked at his company. Then fall came. I went to Ohio, and she went to Virginia, and we fell out of touch."

"I get the feeling she remembered you more than you remembered her." Halsey glances at Ruth, who's left Certaine's table; he and the others are now at the register, paying. She's trading one pot of coffee for another, fresher one.

"Maybe so," I admit. "I'll talk to her, Father."

"Do, Merrick. I rate you a mensch most of the time." He waves at Ruth and mouths the word "coffee." She nods.

"So, how is it you're going to this party if you're not going with Ruth? You and Helen are like me: outsiders. Did you actually get an invitation?" His unexpressive face manages a twitch of curiosity.

"No, not a formal one, not that I know of," I tell him. "Actually, Wylie Stroud's niece is in town, and she asked me to go with her."

Halsey straightens and looks at me. "Tall blonde built of dry ice?"

I smile. "Um…yeah, that fits. How…?"

"I ran into Wylie the other day, and she was with him. She didn't have much to say, and I couldn't get any read on her. How'd she come to ask *you* to the party?"

I knew that would puzzle someone. "Long story, and I have to go; it's not exactly official yet." I pull bills out of my pocket. "Your coffee's on me."

"Thanks, Merrick," he intones, and I can feel him staring at me as I leave. I doubt this conversation is over.

I SPEND THE DAY FOLLOWING UP ON SOME LEADS IN OTHER CASES, nothing worth commenting on. Mostly paperwork.

The conversation with Father Halsey rankles me all morning.

One reason: when I reported I was not sure about Ruth, I hadn't pictured her at all. I'd been picturing Rachel Gunner. But that was crazy. Rachel Gunner was not the one even if I wanted her to be. Desperately. I'd make a brief, character-actor appearance in the glittering Hollywood film of her life, and that'd be that.

But another reason is that Halsey's right. I'm a coward, a dithering coward, and I have been mistreating Ruth, keeping her waiting. Have you figured out that where love is concerned, my shit's not together?

I send Talbot out to get us burgers at lunchtime, and shortly after he leaves, the phone rings. I answer it, not recognizing the number but made hopeful by the location below it: *Burbank, CA.*

"Ford Merrick, private investigator."

"Hey, Ford!" It's *her.* "This is Rachel."

"Yes," I say excitedly, "yes, this is Rachel. That is, you are Rachel. This is Ford. That is, I am Ford."

She laughs again. I hear little bells on trees. I don't know how she makes that happen. Magic. "Thanks for getting that straightened out, Mr. PI. Nothing gets past you, clearly."

I laugh. Why not? "Nothing gets past me clearly."

She laughs at that, and for a moment, I'm ten feet tall. Let's see point-guard Certaine shoot over me now.

"So, I'm calling about Friday. I know we agreed I'll pick you up Friday at seven., but we were going to work out a backstory; what did you call it—a cover?"

I nod and then realize she can't see that over the phone. The woman discombobulates me. "Yes, a cover. Any thoughts?"

"So, you're still willing to help me, to let me hire you?"

"Yes, I am. By the way—the party, what should I wear?"

"Do you have a tux?" she asks hesitantly.

"In Alabama, in the *summer?*"

"Sorry, my uncle likes black tie. He likes formality. Do you have one?"

"No, but I can rent one. Talbot, my assistant—his mother runs a dress shop and rents tuxedos too. I'm sure she has one around that'll fit me."

"Really? You have an impressive inseam."

I open my mouth but can't summon words. How do you respond to that? Is this banter? She's killing me again.

"I've rarely been told that."

"'Rarely'—so you *have* been told it?" I hear a breathy giggle. I never imagined her giggling, but I like her more for it, *dammit.*

"Um"—I fumble evasively, again not sure how to respond—"do you have any cover ideas?"

"Well," she says, drawing the word out, "I've been in Auburn a couple of times shopping. We could say we met at that shop on the corner, the famous one that used to be a drugstore."

"Toomer's?"

"Yes, that's it. The place with the fabulous lemonade, right?"

"Right. We could say we met there, buying lemonade. It's summer in the Deep South; everyone will accept that. We were in line together."

"Good," she says enthusiastically, "and we sat down on the stools and chatted while we drank our lemonades."

"And that's when I asked you out."

"No, that's when I asked you out."

I hesitate, and she notices. "We should keep our cover close to the truth, right?"

I wonder how she knows that when she had forgotten the word "cover" earlier.

"Yes, but I don't think it's...uh...*believable*...that you asked me out."

She is quiet for a moment.

"I think that's one of the nicest, most indirect compliments I've gotten, Ford. But you're the only one who's going to think that. Let's stay close to the truth. *I* asked you."

I shrug as I concede. "Okay, you asked me."

"Besides," she says, her tone conspiratorial, "if it's not believable that I'd ask, why would it be believable that I'd say *yes* if you did?"

I grant that point too. "True."

"And stop this *believability* talk, Ford. If you believe it, everyone else will."

"But I *know* it's not true. You didn't really ask me out."

"Didn't I?" She gives me no chance to answer. "I'll be by Friday at 7:00 p.m. A tux, don't forget." She ends the call before I can respond. I hear her soft laugh as she does.

I spend the rest of the afternoon surrounded by the sound of bells in trees.

After Talbot and I close the office, I drive the short distance to my house, the one I share with Helen.

It's a beautiful, sprawling, two-story house with a wraparound porch. Helen keeps the porch a jungle; she has plants everywhere. The house is always spotless except for my room, and Helen has given up on it entirely. She just tells me to keep the door closed, and she tries to forget it's there.

It's not that bad; actually, it's not dirty, just cluttered. Helen is one of those Zen housekeepers who want the place as bare as possible. I'm no hoarder, but I'm not nearly so Zen. I like my stuff around me at home, ready to hand. Books, papers, whatever. I also like posters, pictures, and guitars. So my walls are covered, and there's not a ton of room to move around. But I don't dare let the clutter escape my door.

I jog up the front steps to find my sister sitting in one of the rockers on the porch. It's late enough in the afternoon to sit out—assuming you do not move or move like a caterpillar, never get excited, and have an iced tea or mint julep handy.

Helen has an iced tea, and she is rocking at a *larghetto* tempo—so slowly, you might not have noticed the rocking at all. She gives me a small wave, more wrist than elbow.

"Hey, Ford!"

My sister is an attractive woman, very tall, with thick auburn hair and clever green eyes. But she doesn't usually do anything to capitalize on her looks. Most days, she manages to brush her hair and put on a clean lab coat over clean gray scrubs, but that's about the extent of her efforts.

Her lab coat is gone; it must be hanging inside. She's still wearing her scrubs although she's kicked off her shoes. They're on the porch in front of her. She's moving the rocking chair with her stocking feet.

"Hey, Sis. How was your day?"

"Fine, fine…" She gives me an unusual, orbiting, satisfied smile.

"Really? Double-fine?"

She laughs and returns to the earth's atmosphere. "Yes, as it happens. You know that guy—that *man*—I told you about, Sam Nettles, the cardiac surgeon, the new one who works at the new cardiac center behind East Alabama Medical Center?"

I do remember. She'd mentioned running into him at the hospital a couple of times, and it was not common for my sister to mention anyone but patients.

"Yes, the one you said was so handsome?"

She blushes and rocks faster. "Right, him. He asked me out today. To that fancy party out at Noble Hall on Friday." Her green eyes flash with pleasure above her gray scrubs.

I drop my chin and look at her. "Do you have something fancy to wear?"

She nods and narrows her eyes. "I think there's an option or two far back in my closet, yeah."

"Well, it happens that I'm going to be there too."

"Oh, Ford, that's great. Ruth asked?"

"No," I say, slightly ashamed, "I'm going with the niece of Wylie Stroud. She asked me."

I don't recall lying to my sister. I dislike it. The words taste rancid, but there's that pesky confidentiality thing.

"I've heard about her. The husband of one of my patients works out there. I was talking to him today in the office. He says she's like a *supermodel*…"

I nod slowly. "If *Supermodel* were the name of a female superhero. She's striking. I ran into her at Toomer's. I went in to get a lemonade to cool off yesterday, and she was in line too. We started chatting, sat down on the stools, and drank our lemonades together. As we finished, she asked me if I would be her date. Very casual, of course."

If I'm lying, I might as well practice, I guess. The taste of the words has not improved.

"Wow, Ford. That's great. But what about Ruth?"

"She asked this morning. I had to say, 'No.' She's not happy with me. So, she's going with Certaine."

Helen shakes her head. "*Ford...*"

"I know, I know. Father Halsey already catechized me about Ruth this morning. At Ed's."

Helen keeps shaking her head. "That's one large, odd priest."

"Tell me about it. He's a realized impossibility," I add without elaboration.

Helen smiles and sips her tea, slowly returning to orbit. "I'm excited about Friday." She repeats herself, her soft voice barely audible over the subtle sound of nighttime insects. "Excited."

I don't say anything, but I am too. Excited. I know better, but I am too.

CHAPTER 4: *Noble Hall*

I mentioned that Opelika means *big swamp.*

Or so I'm told.

I'm told it's a Creek word. I've never checked, not even on the internet. I like to believe it, but I do find it mysterious since there's no swamp, big or little, anywhere in the area—the Auburn/Opelika area as it's called. It's a mystery, and I live with the mystery and sorta like it.

I like the name "Opelika"—the sound of it—the *long-O* opening, and the *short-A* closing. The area has a lot of Creek names: Loachapoka, Notasulga. Music, all.

The Auburn/Opelika area—the two towns blend imperceptibly along Opelika Road and are beginning to blend elsewhere along other, less major roads as the area grows and changes. I guess I've been talking about them as if they were pretty much one place, and they are. Auburn's the white-collar city; the university is there. Opelika is blue-collar; the railroad was there. That's the way the cities used to be traditionally. But, as I said, the cities are blending, the blue and white running together to create a lighter blue. Most differences between the towns are slowly vanishing.

The big difference now is the twenty-some thousand, twentyish students who live in Auburn and attend the university. Their presence gives Auburn a bustling, post-adolescent energy that Opelika lacks. Opelika seems sedate, middle-aged by comparison.

Opelika was nearly the capital of the South in the Civil War. No, really. It was a railroad hub and had a natural claim to the role but lost out to Richmond. (Geographically, Opelika made better sense, I reckon.) Downtown Opelika remains a railroad town in gross anatomy: multiple tracks divide the center of town, and trains rumble through regularly. A large railroad station, refurbished, stands off to the side of downtown beneath an overpass, spiffed up but underused.

I said it's not swampy here, and that's true: no swamps and not swampy except in a general sense of the term. It's green, damp, and subtropical, and in the summer it's just out-and-out, full-on, scalding-damp tropical. The sun blares through air so humid that the sun itself seems fashioned of fire and water, a ferocious ball of yellow steam.

FRIDAY, THE AIR IS INCREDIBLY STEAMY.

With the office closed, I'm distracted all day by the prospect of the party, the prospect of Rachel Gunner. I know that I'm not her date, not exactly, and that I will be technically starting a new case: working, not attending the party, not as the others are. None of that lessens my distraction; it increases it. I've never looked forward to a date so much despite this not being one.

In the mid-morning, I trek to Olive Norton's shop, You Wear it Well, to pick up the tuxedo she'd fitted me for yesterday. Olive, Talbot's mother, rules every space she occupies. She's small with a rounded prettiness, and she moves with a pulsing, radiant energy that makes her seem like a nuclear power plant draped in a cotton dress. She's been a third mom to me: Mom, Helen, and Olive. I was fourteen when Mom and Dad died; Helen was eighteen, and she became my parent. But Olive was there too, helping Helen and raising me alongside Talbot. I owe her.

I open the door to the shop, and the bell above it rings. The sound conjures Rachel Gunner, that black pantsuit, and those cool, blue eyes.

Olive stands up; she's been bent over behind the counter, and she smiles.

"Ford!"

"Olive!"

She hurries around the counter and opens her arms, and I step into them, hugging her. She's so much shorter than I that anytime I hug her, I worry I will miss and close my arms above her head. But I have never missed. She squeezes me hard, and I catch a whiff of her spicy perfume, always a comfort to me.

"So, you're here for the tux for the big party?" She tilts her head back to look me in the face. She has one eye closed as she does when measuring someone. But there's no tape in her hand.

"I am."

"Talbot tells me you are not going with Ruth." I haven't mentioned that to Olive. I've let her assume whatever she assumes. Talbot routinely makes my life harder.

"Ah, yeah, that's true. Wylie Stroud's niece asked me before Ruth mentioned it, and so I couldn't go with Ruth."

Disapproval lurks in the back of Olive's eyes, pulled forward by her rising eyebrows. "You did not anticipate Ruth would want to go with you?"

First the priest, now the dressmaker. "No, I honestly didn't, but mainly because I knew nothing about the party. The first I heard of it was when Rachel told me about it."

"*Rachel,* eh?" Olive says, as if the name spoke itself at a frequency only Olive can hear. "She's a fancy girl, isn't she?"

The term escapes me. *Fancy?* Olive speaks a dialect all her own. She often means something different than her words say.

"If you mean *rich*, I guess so."

Olive wrinkles her nose, an expression shared by Olive and Talbot.

"No, I don't mean *rich*, although Talbot says she drives one of those cars that cost more money than they would hold. No, I meant…" She gestures confusedly, looks at me for help. "You know, Ford—the two blonde girls on *Andy Griffith. What* are they?"

I spent a lot of my teenage years watching *Andy Griffith* with Olive and Talbot. She treats the show as scripture and uses it to interpret her life. Living in Opelika as she does, it mostly works.

"Oh, you mean the *fun girls*, Skippy and…let's see…Daphne."

Olive nods in recognition of the names. "Yes, Skippy and Daphne." She repeats the names to herself in a whisper as if trying to commit them to memory.

"No," I say when I understand, "she's not like the fun girls, except she's blonde. She's tall, well educated, I think, sophisticated. I gather she lives in California, in Burbank."

Olive listens and shakes her head. "She's not the right girl for you, Ford. Don't fall for a woman who has no roots."

"Maybe she has Burbank roots?" I say without really thinking. I still know nothing about Rachel, I realize. I got Burbank from the caller ID on my phone when she called—that, and her Porsche's license plates gave me California.

"No one in California has roots. The ground is too shifty out there." Olive has a settled hatred for both the West and the East coasts. She has a vague notion that everyone in California has a job in the adult film industry and that everyone in New England teaches radical left-wing politics at a university.

"I'm just going to a party with her. It's casual. Barely a date at all." Because it isn't one, I know—Rachel's joking on the phone aside.

I haven't put much thought into the reason I am going to the party, my work for Rachel. I've let myself float along, half deluded into believing that it is a real date. That's not going to work out for me, that half-delusion of romantic grandeur. It's going to render me more than half-unhappy. But I can't give it up, not just yet anyway.

Olive tosses her head skeptically. "Talbot told me about you, your reaction to her, how *money* you've been since you met her."

"How *money*?" I wonder if we are back to the rich thing, fancy girls.

"Yes, you know, daydreaming around, not seeing what's right in front of you."

"*Moony*?"

"Yes, moony!"

A sane person does not keep hearing little bells on trees. I guess I have to agree; I have been moony, a little lunatic.

"I consider myself *warned*, Olive. Now, about the tux?"

She shakes her head, still skeptical. "You will look very lovely in this, Ford. That fun girl won't know what hit her."

I STAND IN THE HOUSE AND PEEK OUT THE DOOR. MY NERVES would have me waiting on the porch, except my tux and bow tie would wilt if I did. So, I stand and peek out the door, then look at my watch. It's almost 7:00 p.m.

Helen's still upstairs. That afternoon, Sam Nettles called to say that work would make him late. So, Helen's using the extra time to get extra ready. It's obvious that my sister is taken with Dr. Nettles.

I hear a car and peek out. The navy Porsche sits in judgment on the street. I can see that Rachel is in it, see her in silhouette. The car door opens, and she steps out, and I hear my own breath catch.

She's wearing a long blue dress, and it's all a-shimmer. Imagine Rita Hayworth in the *Gilda* dress, only imagine it blue and imagine Rita blonde. The dress reveals Rachel's shoulders, and it embraces the rest of her gently. As she moves, she moves me. She's carrying a small silver clutch and wearing long blue gloves. Silver flats flash beneath the long skirt.

Gloves and a long skirt in Alabama—and in the summer.

She does not look like the steam outside affects her. I've never known any woman who could manage this heat so unaffectedly. Alabama summers douse all attempts at elegance. Except Rachel's. Halsey's comment about dry ice comes to my mind. As Rachel gets near the porch, I decide to save her the steps, so I open the door and walk out.

She stops and looks at me, and I feel much shorter suddenly. Her mouth opens a bit, and her eyes shift up, then back down. I guess the tuxedo is a failure, although Helen raved about it.

Rachel steps to the edge of the porch stairs, her eyes on me. I see a faint redness in her cheeks.

"Ford, you look *wonderful.*"

I regain my normal height. I hadn't realized I had been holding my breath since she got out of the Porsche. I breathe again. Her reaction was favorable, not critical, as I thought.

"Thanks, Rachel. And you, I never knew anyone could lay possession to an entire color, but, as of that dress, as of tonight, you *own* blue."

She stares at me for a minute, and the red in her cheeks darkens.

"Ford, you say beautiful things. Thank you. Are you sure you're not a writer?"

I hate the dodge, but I descend the stairs instead of answering.

"I've never ridden in a Porsche," I say to change the topic. That's true. My grandfather has exotic cars, and he lets me ride in them or drive them, but he doesn't have a Porsche. His tastes run to British cars.

Rachel laughs as she turns. She reaches out and takes my hand. I wasn't expecting that, and my breath catches again as I gently squeeze her gloved fingers. She gives me an answering smile, and we walk to the Porsche.

I don't even notice the heat, only her gloved hand in mine.

NOBLE HALL WAS BUILT IN 1854 TO STAND TALL ABOVE A TWO thousand-acre cotton plantation. Slave labor built it, and I admit that slavery haunts the place for me. In the South, if you're white, it's hard to go anywhere without returning to the scene of a crime.

I've never been inside Noble Hall although I have passed it many times, walked around it once, and been told about it often. It's my symbol of the area and has been since I was a boy. The house itself is a massive, Greek Revival reminder of the Old South with monumental Doric columns in the front guarding two full-length, cantilevered balconies. Inside the house, I'm told, are twelve-foot-high ceilings, and the exterior walls are eighteen inches thick. It's a hell of a place—a Dixie excursion against eternity.

During the Civil War, the house was used to shelter injured Confederate soldiers. Toward the end of the war, Union troops were prepared to ransack the house but were dissuaded when one of the residents of the house showed a Masonic ring. The Union soldiers left, taking only the horses and mules. That's the story anyway.

Near the main house is the exterior kitchen, built outside to isolate the heat of cooking. Behind the house stands a much smaller one for the overseer. It's surrounded on both sides by wide green fields, and in the rear by dense woods.

Rachel pulls into the half-circle driveway and drives to the back of the house. She parks the Porsche in front of a white fence surrounding the overseer's house. We've chatted pleasantly if purposelessly on the drive. She asked about where I got the tux, so I entertained her with tales of Olive. I omitted the fun-girls part.

Lines of nice cars are parked neatly behind the house. A few party-goers stroll the manicured lawn, taking in the house. A white-coated waiter stands outside, a tray of iced drinks in his hands.

Rachel and I haven't talked about my reason for being here, her office visit. I expected her to want to discuss it, but she did not seem to. And I'm still enjoying my half-delusion of romantic grandeur; I have no desire to rid myself of that. Noble Hall makes everything dreamier.

But after we leave the car, I see her inhale deliberately and smooth her dress. Then I remember sensing *artifice* in her although I had forgotten it until now. She takes my hand again and glances at me. "So, let's go meet Uncle Wylie."

She leads me into the house. The back door we use leads into the small interior kitchen. More waiters move about in the small space—a dance of white coats—and the counters are heavy with trays of food, fruit, and drinks. We pass from there through a fancy dining room with a table big and shiny enough to host a hockey game. And then we enter the large, formal, living room, a regularized cavern, and are greeted by the sound of voices and an increase in temperature—too many talking bodies crowded into the space.

Despite the crowd, we do not enter unnoticed. The room momentarily hushes as everyone turns to gaze at Rachel. She had dropped my hand just before we entered the room. The only eyes I see on me are Wylie's.

He stands at the center of the room, the center of the crowd, the centerpiece of the party—or he was until Rachel walked in. I can feel him examine me; he seems surprised to see me with Rachel.

His tuxedo exudes expensiveness. His blondish hair has been combed back; his teeth shine whiter than my memory of them. He's smiling at us now, his surprise gone or hidden. Rachel starts toward him through the path made by the parting crowd. I follow her. The sound of the room slowly returns and builds.

As we walk to Stroud, I see Doug Certaine and Ruth standing off to the side. Certaine stares at Rachel; Ruth stares at me. I missed her earlier. Near them, I see Ruth's dad and mom. Big Jim Sutton has never liked me much. He seems happy to see me with someone other than his daughter. But his wife, Ruth's mother, Laney, looks from Ruth to me and back to Ruth with concerned sympathy.

As I reach Wylie Stroud, Rachel takes his hand and, holding it, half turns to me, presenting me. "Uncle Wylie, this is my date, Ford Merrick."

"Ford Merrick," he says, but to himself, not to me. "Oh yes, the private detective in Opelika. We've been introduced, I believe." His smile seems to have a gravitational field, and I'm inside it, tugged toward him.

"Yes, we have," I say, making myself smile, mine a weak shadow of his. We shake hands.

I'm reminded of the reason I didn't like him when we first met. He's too charming. A dessert that's too sweet—he's like that, but with charm. Or someone wearing too much of a nice-smelling cologne. He isn't, but he's like that. Too much of a good thing. Charm overload.

I do my best to hide my reaction, to appear as charmed as he obviously expects me to be. The great man remembers the mere plebe and condescends to smile.

"Noble Hall is all I expected," I offer, not sure what to say but remembering that my job is to make sure he likes me. "It must be an amazing place to live."

I don't think so. It's beautiful and all, but it drags its spooky history behind it.

He seems pleased by my words though, and he takes an expansive glance around. "Yes, history in rock masonry. It's a wee bit overwhelming to think it's mine."

"I can imagine." I can't, but it's the proper response in conventional conversation. Rachel has been pulled aside by an older woman; so, for the moment, it's just Uncle Wylie and me.

"How did you come to buy it?"

He looks at me for a moment before he answers. "I was tired of the West Coast, tired of LA. I wanted someplace slower but warm. A retirement place. And I wanted a place where my niece could visit me—she's my only living relative—a place that would take her away from California. She's tired of that life, I believe. She's been hoping to slow down herself. Anyway, the man I hired to find me a place located Noble Hall, and as soon as he sent pictures, I knew it was what I wanted. Price was no object," he adds with a sincerity that both impresses and annoys me.

"Do you ride?" I ask. I'd seen horses in the fields beside the place. I wonder if they're descendants of the ones the Union soldiers confiscated.

"Yes, I do, but the horses aren't mine. The previous owner rented out the fields, and I've continued the arrangement with the proviso that Rachel or I or our guests may ride the horses now and then. Do you ride?"

I smile and laugh. "It depends on what you mean by 'ride.' I've been *aboard* a horse several times, but each was less a case of riding than of being carried."

He chuckles. "Well, if you are ever here and want to ride, feel free. Rachel rides; she's a skilled rider."

Of course she is. Of course. Rachel rejoined us in time to hear the last few remarks. As she smiles at me, I realize that I am getting to know her uncle, doing precisely what she wanted me to do, and he seems to like me. I wish that her pleased smile were for other reasons though.

"No, Uncle Wylie. I'm passable, nothing more."

It's nice of her to pretend for my sake. The gap between us already feels like the Snake River Canyon. No way across. And all I have is a short rope and a grappling heart.

Music swells, and I realize that a four-piece band has taken up position on the front porch. The room we are in has massive windows that reach almost from floor to ceiling, and one has been opened to allow the music to waft inside.

Wylie turns from me to address the crowd, throwing out his arms theatrically. "Feel free to dance."

Rachel takes my hand and homes herself in my arms before I can react.

I dance about as well as I ride. I've done it, just never well enough to feel like I've succeeded. But Rachel whisks me into the dance. The music plays, and she moves, and I move with her. She looks into my eyes, and hers no longer seem cool, velvety. Her gaze is warm and intricate. Different things, things I can't name, dance in them at different levels.

I glance away, overcome, and see Uncle Wylie watching us dance. Rachel presses her body against me, not hard but insistently, and she frowns as Wylie looks away.

I still don't know what to make of the two of them. I had begun to believe he was her uncle, but doubt has slithered back into my head. Rachel reaches up and turns my face back to hers: I had been staring at Wylie although he did not notice. I gaze into her eyes, held by her eyes, and I realize I am dancing. Successfully. I *am* dancing.

A sermon I heard Father Halsey practicing one day comes back to me. I'd shown up early for choir practice just to enjoy the cool, woody quiet of the church sanctuary, and he was standing in his office, working on his delivery. The sermon was about Jesus walking on the water. Peter, the disciple, the ever-overeager one, sees Jesus, and Peter manages the miracle too, but only for so long as he has faith, only for so long as he looks at Jesus. When he, predictably, begins to worry about the water and wind, he sinks.

I now know a little of what Peter must have felt. If I look into Rachel's eyes, I dance; if I look away, I falter.

I keep my eyes on hers; we spin and spin and spin, and I lose track of everything—Uncle Wylie, the twelve-foot ceilings, and the eighteen-inch walls—and I am simply with her, dancing and dancing, footloose and free in the endless blue of her eyes…

…until I feel a hard finger on my shoulder, a tap that is more a poke. I turn to see Doug Certaine. He's not looking at me; he's looking at Rachel, hungrily, and he deliberately speaks to her, not to me. "Mind if I cut in?"

Rachel frowns but nods her willingness. Certaine smirks at me.

He dances her away. I stand motionless, feeling like all the magic has vanished from life. And then I hear Ruth delicately clear her throat beside me. "So, she's the plan you made?" she asks, referring to our conversation at the diner. She's staring at Certaine and Rachel as they dance.

"Yeah. Yes, she asked me the day before you did. I really didn't know about the party until she asked."

Ruth looks at me for a moment as if trying to decide whether I am telling the truth. She glances down. "I suppose I should have mentioned it to you sooner, but I was almost sure you would get an invitation. Stroud talked to Dad and Mom about who to invite."

I raise an eyebrow. "Did he talk to your Dad *and* Mom, or just your Dad?"

Her face shows surprise. "Now that you ask, it probably was only Dad. Mom was ill the night Stroud visited them."

I shrug to say, *There's the explanation.*

She nods. "I'm sorry, Ford. And Christ, am I sorry I came with Certaine! He's worse than I imagined."

"Think of him as penance for some sin of your childhood."

She gives me a flat look. "You spend too much time with that hulking priest. You need new friends, Ford Merrick." I see the thought form in her mind, and she looks out to the dance floor at Rachel—pushing Certaine away, holding him at arm's length. "But I guess you're working on that, aren't you?" Her voice is quiet, and I know she doesn't really want me to answer the question.

The music ends, and Rachel walks back to me. Certaine follows close behind, but Rachel does not acknowledge he is there.

"Who's this, Ford?" Rachel asks as she looks at Ruth.

"This is my…friend…" Ruth stares hard at me. "…my *old* friend…" Then Rachel shifts her gaze to me, a question in it. I start again. "This is Ruth Sutton. Ruth, Rachel Gunner." Neither woman seems happy with me, but I step back and let them talk.

They manage a few cordial but awkward sentences; then Ruth motions to Certaine, and they leave. Rachel watches them go. "So," she says as she turns around, her eyes different now—deep, "how long has Ruth been in love with you?"

I'm sipping a drink lifted from a passing tray when Rachel asks her question. I keep it to my lips for a time, trying to decide how to answer.

"Her? In love with me? She's here with Certaine." When asked a hard question, here's a tactic: respond in the interrogative, then remark on something obvious. Pretend it's an answer.

"I see that. But he's a tool. She's with him but not *with* him."

I give her an arch response, still hoping to avoid her question—hoping to be funny. "There's a bit of that going around, huh?"

It takes her a split second to understand. She hadn't foreseen her phrase applying to us. A flash of hurt shows in her eyes when she understands, but they are cool velvet afterward.

"I suppose so." Her manner shifts, now in concert with her eyes. "You made a good impression on my uncle. He doesn't like folks who come on too strong, and he doesn't like braggarts. Coming on too strong and bragging are reserved for him." I see her eyes find her uncle and see the frustration on her face. "I would say our mission's accomplished."

I'm about to comment when I see Helen enter the room. She's on the arm of a tall, athletic man. Impeccably dressed. He's *Gentleman's Quarterly* pretty. *Sam Nettles, I presume.* I see what Helen sees in him.

But my gaze shifts to her and stays there.

She has a green ribbon in her hair, and her hair's been brushed lustrous. Her gown, simple and elegant with delicate straps on the shoulders, is green too, as are her shoes. She has on a simple string of pearls and wears no other jewelry.

Helen recreates the hush that greeted Rachel; everyone looks at Helen admiringly. Rachel sees me staring and whispers to me. "Who's that, Ford?"

"My sister, Helen," I answer proudly and see Rachel smile at the answer. Helen sees me, and she takes Sam's arm and leads him toward me—toward me and Rachel.

Helen studies Rachel as she and Sam cross the room. She shoots me an approving glance, one I return. Just before they reach us, the music starts again, and suddenly, Doug Certaine has his hand on Helen's arm. "Dance, Dr. Merrick?" He pulls her onto the floor without waiting for a response.

Helen's face falls, she glances at me for help. Sam, new to all this, seems unsure of what to do. I step forward, put my hand on Certaine's shoulder, stopping him, turning him toward me. I should have known that was what Certaine wanted. He'd humiliated Ruth to get to me, danced with Rachel to get to me, and now he'd manhandled Helen to get to me.

He'd gotten to me.

He turns with a punch already traveling. My feet were not quick enough for basketball, and I may not ordinarily be a dancer, but I am far from immobile. It helps that he's broadcast the punch by dropping his shoulder as he turns. I duck, and he misses, the force of the punch carrying him forward.

As I duck, I get a glimpse of the floor, and I see a silver shoe snake out and trip Certaine. Certaine lands hard and against the legs of a waiter who loses control of a tray of empty glasses. They crash to the floor, not quite in unison, glass shattering. Before I straighten, I see the silver shoe stomp on Certaine's hand. It all happens so fast, I half believe it was a hallucination. I'm already suffering from half delusions.

Certaine sits on the floor, nursing his hand, miserable. Laughter fills the room as the shock ends. Ruth appears, breaking through the crowd to the vacated spot on the floor around Certaine and the broken glass. I see her face cycle through various reactions but settle on sympathy. She walks to Certaine carefully through the shards.

"C'mon, Doug, it's time for us to be going." She reaches down to him and helps him up.

I've never admired her more. After the way he treated her at the restaurant, after his behavior here at the party, she helps him up, helps him save face.

Decent. Ruth Sutton is *thoroughly decent*, and she deserves better from me.

Rachel is watching me watch Ruth. Ruth leads Doug out of the room, and waiters sweep up the glass. Music begins again, the party less Certaine.

Rachel leads me out the front door and onto the porch. The open window for the musicians makes the living room hot; the central air is overworked. But the sunlit porch stifles in comparison.

As soon as we step out, my tie feels like it has come alive and has concluded it must choke me. I feel sweat beading and running down my back, soaking into my shirt and the top of my pants. I worry that soon my feet will start to slosh in my shoes.

Rachel looks cool, still. She continues to wear the gloves. I want to ask her about her footwork with Certaine—it was her silver shoes—but I don't quite know how to ask. I decide to let her mention it if she wants to discuss it. The more I think about it, the more her footwork seems impossibly fast and effective.

She leads me to the edge of the porch. A breeze, weak, begins to blow. She turns to me. "So, you never answered my question about Ruth. How long?"

I tug at my tie, my collar. "A while, I guess."

"You guess, but you don't know?"

"No, I guess I know."

She sighs. "Ford, I'm not going to chase you all over the English language. *Guess* or *know*?"

"*Know*. She's…had feelings for me for a while."

"And you for her?"

I could say *no*. A part of me wants to say *no*, but after what I witnessed, that seems a betrayal—of fact and of Ruth. "I don't know."

Her eyebrows sink to glower, and I go on. "No, no, that's not an evasion. You saw her a few minutes ago. She's a friend, plus I really admire her. I've known how she felt for a while; I've just not done anything about it, not really."

I want to say that Ruth never makes little bells ring on trees. I want to say that I've thought of only Rachel since she was in my office. I want to say that I have to keep reminding myself this isn't an actual date. I want to say all of that, but I say none of it.

She bites her lower lip and applies her attention to the porch floor.

As she finally looks up at me, Uncle Wylie finds us. They make eye contact, and something I don't understand passes between them.

He smiles at us. "Is everyone all right? That Certaine fellow knows how to have a party, eh?"

We both nod. Wylie goes back inside after one more significant glance at Rachel. Rachel's face has changed. That look from her visit to my office is back, the look that suggests contempt, the look for which I don't have the right word. She looks out across the manicured lawn and shakes her head.

"All this is none of my business, Ford; I'm sorry to have insisted. Curiosity. But ours is a business arrangement, and you don't owe me any personal revelations. Again, I'm sorry."

I'm sorry too. Much sorrier than she knows, much sorrier than I confess because I say nothing. I just nod. My half delusion can't be maintained any longer.

I'm her employee, not her date. I chat a time or two with Wylie again and dance with Rachel, but the magic's vanished. The endless blue of her eyes is inaccessible to me—if it ever *was* accessible to me.

She's pleasant and fun, but it's not the same. She drives me home and drops me off. She doesn't get out of the car.

Helen is still at the party. She and Sam seemed to be enjoying each other thoroughly.

Wylie invited me to lunch at the country club Sunday as his guest; that'll be my chance to get to work on the case. I didn't mention his invitation to Rachel; things were businesslike enough on the drive home.

Olive Norton has an odd gift. In one evening, I've gone from moony to money.

CHAPTER 5: *Clubbable*

I peel off my damp tux and hang it to dry on my closet door.

I step back and squint at it.

Even though it did look good on me, it just isn't me! Hanging there, it seems like a skin I sloughed off. Noble Hall—beautiful though it is—is not my sort of place, but Rachel Gunner it would fit like a glove.

I slip on an old, holey Oberlin T-shirt and gym shorts, collect my trusted old Parker fountain pen and the yellow legal pad I'm currently using, and descend the stairs. I leave the pen and paper on the large dining room table then walk into the kitchen. Like the rest of the house, there's little decoration here, although I suppose the utility items double as décor. Large old colorful mixing bowls, nesting largest to smallest, sit heavily on one counter. Helen's prized, intimidating Griswold cast-iron pan stands guard on the antique gas stove, seasoned to perfection and glistening like black glass.

I open a cupboard, grabbing one of the Mason jars we use as glasses—a big one—and open the refrigerator with a silent prayer. My prayer is immediately answered; a large pitcher of Helen's sweet tea fronts the central shelf, gleaming in the fridge's light. Are answered prayers a perk of having that "hulking priest"—Ruth's memorable phrase—as a friend?

Filling the Mason jar with ice, I add the slow-moving tea and return the pitcher to the refrigerator. I sip the tea as it's too sweet to gulp—closer to a solid than a liquid and really closer to a topping for pancakes than a drink. Returning to the table, I pull the legal pad over, uncap my pen, and sit down. I begin to consider the scene I am writing in *Do I Not Bleed?*—my latest detective novel. Quite a title, huh? Almost an educated reference. Good old William Shakespeare. Inexhaustible.

Educated reference. That's part of what I like about the best writers in the genre, especially my heroes: Chandler, MacDonald, Davis, and Rice. Educated men and women, reference and allusion, crowd their novels thick as corpses. My detective, Burnishaw Lennox ("Burney," his friends call him), violates norms of the genre. My comment to Rachel about being a soft-boiled detective was a moment of self-quotation; Burney calls himself that in this novel. Burney's short, a smidgen overweight, but he's also patient, quick, winning, and insightful. I like writing him; he comes naturally to me. I'm just starting to reimagine the current scene when I hear the door open and hear whispers, laughs.

Helen floats into the dining room light from the front-room dark a moment later. Her lips are red, swollen, and parted; she's panting a little. Her color is high, and her eyes, like her thoughts, elsewhere. It takes her a moment dimly to see me, see the room. She blinks at me and then smiles her warm, generous smile. That smile kept me alive when Mom and Dad died.

"Someone had a good time," I say, teasing her.

She looks down at herself, smooths her dress, and bites her lip. She hadn't quite intended for me to see her slightly disheveled, unmade. "Um, yeah, Ford. I had a great time. Sorry we didn't get to talk more, that I didn't get to know Rachel. But Certaine showed his ass—not that he has anything else to show—and then Sam and I seemed on opposite sides of the room from you and Rachel for the rest of the evening. Did you have a good time? Rachel Gunner's dead-in-your-tracks pretty, brother of mine."

She's spiraling, or as close as Helen gets. Spirals are my thing. I find it adorable in her (deplorable in me). I haven't seen her this excited, particularly about a man, since *ever*.

"Dr. Nettles isn't just a big brain," I say in response.

She sighs and answers unselfconsciously. "He sure isn't." She catches herself then and gives me a quick embarrassed look. "Not that I...I mean that we... He kissed me in his car, then on the steps, on the porch, and again at the front door. But nothing...you know...that is... nothing else happened. He was a gentleman."

Her awareness of her surroundings, of me, increases, the dimness gone. She looks at the pad, the pen in my hand. "You don't seem as happy as I expected you to be after playing beau to the belle of the ball..."

I can't tell Helen the truth—*confidentiality*—so I shrug. "The Certaine thing threw me off. And then Ruth. I don't think Rachel likes me as well as...well...as well as I'd hoped."

Hope is the thing with feathers that perches in the soul.

Emily Dickenson wrote that. Tonight, I feel like hope's a thing with horse feathers. I try to shoo it from its vantage in my soul, vulturous old bird.

"Sorry, again, Ford." Helen smooths the back of her skirt and sits down opposite me at the table. Her face is puzzled. "For what it's worth, every time I saw her, Rachel was looking at you—*gazing* at you—trailing you like a sunflower the sun. She sure seems to like you. Why do you think she doesn't?"

I shrug again. If Father Halsey can have a language of grunts, I can have one of shrugs. "She made it pretty clear. I was her date because she doesn't know anyone else yet. The one fish in an as-yet-unstocked pond."

Helen presses her lips into a line as she often does when she thinks hard, but she doesn't share her thoughts with me. After a moment, she shifts in her chair and launches in a new direction. "I saw you talking with Ruth."

"Yeah, we talked a little. She was complaining about Certaine."

Helen nods. "Undoubtedly. How's she, otherwise?"

"Okay."

"She spent a lot of the evening watching you and Rachel. Seeing you two together was harder on her heart than Certaine was on her feet."

It's my turn to nod. "I'm going to make things right with her. I will. No more dithering."

"You *like* Rachel, don't you? Really like, *like* her."

"Geez, Helen, I'm not eight."

"Well, then you're *interested* in her."

I grope for a way to change the subject. "Why'd you let Certaine yank you onto the dance floor?"

"Oh, that. He surprised me, first. And second, I didn't want to be bitchy in front of Sam; Certaine would have forced me to be bitchy. I knew you'd step in, but I didn't expect things to go the way they did. Sam was impressed."

"I suppose," I offer, "but it added to Ruth's humiliations."

"I know. She was a trooper though, helping Certaine up and leading him out, head high."

I picture the scene. "Yeah, she was."

Helen gestures at the pen and paper. "Communing with Burney?"

"Trying to."

"Do you think you've ever written a woman more fit to be the leading lady in a detective novel than Rachel Gunner?"

"No," I admit, "my imagination's not that strong."

SATURDAY RISES HOT AND THEN HEATS UP.

I spend the heat of the afternoon with Talbot. Olive's house is old and sprawling, but it has a pool behind it, Olive's only splurge. She made us ham sandwiches before she left to play bridge with some friends. I'm eating one in a deck chair I've pulled into the scant shade. Talbot floats, his eyes closed, supine on an inner tube in the shallow end of the pool.

He paddles with his hands every so often, his eyes remaining closed, to keep the inner tube centered in the shallow end.

Tal's afraid of the deep end.

"Ford," he says in a contemplative tone, paddling gently, "tell me again. She had on a blue dress, Rita Heyworth, and long, long blue gloves?"

"Yeah, Tal," I say around a bite of ham sandwich. Olive's occult gifts extend to processed meats. "Long, long blue gloves."

"And you held her hand while she was wearing the gloves?" I see one of his eyes open a bit to gauge my reaction.

"Right, I held her gloved hand."

"Jesus," Talbot says, extending the name to sentence length. "Jesus. Tell me again."

"Tal, this is getting disturbing. I can't tell if it's Rachel or her gloves."

"I wouldn't want to," he sighs, closing the eye. Then I notice him consult the front of his shorts, and I look immediately away. I don't need to know the full extent of his reaction to the thought of Rachel's gloved hand—don't want to know.

"Hey, Ford," he says again in his continued, dreamy voice, "would it be all right with you if I looked into…a matter…for Big Jim Sutton. He asked me…"

One of the curiosities of the known universe is that Big Jim Sutton likes Talbot as much as he dislikes me. Other than me and Olive, that makes the total number of people who like Talbot countable on one finger.

"A…matter?"

"Uh-huh. Mm-hmm. Evidently"—whenever Talbot tries to play PI, he lards sentences with *evidently*—"some small items have disappeared from the Briggs and Stratton employee locker room in the last few months. He asked me if I would just check around, talk to the folks, you know, see if I notice anything."

"Tal, you know that to be a licensed PI in Alabama, you have to meet certain requirements; among them is a test you have to pass."

He waves his hand lazily, his eyes remaining closed. "I could pass that test, no problem. I've seen every black-and-white detective movie ever made. I proofread your novels. I work by your side."

I reverse the order of his list. "You sit in my waiting room and play video games. You read my novels and add your misspellings. You watch detective movies, but you never get the details right and always get the perp wrong. You suck at all known forms of testing."

He continues to wave his hand in sublime unconcern. "Short hurdles."

"Short hurdles are tall when you're even shorter."

One eye opens. "Way to buoy my confidence, best friend." He splashes water at me, but the droplets far fall short of his target.

I laugh. "I'm just giving you a hard time, Tal. If you got serious, you could pass the test, no doubt. But remember"—I take on a sober tone—"to get a license, you must also have committed no crime of moral turpitude, and the licensing board decides the final definition of 'moral turpitude.'"

Tal looks at me, puzzled. "Moral *what?*"

"*Turpitude.* Inherent baseness or vileness, shameful wickedness, depravity."

He still looks puzzled. My synonyms list seems not to have helped. I sigh. "The sort of thing you were imagining with Rachel Gunner's glove…"

"Oh. Oh! That is a high hurdle."

I laugh again. "Just your browser history would convict you."

"Leave my browser out of this."

"Seriously, Tal," I say, losing both the loud and the joking tone. "If you want to help Big Jim, that's fine. But you can't do it for pay, and

Kelly Dean Jolley

you can't link what you are doing to me or the office. You're just a private guy helping out a buddy."

"A private *dick* helping out a buddy," he says.

"From your mouth to God's ear, Tal."

Confused, he looks meekly up into the hot blue sky, then scoffingly across at me, and paddles away from the deep end. He'd been drifting toward it.

THE LEE COUNTY COUNTRY CLUB IS NOT EXACTLY TERRA INCOGnita. I've been there. Honestly, I have.

Of course, I'm not a *member* and almost certainly never will be. But I went once with Ruth to a dance during the summer after our senior year, and I've had to go occasionally on business. The club has its fair share of intrigue, and I have sometimes been involved in it.

The club is on one edge of a massive, breath-taking, golf course of emerald perfection. It is surrounded on the other side by tennis courts and an Olympic-sized pool. A small building that stands alongside the pool and gets called "the cabana" although it's too ornate to seem particularly cabana-like to me. The club and the cabana are both fluorescent white. (I know, I know…)

I meet Wylie at the front door. He's just gotten out of his Mercedes and handed the keys to the valet. The valet parked my Camry, dust and all, a few moments earlier, and I've been standing, chatting with her. She's a tall, attractive, redheaded, Auburn student named Kip Mott who's finishing a degree in hotel and restaurant management.

I'm surprised when she recognizes me and asks about Talbot. Turns out, he met her a few nights ago in the Avondale, a nice, quiet, upstairs bar in downtown Auburn, just up the street from Toomer's Corner. She recognizes me from Talbot's description, and she asks how Talbot's doing. I tell her fine. I omit his turpitude.

She seems under the decided impression that he is my partner, in fact, my *senior* partner, but I don't disabuse her of that mistake.

She seems perfectly able to handle herself, and why spare Talbot the bruising he deserves?

"Ford," Wylie says as he glances at Kip rounding the front of his car, "good of you to come. I'm still trying to get to know folks in the area, and you seem like someone worth knowing. My niece certainly seems to think so."

My immediate thought is that that's a lot of *seeming*, but I don't speak it. I just nod and shake Wylie's hand. "Glad to be invited. It always seems cooler out here even though I know it's not."

He nods. "It does. I hope you're hungry. I am."

We walk into the club and through it to the restaurant inside. As we walk, we chitchat about the party and the Alabama weather. Several well-preserved, tanned, middle-aged women pass us, or we pass them, and they all have eyes for Wylie. He gives each his Bob Barker smile and nods.

A young man seats us in the restaurant and gives each of us a menu. We're seated by a large window that looks out onto the pool.

"Price is no object, Ford-boy," Wylie announces in a somewhat unexpected *we're-best-chums* voice. It's the second time he's told me that, and if he keeps saying it, I'm going to stop believing it. I adhere to the reverse of Carroll's line from *The Hunting of the Snark*: "What I tell you three times is *false*."

"Thanks, Wylie." I pretend to consult the menu, but I am instead watching as Wylie settles into the scene. His eyes are quick, intelligent. He sizes up everyone in the room in a few seconds. Despite his over-the-top, slightly foppish charm, I get the unsettling feeling that he is no fool. I'm going to have to be more careful than I was at the party. There, I had Rachel and the other partygoers to provide distraction. Here, I'm his focus. He settles his eyes on me and the menu. "Really, Ford-boy, price is no object."

"Say," I begin casually, letting the third time pass, "what do you do? Rachel never actually told me."

He smiles too easily. "It's not easy to say; that's probably why. You might say I'm a professional *dabbler*. I inherited a lot of money from my father, who'd already diversified the family holdings, and I've diversified them more. Mostly, I've worked in corporate finance, but of late, I've not been in an office much. I'm at the point where I just don't need to work. My money makes money for me."

"So, it grows, like the desert?" I grin.

He stares at me. "You're a complicated man, Ford-boy."

"Most people call me 'Ford,'" I say with a hint of flatness.

He nods. "No doubt, Ford-boy, no doubt," he says, either not hearing or not caring.

I notice his eyes narrow a bit, and I follow his glance out the window and to the pool.

Rachel Gunner is climbing out of the pool wearing a red bikini. I was right, what I said to Helen: my imagination's not *that* strong. My gulp, luckily, is inaudible.

My immediate, irrevocable judgment is that Rachel Gunner owns all the colors she wears. Black, blue, red, whatever.

Her hair hangs down, dark and wet, and she uses her fingers to comb it back from her face and then her hands to squeeze water from it. She turns and speaks to a man who is climbing out of the pool behind her.

The man's an ad for an abs machine. He's not tall, but he's pretty, maybe prettier than Sam Nettles. He smiles at Rachel beneath his Ray-Bans; he's certainly daintier than Sam despite the dark tan and definition. I cannot see her reaction to his smile. She's facing him, and I will not stare at her back, her backside. Her reaction does not reinforce the man's smile. Wylie turns to look at me.

"Huh…my niece is here too. I didn't know she was coming, but then again, she didn't know I was. We haven't talked much since the party. Lake Thornton," he says, nodding in the direction of the ab ad, "showed up unannounced yesterday morning, and she's been tied up with him since. He's staying at the hall."

We're both looking at Thornton. A definite note of disapproval sounds in Wylie's voice.

Wylie sips his water, and the waitress arrives and takes our orders. Thornton has dampened our spirits as well as the pool deck.

When the waitress leaves, I look back out. Rachel's reclining in a deck chair, and Thornton sits in one beside her.

Kip Mott walks by, and I watch as Thornton inspects her backside through his sunglasses. Rachel sees it too and frowns, although she turns her face from Thornton so he cannot see her reaction.

Wylie clears his throat. "So, your family's not from the South?"

I'm unsure how he knows that, but I let it go. "Not originally. My parents moved down here a few years after meeting each other in Boston. My mom's family is from Boston. Her father, my grandfather, is still there."

"Oh, are you close to him?"

I pick up my water and sip it again. "Yes, now—closer to close, anyway. He and Mom didn't agree about Dad. She loved Dad; Grandpa...didn't..." I shrug.

I see Wylie's eyes stray out to Rachel and Thornton. He nods in understanding. "Right, too bad. But things are better now?"

It's a long story and complicated; I don't want to tell it now, especially while watching Thornton-o-vision, all-abs-all-day TV. So, I shorten and simplify the story "Yes, it took some time after Dad and Mom were killed but, yes. Things are better now."

"Good," he says, as he moves his glass so the waitress can put his salad down. "Family matters."

"It does," I agree. "Is Thornton family?" I hope as I ask.

"No, no. He and Rachel were...an item once, but he's part of what she needs to get away from—*California*."

Somehow, I understand him. Thornton is California personified. Olive would hate him. I certainly do. I adjust my chair so I cannot see so easily out the window.

"So, Wylie, you've not got *any* business keeping you busy here?"

He smiles. "You're a good judge of character, Ford-boy. I can't be completely idle, don't have it in me. I've got a thing or two going here, angles, but nothing far enough along, developed enough, for comment."

I take a few minutes and try to get him to comment, but he never does. He splits his attention between me and Thornton-o-vision but keeps his conversation vague.

We finish, stand, and are about to walk out when Rachel and Thornton enter the restaurant through the double doors that lead out to the pool. Rachel sees us immediately; it's evident that she does not like to be surprised, but she overcomes it, smiling as they approach. I am just thankful that Rachel has put a wrap over her bikini!

Unfortunately, although he has a shirt in his hand, Thornton has not put it on. Why would he? The abs are more depressing up close.

"Ford, Uncle Wylie! I didn't know you'd be here. It's nice to see you, Ford." She sounds like she means it, but she glances at Thornton as she speaks. "Um, Ford, this is Lake Thornton. An old friend of mine… that is, a friend of mine."

Thornton reaches out for me, the Rolex Submariner on his wrist flashing. I shake his hand. His sunglasses are pushed back on his head, and I see that he has bright blue eyes. I hate him more every moment.

"*Ford*, is it?" He asks this as if he's a Chevy man.

"Yes, good to meet you." I'm spitting the words like sawdust, but I sound like I mean it. I don't.

"Rachel mentioned that you were her date at the party the other night."

"Yes, she suffered through dancing with me," I report with a wavering smile.

She gives me a split-second look of annoyance, and it tinctures her tone. "No *suffering* involved. Our dancing was…memorable."

Thornton gives me a more respectful glance, measuring me, and straightens himself. "Our Rachel loves to dance."

I have no clue how to respond to the "our." She's not mine. She once was his, or so he seems to think—maybe still does. I can't tell what's true now.

I've had enough of the club. Enough. I imagine beating Thornton into submission with his Submariner.

"Thanks kindly for lunch, Wylie. Rachel, Lake, nice to see you again and to meet you, respectively." As I leave the restaurant, I hear sandals slapping behind me; then a hand lightly grabs my arm.

I turn, and Rachel's standing there; it's her hand. Her cheeks are faintly red again like when she picked me up for the party. Probably the sandalled sprint to catch me. I have long legs; I gobble ground with each stride even if I'm not hurrying, although I was just then.

"Ford," she says softly, looking around and behind her, then facing me, "I'm sorry about the other night, the drive home. I stopped being good company. But you didn't. I know this is confusing—you working for me and all—but could we meet later this week?"

I honestly can't tell whether she is asking me for a date or asking me for a PI-client discussion. Now, I don't care. I'll take what she gives.

"Sure, how about tomorrow?"

She smiles at me and dissolves me in my shoes. "Great," she says. "I'll call you."

I nod, look past her, and glimpse Wylie talking to Thornton. They aren't talking as buddies. Seeing that makes me dislike Wylie's "Ford-boy" less.

I part with Rachel and step outside. Back at the valet stand near the door, Kip takes my keys and fetches my Camry.

CHAPTER 6: *Courthouse*

Monday morning divides itself into alternating sudden thunderstorms and rapid-boil sunshine.

Each thunderstorm darkens the sky as if the clouds were dyed with India ink, dumps rain, whips it about, and then, at impossible speed, the inky clouds disperse. The sky blues, and the sun boils the standing water, chasing it back skyward as steam and humidity. Everything in the distance wavers until the sky begins to darken again.

The whole damn display mocks my shifty moods over the last week.

I spend the early morning planted at my desk, staring out the window, mixed with the weather. Yesterday's lunch at the club still nags me—my failure to get anywhere substantial with Uncle Wylie—but also, and admittedly worse, my memory of Rachel Gunner with Lake Thornton.

Thornton-o-vision.

I'm embarrassed by having imagined beating Thornton with his watch. A PI I am, but a violent man I am not. I don't even carry a gun.

Talbot hates that and constantly tries to scold me into carrying one. Says I'm not *legit*, and so he's not either. Of course, I do own a gun;

it's in the filing cabinet in my office. I keep it cleaned and oiled, but I've hidden the bullets in my desk.

Father Halsey's Cambridge Bible came in a decorated box; he gave the box to me, and that's where I keep the bullets. It's a box I'm confident Talbot will not open. Once a month, I take out the gun and the bullets and drive to the range on the edge of the Tuskegee for precautionary target practice.

I am still staring out the window when I hear voices in the waiting room.

Talbot took the morning off so that Olive could drive him out to Briggs and Stratton. He's back; one of the voices in the waiting room is his.

The door to my office opens, and I recognize the other voice: Miller Solomon, my lawyer landlord. Talbot opens the door and waves at me.

"I'm back, Ford. Mr. Solomon wants to talk to you." He gives me a barely perceptible shrug; Talbot doesn't know what Solomon wants.

"Send him in, Talbot."

Solomon strides into the office. He strides; he doesn't walk. Ever. He's tall and intense. As I said, he's a good guy, but his goodness hides deep inside. I stand to greet him. It occurs to me he's never been in my office before, despite being my landlord and neighbor.

"Hey, Merrick. How're cases?" He looks at me closely.

I frown. "To be honest: *case*. As in one. As in *not plural*. And it's not going well."

He nods, his face grave. "Sorry to hear that. But I've come to get you to two, get you to *plural*."

I gesture to one of the straight-backed chairs, and he sits. I do too, in my desk chair. He glances at my *Blade Runner* poster and shakes his head. "Do you like the theatrical release or the director's cut?"

"The voice-over one, the theatrical release," I say immediately. "It's the one that feels like a detective film. And I hate the unicorn sequence. I didn't know you liked the movie."

He gives me a brief, shallow smile. "I do. And I prefer the theatrical release too."

I chuckle. "But, as much as I like Harrison Ford and the voice-overs, it's Sean Young who…" I let my sentence dangle.

He nods. "Yeah, she's lovely in that film, those angular clothes."

We sit for a moment in respectful silence; then he clears his throat. "So, as I said, I'm here to see about hiring you."

I give myself a shake. I'd been lost in memories of Sean Young's Rachael—and in delayed surprise at Solomon liking the movie. He always seemed too serious for sci-fi. "Is it connected to a case of yours?"

"As you'll understand, I can't say one way or the other. Here's what I can tell you. I want you to look into the death of Jane Pimberly."

"Jane Pimberly? The woman who owned Noble Hall?"

Miller nodded. "Yes." He adds no more.

I straighten in my chair. "Is there a mystery about her death? I heard her son, Wade, found her dead in the mansion, massive heart attack. She'd had heart problems for years, right?"

"Right. She had, she did. No one thought there was any mystery about it, and maybe there isn't. The police were involved, but pro forma. Let's just say that someone is curious about her final days and would like to know more." He leans forward, hands on his knees. "Did you know Jane?"

"No, not really. I met her a few times, saw her in Ed's a few times, but no, I never *knew* her. I heard stories, lots of stories."

Miller huffs, smiles. "Probably all true. Flannery O'Connor wrote Jane's life."

I take an ink pen from my desktop drawer and pull a notepad toward me, interested. "Okay, okay, so…they found her in her house. Had anyone seen her lately?"

"No, not for forty-eight hours. The last time was when someone saw her at the Piggly Wiggly. A neighbor stopped by to check on her the day before she was found, but she did not answer the door."

"Maybe she was already…"

"Maybe," Miller says. "Her car was there."

I knew the car, a shining and massive old yellow Cadillac that Jane Pimberly commanded from port to port. I made a note of that.

"Mm-hmm. Who was her doctor?"

"She'd just started seeing that new doctor—Nettles, I think that's his name—not long before she died. But she was a long-time patient of Dr. McCombs'. She complained about everything, a *hyper* hypochondriac, so she saw *lots* of doctors. Her pastime."

"Did she have many friends—any?"

He shrugged. "Not sure how to answer. She knew people, lots of people; she had money, influence. But she was a bizarre old woman, hard to get on with. I'm not sure anyone would count as a close friend. Cats—she had cats. Noble Hall was a cathouse."

I look up after writing "cats." "You're joking?"

"Yes, about the cathouse, but not joking about cats. Twenty. Wylie Stroud burned stacks of money getting the scent of cat piss out of the house."

"I was out there, at the hall, Friday night," I say.

"Oh, the party? My wife and I were going to go; we were invited, but I got called out of town. How'd the place smell? What do you make of Stroud?"

"Smelled fine, I guess. The house, that is. Stroud's…um …opaque. Charming, handsome, but too…*too.*"

Miller gives me a look. "All hat, no cowboy?"

I'm not entirely sure what that means, and it does not seem like a Miller Solomon comment.

I must stare at him funny because he laughs. "Look, there's no particular hurry on the Pimberly thing. But still, I'd like to know what you find out sooner rather than later."

"Okay, I'll start on it. Say, does Wade Pimberly still live over in Georgia, in LaGrange?"

He stands. "Yes, still does. Up on West Point Lake."

"Thanks for the business, Miller." I come around the desk and shake his hand.

"No problem. I doubt anything comes of it."

"Thanks, Miller."

"*Thank you*, Merrick." I open the door, and he strides through the waiting room and out with a quick nod to Talbot.

.

I DO NOT GO TO ED'S FOR LUNCH. I'M NOT UP TO FACING RUTH JUST yet. I still haven't decided what to say to her.

Talbot walks over to Ford's BBQ and brings sandwiches and potato chips back to the office. That's the place's name, really—"Ford's"—the last name of the family that's owned it forever. Dad loved it so much; I sometimes wonder if he named me after it. He never admitted it.

The most recent thunderstorm lasted a while, and the sky has brightened but remained gray, overcast. The temperature, for now, is bearable. Talbot arrives with his bag, but it's not soaked in rain or sweat.

As we eat in the waiting room, he catches me up on his visit to Briggs and Stratton.

"So, Big Jim gives me the tour and then takes me to the employee locker room. It's just a big cement room with two rows of lockers, a long bench between them, and two doors—metal—one on each side of the room. I looked at the lockers that had been stolen from, but I couldn't see any sign of forced entry. Whoever took the stuff knew the codes; Briggs and Stratton have little safe-thingies on the doors."

"A tumbler," I say, naming the thingy.

"Yeah, and there's a combination assigned to each employee; no one knows those but the employee, although there's a record in a locked filing cabinet in the main office. Big Jim showed me the cabinet too, and it was clean, no forced entry. So, someone must have been able to unlock the filing cabinet and get the records. At least, that's my guess."

"Who normally has the key to the office, the filing cabinet?" I ask, crunching on a chip.

Talbot takes a bite of his chipped pork sandwich and chews it before answering. "Each shift leader. Four people total. One or two of them's always there when the place's open."

I take a drink of my sweet tea. "Any of them misplace their keys, lose them?"

Talbot grins, pleased with himself. "Evidently not. All four said they've had their keys all along."

"Any ideas?" I ask, curious what he thinks.

He knits his brow theatrically. "Not yet, but the ol' noggin is percolating away. Glub, glub." He taps his temple with each "glub." Talbot often resorts to vocables instead of words, sounds instead of units of meaning.

"What was stolen, by the way?"

The knit becomes less theatrical, more genuine. "That's actually the weirdest part. No cash, no wallets, it turns out. I have a list here…"

My phone rings as Talbot reaches into his pocket for his notebook. I recognize the Burbank number: Rachel Gunner. "Hold on, Talbot. I've got to take this."

I leave my sandwich and chips on one end of Talbot's desk and move into my office, tea in hand. I kick the door closed gently.

"Hey, Rachel!" I walk over to the window, phone to my ear.

"Ford, hey! How are you?"

"Fine. You?"

"Fine. Say, I have some free time, and I'm downtown in Opelika near the courthouse. It's not bad outside right now. Meet me at the fountain out front?"

"That's a public spot. People will see us together."

She laughs. God, that sound! "Ford, we went to a party together Friday. We chatted in the restaurant of the club. People have seen us together. It's perfectly fine with me if people think we're an item."

I shake my head, glad she can't see me. "Including Lake Thornton?"

It's a question I know better than to ask, but it's been on my mind since yesterday. A lot on my mind. I try to ask it as if I'm just making conversation, but it feels like I fail.

She says nothing in response for a moment.

"Sorry, Rachel, not my business. Forget I asked, please."

Another moment of silence.

"Lake *showed up* Saturday morning, Ford, not at my invitation. Not at anyone's invitation. He does that sometimes—just materializes like a mushroom, or a mushroom cloud."

She's annoyed, but I can't tell whether it's with Lake or me or both of us. "As I said, Rachel, I shouldn't have asked."

She sighs. "Ford, Lake and I...we...dated for a short time. We've known each other a long time, kind of grew up together."

I want to know so much more, and I don't. No need to provoke my already wretched imagination. Retreat is the best option. "So, the fountain across from the courthouse? I can be there in ten minutes."

She seems past her annoyance when she answers. "I'll be on one of the benches near the fountain. Can you be away from the office this afternoon?"

"Um, sure." I had planned to drive to LaGrange, talk to Wade Pimberly, but I can do that tomorrow. "Why?"

"I'll explain when you get here. See you soon." She ends the call.

As I replay the conversation in my head, I hear Talbot knock on the door. "Do you want to hear the list of things stolen, Ford?"

"I do, Talbot, but not now. Case. Gotta go. Hold down the fort."

"Always do, Ford, always do."

I park in the lot next to the fountain across from the Lee County Courthouse.

The courthouse, framed against the gray sky, seems aglow. Its red brick and white ornaments jut from against the gray backdrop as if only the courthouse is three-dimensional, monumental; everything else, all the rest, me included, are two-dimensional, slight.

I take a moment and gaze respectfully at its six fluted columns, each extending the two-story height of the building. It's got the same general architectural look as Noble Hall.

The courthouse was built in 1896. It has a central section and two wings. Atop the building is a cornice with dentil work, and atop the cornice is a clock surrounded by scrolling. Above the clock, a simple circular cornice surmounts a circular dome capped with a small ornament. The tall clock tower gives the building a churchy feel that radiates a distance from the building itself.

According to the tower clock, I'm right on time, ten minutes since talking to Rachel. I get out of the car and see her seated on one of the benches that faces the courthouse. She seems to be admiring the building. In her hand is a to-go cup, and I recognize the logo: The Breezeway. She's sipping from a straw, lips tight around it. I make myself take no notice of that fact.

She sees me, smiles around her straw, and waves. I wave back, wondering what sort of lanky spectacle I present. I'm wearing what I rate as my summer Alabama-detective wear: a plain tan T-shirt, jeans, and low black sneakers. It's too hot in the summer here for the high tops I prefer and wear during our few weeks of snowless winter.

Certaine, my competition, always has on a sports coat. Talbot has pointed that out a few times—mainly, I believe, because he hopes, if I took to wearing a sports coat, I'd wear my gun beneath it. I wouldn't. I watch Rachel's face as she watches me walk toward her. She puts her cup down beside her feet and motions for me to join her on the bench.

As I sit, I nod to her cup. "The Breezeway?"

She looks at the cup and then glances behind her. The Breezeway, a local restaurant, stands quite near where we are.

"Yeah, I don't normally eat fried food, or"—she nods at her cup—"drink things with processed sugar, but I kept hearing about *chicken fingers* and *sweet tea*, and my curiosity overwhelmed my resolution."

I grin. "And your verdict?"

"Damn good. What was that sauce you dip the fingers in?"

"That's a Southern state secret; if I told you, I'd have to kill you, and then honor would demand I kill myself."

She laughs for a moment and then fastens on one word. "Secret, huh?" Her expression becomes serious. "Are you a man with lots of secrets, Ford?"

"Me?" I ask as if the very idea is absurd. It is, except for my detective-novel writing. And the confidential work stuff, like my job for her. But that last is a secret she knows.

She examines me closely, that look stealing back into her eyes, the contempt-like thing although that is still not the right word. It's a detachment, a coolness, a withdrawal; it feels like disdain, but it isn't. But I feel again like a specimen beetle in a box: wholly objectified. I squirm a little under that dissector's gaze.

"Are you sure, Ford? No secrets?" Her gaze warms after a moment and releases me from the box I felt I was in. I want to wipe my forehead and blow out a breath, but I don't.

"No secrets. Well, I keep a few secrets for Talbot, but that's just public service." Like Talbot daydreaming about Rachel's gloved hand. A secret I keep trying to forget.

"I can imagine. Just sitting with him in your waiting room the other day was…interesting."

"Did he say something to you?"

She shook her head, picking up her cup. "No, he didn't say anything, really. He just *looked* at me. For a long time. But I could, I don't know, *hear* his brain working."

"Glub, glub?" I ask, and she looks at me like I've lost my mind. I rush on to words. "That's the sound Talbot made today, the soundtrack of his brain *percolating*."

"I'd rather not be the cause of that, of his *percolation*."

"That I understand completely. I'm sorry about him."

She laughs. "It's okay. I suppose I've caused percolation before." She says it with no hint of self-compliment.

"Probably the result of resisting fried food and processed sugar."

She laughs again and shoves my shoulder. I laugh with her.

When we stop, she gives me a look, glances up at the clock tower, and then back to me. "So, are you willing to do a little spying with me?"

I boggle. "Spying?"

"Yes"—she rushes on past the word—"I overheard Uncle Wylie on the phone this morning; he didn't know I did. He was talking to someone secretively, and he made an appointment to meet the person at 2:00 p.m."

I look at the clock tower. "That's fifty minutes from now."

"Uh-huh. I didn't hear the name of the person he was talking to, but I'm sure it's connected to whatever it is he's up to…"

"I assume you overheard where he's meeting this person?"

"The Auburn Coliseum."

I boggle again. I can hardly imagine a more unlikely clandestine meeting place. "Really, that mausoleum?"

She looks confused. "I thought it was the *coliseum*."

"Oh, it is. You'll see why I called it a mausoleum. If we're going to be there in time, we should go. I'll drive this time."

She nods and follows me to my car, slurping the dregs of her tea. I turn to look at her.

"Not wasting any?"

She shakes her head. "When I splurge, I go *whole hog*."

That phrase seems stranger from her than the hat-cowboy line did from Miller Solomon.

She glances one last time at the courthouse. "A beautiful building."

It's beginning to rain again as we get in the Camry. The earlier rains had washed off the dust.

THE AUBURN COLISEUM IS A GIGANTIC, FORGETTABLY UGLY BUILD-
ing just off-center of the Auburn University Campus.

We park on the edge of the vast parking lot surrounding it, a
concrete sea.

I have a couple of ball caps in the trunk of the Camry, both Auburn
caps, and I give Rachel one and take one myself. With another of her
graceful gestures, she sweeps her hair up so that it no longer shows
beneath the cap.

She steps toward me, her face close to mine, and asks, breathlessly,
"How do I look? Like an Auburn fan?"

The sun has come out again. The impulse to kiss her overpowers me,
and I feel myself wobble toward her. She moves toward me, lingers
there, face up to mine, her eyes staring into mine. Her tongue darts
out; she licks her lips.

A student walks by, and I lose my nerve. "We should get inside. It's
a big building. Any idea where they're meeting?"

She's blinking. "Wylie said something about a *court?*"

"Oh."

The coliseum is where Auburn's basketball team used to play. It is
as dark and cavernous inside, even with the lights up, as its outside
promises. The team now plays inside a new building, The Auburn
Arena, across the street, a state-of-the-art facility. By rights, and for
the sake of student and faculty ocular health, the coliseum should
be destroyed. However, it still stands defiant and mute, its rooms
serving as makeshift classrooms, and its basketball court the scene of
graduations or other events.

Rachel and I hurry across the parking lot and enter a door she
points out. The building is cold and dim inside. We stand in the cool
dimness for a moment. Rachel looks at me again then steps close to
me and takes my hand.

She's not wearing gloves this time.

I know the coliseum well; I went to games there often as a boy.

Holding Rachel's hand, I lead her down the hallway into the dimmer fastness of the building.

CHAPTER 7: *Pyne Park*

No one's in the long hallway we walk down, heading toward the basketball court. The dimness of the lights intensifies the coldness of the AC.

"I wish you hadn't called this place a *mausoleum*," Rachel whispers to me, pressing herself against my arm and tightening her grip on my hand.

We walk close together until we reach two large wooden doors. Each door contains a rectangular window, but not much can be seen. The lights are not on above the court. I stop and motion for Rachel to stand where she is. I walk to one of the windows and peer through it. Out at midcourt, I see Wylie Stroud. He's standing close to another man; they are talking intently. A facilities employee is sweeping the floor on the far end of the court, but he pays no attention to the little midcourt enclave. A few people are walking up above the court, above the seats, but they pay no attention either. The speed at which they are walking suggests they are there for their health, using the long, enclosing oval to shield them from the outdoor heat.

Wylie puts his hand on the shoulder of the man and addresses him earnestly. I push the door open a crack, but they are too far from me for me to hear them as anything but a low murmur. I feel Rachel lean against me, her front flattens against my back. Wylie could be screaming, and I wouldn't hear. All I hear is my heart's drumbeat in my ears, my blood's lusty whoops as it marches double-time, flags flying, toward far-flung parts of my anatomy.

She leans harder against me and whispers into my ear. "Do you know that man?"

Now, I know one thing and one thing only: Rachel Gunner. The warmth of her eclipses the rest of reality.

I finally take enough control of myself to choke out an answer. "No, never seen him before."

I reach into my pocket, grab my phone, and take a photo of the two men. I look at it on the screen; Rachel does too, sliding herself from my back to my side.

"Good clandestine photo, Superspy." She giggles softly against my ear, breathy again, her lips brushing the lobe.

It's too much. I turn to her, my arm encircles her, and I kiss her, lightly, but on her full lips.

I pull back, afraid I've overstepped, that I will see that unnamed look in her eyes. But I don't see it. She wraps her warm hand around the back of my neck and pulls me to her, kisses me, my lips, and not lightly. I hear Auburn's pep band playing, even without a basketball game, even without the pep band.

She does finally pull back. Her eyes are large. Surprise shows in them despite the coy smile on the lips I just kissed. "Are you this eager with all your clients?" She's not giggling, but a hint of it lingers in her voice.

"When *I* splurge, I go *whole hog.*" The words are out before I consider them, and she recognizes them. She's about to laugh, or I think she is—hope she is—when her face changes. She can still see through the window over my shoulder.

"He's *coming!*"

I don't take time to look to see who she means, Wylie or the other man. I grab her hand, and we run the way we came but turn into an open doorway, a classroom. I swing the door closed but not shut, and we put our backs to the interior wall of the room. A moment later, footsteps echo past.

I put my finger to my lips and then gesture for Rachel to follow me. She gives me a confused look but nods. We go out of the room and into the hallway. The man is just going through an exit out into the sunlight.

I let him get several strides into the parking lot and follow him. Rachel is behind me. "What are we doing, Ford?"

"I want to know who that is."

The man walks to a rusty, red, Ford pickup and gets in. He's parked not far from my Camry. He pulls out, driving slowly, and I gesture for Rachel to stay low. No one is near us to wonder what we are doing. Keeping cars between us and the pickup, we make it to the Camry just a few seconds after he passes it. We get in, and I pull out. The pickup is getting ready to leave the lot. I do not hurry. It's a Monday in mid-summer; the campus is not crowded, not busy. The pickup turns out of the lot. I let a university bus, orange and blue, pass before I pull out after the pickup, the bus between us.

"Ford, what are we doing?" Rachel repeats her question.

"We're following this guy. I'm hoping we can figure out who he is, where he's going." I reach over and push the lock on the glove box. It falls open, revealing a couple of small notebooks and a few ink pens.

Rachel stares into the glove box. "I thought there'd be a gun."

"I don't carry one," I confess but do not mention the one in my office. "Grab a pen and a notebook, please, and jot down the pickup's license plate number. It's an Alabama plate."

Rachel gets a notebook and a pen and stares ahead. She writes down the number. "Got it." She looks at me expectantly. I keep following the pickup.

The man turns onto College Street, the main road through Auburn, heading south. I keep after him.

Rachel keeps looking at me, at the truck, and back at me. "Why are we following him? We have the plate. Isn't that enough?"

"Nope," I say. "I want to know where he goes after his conversation with Uncle Wylie."

"Maybe he's just going to get coffee or get gas," Rachel responds.

"Maybe, but let's see."

She says nothing more, but the atmosphere in the car has become less comfortable. She keeps stealing glances at me out of the corner of her eye. She's regretting the kiss and wishing she could get away from me instead of being trapped in the car. Or so I figure. To make things easier on her, I decide to pretend the kiss never happened and intensify my focus on the pickup.

The pickup travels down College Street a distance then turns onto I-85 north. He'd gone south to go north, but that was the quickest route to the interstate.

Rachel fidgets as we follow the truck onto the highway. "This is above and beyond. Who knows how far this guy might go—how far he might drive?"

I nod but do not change course. "If he goes too far, we'll stop. But I doubt he took that old beater on any around-the-world cruise. He's not going far—no more than an hour, I bet."

Rachel looks at me and shakes her head, but I have the case between my teeth now, and I'm not about to let go. I may be soft-boiled, but I *am* a serious detective. Wylie stonewalled me at the club, but this fellow I am following feels like a loose thread. Tug him, and I'll find the answer Rachel hired me to get, earn my pay.

I drive on. The man clearly has no worry about being tailed, and I make no effort to be fancy. I just get in the left-hand lane and follow him a few cars back.

We drive for twenty, thirty, thirty-five minutes. Rachel's not said much. Neither have I. She suggested we stop a couple of times, but I just shook my head. I know she's annoyed. I hate it when I must piss off a client to do the job for them. I hate that generally, but I hate it in this case so much it makes my stomach hurt.

When we get to forty minutes, my heart starts to sink. We're near LaGrange, Georgia. We crossed the state line a while back. The truck took the exit to the massive Kia plant, and I thought he might be going there, but he went on past it toward West Point Lake. I have a hunch—sort of.

We wind through some back roads; then, to my relief, the pickup turns on its blinker just before getting to the entrance to Pyne Park. It's not where I feared he was taking us, and I'm surprised this was his destination. I'd been to the park before a couple of years ago. Helen and I went out for a drive one Sunday and ended up here. There's not much to it. West Point Lake is huge and beautiful with lots of lakeside, a dock, a couple of permanently closed restrooms, and a couple of piers. Concrete picnic tables stand, half gray, half mossy green beneath old, tall pines at various spots in the park

The pickup drives to the parking area near the park's defunct restrooms. A car is already parked there. It's a shining and massive old yellow Cadillac. The man gets out of the pickup, and Wade Pimberly, Jane Pimberly's son, gets out of the Caddy. I want to yell, *"Shit,"* but I don't. But my damn hunch (I don't believe in them, by the way) was correct. My conversation with Miller Solomon floods back into my mind. *Shit, shit, shit.*

Rachel studies Wade Pimberly through the windshield. He's at a distance but easy to see in the bright sunshine. I can tell she has no idea who he is; at least, it looks like she doesn't. She noticed me tense up when Wade got out of the car.

"Who is that, Ford? Do you know him?"

I'm not sure what to say. I'm not sure what case I am now on: Rachel's or Miller's. Miller wants what I was doing for him to be confidential. So does Rachel. But Wade's identity isn't confidential, just each side of the dual-case nature of my interest in him.

"That's Wade Pimberly. I don't know him personally, but I know him by sight."

Rachel stares at him for a moment then turns to me, her beautiful face a question mark, her faint freckles noticeable. "Pimberly? Like *Jane Pimberly,* the woman who owned Noble Hall?"

"Yes." I nod, trying not to seem too interested in this fact or too disinterested. Like Goldilocks, I want to be just interested enough—interested *just right.* "He's her son. You've never met him?" My tone is flat but not bored.

She shakes her head convincingly. "No, never seen him. Wylie once mentioned that the woman had a son, but he never mentioned him by first name. Why would this fellow meet with Wylie then meet with Pimberly?"

"I don't know," I venture truthfully, "I don't know." But it worries me. Shit, it worries me.

"Are we done now, or do you want to keep following rusty pickup guy or start following Wade Pimberly?" Rachel seems rattled.

"I guess we're done. But, since we're up here, and since the rain is gone, let's go to one of the other parks—they're everywhere around the lake—and walk a little, stretch our legs?"

I cross my fingers mentally. My hands are in full view on the steering wheel. I'd like to spend more time with her, see if she says anything about that kiss. Or, better yet, if she'd like to try it again. It's steamy outside, but that's sorta my idea.

She shakes her head. "No, I need to get back. Thanks, Ford."

I nod, swallowing disappointment, and we drive out of the park. As we head back to the interstate, Rachel asks, "Can you use the license plate number I wrote down to find out who the guy in the rusty pickup is?"

"Probably."

"Probably?" The note of annoyance is back in Rachel's voice.

"Well," I begin, "I have a friend at the DMV…"

She waits. "And…"

"Not so much an 'and'; it's more a 'but.'"

"*But*…" she says angrily.

"But she's unpredictable. I have to trade favors, and her trades always work out in her favor."

"She? And your favor is in her favor?"

"That's about the size of it. So, I don't ask often." I shake my head to underline my comment.

"Who is this? It's not that…Ruth, is it?" Rachel narrows her eyes.

"No, not Ruth. She works at Ed's Diner. No, this is a woman, but she's more my sister's friend than mine. Helen went to school with her. Her name's Michelle. Michelle Trenton."

"And she's more Helen's friend?"

"Yeah. I had a crush on her when I was younger. She used to come to the house, and I would sneak around to get a peek at her in her shorts."

"Is that still how it is?" I can't tell whether she's still angry or now just toying with me.

"No, no. She's married with two kids. I like her husband, Will. He's a chemistry prof at Auburn, but I feel sorry for him. She's…let's say Michelle's not low maintenance in *any* aspect of her life, not just the DMV."

Rachel doesn't say much for the rest of the drive. I don't take her all the way back to Auburn—just to Opelika. Her Porsche's parked across from the courthouse. She never mentions the kiss, and I don't either. We make small talk about the weather, the kudzu, but mostly we ride in silence.

I cannot figure her out. To say she runs hot and cold is too household-ish. She's not some mundane faucet. She's more like the equator and the Arctic Circle or a blast furnace and a meat locker. She melts me, and she freezes me. The shifts from liquid to solid have me in a state.

She says goodbye warmly enough but not as warmly as I'd like: no kiss, not even a touch of her hand as she gets out of my car and into hers. She leaves the Auburn cap on the seat.

I watch her drive away.

BY THE TIME I GET BACK TO THE OFFICE, TALBOT'S GETTING ON his bike to go home.

He invites me to dinner—Olive's making baked chicken and sweet potatoes—but I beg off. Hungering after Rachel Gunner and consuming one of Olive's feasts are not obviously compatible. But I'm too empty to face being full, if that makes any sense.

Probably not. I'm babbling…glub, glub. Like Talbot, I should forfeit words and manage with sounds.

I need to finish this case for Rachel.

I need to finish with Rachel. For my own good.

It must be obvious to her that she can have me if she wants me and have me for as long as she's here; no one's indicated how long that will be. It would be better to refuse her, but I'm honest enough with myself to know there's no chance. She may refuse fried food and processed sugar, but I've no power to refuse *her*. She's had me since the first day in the waiting room.

If I were like my detective heroes—Phillip Marlowe, say—I'd be more indifferent to how this plays out. But though I may be able to channel a little of Marlowe's form, I can't really channel his content. He's a harder man than I know how to be—although he's not as hard as his reputation among inattentive readers suggests.

Rachel's harder than I know how to be too. I don't mean she's hard exactly, any more than Marlowe is. But that thing with her eyes—that look I struggle to describe—that's beyond my ken or my reach, so it's probably no surprise I can't describe it. I can't live it; I have no first-person access to it.

My POV can't reach that level of objectivity. I see things in personal terms, and I can't help it. Helen complains about it sometimes. As a doctor, she manages that dissector's gaze occasionally.

Not me. I'm not exactly sorry about that or ashamed of it, but it may be a career killer for a PI.

Talbot pedals away, and I start to unlock the door, then reconsider. I go around the building to Miller's office door. The sign says, "Closed," so I go back to my door, but I don't unlock it.

I get back in the car and go home.

Helen's rocking on the porch, smiling to herself. Mondays are usually hard days for her; crowds of parents with over-the-weekend sick kids show up and overwhelm her. But she looks happy, unflustered.

She notices me as I walk up to the house, and she points to the other rocker. A pitcher of lemonade is on the small table between the rockers. An unused glass of melting ice is sweating beside the pitcher.

"Lemonade?"

She nods and grins. "With gin dumped in. Medicinally, you know."

Laughing, I sit and pour some over the melting ice. I take a long swallow, puckering. I somehow always forget how sour Helen likes her lemonade to be. "You seem in a good mood for a Monday evening."

She grins again. "I am. Dr. Nettles came by and took me to Ed's for lunch. We were kind of hoping to see you there. I really want the two of you to talk. I know you saw each other at the party, but…"

"Right. Talbot and I had sandwiches from Ford's BBQ."

Helen frowns. "You need a meal that does not come between slices of bread."

"I suppose."

"How was your Monday?" Helen asks as she pours herself a little more from the pitcher.

"Surprisingly…surprising. I got a new case, and I believe I made some progress on it and my other case both today."

"That's good. I suppose you can't tell me anything?"

I nod. "Not a thing."

She frowns again. "It's frustrating that neither of us can talk much about work."

"Yeah," I agree, "it'd be nice to know some details once in a while."

"Were you in the office all day? Or were you actually out investigating?"

"Out investigating."

"Say," Helen says, "I talked to Ruth. She asked about you. You didn't talk to her today?"

"No." I kissed Rachel Gunner today, and I wanted to kiss her again and again. But I don't say that. I rock.

Helen gives me a look: half mother, half sister. "How do you think it would feel, Ford, pining away for someone who can't or won't make up his damned mind?"

I give no answer, but I know how that feels—not for as long as Ruth has, but I know.

I take out my phone and text Father Halsey, asking if we can chat tomorrow morning. I could use some wise counsel, even if it comes packaged as abuse.

Jesus—even the Episcopal priest is harder than I am.

CHAPTER 8: *Confessional*

I feel better about things the next morning. Tuesday. Not great, and I'm not looking forward to the task I have planned today, but I feel better about things.

I drive from Opelika to Auburn where Father Halsey is the priest at St. Dunstan's. It's a beautiful brick church rooted beneath tall trees near the center of Auburn and across the street from Toomer's Corner. As I mentioned, I sing in the choir, and we'll have practice tonight, but I want to talk to Father Halsey before I head to Ed's.

I need to talk to Ruth, but I'm still not sure what to say. I hope Father Halsey, direct line to the heavens and all, will help me figure it out. I park my car out front, take the side steps up to the church, and go in the door.

"Ford!" I turn to look into the small room from which the voice issued and see Father Halsey's secretary, Diana Wentworth. She's the only woman—or man, for that matter—I rate a match for Olive Norton. Like Olive, Diana is short in stature but tall in spirit, towering, a woman to be reckoned with. Father Halsey believes that wisdom begins with the fear of the Lord and the fear of Diana Wentworth.

He keeps the commandments of each.

"Hey, Miss Diana," I say in return, waving into the room, "is the big guy around?"

"Depends on which one you want," she says, grinning at me from her desk chair. "One is omnipresent, ubiquitous, and I'm pretty sure that means He's around; the other is located but large enough to take up more than his fair share of space. You'll find him in the Sanctuary."

She looks back down at the paperwork on her desk, done with me for now. Our routine is for me to stop again for more talk before I leave. She doesn't like to latch onto visitors until they've met with Father Halsey.

I walk across the sitting room, in front of the large fireplace, and through the open double doors leading into the Sanctuary. Father Halsey is standing in the back of the large room, looking up toward the altar. He notices me in the wide doorway but does not say anything. He focuses back on the altar, tilting his head side to side.

I watch in silence. He walks slowly toward the altar between the two rows of pews. He stops as he reaches the first pew, the last in the direction he is walking.

"Women's committee wants to put some flowers here on the edge of the altar." He points to a spot near where I am standing and then to another on the opposite side. "They mean well, but I think the Sanctuary itself is beautiful. No need to gild refined gold, to paint the lily."

Shakespeare. Despite Father Halsey's relationship to The Book, I sometimes forget that he's a very bookish man. His manner disguises that fact about him most of the time.

I walk to stand beside him and look at the spots he pointed to. "I'm with you, Father. Unnecessary. Kindly meant but unnecessary."

He glances at me with amusement. "Are you willing to go to their meeting tomorrow and tell them that?"

I gulp and shake my head. He laughs softly. "And they think that Daniel's sojourn in the lion's den cannot be repeated today. Oh, ye of little imagination!"

He laughs again, and I laugh with him.

"What can I do for you, Merrick? Your text last night didn't tell me what we are going to chat about."

He sits down on the first pew. It creaks under him. He unbuttons his gray suit jacket and tugs at his collar. "Gonna be another hot one. I wonder sometimes, Merrick, if that's the secret to the Christ-haunted South: it's so hot no one can forget about hell."

I mull that over without comment and sit down beside him.

"So, Merrick, confess." He faces me and waits.

I breathe in and breathe out. "I'm going to talk to Ruth today, square things with her, and I just wanted to talk to you about it before I do it."

He nods slowly. "You want me to pretend to be her?"

He may be joking; he may be serious. This is one of the dangers of talking with Father Halsey, not knowing until it gets you smacked.

I look at him: his gray coat, his black, tab-collar clergy shirt, his gray pants, his black shoes, and his broad, heavy shoulders.

I don't think I can pretend he's Ruth. Nope.

"No, I just wanted to tell you, generally, what I'm going to say."

"Well, then tell me, generally."

I lean forward onto my elbows, stare at the gleaming hardwood floor. I can almost see myself in it. It takes me a moment to get started. "So, I need to tell her that I don't, you know, right now, don't...um... have any romantic interest in her. Other interests, sure: she's my friend, and I admire her, you know, really, a lot, but I don't...love her, not *that* way, and I don't...um..."

Halsey shakes his head a little and smiles, but he's annoyed.

"Articulate you *aren't*, Merrick. But you can surely spin word salad. Lord, you can't manage to talk without gumming up the works?"

I shrug. "I'm nervous. I spiral when I'm nervous, bog things down with unhelpful qualifications..."

"Yes, you do. But we both agree Ruth deserves better."

I nod my head. "Yeah, we do."

Halsey shifts in the pew, grunts, and stares out the double doors, but not at anything in particular.

"Look, Ford"—his use of my first name is a measure of his seriousness—"is there someone you're romantically interested in?"

My mouth opens and works guppy-like. Didn't see that question coming. Halsey's tone makes it clear he already knows the answer. Heat rises in my face, but I might as well admit it. "Yes, yeah, Wylie Stroud's niece, Rachel Gunner."

He nods. "I ran into Olive Norton at the Piggly Wiggly. She told me you were money."

"Moony?"

"I understood. So, you have a hankering for the big blonde and not the small brunette?" He extends his arm along the top of the pew and drums his fingers on its top. "What do you know about her, the big blonde?"

"Not much. She's from California. Burbank. Her uncle Wylie encouraged her to come here for a visit. He told me he thought she needed to get away from there, to 'slow down,' as he put it. That she wanted, hoped, to slow down."

"And?"

"And...that's all. That's all I know."

"But you've spent time with her? Went to that party? Saw her at the club?"

"How'd you know that?"

"Other women's committee members. It's my version of Sherlock's Baker Street Irregulars."

I chuckle, imagining those wealthy ladies as London street urchins. "Yes, I went to the party with her and saw her at the club where I did learn one more thing about her. Once upon a time, she had a boyfriend named Lake Thornton, and he and his abs are currently in town."

I realize that except for the brief conversation on the phone, Rachel and I never talked about Lake yesterday. Not at all. I'm tempted to feel good about that until it starts to worry me.

Father Halsey is watching my face. "Envy's a deadly sin, you know. The only deadly sin that lacks a honeymoon."

I have no idea what that means, and he can tell. "All the other deadly sins, pride, anger, sloth, gluttony, greed, lust," he lifts his eyebrows a bit, "they all seem like good ideas at the time, at first. A honeymoon. But envy never seems like a good idea, not even at first."

I mull that over, along with his eyebrows lift. "I suppose that's right. Are you hinting, somewhat subtly, that my interest in Rachel is less romantic, more...um...*basic*?"

Remembering my reaction to her yesterday makes the heat in my face intensify.

Halsey regards me for a moment, then answers. "Just trying to get you to examine yourself, your life. I know you; you're not all surface, Ford, like most folks are. I love them all, as Jesus told me, but I know them too, as Jesus did. You'll be unhappy with someone who's all surface, and I confess, after meeting Rachel Gunner, she not only seems all surface to me, she seems all *mirrored* surface. The human equivalent of a pair of sunglasses. All reflection. She's a beauty, no doubt. A stop-and-stare, double-take beauty. But you know *nothing* about her. You managed to tell me all you know in a few seconds. And yet you're choosing her over Ruth? A woman you do know. Because that's what you're doing. If Rachel Gunner hadn't shown up, you'd have dithered a while longer about Ruth, then finally asked her out, started dating her, and married her. And you'd be happily married to her, tiptoeing home for afternoon quickies and keeping her abed all morning on your Fridays."

He pauses for a moment. I'm shell-shocked: I've never heard so many words from him at once—and "quickies" and "abed"?

He's uncomfortable with his own speech, but after readjusting in the pew and looking around us, he continues. "You know that's true. It's why you're having such a hard time. You know the sort of future you'd have with Ruth, and it's no bad future, but you're wondering about something else...a different future."

I don't say anything, but I find I am nodding my head.

"But be honest: do you have any reason to believe you have a future with *Rachel Gunner*? Any reason to think she's here long-term?"

Now I'm shaking my head.

"So, you're planning to follow her back to California?"

This time I speak. "No, I don't want to live anywhere else; God help me."

Father Halsey laughs silently. "God help us both, kid. So, what're you doing? I haven't told you a single thing you don't know, despite your refusal to tell it to yourself. You *want* Rachel Gunner and, priest or no, I'm a man. I *get* that. But do you see anything *real* happening with her? Can you forecast any future? And if you can't…" He shrugs.

I say no more. He says no more. We just sit together in the Sanctuary until, a few minutes later, he stands, squeezes my shoulder, and walks past the altar and out the rear door.

I sit in silence for a few minutes more. My insides are jumbled. I stand and walk back through the double doors, heading back the way I came in.

"Ford!" I stop and enter Diana's office just as she puts her phone down. "You're going to be here this afternoon for choir practice, right?"

I gather myself. "Yes, sure, Diana. I'll be here unless something comes up at work."

She grins at me, her eyes sparkling. "Big case, I bet?"

"No—a couple of things are going on, but I don't know if either is a big case."

Diana devours detective novels. I can see one, an aged paperback, peeking out from under the spreadsheet on her desk, Richard S. Prather's *Always Leave 'Em Dying*. Good book. It has one of the great detective novel lines: "It was one of those rare, smog-free days when you can see Los Angeles from Los Angeles."

Diana's a big fan of Burney Lennox books, but she has no idea he's my detective, that I am *Logan Smythe*, the author of the books. She talks to me about them sometimes because I'm a detective. I plan someday to tell her my secret, but it won't be today.

She gives me a look like she doesn't believe my claim about no big cases. She glamorizes my life. I should have her sit through a long summer afternoon in the office with just me, Talbot, and a few stray flies.

"I know detectives can't talk about their work, really"—she winks at me—"so I *understand* you. Say, do you know when the new Burney Lennox novel will be out?"

I picture the legal pad back at the house. "No, but I read somewhere it may still be a few months, maybe a year."

"Shit," she says, then turns radish red and looks around to see if anyone else heard her, "I mean, shoot. I've re-read all the others. I'm ready for a new one."

"Me too," I say, meaning something other than what she means. I need to finish *Do I Not Bleed?* I've been fiddling with it too long. When I was working on it the other night, I kept trying not to turn the central female character into Rachel Gunner, so I made little headway. "Will you still be here when choir practice starts?"

"Probably. It's a busy day around here. Father Halsey has a lot on his schedule—you're just the start—and I have to keep him straight and keep the church running."

"He depends on you."

She beams. "Like to think so."

"See you later, Diana."

"You too, Ford."

I SUSPECT THAT DETECTIVE NOVELS ARE A BIG PART OF MY PROBLEM. Problems.

I suspect they're part of my problem with Ruth. Father Halsey's right. I could be happy with Ruth. I'd almost certainly come to love her. But I can't imagine Ruth as the central female character in one of my novels or one of the novels I admire.

Don't get me wrong. I'm nursing no obsession for so-called femme fatales. I'm no fan of that archetype in stories or life. Maybe there are seductively deadly women out there, but I doubt there are many, and they wouldn't interest me anyway. I'm not chasing a touch of evil.

But I am chasing what Rachel Gunner can do to me—has done to me—her ability to make everything vanish but her, to recreate my world in her image. Maybe I shouldn't chase that, and I don't know if I understood I had wanted it before she appeared in my office, but I do and now know I have been.

Ruth doesn't do that; she's lovely, she's good, but she can't make the world disappear.

And, despite my respect for Father Halsey, I don't reckon the difference is a difference between a woman I'm lusting after and one I'm not.

I can't deny I *want* Rachel, but that desire, intense as it is, is not what allows her to make the world disappear. The truth is, I want Ruth too. Or I did. Maybe not as intensely, but intensely enough. I was just too cowardly or diffident to act on it. But, even when I wanted her, Ruth couldn't make the world disappear.

I've been pondering this on the way to Ed's.

I park, get out, and take a deep breath. Purposely, I'm here after the breakfast rush.

Time to talk to Ruth.

As I expect, Ed's is nearly empty. Ruth's leaning against the counter in front of the coffee maker. She's got a cup of coffee in her hand, sipping it. She half-smiles over it at me as I enter.

"Hi, Ford." Her tone's reserved, but I expected that.

"Ruth, hey! May I have a cup of coffee?"

"Sure. Anything to eat?"

"No, I don't think so. Just the coffee." I slide into a booth away from the few other customers.

Ruth places her cup in a bus tray, puts a cup and spoon on a saucer, pours coffee in the cup, and brings it to me.

"Can you sit for a minute, Ruth?" I ask softly.

She nods, but there's dread in her eyes as she slides into the opposite seat. "What's on your mind, Ford?"

I still don't have a plan, a speech, but I will do the best I can. "Ruth, I'm sorry about Friday night. About the mix-up about the party, about the dust-up with Certaine. About it all." She's looking at me intently as if waiting. "I'm sorry about Rachel."

A slight shift in her expression reveals that the last was what she was waiting on, dreading. She blows out a sigh. I stir my coffee cup but don't take a sip.

"I saw you with her at the party, Ford. Saw you dancing with her, saw you look at her. I'm not a dull girl. A woman who's worth her salt knows when she's lost on points, so she should know when she's lost by knockout. And I do know, but I appreciate you coming to tell me so. I know you; this isn't much easier for you to say than it is for me to hear. Maybe we missed our chance back during that summer after high school." She shrugs sadly but smiles through it. "I don't know. Timing matters."

"I don't know either, Ruth. And I am sorry—for everything."

She's controlling herself; her effort's obvious. I stir my coffee again, finding it hard to look at her.

"So, Rachel's relocating to Alabama?" she asks.

Ouch. "I don't know. I haven't heard that she has plans to stay. I don't know her plans." I'm embarrassed admitting this after what just passed between us.

Ruth leans forward. "But you know *her* already?" I can tell she regrets that last word as soon as she says it.

I don't have a clear answer to that—though perhaps that *is* the answer, perhaps that means the answer is *no*.

But—well, here's the thing. For all the hot and cold, the kisses, the dances, and the distances, I do right now feel like I know her. I can't describe what I know. She swamps my descriptive categories, and yet I know her. In the past few days, I've glimpsed *her*. Not continuously. Maybe not deliberately on her part. But I've glimpsed her; I know I have.

That's the faith that's within me. What's the line? Father Halsey said it to me weeks ago in a different context. *"Now faith is the substance of things hoped for, the evidence of things not seen."*

This is going to end badly for me, likely. I foresee it coming; maybe I even expect it. But I'm hoping for another outcome. No risk, no faith.

"I believe I do, Ruth."

She looks at me doubtfully but doesn't challenge me.

Ruth and I manage a few more cursory remarks, but neither of us wants to continue our conversation now.

I excuse myself, pay for my coffee, and leave.

I drive to the office and walk inside. I've got my notebook from the glove compartment in my hand. Talbot's eating an egg salad sandwich, drinking black coffee, and playing some video game, but I don't look carefully enough to know which one. I return his wave and retreat into my office, shutting the door.

As I sit down, hoping work might make me feel better, I pull out my phone and call Michelle Trenton at the DMV. It takes me a minute to get her extension.

"Michelle Trenton," I hear her say.

"Hey, Michelle. It's Ford. I'm hoping you will do me a favor."

"Indeed? You know the drill. Tit for tat. What's your offer?"

"I'll watch the boys Friday night—let you and Will go out to dinner." Her boys are five and seven. I like them, but they are not fully domesticated. Michelle considers the offer.

"Really? From when to when?"

"Um, from 5:00 p.m. until you two get back."

"You must want this information."

"I do." She knows I once had a crush on her. I worry that she still likes to think I do.

"Ok, deal. Give me the plate. I'll call you later."

I give her the number and hang up. I pass on lunch and spend the afternoon shut in my office, studying the music for choir practice, and making notes for *Do I Not Bleed?* But mostly, I am waiting for the expected call from Michelle and the hoped-for one from Rachel.

The second never comes, but the first does just as I'm getting ready to leave the office.

"The vehicle, a Ford pickup, belongs to a man named Bill Peppers."

She gives me his address and place of employment, and I underline that he works at Briggs and Stratton.

I'm already late when I get off the phone, so I don't follow up on Mr. Peppers. I rush out to the car and drive back to St. Dunstan's.

I take the side stairs in a leap and hurry through the door.

"Ford!"

I turn at the door to Diana's office.

Rachel Gunner stands beside Diana, and Rachel holds a hymnal in her hand.

"Hey, Ford, meet Rachel Gunner. She just joined the choir!"

CHAPTER 9:
Hymn, Her, and Fireflies

Rachel Gunner in the choir?

Father Halsey asked me this morning about forecasting the future. I didn't forecast this.

Rachel smiles at Diana. "Oh, I *know* Ford, Miss Wentworth. We're dating."

Diana's mouth drops like her jaw hinges have been freshly oiled. "Dating?"

Rachel laughs. "Yes, you could say that."

Diana looks at me in wonderment. "Dating." It's not a question now. "Ford, you never said."

Rachel slips against me and takes my hand. "It's *new*, Miss Wentworth. We're both still…adjusting…to the idea."

For the first time that I've seen her, not counting the club, Rachel is dressed for the Alabama heat. She's got on a white cotton dress and white leather sandals. Her hair's held back from her face by two small white barrettes.

She smiles at me and squeezes my hand. I still haven't spoken.

Diana's gazing at us. Together.

Wonderment.

Words, I used to have words. None now, nope. "I…we…" I manage nothing remotely coherent, only than to smile back at Rachel.

Diana laughs. "Fear not, Ford"—she glances at Rachel—"Rachel just brought you tidings of great joy!"

Both women chuckle at me. I'm still waiting to be revisited by language. "I…we…I didn't know…" Words begin to return, and I change the destination of my sentence. "I didn't know you sang."

Rachel reaches up and straightens the collar on my shirt. It's a small thing, done without fanfare or comment, and yes, we've held hands, danced close, and kissed, but this is somehow the most *intimate* thing that has passed between us. Diana notes it. And then I begin to wonder about it and about the whole scene, to wonder what's happening, what Rachel is doing. Was the straightening for my benefit or Diana's, or both?

"Oh, there you are!" A new voice.

Rachel looks past me, and I see her face shift, but I turn before deciphering the shift.

Lake Thornton stands in the door to Diana's office, gleaming. His smile hangs in the doorway like the Cheshire Cat's in *Alice's Adventures*, except that his seems to arrive before him, not linger after him.

Neither Rachel nor I speak for a moment, so Diana does. "Hello! I'm Diana Wentworth, the church secretary. You're a friend of…Rachel's?" Diana makes an educated guess.

Lake moves balletically into the room, speaks to Diana. "Hello, ma'am"—Lake says that word with a hint of irony as if he's subtly poking fun at the South, at Diana—"I'm Lake Thornton. Rachel's *friend*, as you say."

Diana nods to Lake and then looks from Lake to me and back again.

Rachel is still holding my hand. I'd expected her to drop it when Lake appeared, but she didn't. Diana's trying to figure out the palpable change in the room's atmosphere, and so am I.

Lake faces Rachel. "Wylie told me you'd be here, so I thought I'd come to hear. Bored out at the farm. Rachel Gunner in a choir was a sight not to be missed." There's an undertone in his voice, unmistakably present but not unmistakably clear, and he obviously expects Rachel to understand it. If she does, she hides her understanding.

I start to say something, but Father Halsey fills the door. He takes in the scene and the players with a quick, sweeping glance. "Time to get started, folks."

He leaves. Rachel, still holding my hand, tugs me forward, past Lake. "Time to sing, Ford."

I follow her out of the office and hear Diana behind me. "Mr. Thornton, you can sit in the Sanctuary if you'd like to listen."

Rachel's face, when she looks back at me, is slightly flushed. But she smiles at me, slows, and lets me lead her.

A temporary riser stands in front of the altar on the near side, roughly where I was standing this morning while Father Halsey contemplated flowers. Several people are already on them. Rachel releases my hand so that I can climb to the top level with the other tenors. Father Halsey, watching, nods toward the altos when Rachel looks at him. She steps up on the lowest level with a quick, bright smile at me. The flush in her cheeks is gone.

I see Lake seated about midway down the aisle. He must have gone outside and come in through the Sanctuary's main door. Diana stands at the end of his pew. She's waiting for me to make eye contact. When I do, she rolls her eyes in Lake's direction and gives me an I'm-on-your-team smirk. I grin back.

She then takes her seat in front of the organ keyboard.

Father Halsey takes his place behind a tall music stand. "Okay, okay, everyone"—the murmuring group quiets—"it's time to start. Let me take a second and welcome our new member, Rachel Gunner." Father Halsey looks at Rachel, and then, as everyone begins to say "hello" to Rachel, he glances at me.

"All right," he goes on, "let's begin with 'When I Survey the Wondrous Cross.'"

I said that my relationship with the church is complicated.

I don't attend, not regularly. Sometimes I attend on Christmas or Easter; sometimes, I slip in the back on a random Sunday and sit for a while, taking in Father Halsey's sermon. Dad and Mom took us regularly when we were small. I suppose their death complicated my relationship with the church. No need to go into that now; it's easy enough to guess how it mostly goes.

I loved the music as a boy, and I love it still. Nothing's changed that. If anything, losing Dad and Mom made the music sweeter, dearer to me. Hymns like the one we're about to sing, the sublime words by Isaac Watts, transport me. I can't give the music up. The choir I'm in does not sing at weekly services—just at special events.

"So," Father Halsey begins, "just a couple of thoughts on what we are about to sing, about the words themselves. We will talk about the music as we work on it. This is a spiritual meditation, a spiritual exercise, a spiritual discipline. The keyword, for our purposes, is 'survey,' the verb of the first line. The song is a visual survey of the scene of Christ's crucifixion. Visual, but also spiritual, an exercise of receptive lucidity. The survey's point is not to revel in Christ's suffering but, rather, to be humbled by it and, humbled, spurred on to life, a better life. Christ's *death*, folks, is always about *life*..."

He says a bit more, and I listen, but I also study Lake. He's trying hard to hide his boredom and his...discomfort. The easy, sure suavity of his manner fails him in the Sanctuary.

We sing through the song once, and Father Halsey stops us to comment on the music, the different parts, and the harmonies. Lake gets up and leaves, hurrying more with each step.

I glance down at Rachel and see her reaction to his leaving—watch her shoulders drop. She does not glance up at me.

WE FINISH REHEARSAL, AND THE CHOIR MEMBERS CROWD AROUND Rachel, introducing themselves and being introduced. I descend from the riser, and Father Halsey meets me. He glances at Rachel then looks at me.

"All mirrored surface?" I ask quietly.

He shrugs uncertainly. "She's got a pleasant voice. Shocked me when she came in, asked about the choir. She came to me first, here in the Sanctuary. I sent her to Diana to get registered, get the music." He pauses. "That woman's a puzzler."

I have no words of dispute.

As the crowd around Rachel disperses, she walks to me and takes my hand again. "Say, Ford, since it's so hot and since we've still got some daylight, why don't you come out to the house for a swim."

"Swim? There's no pool at Noble Hall."

She nods. "True, but there's a lovely little pond in the woods."

The way she says that makes my pulse race. She smiles a slow smile at me. "Can you go home, get some trunks, and head over?"

"Sure. Will it just be you and me?"

"Yes, Ford, just us. Uncle Wylie's at the club, and Lake is going to Montgomery tonight; he's supposed to stay over. So, no worries about unwanted company... See you soon."

Her smile becomes frankly flirtatious, and my pulse redlines. She stands on her toes, brushes my cheek with her lips, and then leaves the Sanctuary through the front doors.

Diana comes up to stand beside me; she must have been close enough to overhear. "Get moving, Ford. That's not an invitation you want to answer slowly."

WHEN I TURN INTO THE DRIVE AT NOBLE HALL, I SEE RACHEL ON the second-floor balcony. She's wearing a wrap over her bikini. She waves at me eagerly then gestures that she's on her way down.

I park in front of the overseer's house beside Rachel's Porsche, which I notice is now dusty as I climb from the Camry.

Rachel comes out of the house in the wrap and wearing beach sandals. She's carrying towels and a small cooler. I have my trunks in my hand, and I changed into sandals myself.

"Hey, Ford," she says. She seems in high spirits. She points to the house. "Go inside, turn right, turn left, and you'll find a bathroom. You can put on your trunks and leave your things there. Oh"—she points to the stoop of the rear door—"will you carry that Bluetooth speaker for me?"

I run inside and change, leaving my jeans in the bathroom. When I return, I am in my trunks. I grab the speaker. Rachel's standing on an extension of the half-circle driveway that leads back to the woods. Against the edge of the woods, an old barn stands and, near it, another small house like the overseer's house. It is unoccupied.

We start to walk in that direction toward the edge of the woods.

"I enjoyed choir practice," Rachel offers, "I haven't really sung since I was in show choir in high school."

That is about the first piece of personal information she's shared with me. I want to know more, but I try not to sound too eager. "Where was high school?"

"Then, it was in Kansas. I was just at that high school one year, just in the show choir the one year, but I wish I could have stayed longer, in Kansas and the choir."

I nod carefully but do not ask anything more. We walk on and reach the edge of the woods. The extension of the driveway ends, but a clear, wide path leads into the woods. The sloping sunlight of the afternoon makes everything seem to glow golden. A rare breeze blows. Alabama summers are typically preternaturally still, and the breeze rustles the leaves around us.

Rachel points to the path then takes it. I walk beside her.

"I moved around a lot as a girl. My parents split when I was little. I lived with my mom, but she got sick—lupus. Pretty soon, after a couple of years, she couldn't take care of me, so I moved to live with my dad. But he changed locations often because of work, so I never settled anywhere. Mom died in my early teens. I didn't feel settled until I went off to college. But even that turned out to be temporary…"

She trails off as we continue to walk. I'm not sure what to say, if anything.

"I lost my parents when I was about the same age…"

She stops and looks into my eyes. She nods, moves the small cooler into the hand carrying the towels, and she takes my free hand in her now free one.

THE POND IS LARGER THAN I EXPECTED. IT'S ENCIRCLED BY WOODS; the green trees and blue sky reflect on the silvery, glassy surface. A graying wooden pier extends out into the water. A makeshift, flat raft is tied to the end.

The breeze had stopped as we walked, and now it returns, disturbing the glassy surface of the water, rippling the trees and sky, nudging the raft.

Rachel walks to the pier and stops, gazing at the water. She sets the cooler down, takes one of her towels, the largest one, and spreads it on the grass just in front of the edge of the pier. I place the speaker on the towel, and she moves the cooler beside it.

She looks at me, her eyes as warm and accessible as during our dance at the party. She kicks off her sandals and shrugs off the wrap. Red bikini. I work not to stare. It helps that I blind myself for a moment by taking off my T-shirt, and then I become self-conscious—too self-conscious to look at Rachel for fear I'll see her looking at me. I have no abs like Lake to offer. I'm not out of shape, far from it, but I've never made any effort to *sculpt* myself. Narcissus and I have never been that close. But maybe he and I shouldn't have been so distant.

I finally look at Rachel, and she is looking at me, smiling. "Ford, if you have your phone, why don't you turn on some music? I'm never good at choosing."

Turning on the speaker, I pull my phone from the pocket of my trunks and pair them. I flip through my music; I have a lot, and I want something that fits the scene. I choose Matt Pond PA's album, *Still Summer*. The first song, "A Spark," comes on, and Rachel tilts her head listening.

"I like that," she says, closing her eyes and swaying to the song. I watch her for a moment, understanding suddenly just how serious my condition has become—like life threatening, cardiac. She opens her eyes and laughs. "C'mon!"

She runs effortlessly to the end of the pier and dives into the pond, knifing perfectly into the air and cleaving the water with no splash. I plunge in behind her, with less grace and more splash.

The water's cold, colder than I expected, and it shocks me for a second. I sink; the water's deeper than I expected too. Dark.

And then I feel Rachel around me, warm and strong. We break the surface together, gasping and then laughing together.

No matter what happens, I will always have this moment: the sinking golden sun, the soft breeze, the cold water, her warm skin. I turn to her; she blinks water from her eyes then kisses me and swims away. I swim after her. She lets me catch her, and we kiss again. She swims to the pier, climbs out of the water, and sits down. I climb up after her.

"Get us a beer, Ford?"

I nod, assuming that's what's in the cooler. I pad wetly to it, leaving footprints on the pier. I dig two beers out of the ice and carry them to her, sitting down cross-legged next to her. I open one and hand it to her. She takes a drink as I open mine. The title song on the Matt Pond PA album starts, the opening lyrics floating on the air.

"Ford," she says as she listens, her voice soft and dreamy as she stares into the water, "do you ever think about a different life?"

She turns to face me, her hair darkened by the water, her eyes deeper than the pond. I take a sip of my beer. "Different how?"

"Like, I don't know, a reversal. A one-eighty? Can a person do that: change direction?"

I look out over the water. Dusk is settling on us and bringing fireflies with it. As each glows above the water, its light is reflected. Doubles, reflections. Rachel looks, and I hear her breath catch.

"I don't know," I begin softly, trying to answer her question with a seriousness that matches the question and the transcendent moment. "I think so. Habits can be hard to break, that's sure, but people get mixed up. The problem's not breaking the old habits as if you were going back in time. We break old habits by creating new ones, going forward in time. The new habits, if we make them, shoulder the old ones out."

She does not look at me; she's staring at the water again, the blinking fireflies and their blinking reflections. She gives herself a shake after a few minutes pass.

"So, did you talk to your friend at the DMV, your old crush, about the rusty pickup?"

I hadn't thought about that since I found Rachel in Diana's office. "Yes, actually. The man's name is Bill Peppers. He works at Briggs and Stratton."

She gives me a puzzled look.

"It's a factory on the south end of Auburn. They manufacture small engines, mainly for lawn mowers and suchlike. It's been an important local employer for years. Anyway, the Peppers guy works there. I plan to go out there tomorrow afternoon and see if I can find out anything. I guess I'll take Talbot with me."

"Really? Does he detect too? I thought he just did…well, whatever he does in that front room."

"The boss out at Briggs and Stratton is Big Jim Sutton. He doesn't like me, but he likes Talbot."

Her puzzled look returns. "Doesn't like *you* but does like *Talbot*?"

"Big Jim is Ruth's father."

"Oh," Rachel says simply. She sips her beer then follows the new line of conversation. Her tone is light. "Ruth seems like she's nice."

"She is. We've been friends for a long time. We dated a little as high school ended."

"Not since?"

"No, not really. We've gone to some things together but never as a couple, a real couple."

"Because of her dad?"

I chuckle. "No, it's sort of the other way around." I don't explain that.

Trying to match her tone, I say, "Lake seems like he's…nice." I can't keep the pause out of my comment.

Rachel chuckles. I love that sound. Little bells on trees. "Lake is Lake."

"You say you two grew up together?"

She sighs. "In a manner of speaking, yes."

"But I thought you moved around a lot."

She nods, glances at me, and then away. "My dad sort of adopted Lake. He ended up moving around with us for a while."

I don't quite understand that, but I don't ask for an explanation. I just nod and sip my beer.

Rachel scoots closer until she is against my side. She reaches for my arm and makes it clear she wants me to put it around her. I do and pull her close. She turns quickly and kisses my ear, then rests her head on my shoulder.

To say that I'm not sure exactly what's happening—that I've been lost since Rachel told Diana we were dating—would be an understatement. This, as darkness gathers, doesn't just feel like a date; it feels like us *together*.

But we've never actually dated, so how can we be together? I don't pursue the question. Rachel lifts her head, we look at each other, and serious kissing commences.

Matters are about to get out of hand—because matters are about to get in hand—when Rachel pulls back. She gives me a teasing laugh and stands, brushing her bottom before stepping carefully off the pier and onto the raft—all of this without a hint of losing her balance.

She crooks her finger at me as she sits down on the raft. I step out, surprising myself by not falling in or upsetting the raft, and I sit down beside her. She unties the raft and paddles with one hand on her side. She gives me a look, and I start paddling with one hand on mine.

The raft moves slowly away from the pier. Rachel stops paddling after a distance, and I do too. She stretches out on the raft and motions for me to do the same. We are beneath the fireflies now. Their lights shine down on us, as do the now-visible stars above the winged beetles.

I try to sharpen all my senses, to etch this in my memory. I survey it all.

We drift for a while. Then Rachel asks, "Bill Peppers?"

"Yeah, does that name mean anything to you?"

"No, I've never heard it before. I'd never seen him before yesterday."

"Mm-hmm."

"So, what did you have to trade your old crush for the information?"

"Michelle? I'm babysitting her boys, five and seven, on Friday night."

Rachel rolls carefully onto her side, looking at me. "Want some help?"

There are so many things I should ask her, so much I don't understand. But some nights should just *be* and not *mean*. I roll over carefully, say *yes*, and serious kissing recommences.

CHAPTER 10: *Risk*

No risk, no faith.

I feel the risk this morning as I wake up.

Last night: the pond, Rachel. Serious kissing that didn't lead to anything more serious than an occasional lightning moment of contact, a warm caress over damp cloth.

We walked hand in hand from the pond. I put on my jeans in the bathroom, and after one last lingering kiss, I left Noble Hall.

I wake to the sound of a storm: pelting rain and rumbling thunder. I would like to just stay in bed, relive last night, and enjoy the warmth of my blanket in my air-conditioned bedroom, but Helen won't have it. She knocks on my door.

"Ford!"

"What?"

"It's here; it's in my kitchen, and it's alive!"

Shit, Talbot. Before I went to sleep, I texted him to come over so that we could drive out to Briggs and Stratton together. I changed my mind about the time. I want to go this morning, not this afternoon, and I told him so. But I forgot; my blanket is so warm.

Helen's not a fan of Talbot. Not at all. It doesn't help that Talbot used to spend hours spying on her each summer, memorizing each bikini she wore when sunbathing behind the house. He once showed Helen *The Bikini Diary* as he called it, fully illustrated and colored with colored pencils, each detailed picture surrounded by lavish commentary.

I suppose he thought it was a compliment. I warned him—seriously *warned* him. Helen erupted like Vesuvius. Talbot was nearly vaporized.

Helen's never forgiven Talbot. She normally pretends he is not my friend, that he does not work for me, and that he does not exist. When she is forced to admit his existence, she calls him "it."

"Be down in a minute."

I roll out of bed and dash to the bathroom. I run under and out of the shower water, soap makes a brief appearance in between, and then I towel off, brush my teeth, and dash back to my room. I throw on clothes and am downstairs in under five minutes.

Talbot sits at the small kitchen table, trying not to fidget, and failing. No doubt Helen told him she'd kill him if he moved. Helen stands scowling by the gas stove, her beloved frying pan stuffed with scrambled eggs and maple sausage links. She holds the spatula like a weapon of war. The kitchen smells wonderful despite the atmosphere threatening bloodshed. Talbot and Helen both sigh in audible relief when I come in.

Thunder rumbles.

Helen places scrambled eggs and a couple of links on each of three plates.

She sits down with hers and leaves me to get my own plate and give the last to Talbot. Talbot glances at Helen and thanks her, but she does not acknowledge him or his cautious thanks. Helen glares at me and takes her plate from the kitchen table into the dining room.

"So, Talbot," I say to cover her relocation, "do you still have that list of items missing at Briggs and Stratton?"

He stares at me while chewing, not understanding the question for a minute. Then, he holds up a hand, his index finger. He puts down his fork and yanks his notebook out of his rear pocket. He flips the yellow cover open and reads while hunting blindly for his fork with his other hand.

"Evidently, the following items went missing and were reported over a period of months. A pair of Maui Jim sunglasses and case; a corduroy jacket, olive drab, medium; a Cabela's cap, black, plain, five-panel; a pair of work boots, size ten; an old Timex digital watch; a pair of leather work gloves; an open package of Q-Tips; a small bag of red delicious apples, a couple of cans of tuna; and a paperback copy of the first Harry Potter book."

I eat my sausage as he reads. He finishes and flips the cover closed. Finding his fork, he resumes eating, but he's got one eye on me. "What do you think, Ford. It's like a weird Mensa test, huh: *Which of the Following Does Not Belong?*"

I nod, finishing a bite of sausage. "Yeah, that's a bizarre list." Pondering it, I ask, "How many different lockers?"

He flips the cover open. "All different, except the tuna and the *Harry Potter*; they were taken from the same locker the same day."

"Ruining someone's quasi-literate, pescatarian lunch break, I'm guessing. Nothing on that list is worth more than a few dollars except the sunglasses."

Talbot speaks around a bite of egg—a yellow, scrambled, "I know." He probably *doesn't* know what "pescatarian" means. "And no wallets are missing—no money, no credit cards, no jewelry except the Timex, if that counts."

"Don't know what to say to that. So, Tal, I have reasons to go out there today, reasons connected to the case I took from Miller Solomon." I quickly relate the substance of Solomon's visit. "I need to find out about an employee. It'd be easier for me if you asked Big Jim about it."

"Okay, who is it?" He fishes a pencil from his front pocket.

"His name is Bill—*William*, I assume—Peppers." I give Talbot a brief description of the man. "He drives a Ford pickup, older, red. Ask, but don't be obvious about it. Treat it as tied to your investigation. I'll wait in the car."

Talbot nods. "Big Jim still *hates* you?" Outside, the rain stops. "Evidently."

NO RISK, NO FAITH.

I'm sitting in the car in the Briggs and Stratton lot. We arrived late. Talbot took forever to eat. I expected to be here around the time for the dayshift to begin, but we're here closer to lunch than breakfast.

I was lucky and found a patch of shade off on the edge of the otherwise sun-hammered lot. The morning storm's gone; it cleared off during breakfast, and now the rainwater has migrated to the air. Sitting feels like bathing. I've rolled down a window, listening again to that Matt Pond PA album and letting myself drift, eyes shut, floating on the aftereffects of last night and the aftertaste of kisses.

I hear a car door shut, open my eyes, and lean forward. Wylie Stroud has just gotten out of his Mercedes. So has Rachel Gunner. She scans the lot, and I'm tempted to duck but don't. She doesn't notice my Camry—too far away.

They walk together to the door of the Briggs and Stratton office. He opens the door and holds it for her; she nods at him and walks in. He follows her, releasing the door and allowing it to swing slowly shut behind them.

Wylie was wearing a seersucker suit jacket over jeans. Rachel was wearing a pastel orange sundress.

What the hell? My chest feels tight. Now I can't sit without fidgeting. A moment later, a massive, shiny, yellow Cadillac pulls into the empty spot beside Wylie's Mercedes. *Double hell!*

I watch, but no one gets out of the Caddy. It sits like some giant, beached, Beatle's submarine, engine running, oily exhaust puffing. A moment later, Wylie and Rachel come out of the office. Wylie sees the Caddy and points it out to Rachel. They walk to it and stand beside the driver's window. I know the window is down because I see an elbow sticking out of it.

I try to make out what is happening, but before I can, a delivery truck pulls in and stops, cutting off my line of sight.

"Goddamn it!" I hiss and smack the steering wheel. A minute passes, two. And then Wylie's Mercedes comes into view. He and Rachel are in it; I can see both silhouettes.

I drop down in my seat even though neither seemed to be looking in my direction. I count to forty; then I sit up. The Mercedes is gone, and the truck has moved, but the Caddy is still there. The elbow has disappeared.

Talbot comes out of the office. Near the Caddy, he waves at me, holding up his notebook in victory.

"Shit, Tal, stop!" I command though he cannot possibly hear me at this distance. The Caddy pulls forward just after Talbot goes by, and I see Wade Pimberly staring at my car as he leaves the lot. *Shit, shit.*

Talbot reaches the car and jumps in, oblivious to all that's just happened. "Got some info on Peppers."

"Did you see Rachel Gunner and her uncle in the office?"

Talbot looks confused. "No, but I wasn't really in there. I left through it, but I was back on the factory floor, talking to Big Jim. Why would they be here? They were here?"

"Yes, they left just before you did."

"Really?"

"Yes, after they talked to Wade Pimberly, the guy driving the massive yellow Cadillac."

"What Cadillac?" Talbot asks. I start the car to keep from throttling him.

LATER, AT THE OFFICE IN THE FRONT, I CALMLY SIT DOWN WITH Talbot and explain what Solomon asked me to do, the suspicions about Jane Pimberly, and about following Peppers to a meeting with Wade

Pimberly. I told him what I saw while he was in Briggs and Stratton. He listens carefully; his face reddens, and his crest falls.

Digging out his notebook, he holds it toward me, head down. "If you wanna fire me, drum me out, go ahead. I deserve it. Dishonorable discharge."

I shake my head although I admit I'm half-tempted. "It's okay; I should've told you all this before. But you have got to keep it to yourself. And you've got to *think*, Talbot."

He gives me a sober, earnest look. "I'll do better." He quickly tells me what he found out about Peppers from Big Jim Sutton.

The phone rings. I had set my cell to redirect calls to the office phone, the old cordless one. We both start to pick it up, but he stops, yielding it to me. I shake my head and let him answer it.

"Merrick's office." He listens then says, "Yes, just a minute."

He mutes the phone, and shows me he has. "It's Rachel Gunner, Ford."

I take the phone and walk into my office, shutting the door.

No risk, no faith.

"Hi, Rachel; it's Ford."

She laughs. "I've been looking forward to talking to you all morning." Her breathy voice steals mine for a moment. "Are you still there?"

"Yes. Yeah, I'm still here. Sorry. Just…um…"

She laughs again, and her voice sinks to a whisper. "Me too. I don't think I slept at all last night." She pauses. "I preferred that raft with you to my bed without you." She pauses again. "I tossed and turned all night. At about 3:00 a.m., I walked back to the pond with a blanket, and I finally went to sleep out there."

"On the pier?" I ask, my body responding to her intimate whisper, but my mind featuring pictures of her in the pastel orange sundress. "You'll fall in."

Her whisper continues. "Too late, Ford. I *fell in* out there earlier, underneath the fireflies. I went out to the pier because I had. The fireflies were gone, but you felt close."

Part of me wants to shout for joy. I want to believe her. I saw nothing this morning that makes anything she's so far said false.

"Last night was…" I say to her, searching for the right word.

"Yeah," she agrees despite my not supplying the adjective. "Yeah. Thanks, Ford. I felt…last night was…*special*."

I don't try to find a better word. Her inflection of that one makes it a mot juste.

She stops whispering abruptly. "Say, it's late for lunch, but, by any chance…?"

"I haven't eaten, actually."

"Oh! Well, let's eat together, okay?"

"Sure. Any place in particular?"

"You choose."

I mention the first place that comes to mind after Ed's. "There's a place right near here. Ford's BBQ."

"That sounds great, just exactly what I'm hungering for…*Ford's*."

Is this banter? Because that *felt* like banter. The pictures of her this morning are eclipsed by memories of her against me last night. I offer banter in return. "They say it's delicious."

"Oh, *they do*, do they? Is it offered to just *anyone*? Who might this *they* be?"

I stifle a laugh and put on a TV announcer's voice. "Obviously, women of taste who enjoy a delicious situation."

She chuckles, low, and it kills me. "I see. And your detective life is no doubt full of such women, *vamps*?"

"I'm afraid it would be ungentlemanly of me to answer that question, and for more than one reason."

"Will you explain those reasons to me while I enjoy my *Ford's*?"

"If you are capable of speech at such a moment, of anything other than rapturous noises."

"We'll see how it goes. I can be there in thirty minutes. I've lazed around the house all morning, but I did manage a shower."

I had been laughing, but now my laughter sticks in my throat. *All morning?* My mind begins to whirl. My chest tightens again.

"Ford, are you still there? Ford? Still want to?"

"Yes, yes. Sorry. Yes. Meet me here, and we can walk over together."

"Sounds good." Her whisper returns. "Can't wait to see you."

She ends the call.

No risk, no faith.

I'm standing with my phone and heart in hand when Talbot knocks on the door.

"Ford, Miller Solomon to see you."

"Send him in, Talbot."

I stare at the Judas phone and hang it up.

Talbot opens the door, and Miller strides in. "Hey, Merrick."

"Miller. What can I do for you?" He sits as I ask.

"Two things, it turns out. First, do you think that you and Helen could meet with me tonight? I have something I need to discuss with you, but I'd like to do it with the two of you together. Say, at your house?"

"Let's see. It's Wednesday, right?" Miller nods. "We should have time after dinner. Say, 8:00 p.m.?" He nods again. "I'll call if there's a problem, but there shouldn't be."

"Good. Second, any news on the case I hired you for?"

"I have a lead, I think, maybe more than one. Does the name Bill Peppers mean anything to you?"

Miller stares at the *Blade Runner* poster, thinking. "You know, I think Jane had a handyman named Peppers who worked for her a year or two ago. She fired him for something or other; she could never keep help. But I've seen check stubs made out to that name."

"You don't know why she fired him?"

He stares at the poster again. "No, I don't think she told me. She was funny about it now that I recall."

"Mm-hmm. Did Jane have any ties—financial ties—to Briggs and Stratton?"

Miller takes a moment, deliberating. "I'm trusting you with this, Merrick. Yes, she did. A healthy portion of the stock."

"And now Wade has it?"

He nods.

"What happened to her cats?"

Miller jerks a little in the chair. "Huh? Cats?"

"The twenty cats you said she had. I assume they were gone before Wylie moved in?"

"Yes, of course. They were caught and taken to the Lee County Animal Shelter. I don't know what happened to them after that. I hope they found homes, but most of them were feral, or nearly so, at least for anyone other than Jane."

"Okay. I'm going to go see Wade Pimberly tomorrow and check on a few other things."

"Good. Well, I'll see you tonight, Ford. Call me if that's a problem."

He gets up, and we shake hands. I walk him out of my office, closing the door; a moment later, while sitting down, I hear the outer door close.

My head is so full of Rachel, Wylie, Bill Peppers, and Wade Pimberly that it takes me several minutes to wonder why Miller's coming to the house.

I HEAR A KNOCK ON MY DOOR AGAIN AND ASSUME RACHEL HAS arrived.

"Ford, Father Halsey's here."

That's a surprise. I get up and open the door. I had forgotten that Wednesday was his day off, his *Sabbath*, as he likes to call it. But I remember when I see him in the straw hat, electric-blue golf shirt, and khaki pants he's wearing.

"Hey, kid. I was just over this way playing golf and thought I'd stop by and see how you were doing."

"How I'm doing?" I ask as I walk back behind my desk.

He closes the door, sits down, and takes off the hat. He pulls a handkerchief from a rear pocket and mops his forehead.

"Courses down here are sure gorgeous, but they're better from the club with a beer in hand than from the green with a club in hand."

I smile and shrug. Other than watching the occasional major ones on slow Sunday afternoons, I have no truck with golf. I wait for him to answer my question.

"I had a chat with Diana last night. It...worried me a little bit. She told me to keep my big nose out of it, but..."

"What is it, Halsey?"

"It's the Gunner woman." He sighs. "I just have a bad feeling."

"Father, I know we're friends..."

"News to me," he says with a frown. He waits for my reaction—dismay—then laughs. "Yes, we're friends, Merrick."

"I know we're friends, but this is *my* business. Don't be a women's committee busybody, Father."

He grimaces. "I deserve that, but listen. We're friends, and I'm worried. And I just want you to know: one white-dressed rehearsal with a choir does not an angel make."

"*Ecclesiastes?*" I deadpan.

He laughs. "Not exactly. But I'd want you to do the same for me if our roles were reversed. Friends are honest, right."

I can't argue with that. "Okay, say your piece."

"I've actually just said it. Look, if Samson had a friend, and the friend had gotten a bad feeling about Delilah, wouldn't a heads-up have been a help?"

"No scriptural pun intended?"

He looks at me, replays his own words. "Ha! No, none intended." He stands. "I'll leave this alone now. But I didn't want to hold my peace when I was worried about yours."

"Thanks, Father."

"See you, Merrick. I can show myself out."

He leaves the office and says goodbye to Talbot.

I stand and take a deep breath. Rachel's supposed to be here soon. *No risk, no faith.*

DESPITE THE WET HEAT, I GO OUTSIDE TO WAIT FOR RACHEL.

The office felt like it was shrinking.

Rachel lied to me. It might have been a white lie; its color remains to be determined. So much does. But she did not laze about all morning. She was up and about: pastel orange and at Briggs and Stratton and talking with Wade Pimberly.

That's a lot of conjunctions for a lazy morning at Noble Hall.

I want so desperately for the phone conversation to be real because if it was, if there was only the one isolated white lie, then last night was real, and maybe Rachel's a cardiac patient too.

It's time to start asking questions, finding explanations, right?

Rachel's Porsche crunches damp gravel in the parking lot, stops, and Rachel gets out.

I expect the orange pastel dress, but she's wearing a Southern Cal T-shirt, cardinal with gold lettering, white shorts, and white leather tennis shoes. With her blonde hair hanging loose, she looks like a photograph from a USC campus brochure. She would single-handedly double enrollment.

She hurries from the car to me, and I can't tell if she's jogging or skipping or both. She grabs me, her breath coming in soft gasps, and she kisses me quickly.

"I'm ready for my *Ford's*!" Her wide smile's contagious, and I catch it; I smile too.

No risk, no faith.
Double hell.

CHAPTER 11:
Far from the Wicked

I'm standing still, lost in thought, worry, and excitement—all spinning in an internal blender. Rachel notices, reaches down, and takes my dangling hand. Her wide smile widens. "Take me. Take me to my Ford's."

The banter's not done. I squeeze her hand; I can't stop myself despite an urge to resist her. *Passion and Reason self-division cause.* Somebody said that—not me, but I quote it to myself. It doesn't change anything, but I quote it to myself.

Self-division.

Rachel is light on her feet as I lead her in the direction of Ford's BBQ, just down about a half block and one street over. The impression that she's skipping I can't shake, although I know she's not. But there's an exuberance, a youthfulness in her movements today, in her, that I haven't seen before. It's as contagious as her smile, and I swear I feel a little like skipping myself.

Except she lied to me, and I don't know why. I don't know why she was at Briggs and Stratton with Wylie, why they spoke to Wade

Pimberly, why she changed her clothes.

She stops me with a tug on my hand after crossing the street. "Hey, are you okay? You seem preoccupied."

I smile self-dividedly, hoping she can't see my two in one. "Sorry, just thinking about a case."

She gives me a look. "No work for the next little while, Ford Merrick. Just me. Only me." Her horizon smile returns. "And my Ford's."

I can't resist and don't want to. I yield. "You seem particularly hungry."

Her smile becomes a smirk. "Whetted my appetite last night…"
"*Whetted?*"

She tosses her head and tugs me into motion. "Seems like the right word."

Oh, it's the right word. I feel its rightness all around my circulatory system before my blood begins to pool in the right but wrong area. I try not to think about the word, "wet," Rachel's damp, warm body in my arms at the pond. No success. *Whetted.*

I retake the lead, and we turn into a short alley that opens onto the back of Ford's BBQ parking lot. An old screen door guards the rear entrance, the screen rusty. On both sides of the door are high stacks of wood for the pit. The tangy smell of BBQ fills the air, and traces of smoke wisp out of the chimney as if declaring the choice of a pope.

Rachel stops me again, and she inhales, long and slow. "God, that smells good!"

I laugh, forgetting my self-division, reuniting, and now I tug her. "C'mon, and keep God in mind."

"What?" She says in a giggle as I pull her forward.

We don't use the rear door. I want her to see the restaurant's sign. Heading to the front, we walk around the side, between the building and the parked cars. I point to the tall sign with the white letters spelling out Ford's Bar-B-Que; beneath is the gold-lettered slogan: *You never had it so good!!*

She looks at the sign for a second, and I clear my throat, commenting with marked formality and exaggerated humility: "You see before you, in golden letters, the unanimous sentiment—note the exclamation mark, note it well—the sentiment of those who've had Ford's."

She shakes her head at me, grinning happily, and looks again at the sign in pleased disbelief. But then her grin loses its shape, and her body language changes subtly.

She nods at the sign. "Interesting quotation."

Like lots of businesses in the South, Ford's BBQ almost always has a verse of scripture on the sign. It changes now and then on a schedule I've never understood. I hadn't paid any attention to today's. I'd been anticipating only the slogan, how it would fit into our banter. But I look now and read: "*The Lord is far from the wicked. Proverbs 15:29.*"

I turn back to Rachel. She's staring at the sign.

"You okay, Rachel?" I ask softly.

She stares at the sign a little longer. "Did you see that movie, a remake, I guess? *True Grit?* Not the John Wayne one; I've not seen it. The other one."

"The one with Jeff Bridges?"

"Yes, him. I don't see many movies. Anyway, do you remember that Bible verse, the epigraph at the beginning of the movie? *The wicked flee where none pursueth...*"

"Right, right," I offer, trying to gauge the sudden shift in her mood, the shadow that's fallen on her, "that's *Proverbs* too, probably. *Proverbs* kinda goes on about the wicked."

She reorients on me and blinks. I can see her trying to rally and recover her high spirits of a minute before. "I suppose. I can't say I've read much of the Bible. A little, here and there, of course. Bored in motel rooms or assigned it in a college lit course."

Changing the subject, I nod at her shirt. "So, was USC college for you?"

She looks down at her shirt as if she'd forgotten what she had on.

"Oh, yeah, I was there. I...I never graduated, but I was there."

Rachel's mood's shifted again. I'm not sure what happened with the sign, but the mention of USC makes her patently wistful. "I liked it there. Liked the classes, did well. But mainly, I liked having a dorm room, a place of my own. Home."

She looks up from her T-shirt. "Sorry." She attempts a grin, and I can see it become more sincere as her mood continues to shift. "So: *You've never had it so good,* huh?"

I nod, resuming my earlier formality and humility. "Indeed," I respond in a low voice but with raised eyebrows.

Her smile is seasoned with desire as she stares into my eyes: "I'm all anticipation."

Hiding my gulp, I bow and gesture toward the door. "No time like the present."

Her sudden, surprised laugh marks the return of her high spirits. She bounces to the door, and I catch up and open it for her. She makes a slight bow of thanks, and we go inside.

ENTERING FORD'S BBQ IN THE SUMMERTIME RESEMBLES DESCEND-ing into Plato's Cave, if the fire in Plato's Cave were used to cook BBQ. It's dark inside; they keep the blinds closed in the summer, proof against the heat, and the scent of BBQ not only fills the air, but it has sunk deeply into the walls, the booths.

Talbot once remarked that a sliver of the paneled walls would taste like chipped pork.

There's a regular menu on one side of the seating area and a list of specials on the facing side. A line, always there near lunchtime, runs behind the first set of booths and turns left to continue between the first and second set. A few moments inside add *cold* to *dark*. I've never quite figured out how they manage to keep it so cold with the pit fire going constantly: air conditioning in the Inferno.

We join the line—it's not too long—and Rachel gawks around.

"Wow," she whispers, leaning close to me, the light scent of her fruity shampoo contrasting with the heavy tang of the pork, "this is the *South*." I nod.

The roomful of trucker caps and sleeveless shirts turns to stare at Rachel, a blue-eyed, blonde, blue-state beauty standing in a red-state, red-meat stronghold. Rachel notices the stares. "Do you think it's my *shirt*?"

I laugh noiselessly. "Sort of."

She looks down at the logo again and then back up at me. She blushes deeply enough for me to see it in the darkened room. "Oh."

The stares finally die down. I order my usual chipped pork sandwich with plain potato chips when we finally reach the counter. Rachel asks the waitress to make it two. The clerk looks at Rachel, and the waitress's face mixes sudden admiration, annoyance, and envy.

We take our receipt to a booth in the corner and sit down, Rachel across from me. I reach up and crack the blind, and streaks of sunlight decorate our table.

Rachel sighs. "This is nice."

"Even in the shooting gallery?"

It takes her a minute to understand that I mean the stares and glances down again. She shrugs. "You get used to it."

I raise an eyebrow. "*You* do. I've never known the struggle."

She laughs quietly. "That's because women stare more artfully."

Chuckling, I ask: "'Artfully'?

She grins. "I have spoken."

So she has.

There's a pause in our conversation, and the waitress calls out our order number. I get up and get it, stopping at the corner of the front counter to fill two Styrofoam cups with sweet tea.

I bring the tray to the table, and Rachel takes her share. She unwraps the sandwich and delicately lifts the top bun, looking under it. "Did I order the pickles and the slaw?"

"It comes on the sandwich. You have to *not-order* it."

She nods and drops the bun. She lifts the sandwich to her mouth. I expect her to take an exploratory bite, but she dives into the sandwich, a mouthful. When she realizes I am watching, she puts her hand in front of her mouth. After a minute, her hand still in front of her mouth, her eyes wide, she says. "You were right. My Ford's delicious. So, so good."

Pleased, I unwrap mine and start to eat too.

WE EAT IN SILENCE. AS SHE FINISHES—SHE'S DONE BEFORE I AM—I gesture at the ruin of the wrapper, empty chip bag, and used napkins before her. "You were hungry."

She picks up one of the napkins and wipes her lips again.

She leans toward me as she puts the napkin down, her beautiful face striped by sunlight. "I was. But there are different types of hunger. A woman cannot live by bread alone, Ford."

She grins as I blush.

"So, you just lazed around the house this morning?"

She turns her head, looks out the cracked blinds then back at me. "Yeah," she says without elaboration, her tone not inviting me to continue with that topic.

"I took Talbot, and we went out to Briggs and Stratton this morning."

She braces slightly. "This morning?"

"I mentioned it last night."

She makes a face, trying to remember. She does. Evidently. "You did. I forgot. Other things from last night stood out for me."

She glances out the blinds again, seemingly thinking. "So..." she says, the word taking the place of the exploratory bite I expected from her before. "Did you see anything interesting there?"

I make no telltale expression. "Talbot went inside. I stayed in the car. He got some more information on Bill Peppers, but it's not of much interest. The date Peppers was hired: a year or so ago. His job:

he's on the custodial staff. A solid but unremarkable worker."

She nods but changes the subject. "So, Talbot went in? That's right—you said that the man who runs the place likes Talbot."

"He does. Big Jim Sutton."

"I'm surprised anyone likes Talbot."

"Including me?"

"Yes, you seem so *nice*."

"Nice?" Helluva a word for a working PI.

She nods vigorously as if defending her comment. "Nice."

Letting that description go, I ask: "But Talbot seems *not-nice*?"

She screws up her face. "No, not mean or threatening, just..."

Talbot's floating discussion of Rachel's gloved hand forces itself back into my mind. "Disturbing?"

"Uh-huh."

"Well, I understand. My sister would absolutely agree that he seems that way; she calls him 'it,' a shortened version of Itt—two *t*'s—Cousin Itt from *The Addams Family*."

"Who? I saw that new *True Grit,* but I am not the pop culture girl. I think you only get to be that by having friends, sharing pop culture at a certain age."

I nod sympathetically. "And you moved around too much to have friends then?"

She looks at me. "Yes, that was a big part of it...but I don't want to think about that time. You were going to tell me more about Talbot."

"Right. Talbot does seem disturbing. He's never quite figured out what thoughts he should share and what thoughts he shouldn't. You were lucky he kept his mouth shut when you were in the office."

She shudders. "I'm sure. He seemed very interested in my shoes."

"Um, yeah, that's a thing. But, really, he is harmless—he intends no harm. If he'd ever have a girlfriend, she'd likely straighten him out quickly."

She nods. "But until he gets straightened out..."

"…he'll never have a girlfriend."

"No chance."

"I know, I know. I've told him, I tell him, but he…"

"…keeps being disturbing?"

"Yeah. But here's the thing: my parents got killed in an auto accident, hit by an eighteen-wheeler, and Helen and I were a mess. Helen suddenly had everything on her, me included, and she's at Auburn, majoring in pre-med. Talbot comes to the house—we hadn't really been buddies before—and he keeps me busy, takes me to his house, introduces me to his mom, Olive, I told you about her, and they take me in: feed me, let me stay over, go swimming, give Helen some space and time to adjust. He's been a fixture in my life since then, and I apologize for him, but…I can't give him up, despite his disturbing nature."

She sits for a moment, contemplating what I've said, then gives me a gentle smile. "See, you're nice, Ford."

"I guess that's going to stick."

She gives me a frank, direct glance. "Me too."

We gaze at each other; then both of us look out the blind. The parking lot's emptied, as has the seating area. The line's gone.

"Can I ask you something?" I manage the words while feeling as if I am holding my breath. I don't give her a chance to answer, although she tenses. "What did you mean about a different life last night?"

She blows out a breath and ponders the tabletop. When she looks at me, her eyes have dampened. "I'm not proud of the person I have been—maybe still am. My youth was, as they say, *misspent*. Did you notice we only use the word in that way? Misspent, wicked." She laughs weakly. "Far from the Lord…"

She stops to lift a clean napkin from my stack and dabs her eyes. She turns from me, her whole body, and looks out the blind. "Anywhere you go, you take the weather with you," she comments quietly. "Do you think that's true?"

I ought to push her, ask her point-blank about this morning. But

I'm caught in her current mood, and I'm in love with her, and I can't bring myself to do what I ought.

I stand and move around the table to her side of the booth. I slide in, slide to her. She leans back into me, still facing the window. "No, Rachel, I don't."

She nods. "Thanks, Ford." She turns and takes my hand, kisses it. The kiss is so unexpected I am unable to respond for a moment; my mouth hangs open. She laughs, that laugh that always kills me. "Let's go, okay?"

We leave, holding hands. She doesn't drop my hand until she reaches her Porsche. It's dustier than the last time I noticed. It no longer looks like a slumming Seraphim, like it belongs to a different order of beings than my Camry.

She gives me a warm but brief kiss. "So, babysitting on Friday night?"

I nod, remembering. "Yeah, if you really *want* to."

"I do. I *really* want to."

I watch her drive away, angry at myself and not angry at myself all at once.

I'm in love—yes, I noticed that too when I realized it earlier. I'm in love with a client I barely know who's lied to me, who I trust but shouldn't.

I don't know what the hell I'm doing, and yet I feel clearer about myself than I ever have.

TALBOT GIVES ME A WILD LOOK AS I COME INSIDE. HE GESTURES with a shoulder toward my office and spits out one word: "Certaine."

Shit. Shit. The door's closed, so I take a breath before I go in.

I find Doug Certaine seated behind my desk in my chair. His navy sport coat is open, his hands are finger-laced together behind his head, and I can see the holster at his side beneath his shoulder. He gives me a catbird-seat smirk. It occurs to me he probably has great abs.

I close my door.

"Ford, Ford. Some name. The name for a dipshit, not a detective."

For Certaine, that's cerebral humor, scintillating.

"Doug, get the hell out of my chair. You don't belong there." I walk to the front edge of my desk, allowing it to emphasize my height. Certaine can probably take me, but he'd pay for it, pay a lot. I want him to know that.

He looks up at me then stands with a smirk. "Too small, anyway."

"Too small for anyone who's all ass."

We trade places, circling opposite ends of the desk. I sit back down but do not invite Certaine to sit. He leans down on the desk, eyebrows forward.

"So, a client of mine thinks you're following him, Merrick."

I look up at him and deadpan: "You're lying."

He glares. "How do you know what Wade said?"

Moron. Makes Talbot look like Sherlock Holmes. "I meant you are lying because you *have* no clients. But I guess you do: Wade Pimberly."

This is a fascinating piece of news. I feel wheels turning all around me.

Certaine understands his error, and his face reddens. It makes him hate me more. "Fuck you, Merrick, you and all the other smart boys. Look, I'll make this short. Stay the hell away from Wade Pimberly. He's a law-abiding citizen, and if he sees you behind him again, or if I do, I'll make sure you and your stupid secretary both pay, do you hear me?"

I'd love to deem the threat idle, but I know Certaine and his PI history. He's as much a strongman, an enforcer, as he is an investigator. More: he's hurt people in the past, and he's good at it, good at getting away with it. I'm not afraid for me, but I am for Talbot. It's typical of Certaine to bring Talbot into this, although perhaps that was Pimberly's idea. He saw us both at Briggs and Stratton. *The wicked flee where none pursueth...*

"I hear you, but I'm going to do what I'm going to do, Doug. And if you touch Talbot, I will dedicate my hours and my big brain to making sure your life goes wrong—wrong in ways you'll suffer but be unable to understand."

He blinks, not understanding. But he gets that he's been threatened back.

"Watch your step, Merrick. I'll be watching it too." He wheels and yanks the door open. He pauses by Talbot's desk, looking back to make sure I witness it, then snarls, "I'll hurt you, you creepy little shithead."

He leaves.

Talbot waits for the outer door to close, then he runs and locks it. "Jesus, Ford, what's going on? What have we stepped in?"

"I don't know. But this morning kicked something into motion. Don't worry about Certaine."

He gives me an earnest look. "Why would I worry about Certaine when you're on my side?"

He's disturbing, sure, but I love him.

I CALL HELEN TO TELL HER THAT SOLOMON WILL VISIT TONIGHT. I'm hoping she will know why he's visiting, but she has no idea either.

I look at the clock on my desk: 2:45 p.m. It'll take me about forty-five minutes to drive to Wade Pimberly's house. I can be back in time for dinner. Might as well pluck the chicken while he's clucking.

Someone said that. Not me. I chuckle anyway and tell Talbot to take the rest of the day off.

CHAPTER 12:
Baby, Banana Bread, and a Briefcase

I get into the Camry, a preheated oven. My big complaint about my office is that no shade trees border the gravel parking lot. It's like leaving a car in an equatorial jungle clearing; I'm sweat-soaked before leaving the lot. The AC blows desperately, trying pitifully to match the moist, accumulated heat in the car.

At the first stop sign, I take out my phone and start the Matt Pond PA album I played for Rachel last night. Listening, cooling gradually, I merge onto I-85 north and point the Camry at Wade Pimberly.

As I drive, I ponder. I haven't had much time to ponder. Too much going on, too many visits, too much feeling. Since Rachel Gunner first visited my office, I've been ballooning skyward, struggling to add ballast, cool my burners, and return to the ground.

I haven't been investigating actively; mostly, things have happened to me. I've been drifting along. Since I've never been in love before, I didn't anticipate what it would do to me. It's like the entire world around me was destroyed in the blink of an eye then recreated exactly as before.

Everything's the same, but everything's different.

Certaine's riled me though. Pimberly's riled me, stirred me to activity, and shaken me from my dreamy stupor, one I've connived at for over a week. I don't take kindly to being leaned on. If Pimberly is agitated enough to dispatch Certaine as a messenger, I need to seize the initiative, the advantage. He won't expect me.

Of course, he might not be home, but I'm not going to pay a call, announce my arrival. I want the added advantage of surprise. So, I'm rolling the dice.

That image of rolling dice sticks in my mind. It's time for me to face facts. A connection exists between Wylie, Rachel, and Wade Pimberly. But what connection—of what kind?

Wylie owns Noble Hall; Jane Pimberly and then Wade Pimberly owned it before Wylie. So, he must have purchased it from Wade Pimberly. Perhaps Wylie had a question or an issue about the house or land to discuss with Pimberly; maybe that was all that was going on. Perhaps that explains the meeting with Bill Peppers. But why go to such lengths with an intermediary and a campus meeting? Why the intermediary; why the campus meeting? As for Briggs and Stratton, Rachel might have just been along for the ride; she might not have known anything about Pimberly. The meeting at Briggs and Stratton might have been a coincidence. Pimberly might have shown up on some unrelated matter. Wylie saw Pimberly and took a minute to speak to him. But why was Wylie there? Why was Rachel with him? Did Rachel already know Pimberly though she denied it? Why didn't she tell me she was at Briggs and Stratton with Wylie and that they saw Pimberly there? She *chose* not to tell me at Ford's; she didn't just *fail* to tell me as might have been true on the phone.

And here's the main thing, the question that jostles all the others: Why would seeing me in the parking lot have caused Pimberly to sic Certaine on me? Certaine showing up changes everything.

I wonder who sent Miller Solomon to hire me, encouraging him to ask questions about Jane Pimberly's death.

I set my cruise control and let the questions meander in my mind as the music calls up memories of night swimming.

Rachel Gunner has me flummoxed. I don't understand the supposed case she has hired me for. I need to talk with Wylie again, and I need to do it when she's not around. Maybe I can make that happen tomorrow.

Eventually, I will ask Rachel the questions I need to ask her, ask her directly, and not let her bedazzle me out of a direct answer. I admit that I've not asked because I fear the answers, fear that they will chase away the dream.

I PUSH THAT FEAR ASIDE AND TURN DOWN THE MUSIC, DO A QUICK Google voice search for the phone number of the Lee County Humane Society, then call it.

"Lee County Humane Society," a pleasant female voice says when there's an answer.

"Hi...um...look, this is Ford Merrick. I'm calling with a peculiar request—"

"Ford? Hey, this is Kip—you know, from the club."

The redheaded Auburn student at the valet stand. "Oh, right! Hi, Kip, how are you? I didn't know you worked at the Humane Society too."

She laughs. "I'm fine, thanks. I volunteer here to clear my head after working long hours with the Daughters of the Confederacy at the club. So, did Talbot send you out on a big case? How does it involve the Humane Society?"

"Have you...seen Talbot lately?"

"No, but it's funny you called. He called a few minutes ago and asked me to dinner. I'm meeting him later at Cafe 123."

I almost swerve out of my lane. A date? Does Talbot have a date? And she's attractive, smart. And he's taking her to a nice place? But she thinks he's the detective. And she's too smart for him to fool her for long. I'm not sure what to do.

I can't remember the last time Talbot had a date that Olive did not arrange. I decide to stay out of it for now.

"That's a good place." I change the subject back to the Humane Society. "I'm calling to find out about some cats that were picked up by the Humane Society a while ago. Twenty of them, I think. They belonged to a woman named Jane Pimberly. She died, and you folks went to her house and took the cats. Would you have a record of that, a way of finding out what happened to the cats?"

"Yeah, there should be." I hear her rattling papers. "It may take a second. The operating system here is the one Noah used on the Ark."

I laugh. "Take your time."

She makes a low, humming noise. I hear keys clacking. "Okay. Pimberly. Cats. Twenty, really?"

"So I'm told."

"Is she the woman who sang naked on her balcony?"

"Mm-hmm. The same."

"Figures. Okay, okay. Right. Here it is. Jane Pimberly. But it wasn't twenty cats—not exactly."

Not exactly? I imagine half-cats.

She clears her throat. "When our people got there, two of the cats, older ones, were dead. They captured eighteen, and they retrieved the corpses of the other two. They brought the cats here." She pauses, and there are more key clicks. "The live cats were a mess—mostly feral, diseased. Vets attended to them, but three more died within a couple of days. The rest improved, and the younger ones ended up getting adopted. But several never did; they were put down. This was a while ago."

"Yes, it was. The five that died—all old cats?"

More clacks. "So the vet notes say, yeah."

"Thanks, Kip. I hope you have a good time tonight. A good place to eat."

"Talbot's kind of an interesting guy, isn't he, Ford?"

"That he is, Kip. That he is."

I LEAVE THE INTERSTATE AND TAKE THE WINDING COUNTRY ROAD to Pimberly's house.

I don't know much about Wade Pimberly. He was Jane Pimberly's son, and they were never close, or so small-town talk has it. He lives on West Point Lake. He owns a big construction company based in LaGrange, but the company does work all around the area, often on Auburn's campus. I've heard occasional rumors that he's mixed up with members of the university's board of trustees; the implication is that he has an inside track to winning bids on campus contracts and is often in a trustee luxury box at football games. I'd never given any of that, or Pimberly himself, much thought until Solomon visited me.

Pimberly and I met once at a local business luncheon, so we know each other by sight. He's medium tall, thick-waisted but narrow-shouldered, and balding. He has a high voice, nasal, and his typical expression suggests that he's just sipped soured milk. He dresses to impress, but he's not impressive.

I SLOW AS I APPROACH PIMBERLY'S HOUSE. THE HOUSE IS BUILT OF brownish bricks, and, although one-story, it is vast, with brick courtyards, gardens, and seating areas. Large oaks overhang the house. It looks like a dwarfish castle.

The yellow Caddy sprawls in the driveway. Behind it, a newish steel-blue BMW sedan sits collectedly. The vanity plate on the BMW reads *TFYWIF: trophy wife.*

A newish Chevy pickup is also stationed in the driveway on the other side of the Caddy. It has a Pimberly Construction logo painted on it.

Behind the house, in the distance, sits West Point Lake.

I pull in and park behind the vanity plate and put my phone in my pocket. A tiny dog appears at my feet, growling and snarling as I get out, but it makes no move to bite me. I speak to it kindly then walk toward the front doors. The dog trots along behind, still growling and snarling, but now the noise seems like marching music.

The doors are large, dark brown. A shiny gold "W" is attached to one, a "P" to the other. Squaring up to them—the dog still behind me and still making unexecuted threats against my ankles—I poke the doorbell. A muted ring sounds deep inside the house.

The ring quiets the dog. It stops threatening and begins to scratch itself, its decorative collar and tags making a tinkling sound. A moment later, the *W* door opens, and a woman stands in the doorway, a tall, iced tea in her hand. She's wearing a surprisingly narrow, red polka-dot halter and, beneath it, a surprisingly narrow pair of red polka-dot shorts, narrowed more by the legs being rolled up. She's also wearing mirrored sunglasses. Her hair is black, as though night fell on her forehead.

She looks at me, and for a moment, I fall prey to the illusion that the sunglass lenses are her eyes. She's thin and deeply tanned, long-legged and long-armed, and she strikes me as a nearly nude praying mantis.

The dog runs between her legs and into the house, and the woman makes a surprised noise: "Whoops!"

"Hi, I'm here to see Wade Pimberly. This is his house, isn't it?"

She nods and shrugs simultaneously, and I don't know what that means. After a moment, she pushes the sunglasses down her nose, revealing a very large pair of forest-green eyes.

"We're out back. Who's calling?" she asks but does not wait for an answer. Instead, she turns and slinks into the house, taking off her sunglasses and putting them on a table near the door.

I'm supposed to follow, I suppose, and so I do. Her long, thin legs are subtly well shaped, and her red heels make them seem longer still. We walk through the house quickly. So as not to glance at her bottom—as if I were following it and not her—I glance around the house.

The decor's a self-satirizing phantasmagoria of atrocious taste.

Shag carpet—I didn't know anyone made that anymore, much less bought it—chokes the floor. It's white, *white*, and I have the strange conviction that I am trekking across coconut cotton candy. Pictures on black velvet adorn the walls along with various slogan plaques. *Live, Laugh, Love. Eat, Pray, Love*—that kind of thing. Lots of love.

A faint scent of incense colors the air. The overlarge, ugly furniture appears to be seconds from the Tomás de Torquemada collection—torture for the eyes as well as the body. Trophies line the mantle beneath a large, framed picture of the woman who answered the door. In it, she's younger, her black hair piled on her head, and she's snug in a daring evening gown, a sash around her that reads, "Miss Sarasota." She's wearing a crown and cradling a bouquet of roses.

We cross through the house to a pair of glass sliding doors. Behind the house is a massive deck built to take advantage of the wonderful view of the lake. In the distance, I can now see a large boathouse and an expensive motorboat tied alongside it. A pier runs from the boathouse out into deeper water.

At a large table on the deck sits Wade Pimberly. He sees me and jumps before he can control himself. A moment later, though, he gives me a *do-I-know-you, don't-I-know-you* look. The look's too late, but he doesn't seem to realize that. I play along for the moment as if the look had been timely.

"Hi, Mr. Pimberly, I don't know if you remember me, but I'm Ford Merrick. We met once a while back…"

He gives me his soured-milk look but twists his lips into a facsimile smile. "Oh, yes…I remember." He looks from me to the woman. "This is my wife, Patty—Patty Pimberly." He accents her last name, *his* last name.

I nod to Polka-dot Patty, she poses in response, and both she and her husband wait to see whether my eyes travel the tanned length of her. I, instead, pointedly gaze out at the water. "Beautiful place you have here!"

"Thanks. Can we get you a drink?" He says *we* but means *Patty*. She's older than her picture inside. He's quite a few years older than she is.

"Sure, some iced tea if you have some."

Patty holds hers out for display, a shift in poses. "Mine's sweet, Mr. Ford. Most say it's the sweetest they've *ever* tasted."

Her throaty tone flirts, but I keep mine businesslike. "Thanks, Patty."

She gives me a look as if disappointed, expecting more of a reaction. I quickly face Pimberly. As I do, I hear Patty huff quietly as she goes back inside, sliding the glass doors. Pimberly pretends not to hear her huff.

"Mr. Pimberly, a visitor stopped by to see me today. Doug Certaine. He does remedial detective work around Opelika. He told me that I was to stay away from you. You and I saw each other this morning at Briggs and Stratton. I'm curious why seeing me would cause you to unleash Certaine?"

He isn't expecting this, and it takes him a second to react. He shifts in his chair. "You say we saw each other. *I* say you were following me."

"I was there before you, Pimberly."

He blinks at me. "Well, you were watching me. And you've got no right to do it."

"To watch someone who drives into a parking lot in that mustard monstrosity in the driveway? How could I not?"

"So, you're telling me you just happened to be there, just happened to be looking at me?" He's not mentioned Talbot at all. That's interesting.

"Just happened, yeah."

He gives me a long stare, and I return it. He shrugs, and the shrug occurs just as Patty comes back outside with a glass of iced tea. She hands it to me, contriving to make her hand and mine touch.

I turn from Patty's small and quick, yet coy, smile to the bristling Pemberley while I sip my tea. I almost gag. Helen's tea is sweet, but this is iced sugar with a spoonful of tea.

I put the glass down, and Patty puts hers down too. The dog had followed Patty into the house and back out; it starts growling and snarling again. Patty reaches down and scoops it up. "Quiet, Baby."

"The dog's name is *Baby*?" I ask, mainly to keep from having to take another sludgy sip of the tea.

"Yes, she's my little terror." Does Patty mean *terrier?* Her expression is so blank I can't tell.

Pimberly grunts as if he knew the language of Father Halsey. "Terror is right. That dog needs to be put down."

Patty pales and holds Baby closer. "Wade, you won't hurt my little dog."

Pimberly eyes her in a way that makes no promises, and he stands up. Patty hugs the dog closer.

I reach out slowly and extend my hand toward Baby. She gives it a puzzled look, then a halfhearted sniff, growling all the while. I pat Baby's head, and she endures it.

"She likes you," Patty exclaims. "But I can see why. I like you too."

I can't tell whether she's just naturally this flirtatious or it's aimed at Pimberly, the continuation of some old quarrel or the beginning of a new one. She reaches beneath her arm with her empty hand and readjusts that side of her halter. She eyes me, wanting me to watch. I look at Pimberly, who narrows his eyes and watches her greedily, but he speaks to me: "Is there anything else, Merrick?"

"Call off Certaine, Pimberly, or I'll *start* watching you, and when I watch, I *see* things."

Pimberly shakes his head. "I do what I want."

I stare into his eyes, saying things silently. "I'll show myself out."

"No, no," Patty says. "*I'll* show you out." She bends over deeply in front of me, putting Baby down without bending her knees. Then she stands. "Follow me, Mr. Melvin."

"Merrick."

She slides open the glass door and smiles back at me. "I never get *names* right. I'm better with numbers." The comment is salacious, and she leaves me to guess the numbers.

As we reverse our course through the house, I ask Patty a question. "That's your BMW outside?"

She gets to the door, stops, and turns to me. "The blue one?"

I nod. "The only one."

"Yeah, that's mine."

"How long have you and Mr. Pimberly been married?"

"Four years," she says with a heavy sigh. "Four *years*." She leans toward me after checking to make sure Pimberly did not follow us. "I guess my itch is three years early." She adjusts the other side of her halter as she gazes into my eyes.

Opening the door for myself, I step out and glance back. She picks up her sunglasses and puts them on. "See you around, Mr. Melvin."

She watches me leave with her mirrored, preying eyes.

I DRIVE SOUTH WONDERING ABOUT THE SCENE WITH PIMBERLY, Patty, and Baby. Pimberly might call Certaine off; he might not. But the trip wasn't wasted.

Pimberly's hiding something—that's sure. What he's hiding is unclear. I can't assume it has anything to do with his mother's death, officially a death by natural causes—heart attack, remember?

Pimberly certainly strikes me as a man who cuts corners; he might be hiding sharp business dealings and nothing like murder. Matricide. His wife's done with him but also afraid enough of him to stay.

My phone rings. It's Helen.

"Hey, Ford!"

"Helen, what's up?"

She pauses for just a beat. "I've invited Sam for dinner, and I finished up early so I could cook it. I just wanted you to know."

"That's great, Helen. I'd like to get to know him since you are."

I can feel her blush over the phone. "Ford," she says warningly.

I laugh. "Sorry—but that's great. Just, we have Solomon coming over later."

"I know. Sam's gonna be here early. Five thirty. We can eat, and he can leave before Solomon arrives. I'm baking banana bread."

Okay, the big guns are out. My sister likes this man. She likes him

KELLY DEAN JOLLEY

banana-bread much, and that's a lot. Helen's banana bread is better than her iced tea.

"Sounds delicious. But you didn't need to call me about this."

"No, I know. I was just hoping you might invite someone. Rachel?"

"Oh, well, maybe. We had lunch together."

"Right. One of my patients today was there. He told me all about it, about her. She shook Ford's."

Me too. "I'll ask and text you the answer."

"Good, see you in a bit."

"HEY, FORD," RACHEL SAYS CHEERFULLY WHEN I CALL.

Nerves attack me as I start to talk. "Hey, I'm calling because Helen invited Sam to dinner and she's made a lot, I'm guessing, including banana bread, which is worth it all by itself, and anyway, she wondered if you would come to dinner too because she really likes this man, but she's nervous about having him to dinner, about the awkward *threesome*—um, not the right word—the *triangle*—um, not the right word, either…"

Rachel laughs. "Ford, slow down. Are you really this nervous about asking me to dinner after the lunch we had?"

"I guess. *Me* twice in one day is kind of a lot."

"That sounds good. Banana bread sounds good. What have you been up to?"

I freeze for a second. I don't want to have this conversation, and I especially don't want to have it on the phone, unable to see Rachel's face, her actions. "Just some case follow-up."

Her answer is teasing, but there's a note of worry in it. "Very mysterious."

"What about you?"

Now she's guilty of a prefatory silence. "Oh, not much. Lake got back from Montgomery, and we're having drinks on the upper balcony."

That information sinks into my lower gut like a knife. "Oh, Lake is back."

140

We're both silent for a moment. "So, you'll come to dinner?" I ask. "Your place, right?"

"Right."

"See you then. I'm really pleased Helen suggested it. I'd like to get to know her better."

That makes my gut hurt less; the stabbing pain subsides. "Okay— five thirty? Helen and I have someone stopping by later about a business matter, so we won't be able to make an entire evening of it."

"That's fine. See you in a little while. And, Ford"—her voice sinks—"I was already missing you."

I hardly know what to say, so I say what I feel, surprising myself. "God, I was missing you too."

A KNOCK AT THE FRONT DOOR HERALDS THE ARRIVAL OF DR. Nettles.

Helen's still busy in the kitchen with some last-minute prep, so I open the door. I can see him through the glass.

"Hey, Ford," he says when I open the door, shaking my hand, "good to see you again."

"You too, Sam. Come in. Helen'll join us in a minute. Drink?" I move us into the living room and sit down on the end of the couch. He's wearing an orange polo shirt, jeans, and brown casual shoes. He has a winning smile.

He looks around. "Sure, a gimlet. Beautiful place, Ford."

"Thanks, but the beauty is all Helen." I make his drink at the cupboard where we keep the alcohol. "She chose everything, arranged everything. The only room I control is mine, and you'll note, if you see it, that it's the only room with a closed door."

He laughs and then gives me a pointed look. "Helen tells me you're a private detective?"

"That's what it says on my office door." I offer him the drink with a smiling shrug.

"How'd that happen? Helen said you went to Oberlin. Did you major in *noir?*"

I shake my head, smiling too. He sips as I speak. "Yes, I went to Oberlin. No, I didn't major in noir. But I probably would've if I could've. I double-majored: literature and psychology. My dad was a big detective buff, and he got me started reading detective books young. He was really a big fan. Movies too. You might say that Dad, *Encyclopedia Brown*, and *The Maltese Falcon* are to blame—and *Blade Runner.*" I stop. "Well, after I finished at Oberlin, I came home, and I couldn't decide what to do, what to be. Dithering's...um...my strong suit. I considered going to grad school but decided I'd had enough time in the classroom. I wanted to work but to be my own boss."

I stop and laugh. "I felt a little like Lloyd Dobbler: 'I don't want to sell anything, buy anything, or process anything as a career...' Anyway, one day a woman asked Helen if there were any reputable private detectives in town. Helen mentioned the question to me, and it was like tumblers moved in my head. I thought, *'Why not?'* Soon, I found an office and put up my sign."

Sam listened carefully, chuckling at the Lloyd Dobbler reference. "Love that film, *Say Anything.* That's fascinating, Ford. It must be a job full of excitement and intrigue."

I shake my head. "Not really." I recall Rachel showing up in my office. "It has moments, but they're few and far between. Mostly, a detective is a harmless drudge."

"A doctor is too," he says. "TV makes it seem like we run around restarting folks who've coded like we're constantly in a maelstrom of ER drama. But it's not like that really—"

There's another knock on the door. "That must be Rachel. Excuse me, Sam."

My heart's racing, and my palms are sweating as I walk to the door. For some reason, the thought of Rachel crossing the threshold here, entering the house, having dinner with Helen and Sam—it all hits me at once. How much I'd like this to be my life. Helen happy with Sam, me with Rachel, all four of us together, friends and family.

But I have no idea what Rachel wants—except she said she'd "stick."

I wipe my palms on my pants and open the door. She's in her third outfit change of the day. I realize what a long day it's been—its revolutions marked by her wardrobe. She has on a white linen blouse, light blue slacks, and white sandals. Her hair has been swept up but not into any tight bun. She's a standing summer evening.

"Hey, Ford, here I am." She puts her hands out, they're cool against my cheeks, and she gives me a warm kiss that becomes hot against my lips.

Helen clears her throat behind me. "There you are, Rachel—welcome!"

We break the kiss, and I turn. Helen's standing with Sam, holding his hand. He's pleased by that fact, and he flashes his GQ-cover smile.

"Hi, Helen, Sam," Rachel says, slipping past me.

Rachel's ill-prepared for the next moment when Helen drops Sam's hand and pulls Rachel into a tight hug. When Helen releases her, Rachel blinks for a moment then smiles.

"Let's go to the dining room," Helen says. "It's all ready."

It is. Helen's used our mom's wedding china, the golden candle holders, and the lace tablecloth: a table for royalty, displaying our dearest, finest possessions. We've only used these once before, and that was when my grandfather—my mom's dad—visited after I graduated from Oberlin. I notice that Helen is wearing Mom's silver, floral hair comb in her dark hair and a plain-cut but form-fitting gray dress. She looks queenly. Sam steals glances at her as she seats us all.

The table is heavy with food. My sister is amazing: works all day then somehow pulls this off. It's magic. There's cold chicken, kale salad, a bowl of freshly cut mixed fruit, and warm bread. A pitcher of iced tea stands on one end of the table, ice water on the other. In between are two bottles of chilled white wine.

We begin to eat, and the conversation is free and easy—light, like the food. Helen tells funny stories about waiting room behavior on the part of patients. Sam talks about growing up in Detroit. I relate a story of taking too many No-Doze before an exam, worried I'd go to sleep during it because of my studying all-nighter, and how I'd written an entire bluebook full of complete No-Dozing gibberish.

Rachel listens to everything, comments, laughs, and asks questions, but she tells no tales about herself. No one notices but me, I think. At one point, she looks at me, and I can tell she's wondering if I've noticed. I do my best not to let on.

"So, Sam," I ask, dividing my attention between him and Rachel, "were you Jane Pimberly's doctor?"

Sam is surprised. Rachel's hand tightens on her fork; the tips of her fingers whiten.

"Yes," Sam says, "or, rather, I was one of her doctors."

"That's a strange question, Ford," Helen says, a reprimand encoded in her wording. Rachel picks up her napkin and wipes her lips.

"I was just thinking about Jane the other day," I explain, "I guess because of the party at Noble Hall. I mentioned her to Miller Solomon, the lawyer, and we talked about her for a minute. He mentioned you had been her doctor, one of her doctors."

"She was an unusual woman," Sam offers. "It was hard to tell which ailments were in her head and which in her body."

"But she had a bad heart, at least that's what everyone says, and that's what it said in the newspaper about her death: heart attack."

Sam shrugs. "Yes, that's what the paper said, and that's what I heard from Dr. McCoombs, who was her longtime doctor, her primary physician. So, I assume that's what happened."

"Assume?" I ask.

Helen gives me a sharp look. "That poor old woman. Ford, this isn't appropriate."

"I'm sorry. She was such a character, all the stories about her. There's that one about her walking the grounds of Noble Hall at night, carrying a lantern…"

"Ford," Helen says, exasperated.

"…and all the cats. Twenty cats."

"Twenty?" Helen asks without thinking, and then I can see her kick herself under the table.

Rachel's been sitting still through the conversation, listening.

"She did have cats," Sam agrees, "but I didn't know how many. She was always scratched up, her hands and forearms. Sometimes it was bad. I guess they weren't all tame."

"Speaking of *unhousebroken*," Helen says loudly, redirecting attention to herself, "Doug Certaine showed up in my waiting room at the end of the day today. My receptionist told me he was there. But when I came out, he was gone. That's weird, even for him."

Sam nods; Rachel looks at me. I understand. The bastard visited Helen for my benefit. He wasn't just threatening me and Talbot; he was threatening my sister too.

I fight back my anger, but I believe Rachel sees it. Helen misses it as Sam is asking her about Certaine; he's angry too, though not for the reason I am. Helen is trying to discourage his anger, but I can tell that his emotion flatters her, reassures her. It strikes me just how important this evening really is to her—how important Sam is.

"So, Helen," I say, interrupting, "there's banana bread?"

She squeezes Sam's hand then nods at me, smiling. "Yes, there is. Would you and Rachel like to get it? It's in the kitchen. Just grab some dessert plates and forks. You can make coffee; everything's set up. Just turn it on."

I'm sure my sister is planning to make out briefly with Dr. Nettles while we are in the other room. The smile Rachel gives me as we enter the kitchen and close the door reveals that she has the same thought about Helen's plan.

"So, what can I do?" Rachel asks. My answer is to swoop her into my arms and kiss her the way I've wanted to kiss her all day—brief, passionate kisses, one after the other like Cary Grant and Ingrid

Bergman in *Notorious*. When I finish, we are both breathless, our eyes dilated.

"Ford," she says, elongating my name—her chin trembling just perceptibly—and stepping away from me around the counter. "I can't come back from another of those."

"No, me either," I confess, glad to have the counter to stand behind. "We should get the banana bread, turn on the coffee."

"You mean we didn't already? I figure every appliance in the house is turned on." She fans herself with her hand, and we laugh—our laughter, *shared, intimate.*

A few minutes later, we take the dessert and coffee into the dining room. Helen's hair comb is crooked in her hair.

HELEN AND I ARE CLEANING UP AFTER DINNER, EACH LOST IN OUR own thoughts and feelings, a warm, mutual hush between us.

For the third time, there's a knock at the door. Helen goes to answer it and brings Miller back to the dining room with her. He's carrying his briefcase. We'd left out the banana bread and coffee. I offer some to Miller as he sits.

"Thanks, but no. My wife stuffed me before I left the house."

He opens his briefcase, takes out a thick folder, and puts it on the table. He looks at us both, and I can see a hint of a smile on his face, a rare thing.

"I know you two must be curious about why I'm here, so I'll get right to it. Your maternal grandfather has decided to retire. He cashed in his stocks and other holdings and liquefied much of his fortune. It's been very hush-hush. As I understand it, he bought a rather large yacht and plans to retire to sea. He has no desire, he says, to take his fortune with him, to keep more money around than he could spend, or to make people wait like vultures for him to be dead, though of course you two wouldn't.

"Anyway, I have worked with his lawyer in Boston at your

grandfather's request." Miller opens the folder, takes out two pages, and hands one to me and one to Helen. "Two accounts have been set up at Auburn Bank, one in each of your names. Again, hush-hush. Each of the two accounts contains ten million dollars. I know your financial situation, I know you have not been scraping by, but you are both now and officially *wealthy*. I feel a little like the guy with the Publisher's Clearing House checks."

Helen gapes at me, and I gape at her. We each mouth, *"Ten million dollars?"* as Miller chuckles.

CHAPTER 13: *Windfalling*

All that great wealth generally gives above a moderate fortune is more room for the freaks of caprice, and more privilege for ignorance and vice, a quicker succession of flatteries, and a larger circle of voluptuousness.

— Samuel Johnson, *Rambler #38*

Swamped, swallowed, engulfed.

I mentioned Opelika means *big swamp*, right? Except there is no swamp, big or little, except in our house—mine and Helen's.

For a long time after Miller leaves, we sit silently like statues. We're at the dining room table, the remaining banana bread untouched on a tray. The dregs of the coffee overcooking in the kitchen provide a background odor.

The clock on the mantel in the living room ticks as if it were in the money.

Moony.

Helen shakes her head and swallows; her voice is shell-shocked. "I suppose we knew he might leave us something..."

I recall telling Rachel about my grandfather's collection of English sports cars. I didn't mention he has *fourteen*.

"Yeah, but *leave* us something. He's been in dandy health as far as I know." Helen nods her agreement. "And I never imagined anything like this. He'd always said he would die in the office and that he was leaving his money to charity. I believed him on both counts."

"Me too," Helen says quietly. "I know we're on better terms with him than we were before…well, before Mom and Dad, you know…but he's only visited here twice, for my graduation and yours, and he never seemed to forgive us for not going to Harvard, as he did, as Mom did."

"Right," I say as I stand up, "and forgiveness isn't his métier. He never forgave Mom for Dad. He sorta forgave us for being Dad's, but… Shit, Helen, ten *million* dollars. I don't want ten million dollars."

Here's the weird thing—I don't. Really. I've never cared about money. Neither has Helen. We don't want to be poor; don't misunderstand. But there's a point with money past which it's way more burden than blessing. It's not like I have a list of items I need or even want. I have no visions of sugarplums dancing in my head.

Being a detective offers regular proof that if money itself isn't the root of all evil, the love of it surely is. (I don't just read detective novels.)

Ten million dollars.

"We can't tell anyone, Helen. No one."

Her face shows incomprehension, then she nods slowly. "No. It would change everything: my practice, your work. You're right; we can't tell anyone, our friends. We need time to consider this, decide what to do."

Helen already donates a lot of her money to charity; I guess I said that. She makes a *ton* more than me. I sell books, but genre books through a small publisher. I couldn't live on what I make from writing alone.

Or from detecting alone.

But I don't need ten million dollars.

"Right," I agree. "We don't tell anyone until we decide what to do."

Helen sighs then glances at me. "Help me finish clean up?"

I nod.

Later, Helen goes to her room, and I go to mine, but I hear her moving around. She doesn't sleep, and neither do I—at least, I don't expect to.

MY PHONE RINGING WAKES ME, SO I DID SLEEP. AS IT RINGS, I realize I dreamed of ringing cash registers, Scrooge McDuck, church mice, gold doubloons, and plug nickels. I pick up my phone and see that it's Rachel. I added her name to the Burbank number.

"Hey, Rachel," I say, my voice cracking from a night's disuse.

"Ford, hey, I'm sorry if I woke you; I was just worried about you."

I push myself toward the headboard of my bed enough to sit up. "Worried about me? Why?"

"Last night at one point, Helen mentioned Doug Certaine, and I saw you get angry. Helen deflected the conversation, but I wanted to ask you about it." No surprise that Rachel noticed Helen's deflection. Rachel's the mistress of deflections.

"Oh. Yeah, I guess that's right. I forgot about it."

"Forgot?" She sounds surprised.

"Um, we…Helen and I…we had a visitor last night with…news. It distracted me."

"*Bad* news, Ford? I hope not." Her concern touches me.

"No, not bad, just unexpected. I can't really talk about it right now, but as soon as I can, I'll tell you."

"Okay, and the thing with Certaine, his visit to your sister? You took that as a threat, didn't you? Is it because of what happened at the party here?"

"No. That's part of the history, but Certaine and I have a long history; it stretches back to the dawn of time: high school."

"Oh, wow. That is way back. I'm going to be busy today, but we're going to babysit tomorrow night, aren't we?"

I had forgotten Michelle's twin terrors. "Yes, but I can do it by myself."

She sounds hurt. "You don't want me there?"

"No. I mean, *yes*. I want you there. I just—"

"Ford, get it through your head that I want to spend time with you: swimming, eating, babysitting. It's all good if we're together."

There's that word. I keep feeling that we are together.

"Rachel, are we dating, or are we pretending to date so that I can figure out what Wylie's up to?"

After the briefest of hesitations: "We are dating, and you are figuring out what Wylie's up to."

"And you've decided we are dating…unilaterally."

That low laugh. "How long would it have taken if I'd left it up to diffident you to decide, or even if I'd only waited for you to go halves on the issue?"

I shake my head and laugh at myself. "Touché."

"Exactly. Sometimes a woman has to take what she wants."

The thought that Rachel Gunner wants me cheers and confuses me. What do I have that she could want?

I push myself farther up the headboard and take the plunge. "Rachel, how long are you going to be visiting Wylie? Don't you have a life to get back to in California?"

"Do you want me to leave?"

"No! I mean, no, I don't. Of course not. But…"

"But you're worried about it? Things are happening fast?"

I blow out a breath. "Yeah."

She takes a minute. "Look, I don't want to have this talk over the phone. Can we postpone it until tomorrow night?"

"Yes," I answer while shouting, *"No,"* internally. "Friday it is."

"And, Ford?"

"Yes?"

"Don't worry. It's okay."

"Okay."

She ends the call. I pull my sheet over my head

TALBOT'S ALREADY IN THE OFFICE WHEN I ARRIVE. HE HAS TWO cups of coffee on his desk; steam rises from both. Mine's black, and he hands it to me as I come in. His is creamed white—and sugared, no doubt. Talbot does his best to make sure his coffee does not taste like coffee.

Despite all that's on my mind, I remember my phone chat with Kip as he hands me the coffee.

"So, Cafe 123 with the lovely Miss Kip, eh, Tal?"

He blushes. I hadn't known that blushing, or embarrassment in any form, was possible for him.

"Kip told me you called the Humane Society."

I sit down next to his desk, and he sits. "She was helpful. I met her at the club."

He nods. "She told me. And hey, Ford...ah...thanks for not giving me away."

I sip my coffee, peer at him over the cup lip, then lower the cup. "She still thinks you're the boss?"

"No, I confessed."

"So, she made you wear the Caesar salad?"

He shakes his head. "No, she was cool. She got in my face—man, she can be scary—and then she said we should eat. We did. After, we walked around downtown and sat by the fountain across from the courthouse."

"How old is she, Tal?"

"Older than you think. She's a senior, but she took two years off between her sophomore and junior years at Auburn. She's twenty-four. An old soul."

I almost choke on my next sip of coffee. "An old soul? Did Olive say that?"

Talbot shakes his head again. "No, Kip said it about herself. She was wild when she was younger—high school, early in college. She worked for the Peace Corps those two years off, and it settled her, she said. She came back and got serious about school, about life."

"And she didn't kill you for lying?"

"No," Talbot says, clearly still shocked by it himself. "She forgave me."

We each say, "Huh," at the same time and sip our coffees.

"Say, Ford, do you think you could help me learn to drive again?"

"Talbot…" I tried to help him once during high school and once a couple of years ago. Both efforts nearly got me killed.

"Please, I need to be able to drive if I'm going to date Kip. And I've been saving for a car."

I can't hide my skepticism. "Tal, I know how much you make. How could you have saved any money for a car?"

"What else do I spend it on? I ride a bike or walk. I live and eat at home—except when you feed me. You buy all the video games, the movies…"

"So, you really have enough to buy a car?"

"Almost, if it's a used one. Please, Ford, no woman has ever been nice to me, much less one like Kip. *Please*, Ford. And a raise?"

It occurs to me for the first time since I left the parking lot that I can afford to increase Talbot's pay since I can afford almost anything.

"Okay, I'll tell you what: I'll give you a raise. But you'll have to find someone else to help you learn to drive. Been there, done that, twice. There are limits even to our friendship."

He grins. "I'll find someone."

I SPEND THE MORNING ON THE COMPUTER, CHASING WADE Pimberly. This is the sort of detection I often do: virtual.

Pimberly's name is linked to construction jobs, several on Auburn's campus. I find pictures of him and Patty at club events and Auburn football games. I'm about to shift to Peppers when I find an old newspaper article written years ago when Pimberly was a boy.

It's an article about Noble Hall. The article doesn't tell me anything I don't know about the place, but the accompanying picture shows

Wade standing on one side of his mother. A man stands on the other side of Jane Pimberly. The caption identifies him as David Diamond, a worker on the grounds.

The picture is grainy, gray and white, but I see a resemblance between Diamond and Wade. I print a copy of it and drive to St. Dunstan's in Auburn.

I want to talk to Diana Wentworth.

DIANA DOES MORE THAN PREVENT WIDE FATHER HALSEY FROM veering off the straight and narrow. She does more than run St. Dunstan's. She also knows more about folks in Auburn and Opelika, particularly the old families—the club set—than anyone else. She's spent her life on their laced fringes.

Diana's mother belonged to the set, but her father did not, and that kept Diana from ever fitting in. Her mother's friends were almost all from the set, and for a time they said they forgave her mother's indiscretion in marrying down. Over time, though, those friends disappeared. But Diana kept tabs on them, their sons, and their daughters. There's a touch of ressentiment in Diana's knowledge; she does delight a little in scandal and misstep. But she's not given to sharing what she knows—more Google than gossip. She knows what she knows, but she doesn't share unless asked.

I vault up the steps and through her door. Diana's at her desk, a cup of tea in one hand, a copy of *The Burnt Orange Heresy* in the other.

She puts the novel down atop a copy of *The Book of Common Prayer* when she sees me. "Ford! Not often that I see you on a Thursday. Father Halsey's at the hospital, visiting a parishioner."

"I'm here for you today, Diana, not him."

She gives me a pleased grin and nods to the chair on the side of the room. I grab it and move it across from her desk, sitting down.

"So, what can I do for you?" She leans forward and eyes me over her teacup. "Is it for a *case*?"

I shrug but smile, and her eyes gleam.

"Ask away, Ford."

"What can you tell me about Jane Pimberly, about her history?"

Diana shakes her head, looks away, and blows out a breath. She pauses for a long moment. "Poor old Jane. All the money in the world, and it bought her nothing but misery." She stops and frowns. "Her family's the oldest in the county, and her father was a low branch on a family tree of hard, vainglorious men. Her great-grandfather obtained Noble Hall during Reconstruction, and old rumors say he swindled it. He drank, chased women, and beat his wife. He seemed to set the standard of behavior for Pimberly men.

"Jane lived in real terror of her father; she never dated and hardly mixed with others, though she was, by their reckoning, ranked first in their set. She tended her father into his bitter old age, and when he died, she had a brief flirtation with wildness, but wildness was never really in her."

Diana pauses again, and I think of my conversation with Talbot about Kip.

"She got mixed up with a man, a drifter really, his name was...?" She drops her chin and stares at her desk, making an effort to remember.

"Diamond?"

She looks up at me. "Yes, that's his name. Jane fell as hard for him as I've seen a woman fall; of course, she was wholly unprepared for love, for a man being warm and kind to her. Wade, her son, is almost certainly Diamond's boy although Jane's mother—usually just an ornament at Noble Hall, almost non-existent as a person—hurried Jane from town. When she came back, a little over a year later, a boy child was in tow. The claim was that the child belonged to a cousin who could not afford to care for it and that Jane took it in, but no one believed that story except Jane's mother, who knew it was false but convinced herself it was true. Everyone was polite enough to *act* like they believed it. But Jane herself made no attempt to keep to the story once her mother passed. No one pretends Wade is anyone's son but hers. Except maybe Wade…"

I let Diana unwind the story, deeply interested in it. In her pause, I fish the picture from my pocket and hand it to her. "That's Diamond?"

She peers and nods. "Yes, that's him."

"So, he left, never came back?"

"Not until after Jane's mother died; then, he started coming back regularly. Jane tried to pass him off as just an employee, but he was sleeping with her when he was in town. Most people figured he came to town to bed her and to beg money from her, and when he'd done both, he'd leave. Then he'd come back for more."

The story is suggesting things to me. "Did Wade know Diamond as his father?"

Diana shakes her head. "I'm not sure. He must have, but he's never publicly acknowledged it. Eventually, Diamond drifted away and never drifted back. Jane's heart broke, I believe, though she couldn't—wouldn't—let on. I've always thought her descent into half-madness was mostly the result of Diamond leaving her and never returning although, Lord knows, her life provided enough causes for such a descent."

"Did she and Wade get along?"

Diana frowns again. "They weren't close. Wade was ashamed of her, I think—more as she got older and madder—and certainly ashamed of Diamond. When Wade was old enough, he left town, moved to LaGrange. Jane loved him, but he was at best indifferent to her. Another misery in her life."

I take the picture back and put it in my pocket. "Did you know about cats?"

"Jane's feline menagerie? Yes, and it was hard to stand close to her in the final couple of years without knowing about them." Diana looks around and leans forward, whispering with sympathy: "She stank of cat urine."

"Was she often scratched up?"

Diana seems surprised by the question. "I didn't see her often, so I can't say. But she was scratched up when I saw her the last time, a week or two before her heart gave up."

Diana sinks into melancholy, and I admit to feeling it too. Not a happy story. It hits me harder because of last night. I suddenly have heaps of money sitting in the bank myself. Jane's didn't make her happy, much the opposite.

We sit together for a moment in what feels like an impromptu wake.

"Is someone poking into Jane's death?" Diana asks quietly but intently.

I just look at her, and she nods, understanding. "Well, good luck, Ford. If something happened to her other than the official story, I hope you unearth it. Jane deserves a good turn."

THE HEAT OF THE DAY ARRIVES EARLY.

I leave St. Dunstan's and cross the street, walking to nearby Toomer's Corner. I enter the refrigerated interior, claim a stool, and order a lemonade. So cold, so sour, so *wonderful*. The rich man in hell would have begged for a drop of this from the beggar's finger if he had known of it. Toomer's Lemonade would make even fiery torment momentarily bearable.

I gaze around as I drink my lemonade, contemplating what Diana told me but then remembering that this is where Rachel and I were *supposed* to have met—here, over lemonade.

And then, as if by a spell-work summons, Rachel walks into the shop. I gawk at her, and when she sees me, she gawks back. "Fancy meeting you here," she says, laughing.

"What's brought you to Auburn," I ask.

She walks to me and kisses me then sits down before she answers. "I was going to go see Diana at the church. Choir stuff. I'm missing some music, but I'll see her in a minute. The lure of lemonade was irresistible. So, for now, I'll enjoy a lemonade with my boyfriend."

I choke on my sip. "Boyfriend?" *Swamped.*

"Sometimes a woman has to take what she wants."

I nod, trying to recover my internal balance as she orders. "Okay, *girlfriend*; I surrender to the title gladly. So, are we going to have that talk now, early?"

Her face darkens for a moment. "No, not here. Not now. Tomorrow, as we said."

I notice her keys on the counter. No Porsche key is on the ring, but there is a Range Rover key.

"Did you get a new car? Range Rover?"

She gives me a spooked look for a second. "How could you know that? I just took delivery this morning. It's another reason I'm out, taking it for a first spin."

I nod at her keys. She stares at me for a minute, and that cool look inhabits her eyes for a second. "You *are* a detective, aren't you?"

I shrug. "What about the Porsche?"

"Traded it. That was California." She doesn't explain further. Her lemonade arrives.

"Oh," I say, not fully understanding and not daring to hope that means the decision involves me.

"It's white," she says, "tan interior. Seemed like better color choices under this taskmaster sun."

I appreciate her phrasing. "Yeah, that's why my Camry's white. It helps—but not enough."

She nods. "The AC in the Range Rover on high will ice you over in about thirty seconds."

"Lucky girl."

She makes a face and then shrugs. She looks at her watch. "I've got to go. Lake is with me. He's at the haberdashery down the street, and I'm supposed to meet him at the car in a few minutes."

To hide the deep green I suddenly color, I seize on a word. "Haberdashery?"

She giggles. "His word. Clothes horse." She sips her lemonade

"He *is* pretty," I offer, a forced attempt at magnanimity that makes even my lemonade taste sweet by contrast.

Rachel tilts her head. "Yeah, he is. No one appreciates that more than he does. And once you know that, it seems less a fact if that makes sense."

I nod, feeling better, fading green. She stands and kisses me again, her lips cold from the lemonade, tart. I kiss her back.

"See you, boyfriend," she whispers in my ear, tugging me against her for a second in a tight hug. And then she's gone.

I DRIVE BACK TO THE OFFICE, TURNING THE WORD "BOYFRIEND" over in my head.

In less than twenty-four hours, I've become a millionaire and Rachel Gunner's boyfriend. An embarrassment of riches, to coin a phrase.

CHAPTER 14:
Entrances and Exits

I'm still processing the morning's conversations when I return to the office, still processing Miller's visit last night.

It's lunchtime when I park and get out. The sun's screaming down at the lot. I unlock the office door; the outer office is empty. Talbot must have biked home to raid Olive's fridge. It occurs to me that's not a bad idea, and then I hear a noise from the inner office. A sliding sound, a sound of movement.

Quickly, I grab the broom from the narrow closet behind Talbot's desk. Holding it reversed, low on the handle, close to the head, I move as quietly as I can to the door to my office.

I push it open and leap inside, brandishing the broom.

Nothing.

The office is empty. I walk around my desk. My chair's not pushed under the desk as is my habit when I leave. The computer is on and displays the password page, but the entry line is blank. The papers on my desk are scattered. The filing cabinet's locked, but there are fresh scratches around the lock.

I feel the heat before I notice the source. The window stands open about five inches or so. I don't usually keep it locked though I normally keep it shut of course. I leave it unlocked because Talbot often forgets his key. But I know he had it earlier when he brought the coffee to the office.

Someone's been rifling my things. But it looks like they found nothing.

I stand the broom against my desk and shut the window, locking it this time. I am considering various tactics for making Certaine's life miserable when I see a rusty-red pickup pass on the street in the distance.

It's Bill Peppers's truck.

And then I'm no longer sure it was Certaine in my office. But if Pimberly has Certaine on the payroll, as he clearly does, why send Peppers to invade my office? Why not send Certaine? Certaine, at least, can claim to be a professional.

Why send Peppers?

But maybe it was not Pimberly who sent Peppers. I also saw Wylie talking to Peppers at the coliseum. Maybe Wylie sent him. But why? What in my office could interest Wylie Stroud?

All things considered, my investigation of Wylie has made virtually zero progress: two unhelpful conversations—one at Noble Hall and one at the club—and one clandestine surveillance at the coliseum. I still have no idea what Wylie is up to; all I really know is that he met in the darkened coliseum with Peppers, who later met with Pimberly out at West Point Lake. That's all I've got. Oh, and Wylie (with Rachel) visited Briggs and Stratton.

It makes me suspicious of Wylie, but I couldn't say what I suspect him of. I suspect him of being suspicious. *Gah!*

I need to talk to Wylie again, talk to him without Rachel around.

After a moment's thought, I send Talbot a text to tell him I will be out of the office for the afternoon, and I head to Noble Hall. If

Rachel's new car is there, I'll just drive on by. If not, I'll stop in for a chat with Wylie.

There is no white Range Rover in sight and no rusty-red pickup, so I enter the hall's driveway.

I admit mixed feelings about the absent Rover. On the one hand, I want to talk to Wylie—*need* to talk to him. On the other hand, if Rachel's not back, then there's a decent chance she's still out somewhere with Lake—some haberdashery where he's probably modeling new Speedos and flexing his abs. Can you flex your abs? Isn't it pitiful that I don't know?

Pushing that question and the pictures that spawned it from my mind, I park beside Wylie's Mercedes.

I walk to the back door and knock.

A couple of minutes later, an aproned, older black woman comes to the door. She's got a broom in her hand and a face of long-tested resignation.

"Can I help you, young man?"

"I'm Ford Merrick. I was hoping I could talk to Mr. Stroud if he's taking callers."

She nods. "Let me check." She starts to leave, then stops and turns around. "Merrick? Are you kin to the lady doc?"

"Yes, she's my sister. Do you know her?"

"She's *my* doctor. I like that girl. Helps my sciatica." She smiles at me, a surprisingly youthful smile.

"Me too," I respond. "Like her, that is. She doesn't help my sciatica. I haven't got sciatica."

She indulges in a long exhalation of sympathy, slowly shaking her head. "Guess we know which Merrick child got all the brains." She walks away.

I laugh and turn around, looking out toward the woods to the trailhead that leads to the pond. I wish I were there with Rachel right now. I taste her lemonade on my lips. I lose myself in thoughts of her and so don't hear Wylie approach.

"Ford-boy?"

Oh boy. I turn back around. Wylie's wearing an untucked shirt, a pair of khaki shorts, and flip flops. Today was clearly a no-shave Thursday. He looks different than at the party or at the club.

"Hello, Mr. Stroud. I'm sorry to bother you, but I was hoping you could help me."

"Help you?" He opens the door and joins me outside.

"Yes, my assistant, Talbot Norton, has been investigating some thefts at Briggs and Stratton..."

I watch his face, but he keeps his puzzled smile in place, unchanged.

"...and suspicion has fallen on a man named Bill Peppers. When Talbot checked into Peppers, someone claimed to have seen his truck parked here at Noble Hall. Talbot was curious whether Peppers has been here since you bought the hall. He once worked for Jane Pimberly, and Talbot thought he might have come back, hoping to get a job here again."

As on-the-spot, on-the-job PI yarns go, that'll do.

Wylie's face goes slack for a second, and his eyes cool. The look in them is close to that look I've seen but can't name in his niece's eyes. Then he smiles. "Peppers? No, I don't think he's been here, but then again, I'm not here all the time. He might've stopped by when I was out, but no one told me he did. I do know Peppers, though. Met him in Auburn a while back at that nice little coffee shop—the one with wine and books?"

"Well Red?"

"That's it. I like that place. Never saw him again until I ran into him a few days ago on Auburn's campus. I'd stopped by the coliseum to talk to the gymnastics coach about becoming a scholarship donor, and I ran into Peppers. He remembered me and chatted with me for a minute. But that's the only other time I've seen him."

As on-the-spot lies *to* a PI go, that'll do. But it is a lie.

Wylie and Peppers weren't chatting, and their body language was the language of familiarity, not of mere acquaintance. I majored in psychology; I graduated smart even if it doesn't always seem like it.

I do my best to act as if I believe him.

I nod. "Well, I'm not sure he's the one who's taken the things at Briggs and Stratton—no one's accusing him—but I told Talbot I'd be out this way…"

"Hoping to see my niece, I take it?" He's happy to change subjects, and he's peering at me curiously.

I blush; I can't help it. "No, not really. I saw Rachel earlier. She said she got a new car, a Range Rover?"

He smiles, shakes his head. "Yes, she traded the Porsche. Got the Rover this morning, and the dealer brought it here and picked up the Porsche. Lake worked it all out for her in Montgomery yesterday."

I wish I didn't know that. Lake is awfully *damn* helpful.

"Oh, I didn't realize."

He puts his hand on my shoulder and pats it. "Don't worry about Lake Thornton. He had his shot with Rachel. Not saying he doesn't want another one, but I'm almost certain she's of no mind to give him one. I believe she's set her sights on *someone else*."

He gives me an avuncular grin—or tries to. He misses slightly, and I wonder what that means.

"Let's walk, Ford-boy. There're some things you need to know, and I need to stretch my legs." We walk on to, then off of, the driveway and start down the road that leads to the pond trail.

He stops and faces me, squinting into the sun. "I told you that Rachel needed to slow down. You need to understand: she's lived a certain kind of life, one not much hemmed in by convention, normalcy. She was a beautiful woman in Los Angeles. With money. She made mistakes; no doubt, she'd reckon Lake is one of them. She wanted a change, but she didn't seem to be able to break all ties with the fast, shiny crowd—to break ties once and for all. So, I invited her here as I told you."

We walk on, and Wylie stops and picks up a long branch beside the road. He uses it as a walking stick. "I'll be honest," he says after a moment, "I didn't really expect her to stay long. I figured I could get her to stay for the party and then she'd get the West Coast itch and be back on the road, back to fast and shiny.

"But I didn't figure on you. Never would've guessed you were her type. I thought I knew her type—that Thornton was it, the paradigm. I met that doctor the other day here with your sister. Nettles?"

"Yes, Sam."

"Now, he's Rachel's type. Or was. But she's not made any noises about leaving, and that Porsche, that car had symbolic not just monetary value to her. Not sure I know what her parting with it means, but it sure is interesting." He eyes me for an instant from the corner of his eye.

"I don't know what it means either," I tell him. "And I find her—"

"Inscrutable?"

I grin at him. "Like the sphinx or ancient runes."

"Girl's been like that since she was a knot of blonde hair and braces. Her dad...my brother...he's like that too. Or he was the last time I saw him. He..." Wylie stops moving.

We've reached the trail. He looks down it but makes no move to walk it.

"Let's head back." Wylie seems to have ended his supply of information.

We reverse course. The heavy heat of the afternoon has us both laboring, sweating. The day's so hot and still that no insects can be seen or heard.

We're the only creatures silly enough to be moving under the sun.

Wylie decides to talk again. "Rachel has some money, Ford." I notice the change in my name. "She's not inexpensive. She has fancy tastes. Oh, she can amuse herself with BBQ, chicken fingers, and sweet tea, but eventually the need for less common things, dearer things, will return. Say, have you ever thought of investing? I mentioned to you that I had some things working, and if they pan out, I'd be happy to give you a chance to get on board, let your money work for you. Nothing's better than when your money makes you more money."

As I contemplate my massive account at Auburn Bank, I know I don't really need any more money, but I'm curious about Wylie's scheme. I haven't told anyone about my inheritance; I told Helen I wouldn't.

Wylie's scheme? This is what Rachel wanted to know—what she hired me to find out.

"Investing? Not something I've done, but if you have a *good* opportunity…"

He puts his hand on my shoulder again and smiles. "Let's see what happens in the next little while. If it looks good, I'll let you know." We reach the house, and he tosses the walking stick into the grass. "Anything else I can do for you, Ford?"

"No, that's all I need. Thanks."

He goes inside, and I get in the car, wondering what Uncle Wylie is playing at.

Do I need money to have Rachel?

I DIDN'T WANT TO GO BACK TO THE OFFICE. IT WAS LATE WHEN I got back to Opelika. For some reason, my chat with Wylie has started things spinning faster inside me.

You need to understand. I'm not an atomistic, fact-by-fact sort of detective—not one of those who works out hypotheses, gathers evidence for each, and weighs it carefully against other hypotheses and the evidence for them. No, I'm holistic: I work with big pictures. Hedgehog detective, not fox detective. St. John, not St. Paul. But it takes me time to get the big picture into focus or to let it focus itself.

Shapes are emerging, but nothing's in focus yet. I can't decide whether I'm working one case or two, and I can't decide about my girlfriend, Rachel Gunner. I still have faith, but…

I park at the house and get out. I'm surprised to see Helen on the porch until I realize it's not Helen. I glance behind me. I missed it: on the opposite side of the street is a steel-blue BMW. *TFYWIF.*

It's Patty Pimberly.

She gives me a finger wave and a smile that promises things. Some of the promised things are on display, tanned, and handleable.

She's seated in a rocker, wearing a red miniskirt the width of a Christmas ribbon. Above it, she has a red crop top so tight that it seems to be paint, not cloth. Her black hair hangs long and loose. She has on her mirrored sunglasses, and reflected in them, I can see what she sees.

She's rocking herself in open-toed, red heels, her red toenails far beneath red fingernails. Her knees are slightly parted, as are her lips. Lubricious.

"Hey, there, Melvin."

"Merrick."

"A rose is a rose is a rose…"

"No, it's Ford, not Rose."

She looks at me hard, as if trying to understand. "Oh, I see. You're funny, Melvin."

That wasn't funny, and I didn't mean it to be. She stops rocking.

"Aren't you going to invite me inside, offer me a drink? It's hot out here as you can see." She gestures toward herself and not the day.

I'm suddenly tired. I didn't sleep well last night, and I've had a busy day. I just cooled down in the car after my steamy walk with Wylie. I don't have much patience for this clumsy red seduction routine from Patty.

"Where's Wade?"

"Oh, who knows? He left the house early this morning. Left me alone all day, left me to my devices. Which made me think of you, so I Googled you, checked your office, and here I am. Ready, waiting."

I sigh silently. Patty's offer leaves me cold despite the heat. I'm in love, remember. But Patty's offer wouldn't have tempted me before

Rachel Gunner. Brief encounters aren't my style, and married women are off-limits.

Then Wylie's phrase shoulders its way into my mind: "the fast, shiny crowd."

Patty belongs to LaGrange's version of that same crowd. The thought makes my stomach turn then ache. No doubt, Rachel's fast, shiny crowd was even faster and shinier. *Damn.*

That thought depresses me so much my shoulders sink, and I feel them do it.

"Look, Patty, I appreciate you stopping by, but I've got things I have to do tonight," I lie, trying to be polite, "and I don't have time for whatever you have in mind."

She reaches up and lowers her sunglasses. I've seen the gesture before. "You don't understand what I have in mind?" she asks in frank, green-eyed disbelief.

"No, and I'm sure I'd be a disappointment to you, whatever it is."

She surveys me from top to bottom, her green eyes above the mirrored lenses. "I don't think so. I'm not good with names, but I make up for it in other ways. I'm good at other things."

"No doubt," I say, "but *no*."

She seems genuinely puzzled, on the verge of anger, unable to accept that I'm rejecting her advances.

She crosses her legs like a man, and her Christmas ribbon skirt now covers nothing, including the panties she's not wearing.

"Look, if you take me inside, I'll let you do *anything* you want. Anything. I'm *very* limber."

She pushes the sunglasses up with one finger, hiding her eyes while everything below is on display.

"I'm sure that you are, Mrs. Pimberly, but as I said, 'No.'"

I'm generally not rude, but I'm not going to be Basic Instinct-ed all afternoon in red, not white—and not on an empty, achy stomach with sinking shoulders. I turn and nod to her car, the vanity plate.

"I'm sure your husband wonders where you are."

She gets up and swings down the steps then turns her mirrored lenses on me, frowning. "Let him wonder. *You* will…"

She slinks down the sidewalk and across the street—long legs on display and hips making suggestions. She glances back a couple of times to see if the view has changed my mind.

I do wonder. I wonder who's watching Baby.

CHAPTER 15: *Surrounded*

After Patty drives away, I go inside and make myself a gin and tonic. As I make it, I receive a text from Helen. She tells me that she's going to dinner with Sam and then adds, in a second text, that she might not be home tonight. Her crooked hair comb at dinner was foreshadowing.

I'm happy for her. She's worked so hard for so long, been so single-minded, it's good to believe that she's found someone, someone who might regard her as seriously as she's always regarded others, particularly me. Sam seems like a real man, one who finds a woman and remains steadfastly hers. Even though he's handsome and successful, he does not seem like the dating app type, the type who confuses romance and shopping. So many people can't get their categories straight.

I carry my gin and tonic into the living room and sit down in the recliner. Speaking of categories and straightening, I have a lot to consider myself.

Here's what I think I know—

Noble Hall is more than a beautiful house with a sad, ancient Southern history. It also has a sad recent history; it's the scene of Jane Pimberly's tragic life. Although I don't have a fiber or bloodstain of hard evidence, I'm growing convinced that Jane did not die of natural causes. Perhaps it's mere fancy, and particularly bad in a detective, but I believe that human lives have a lyric shape—a pattern or meter that shows the lives for what they are, revealing the character that is destiny. (I was also a literature major, you know.) Anyway, Jane's life is a sad lyric, but it ends *too neatly* with a lonely heart attack amid a clowder of feral cats.

For some reason, those cats and Jane's strange behaviors—the midnight lantern walks, the naked balcony singing—are all clawing at my thoughts. Her story ended in a different way, I reckon—less neatly, more darkly.

And I am now sure that Wylie Stroud *is* up to something. Rachel was right to be suspicious. What tie does he have to Peppers, and does Peppers tie him to Pimberly? And if he's tied to Pimberly, what else might Wylie be tied to?

His talk to me of Lake was double-edged. It seemed like he was reassuring me, but the very fact that he chose to reassure me made me less sure. And he just doesn't do the concerned, avuncular bit well. It's forced, unnatural. A bit of bad acting.

Acting.

And that brings me to Rachel, but I'm not going to worry about her now. No, not right now. No worry.

We're going to talk tomorrow. At last. Soon enough.

I sip my gin and tonic slowly, letting my thoughts sink and rise, cloud and clear, pool and eddy. It feels good to stop managing them myself, directing them.

I pour another drink and turn on some music: Richard Buckner's *Surrounded*. When I get to the song, "Beautiful Question," I push Repeat.

I sip, listen, and let my mind go swampy.

Friday dawns with tornado warnings.

The ground is soaked from long, hard overnight rain. Water stands

171

everywhere in the yard when I look out my window. The sky looks like it's sinking under its own weight.

I go to the bathroom, shower, shave, and brush my teeth. When I finish and get dressed, it occurs to me that Helen may not be here.

I shove my rolled socks in my shoes and walk down the hallway to her room. I knock. No answer. I call out her name. No answer.

I crack the door and peek in. The bed's made, unslept in.

She stayed with Sam. I'm happy for her, but I also feel a twinge; we've been a unit for a long time, dependent on only each other. It now feels like things are changing, shifting, and I can't predict how they will end.

I wish she were here to talk about the money. It preyed on my thoughts again last night. More dreams of coins, and a disturbing, chilling image, just before I woke, of Rachel in her red bikini and in Lake Thornton's arms atop a pile of glittering gold.

That image, the threatening sky, Helen's absence—they all blue my mood. I put on my shoes and decide to go out for coffee. Wylie's mention of Well Red yesterday has the shop in my mind, so that's where I go.

Rain squalls off and on as I drive from Opelika to Auburn along Opelika Road. On the edge of downtown Auburn, I turn into the coffee shop's lot. It's already crowded; the lot's small, and the shop's popular.

But my office is closed today, so I'm in no hurry.

I climb the rear ramp leading to the large back porch. The rain has kept the porch empty. Inside, coffee drinkers are already seated. Gathered at a couple of tables are small groups of students, each facing an open Bible, a common sight in local coffee shops. Scripture's not just on signs; it's everywhere—though it's unclear that common life here differs from common life anywhere else. Often, the omnipresent scripture seems more elaborate decoration than existential directive.

Maybe that's just my mood talking.

I walk around the wooden counters that house the baristas and uphold the register and espresso machine; I sit on one of the high stools at a raised section that serves as a bar. I order a black coffee.

The barista, a young woman in a flannel shirt, slides me an earth-toned mug full of steaming coffee. I inhale it, dispelling disturbing dream afterimages, family changes, and the drooping sky.

The tornado watch ends as I drink my coffee. I listen to the baristas talk among themselves.

A hand settles on my shoulder, and I hear my name. I turn around on the stool to find Ruth. She's not dressed for work; she's in casual clothes: T-shirt, jeans, and sandals. An umbrella is in her hand. She smells like rain, and her smile lifts one corner of my mood.

"Hey, Ruth." I should feel self-conscious, but I don't. She doesn't seem to be either.

She grins at me. "I didn't know you came here."

"Not often. I'm at Ed's most of the time, as you know."

"Not in the last few days."

Now I do feel a smidgen of self-consciousness. "I thought you might want some space."

"Thanks, Ford, but I'm fine. Right as rain. Or I will be soon, and I want to keep you as my friend. We've always been friends."

"We have," I agree and smile. "Join me?"

"For a minute," she says as she takes a stool beside me. "Say, Dad says that you and Talbot were out at Briggs and Stratton, though I guess Dad only talked to Talbot."

"Figured it was best I stay out of arm's reach."

She gestures to the barista for a cup, and I gesture for it to be put on my tab. Ruth snickers. "You've never been Dad's favorite, but just lately..."

"Murder?"

"Absolutely. Premeditated, painful, and with no discoverable corpus delicti. Just your body buried in a far-flung, unfindable hole."

"So, he's not given this any thought?"

She snickers again. "Best you stay out of the factory. Death by small engine does not sound like a pleasant end."

I shudder and nod my head.

"Ford, Dad says Talbot was asking about Bill Peppers."

"Yes, he was. Do you know Peppers?" The thought surprises me.

"Not much or not well, or however I should say it. Dad hired him to do some work around my apartment. He did the work, but…"

"But…?"

"But he's creepy. Not in the cartoonish way Talbot often is—always is—but in a serious, scary way."

"What did he do?"

Ruth pauses then goes on: "Do? Nothing. He just kept sneaking looks at me. Certain kinds of looks, hungry and insistent if you know what I mean, although maybe a guy can't understand…"

I bite my lip. "I don't know if I've ever been on the receiving end of one, but I have an idea what you mean."

"Well, when he finished at my place, for the next couple of weeks, I kept having this feeling, this feeling that someone was watching me."

"A Peeping Pepper?"

She shakes her head hard though she smiles. "This is serious, Ford."

I nod and kill my smile. "I know. I just couldn't resist the phrase."

"Words are going to do you in. Do you and Talbot believe he took those things from the lockers?"

"Honestly, we don't know. It's Talbot's case in an unofficial sense. He's been trying to make some sense of it."

"I wouldn't put anything past Peppers. Be careful with him, Ford. There's violence in him along with that hunger. He's not a man you want to cross, not unless you're sure."

"Thanks, Ruth."

We sit and drink our coffee for a minute until she turns to me. "So, how's Rachel?"

"Fine. I'm supposed to see her tonight."

She smiles, but I can see something in the back of her gaze. "I saw her late yesterday afternoon. She stopped in at Ed's. The man with her wanted something to eat." She tries to say it casually but can't quite do it. "He was the most handsome man I've ever seen, but he seemed to me like a high-ticket Certaine."

I laugh as my stomach churns. "That's about right, I think." I glance away. "He's her old boyfriend."

Ruth gives me a sideways look as she sips the last of her coffee. "And that doesn't worry you?"

"It makes my stomach ache."

Her eyes are kind when she looks at me. "She didn't seem like she was *with* him, you know, for what that's worth. She waved at me, wanted to talk, but one of the other waitresses had their table and the guy…"

"Lake."

"Lake took his club sandwich to go. I didn't get free in time to talk to her. Dinner rush."

She stands up. "He's handsome, Ford, but insubstantial. Rachel's not a dull girl either. Thanks for the coffee."

She leaves, and I turn back to the counter. As I sip the last of my coffee, I decide that—good idea or not—I'm going to talk to Bill Peppers.

I drive to Bill Peppers's address. He lives in a rundown apartment complex in a low-lying area on the southern edge of Auburn. Garbage is piled high in the dumpster next to the entranceway and spills out onto the parking lot.

In front of the first apartment, music blares from the radio on a table, but no one seems to be listening to it.

As I get out of the car, a small girl whips by me, towed by a massive brindle pit bull. He turns his boulder head to me and gives me that pit bull smile, the one that seems clownish or killer depending on the context. Luckily, with the small girl on the other end of the leash, jabbering but not upset, the smile seems clownish. The girl has both hands on the leash, and she's ineffectually commanding the animal to reverse course. He seems to have an important destination in mind and continues in his original direction. I start to help her when she shakes her head, her pigtails wagging, smiling with the chocolate milk stain around her mouth.

"It's okay, mister. He does this. He'll pull me back home once he's tired."

They keep going, and I walk down the sidewalk in front of the apartments to the last one in the row: Peppers's. The music on the other end keeps playing. I don't see Peppers's truck anywhere in the parking lot. I knock on his door—forty-one—and wait. I can hear the TV inside: MTV. I raise an eyebrow. Not what I'd have figured Peppers to watch; then again, I'm not sure I know what I figured he'd watch. No one comes to the door, and I don't hear any movement inside. I knock again.

A middle-aged woman opens the door next to Peppers's. "He ain't home, mister. He just always leaves the TV on one of them *Real World* shows—as if this hole ain't real enough. He ain't been around a lot lately. Truck's always gone."

I nod. The woman's wearing a shower cap and a green robe, and a yellow nightgown shows beneath it.

"Thanks. Do you know—does he have a wife, a girlfriend?"

She bares her teeth in a hard-to-describe expression, the whites of her eyes showing. "Peppers? *Hell no.* No woman in her right mind ever wanna be alone with him. That man's broke."

I'm not sure I understand. "Poor?"

"*Hell no.* Not poor. Broke. There are parts in him that are a-spinnin', but they ain't turnin' no other parts."

I'm not sure how much that explanation helps me, but the point is clear. Something's wrong with Bill Peppers. His neighbor is obviously reacting to what Ruth did.

"Huh. Well, could you keep my stopping by to yourself? I'll find him later."

"No skin off my nose. I never speak to him if I can help it. Can't stand them eyes of his. Doan pay to tempt no sociopath. Doan say the Devil's name."

THE SUN COMES OUT FOR THE FIRST TIME AS I HEAD BACK TO Opelika.

Despite the office being closed, I decide to stop by. Hearing about Bill Peppers has made me want to double-check things there. After what I've heard, the thought of Peppers rummaging through my things makes me cringe.

As I shut off the Camry, I hear a horn and crunching gravel then feel a sudden jolt.

I look behind me to see a black car and the red faces of Talbot Norton and Father Halsey. Talbot is screaming. Father Halsey is yelling. The car against mine, I realize, is Father Halsey's old but immaculate Lincoln Town Car.

Father Halsey lumbers out of the car, still yelling, and I can hear him now. "Talbot Norton, you are an offense against Christian theology, against the view that all things work together for good! You are an absurd element in the divine plan, a wrench in God's works!"

Talbot tumbles out, glancing at me but clearly more concerned with Father Halsey, who is livid above his white collar.

"I'm a man," Talbot protests. "I'm not a *wench*."

Father Halsey looks as though he's summoning divine fire. "*Wench*? I said, *wrench*, you blot on all that's holy. No one should let you bike, much less drive. You should never be near wheels, period. No spheres. Olive should take your Spirograph. I can't believe I let you talk me into this!"

By this point, I've checked the damage. Other than the slide ruts in the gravel and a smudge of white Camry on the bumper of the black Town Car, no serious damage has occurred. I wave my hand at Father Halsey, hoping to point this out, but he ignores me.

"Talbot Norton," he growls, one hand fisting in the other, "you are a temptation to my faith."

Talbot cowers and slowly moves behind me. Father Halsey finally looks at where I waved, registering the lack of damage. I see him trying to calm himself.

Talbot peeks out from behind me. "I'm sorry, Father. I didn't expect anyone to be in the lot. The office is closed."

Father Halsey glances pleadingly heavenward. He lowers his head, glaring at Talbot from beneath clenched eyebrows. "That's why we drive with our eyes *open*, Talbot. *'Bring out the people who are blind, even though they have eyes.'*"

Talbot hides behind me again and squeaks at me. "Is he casting a spell? Sorry, Father, I just turned too fast, and it scared me. When I get scared, I shut my eyes." I step out of the way. Talbot's crouched, his eyes closed.

"Jesus," Father Halsey says when he sees Talbot in his vertical, fetal position. Father Halsey kicks at loose gravel, then he shakes his head at me and climbs into the driver's side of the Town Car.

His knees hit the steering wheel, and I hear him roar: "Shit!"

He slams the seat backward then backs the Town Car away from us, turning it as he does. When his door is parallel with us, he rolls down his window and asks reluctantly: "Same time tomorrow, Talbot?"

Talbot nods his head meekly.

Father Halsey rolls up his window, glares at Talbot once more, and drives away.

Talbot looks at me. "I had no idea a priest knew *those* words."

TALBOT AND I SPEND THE REST OF THE DAY IN THE OFFICE, BUT we leave the door locked and don't answer the phone. He's planning to take Kip to dinner at Wok and Roll this evening. We spend some time puzzling over the items stolen at Briggs and Stratton but get no closer to finding a pattern among them.

I tell him that I believe Bill Peppers broke into the office, and we talk about Peppers, about my visit to his apartment complex, about Ruth and the neighbor woman. Talbot's hurt when I slip up and tell him that Ruth compared him to Bill Peppers. At the peak of his righteous indignation, I ask if he still has the *Bikini Diaries*. He doesn't answer, and that is an answer.

"You know, Talbot, if you want someone like Kip to like you, you need to burn that book, and you need to make it up to Helen. Imagine if Kip runs into my sister..."

Talbot gulps. "Damn."

"Exactly. If you want a woman to take you seriously, it's time to start acting like a man."

Talbot looks at me for a quiet minute then nods and speaks seriously. "And stop acting like a wrench."

I GET MY FIRST RIDE IN RACHEL'S RANGE ROVER AS RACHEL DRIVES us to Michelle's.

The car is as nice as I expect, but I admit that I can almost feel Lake in it, smell his scent mixed with the new car scent. He was there first. I don't like being second to Lake, but there's nothing I can do about it.

The fact of him remains even if the scent of him fades.

Father Halsey and Talbot's comedy routine chased my lousy mood away, but it arrived again with Rachel's white Range Rover.

But it's not just about being second to Lake. I'm also dreading the talk we're supposed to have. I've avoided thinking about it all day, but there's no avoiding it now. I've connived at this dream for days, and now it's time to face the morning, the alarm clock.

To make matters worse, Rachel seems to be in a mood herself. She kissed me when she picked me up, but there was something amiss in the kiss, then she looked away, and she hasn't quite faced me since. She's driving—so there's that—but I have a feeling she spoke too soon when she told me not to worry.

Something has changed, is changing.
I feel like Talbot: I'm scared, and I want to shut my eyes.

CHAPTER 16:
Warnings, Jokes, and Considerations

I've called Michelle's boys "twin terrors" but, as I've also noted, Dirk is five, and the other, Brad, is seven. So, they aren't twins in the biological sense, but I think of them as twins in the *meteorological* sense.

The tornado warnings for this morning were probably to alert me to my danger tonight. Each time I see either boy, I'm reminded of the Tasmanian devil, whirling wildly. Each of the boys is like that, a Tasmanian tornado.

A devil.

I always get the short end of deals with Michelle. But at least tonight I have a teammate—or I hope I do—in Rachel. I could not have been more surprised at her volunteering to do this with me. The glamorous woman in the black pantsuit I first met at my office looked like a woman who had never heard so much as a rumor of children. Now, she is wearing a navy T-shirt, cut-off jeans, and flip flops and driving me to a Friday night of babysitting. Plus, she's not just dropping me off; she's staying.

She could be in her Porsche, in that black pantsuit, hurtling cross-country to LA, Lake Thornton in the car beside her doing seated ab crunches or whatever, but she's not. Acknowledging that improves my mood and makes me less fearful about hers.

She could have just canceled, but she's here, with me.

Michelle and her husband, Will, live in Opelika, not that far from me. Michelle and Helen were best friends through high school, and I briefly had a teen crush on Michelle. It's probably not quite right to say that Michelle and Helen are still friends. They are, but not like they once were. Michelle struggled to cope with our parents' deaths, with Helen's grief and sudden duty of caring for me, the house, and so on. She pulled back from Helen, and although my sister understood it and forgave Michelle, their friendship was never intimate. They have lunch on occasion, and Helen is the doctor for the family, but that's the length and breadth of their relationship.

Will, Michelle's husband, is a nice man, a smart man—a chemistry prof at AU as I mentioned. He's abstracted, congenial, a booklover, and an audiophile—absolutely obedient to Michelle.

Rachel pulls close to the curb in front of the house. It's a two-story with an attractive, flower-boxed porch. The flowers are currently in bloom. In the yard lie two bikes, both small, one with training wheels and one without. Rachel bends down to look at the house through my window, and I lean forward and kiss her cheek.

She faces me for the first time since she picked me up. "That was sweet, Ford. Thanks."

"My pleasure—anytime."

Her eyes flash, and she leans in and kisses me on the lips, opening hers slightly, her tongue touching my lips tantalizingly before she leans away. Her color is heightened, and she's breathing deeply. "We have to babysit. Probably shouldn't get too carried away. So, we're about to see the old girlfriend?"

I shake my head. "No, an old crush, I guess. Long over." Rachel gazes into my eyes as if checking, then she moves back to her door.

"She's Helen's friend?" Rachel asks, getting out.

I get out and wait for her to come around the front of the car to me. "Yes, but not like before. You know how that goes."

She looks at me. "No, not really; I never had friends in high school."

I'm pondering that as we walk to the porch steps. Rachel takes my hand as the front door opens. Michelle steps outside. She's dressed for dinner in an olive-green dress and pearls, green heels.

She's smiling until she gets a close look at Rachel, and then her smile straightens. "Ford, who do you have with you?" Michelle doesn't wait for me to answer. "I'm Michelle Trenton."

Rachel nods and smiles. "Hi, Michelle. I'm Rachel Gunner. I'm going to give Ford a hand tonight if that's okay?"

Michelle laughs. "Sure, he'll need you. We haven't met, have we?"

"No, I don't think so. I came to town recently. Ford's been showing me around." Rachel makes a point of swinging our joined hands as she says this. Michelle notices and is annoyed. She likes to believe my crush has continued and will continue, and it's hard to believe that with Rachel standing on her porch, holding my hand.

Before anyone can continue, a sound like an air siren surrounds us, tearing the air, and two boys, one dark-haired, shorter, one light haired, taller, sonic scream as they pass us, managing to scream in discord and shut down all rational thought within earshot.

As the boys leap from the porch and dig for their bikes, Will, chasing them hopelessly, comes through the front door. "Boys!" he cries in an already—always—defeated voice. "Boys!" The boys stand their bikes up, still screaming.

Michelle joins in. "Boys!" The boys each throw a leg over a seat, still screaming.

Still screaming.

"Boys," Rachel says without shouting.

But somehow, her voice knifes through the boys' screams. They immediately shut up and turn to look at her.

Brad, the taller, blond-haired boy, starts to glare at Rachel, but she glares faster, beating him to the draw, and his gaze clatters to the ground. His brother, Dirk, sees Brad's defeat, and he shows no fight either.

Dirk points at Rachel, his hand grimy, the nail on his pointing hand with dirt beneath it. "You're pretty!"

Michelle looks from Dirk to Rachel and back to Dirk. She seems simultaneously impressed and envious. Will is all amazement at both Rachel and the sudden silence. He runs his hand through his blond, curly hair: "Wow."

Michelle quickly speaks. "Will, this is Rachel Gunner. She's *with* Ford, and she's going to help him with the boys."

Will nods to Rachel and smiles warmly. He glances congratulations at me.

"Nice to meet you, Will." Rachel looks from the father to the sons. "Boys, come here. We'll play in the backyard. Stand your bikes up near the porch, okay?"

Both boys do as they're told. Michelle does not try to conceal her amazement. Neither do I. "Shit," I whisper.

The boys pass us, going into the house. Rachel follows them, and I follow her. "We'll see you two when you get home," I say, the tall man bringing up the rear in a short parade.

I'M ON MY BACK IN THE GRASS OF THE BACKYARD. MY GUN IS NEAR me but empty. Useless.

There's nothing I can do now. Nothing. I can barely breathe. Brad's beside me, his shirt matted and soaking, his eyes closed. I don't know where his gun is. I worry it's broken.

Lost. We lost.

I hear another gun, a shotgun, pump across the lawn. I look up, raising only my head, opening only one eye.

Rachel stands with Dirk beside her. He has his emerald squirt pistol trained on Brad. Rachel's squirt shotgun is aimed at me.

"Don't make me end you, Merrick," she says flatly, "you know I'll do it. No remorse. We've already finished your partner. Watch 'em, Dirk."

I can't help it. I start laughing, and Brad does too. Dirk and Rachel join in. Dirk stops laughing for long enough to raise his squirt gun into the air and begin to dance in place. "We win, Rachel, we win!" Rachel tousles his hair and dances with him.

I watch her in wonder. She's wet; grass clippings are stuck to her long legs, her bare feet; her hair's messy, wet across her bangs, and her careless giggle ripples through me head to toe. I look for little bells on trees.

Brad stands up and joins in the dance with Dirk and Rachel. I sit up and shake my head at them; then I join them too.

Rachel is a Tasmanian exorcist.

LATER, HAVING CLEANED UP—THE BOYS FED AND PUT TO BED— Rachel snuggles next to me on the couch. I've found Will's vinyl copy of *Sinatra/Jobim: The Complete Recordings* and put it on, the volume low.

We haven't had that talk; we've been too busy with the boys. But I feel it coming.

Rachel's head is on my shoulder, and she starts talking without moving it or facing me. "You ever imagine kids, Ford—a house, a yard?"

I was trying not to ask her that question, so hearing her ask it of me leaves me speechless. My speechlessness causes her to raise her head and look at me.

"Yeah," I say softly, trying to answer as if on tiptoe, "sure I have. It's what I want, my own version of what Helen and I lost. A home, a wife, kids."

She nods and looks away. "A pretty…ordinary dream…for a *detective*."

I can't tell if that's commentary or condemnation. But I told the truth, and I am sticking with it. "I suppose. But remember, I'm a soft-boiled detective. I'm not the *love 'em and leave 'em* sort."

She takes my hand in hers. "No, you're not that sort."

"I'm the boring sort, I suppose."

"No," Rachel says quietly, "you're *not* boring."

"But I'm not *Lake*." I hate myself for saying it as soon as I do, but there it is. Damn my betraying Benedict Arnold tongue.

Rachel's eyes harden. "Lake? No, you're not Lake. Lake *is* boring. I like him; I once believed I more than liked him, although lately, I've come to doubt that was true…"

Sinatra sings in the background, "Meditation." I wait for Rachel to continue because it's clear she's not done.

"I came here for mixed reasons, Ford, and I came here for mixed-up reasons. I've been unsure about so many things for so long. I've not been the best person. No, that's not right. I've been bad, but I've wanted to be a good person for a long time.

"And now, here"—she glances at me—"with you, I have a chance to live a different life and become a different kind of person."

I exhale, relieved. "Rachel, look, I know this is all new, but I also know I've never felt like this for anyone before…"

She smiles a pleased smile and bumps me with her shoulder. "Not even for Michelle?"

"Not even for Michelle, not even in my teenage fantasies. Not even close."

Her smile complicates itself into a smirk. "When we find a place and the time, we'll see what we can do about those fantasies." She grabs me and kisses me with a passion that steals my breath and almost steals my consciousness.

She takes her time with her thievery.

She pulls back just before she's stolen all of me, and she licks her lips, panting. "We'd better stand up, maybe dance. If we stay on this couch, we will end up doing things no babysitters should do while babysitting. I'll make you forget Michelle Trenton in her own house."

We stand and begin to dance. We spin slowly.

"Ford," Rachel says, leaning back, "will you do me a favor?"

"Anything, Rachel."

She rests her head on my shoulder. "Stop working on my case. Stop pursuing Uncle Wylie."

I stop dancing. "Why?"

She steps back. "I'm the client; if I want you to stop, then you stop, right?" She speaks softly, but there's an edge in her tone. "And I just want you to stop, that's all. I'm sure he's *not* up to anything. It was all my imagination."

Except I don't think it was all her imagination; he is up to something. I worry that Wylie is part of my case for Miller, my investigation of Jane Pimberly's murder. The tie to Peppers is something I can't ignore. *Damn it.*

"I will quit working on your case if that's what you want," I tell her after a moment, hating myself for my internal prevarication. *Her* case—but not *Miller's.*

"Good, it is"—she gives me a quick kiss—"it is what I want."

"Of course, if we're dating, if you're my girlfriend, and if you live at Noble Hall, I'm going to run into him, right?"

"Right," she agrees, "but…"

"But what, Rachel?"

She shrugs. "Don't spend time with him alone. He's a talker when he gets to know you. He talks people into all sorts of things. And there are stories—stories of mine, stories about me—that *I* need to tell you. And I don't want you to hear them from him or anyone else at the hall.

"I'm going to have to work up the courage to tell them to you. I don't know if I can tell them to you until you trust me, and I'm not sure you do. You want to; I can see that. You're trying; I can see that too. But I also know you have doubts."

"Rachel, I—"

"I understand, Ford. It makes sense. You know almost nothing about me. I show up out of nowhere and walk into your office. I'm not the sort of girl you know and have known. Helen, or Ruth, or even Michelle."

I start to speak again, but she stops me with another kiss.

When it ends, she grins, playfulness replacing seriousness. "You're fired, Ford. And think about it this way: no more worrying about whether we're pretending for the sake of the case because there is no case."

We start to dance again. I'm trying to sort cases and non-cases in my head when Will and Michelle return.

RACHEL'S DRIVING ME HOME WHEN MY PHONE RINGS. IT'S OLIVE Norton.

"Hey, Olive, what can I do for you?"

She's crying, wailing. "Ford, it's Talbot! Someone hit him. With a car. On purpose! Someone drove onto the sidewalk and hit my baby!"

I swallow my heart then shake my head, not sure I heard correctly. "Olive, Olive—God, I'm sorry. How is he?"

She erupts into uncontrolled sobs. I try to get her to talk to me, but I hear other voices on her end of the line. In a moment, someone else speaks to me.

"Ford, this is Kip Mott."

"Kip! So glad you're there! How is he?"

"We don't know for sure. The car that hit him knocked him a distance. Airborne. He's badly scraped up, bruised. They're mostly worried about internal injuries. I've been with him the whole time. He was unconscious for a moment but then conscious again. He was conscious in the ambulance. Who'd do this, Ford? It was no goddamn accident…"

"You say a car hit him? What did it look like?"

"I told the police. I didn't get a good look at it. Black, dark blue maybe. Big. It came from behind us as we walked back to Talbot's after dinner.

It could have hit us both, but it only hit him. I was rushing to him; I only glanced at the car as it sped away. I've told the police. They're hunting for the car." She's holding it together, but she's badly upset.

I don't recognize the description of the car. Certaine drives a newish silver Dodge Charger, and of course, Bill Peppers drives that old pickup. But it could have been one of them in a borrowed car or a stolen car.

Or someone else entirely.

Rachel's been listening but hasn't spoken. She does now. "Tell me how to get to the hospital, Ford."

I give her directions. I tell Kip we'll be there in a few minutes; then I call Helen.

WE PARK IN THE BOTTOM OF THE EAST ALABAMA MEDICAL CENTER garage and hurry to the Emergency Room.

We see Kip and Olive talking to Father Halsey when we get inside. I had planned to call him, but he's already here. Olive sees me, and she runs to me, grabs me, and begins to weep and talk all at once. I hold her and say soothing things.

Kip and Rachel seem to be acquainted, and then it hits me: the club. They must know each other from there. They talk quietly, and I succeed in getting Olive to slow but not stop her sobs.

Helen and Sam come in a few moments later. Helen walks to me, and Olive somehow relocates from me to her. Sam nods to me. "I'll go back and see what I can find out, Ford."

"Thanks, Sam."

FATHER HALSEY APPROACHES ME. HELEN'S GOTTEN OLIVE TO SIT down, calm down. Rachel and Olive are on each side of Helen as a concerned Kip peeks down the hall through the small window in the door through which Sam disappeared; you can see the urgency in her posture.

"Who'd want to hurt Talbot Norton?" Father Halsey growls at me.

I'm tempted to remind him that he threatened Talbot earlier in the day, but I don't. I meant to ask Talbot how Father Halsey ended up teaching him to drive, and now I know—Olive. She must have arranged it. Father Halsey's always had a soft spot for her.

"I'm afraid it's a case of ours, of mine. Things have taken a turn. I'm not sure who did this, but I'm pretty sure that in the last few days, we…um, I…have kicked a hornets' nest or two."

Father Halsey gives me a measured glance. "You can take care of yourself, Ford. But Talbot's got no chance. If he works with you, he's got to run your risks. And he'll do it because he loves you so much. Have you thought about that as seriously as you should? Talbot's not built for risks. You are, even if you don't realize it or act like it." He raises his brows. "Or look like it."

I glance at my shoes, self-conscious, ashamed, but not of them. I've avoided thinking about this the entire time Talbot's worked for me, and I've known I was avoiding it. The truth is, I'm guilty of not taking Talbot seriously despite my long friendship with him.

Because I let myself see him as a joke, I assume, maybe even hope, everyone else does and will.

I was wrong about that. Someone took him seriously—seriously tried to hurt him, maybe kill him. No joke.

Kip turns from the window, steps back from the door, and Sam walks through it a moment later. Olive stands up as he reaches her, and so do Helen and Rachel. Father Halsey and I join the group.

"He's going to be okay. He's badly bruised, badly scraped. Raw in places. He's got a concussion. They'll keep him overnight, but there are no internal injuries. He told me to tell everyone"—Sam gives us all exaggerated thumbs up—"and that's a quote."

Olive begins to sob again but in relief. Helen hugs her. Rachel walks to me and hugs me. Kip blows out a long breath.

Father Halsey grunts but in a patterned hush. It takes me a minute to realize he's praying.

Kip, on the edge of tears, seems unsure where to stand.

I tug on Rachel's hand, and we go stand beside her.

As we do, I consider tornado warnings and the gun in my filing cabinet.

CHAPTER 17: *Wave*

After Olive returns from a brief visit with Talbot, Helen convinces Olive to go home. Helen and Sam are going to take her.

I'm impressed with Sam. He fell in immediately with us all even though he didn't know Kip or Father Halsey or Olive—or Talbot. As Olive goes out the ER doors, Helen and Sam follow. I see Sam settle his hand on Helen's back and rub it gently. I'm so tired, angry, and emotional that Sam's gesture brings tears to my eyes. I can be happy for Helen.

I'm trying to blink them away when Rachel notices. She's still holding my hand. "It's okay, Ford. Talbot's going to be okay." I nod. She waits a moment, then continues. "Is it a case? Is that what got Talbot hurt?"

I look at her, my lips pulled to one side of my face as I wipe my eyes with the palm of my free hand. "I don't know. Probably. But I can't talk about it."

She looks into my eyes, concern in hers. "Be careful, please."

I squeeze her hand. "I will."

Kip comes back into the ER. She had gone to see Talbot too. She stops beside us as Father Halsey returns with a small cup of machine coffee in his hand; he sniffs it and frowns.

"He's fine, I think," Kip says, visibly relieved. "I'm just starting to *like* that guy. I don't want to lose him."

Rachel nods at Kip but squeezes my hand: "I know how you feel."

"Kip," Father Halsey says, "can I give you a ride?" He tosses the full cup of coffee in the trash.

"Yes, please."

Father Halsey nods gravely at me, and then he and Kip leave.

Rachel turns to me. "We should go. There's nothing you can do here tonight."

"I suppose so."

She steps to me and kisses my cheek, gives me a gentle smile, and leads me out of the ER.

RACHEL PARKS THE ROVER AT MY HOUSE. HELEN'S NOT HOME YET; the house is dark. Rachel shuts the engine off.

My phone beeps, and I panic, worried about Talbot, but it's a text from Helen. She's going to stay with Sam again tonight if I'm okay. I text back that I am. Rachel's watching but hasn't asked anything.

I face her. "That was Helen. She's spending the night at Sam's."

Rachel nods and searches my face. "Do you want me to stay?"

Everything in me screams, *"Yes!"* "No, believe me, I'd *love* it"—I don't catch myself before I use that word, so I just keep going—"but I wouldn't want...I can't... Not tonight, with Talbot there in the hospital..."

"Ford," she says softly, "we don't need to *do* anything. I want to stay with you, *be* with you."

I feel deranged. I want her so desperately, and yet I don't want our first time to be tonight, overshadowed by what's happened.

But I would like her to stay, be with me. "I just want...I just imagined...our first time to be...celebration, not comfort."

193

"You say the nicest things, Ford. Are you sure you never thought about writing?"

That's a secret I will share with her but not tonight. I lean to her and kiss her. "Come on inside."

Rachel stands and looks around my room. The pad I'm using to write *Do I Not Bleed?* sits on my desk. My guitar stands in the desk chair. Rachel scans it all: the posters, books, and magazines.

"You weren't lying about this room being different than the rest of the house. But I like it too."

I grin and open one of the drawers in my dresser, rifle around. "I could go to Helen's room," I offer, shrugging. "I really don't have any PJs."

Rachel chuckles. "Just a comfy T-shirt—that'll do."

I find her one and hand it to her, folded. She holds it up in front of her and reads it. "Just for Him"?

I blush. I had forgotten that logo was on the shirt. "Um...yeah, sorry. That's a barbershop...um...a *male salon* in Auburn. I was on their softball team one summer. That shirt's my souvenir."

She shakes her head and chuckles again. "How'd your team do?"

"We sucked," I say without thinking. She gives me a flat look.

"Oh, sorry...um...we were bad. Lost every game by mercy rule. It was a sad, sad season."

She looks around, and I point her toward the bathroom. "There're new toothbrushes in the top drawer, unopened. Helen insists I be prepared."

Rachel tilts her head. "Lots of women in and out, Ford—lots of toothbrushing?"

My blush returns, heightened on its second visit. "No," I report and leave it at that.

I dated a couple of women in college, each for a while, though each relationship fell apart eventually. One woman was a lit major;

she dumped me for a tortured writer. The other was a psych major; she dumped me for a psych assistant professor. Since I graduated, I haven't dated much. I've gone out with Ruth a few times and with two other women, nurse friends of Helen's, but only once with each. So, no—not a lot of tooth brushing.

Other than mine.

Rachel shakes her head at me. As she starts for the bathroom, I tell her clean washcloths and towels are on the rack.

When she goes into the bathroom, I kick off my shoes and sit on the end of my bed, putting my phone on the nightstand. I rest my hands on my knees and sigh. I need to figure out Jane Pimberly's death. Everything seems increasingly to center on that. And then it occurs to me: to figure out her death, I need to figure out her life beyond what Diana told me.

A plan of action begins to form.

And then Rachel comes into the room, and no other form matters for a moment. The balance of the universe is dark, without form, void. But she is light.

SHE STANDS THERE IN MY ORANGE, SOFTBALL, JUST-FOR-HIM T-shirt, her blonde hair loose.

She puts her arms out to her sides, wrists relaxed and spins. She lets her eyes smolder for a second when she stops, puts one hand on the words, on her heart.

"Truth in advertising, Ford," she whispers. Her legs and feet are bare. The smolder in her eyes arcs, leaps across from her to me, and I feel it keenly. I stand and kiss her, careful to keep my lower body separate from hers. If I contact her, the smolder will inflame.

She senses my caution and respects our middle distance. I take my turn in the bathroom.

When I finish, I find her in my bed—beneath the sheet and propped on the pillows. She's on my side of the bed, but I absolutely don't care.

The lamp beside the bed supplies a soft glow. She pats the other side of the bed. Wearing one of my Oberlin shirts and some gym shorts, I slip under the sheet beside her. She unstacks the pillows, gives one to me, then rolls against me. She rests her chin on my chest.

She smiles a small smile. "I'm sorry about Talbot. But I'm glad to be here with you, glad...well, just *glad*..."

"Are they going to miss you at Noble Hall? Do you need to call? Text?" I recall my early worry that she and Wylie were involved.

I dropped that thought a long time ago, I realize. He may not be her uncle, but he's not her lover. I've never felt the slightest jealousy toward him, not like Lake.

"I'm a big girl, Ford; Uncle Wylie doesn't monitor my comings and goings." I nod, and she waits, looking at me, expecting another question. When I don't ask, she grins. "And Lake has *no right* to monitor my comings and goings; as I told you, that's done. I'm just waiting for him to leave. Eager."

"You're not alone."

She rolls her eyes. "I'm in *your* bed, and although we're not making love, we both want to. Got that?"

"You're telling me what I want?" I ask, raising my eyebrows and laughing beneath my breath.

"No, the deliberate distance between us in that post-spin kiss told me what you want. I'm just relaying the information on the off chance it didn't travel northward in you."

I take a second to repeat that sentence in my head. "I'm not the only one who should think about writing."

She pushes herself forward to kiss me. I feel her all along the length of me. We both sigh as the kiss ends; then we start laughing at each other.

"Ford," Rachel asks, still laughing, "what was the record you played at Michelle's?"

"The Sinatra album?"

"Yes, do you have it?"

I nod. "It's on my iTunes. Sinatra and Jobim. Jobim was an amazing bossa nova composer, songwriter."

"What was that song, the one where Sinatra sings that really low note?"

I think for a minute. I love the album, but it's not in my regular rotation. I save it for special occasions. "That song's called 'Wave.'"

"Can you play it for us? Since I told you what you want, why don't you listen to the words for me? I loved them when I heard them—when we were dancing at Michelle's. Especially after our talk." She turns her head, resting her cheek on my chest, not her chin—eyes away from me.

I stretch, get my phone, and start the song. She squeezes me as it begins but does not look at me.

Sinatra sings. Rachel squeezes me harder.

Sinatra's voice acts as an allayment as he croons of loneliness leaving when two people dream together.

The wave catches us, and we drift away.

I WAKE UP EARLY AND CHECK MY PHONE.

Nothing. I take that as good news, but I want to check on Talbot. Rachel's wrapped around me, a clinging vine. I kiss her and gently extricate myself. She smiles in her sleep.

I get up and go into the hallway, closing the door. I call Olive. She answers immediately. The cheerful sound of her voice tells me what I want to know before she answers my question about Talbot. She tells me he's fine and that she'll take him home later this morning. I tell her I will stop by their house this afternoon once she has him settled.

I have things I can do between now and then. I need to do something.

OUTSIDE, LATER, I KISS RACHEL GOODBYE AND TELL HER I WILL call her. Things between us feel warm and comfortable—but tantalizingly flammable. She drives away as I start the Camry.

It's sunny but surprisingly pleasant. There's even a hint of a breeze. The standing rainwater of yesterday has evaporated.

I drive out to the edge of Opelika to a large, two-story house surrounded by magnolia trees. Dr. McCoomb lives and practices in the house. A discreet shingle hangs on the porch over the stairs, but he no longer takes new patients. He still sees some of his old ones, but only for minor issues and then mostly only to chat. For more major issues, he now sends them on to younger specialists as he did Jane Pimberly to Sam. I imagine he must have had his hands full over the years with Jane and her hypochondria.

I knock on the door, and it takes Dr. McCoomb's longtime assistant, Mildred, a moment or two to make it to the door. Talk around town for years has been that she and McCoomb were a couple, but if so, they were never seen in public together, and she was never known to spend the night. It was impossible not to notice that they were never seen with anyone else; you could feel their harmony with each other. When Mom took me to see McCoomb, I could feel it even as a kid.

"Why, it's Ford Merrick. It's been ever so long, my boy!" Mildred's voice is the tonal equivalent of Helen's sweet tea, all amber, syrupy, and a sweet treat for the ear.

"Hey, Miss Mildred. Is the doctor in?"

She laughs. "Yes, the miserable old grump is here. He's in his office. He says he's watching the news. I know he's really watching his soaps. He records them, you know. He talks to them too. Worse and worse as he gets older."

She knocks on the interior office door, and I hear McCoomb's bellow: "Don't disturb the doctor!"

"Vance," Mildred says in a voice of infinite patience, "it's that lovely boy, Ford Merrick. He wants to talk to you."

"I don't care!" McCoomb shouts. "I want to 'watch' *The Young and the Restless*, not 'talk' to 'em."

Mildred looks at me and grins. "He'll see you now."

I go inside. Mildred doesn't close the door, but she goes back to her desk.

McCoomb, although seated, seems tall. That's because he is; he's taller than me but long-waisted so that he seems even taller when seated. He's staring at a small television. A soap opera is on and about to go to commercial. There's a swell of dramatic music and a close-up of a generically beautiful brunette with a prolonged look of blank shock on her face, and then an announcer is talking about the scent of new and improved Gain detergent.

McCoomb picks up the remote and clicks it, muting the TV.

He stands, but as old as he now is, standing requires his arms as well as his legs. It takes a minute, but then he steps forward and shakes my hand. "It's been a while, Ford. How are you?" He looks me over—a physician's eyes.

"Well, Doc, I'm not here about my health; I'm here on a case."

"A case? Oh, that's right. You finally became Encyclopedia Brown, didn't you? A late bloomer, I guess." He laughs, and I do too. "How can I help?"

"I was hoping you could tell me about Jane Pimberly."

He gives me a close look. "Jane? She's gone, Ford, and her life was sad enough. Is there really any need to dig her up, so to speak?"

"No ghoulish curiosity or anything, Doc. I'm professionally puzzled about her death. Was it a heart attack?"

He sighs and sits back down, again using his arms as much as his legs. "Yes, it was. They called me after they found her. I went out to the hall. She'd had problems with her heart for a long, long time. Unlike a lot of her ailments, that one wasn't in her head." He shakes his. "She was on the floor in a puddle of urine—her own and feline—cats crawling all over her, sleeping on her corpse, stalking through the house, mewing their heads off. A couple of cats were dead on the floor too. It was like a scene in a goddamn horror movie."

He pauses and then continues. "She loved those cats, but most of them hated her. That was Jane's lot in life, I suppose: to love things that hated her back." He stares at the floor for a moment.

"Jesus, how that house stank! Cats everywhere—cats, cans of food on the floor, on the counters, some food in half-dried piles on the floor. She must have fed them right out of the can—no bowls anywhere. One of the paramedics opened the refrigerator, and I saw inside; it was full of open, half-empty cans. Fancy Feast from hell. She must have lost track of how many she opened."

I regret having heard the story and change the question. "Was she crazy, Doc?"

"Shit, son, this is the South! Who knows who's crazy? Was Jane crazy? Yes, more than half. But it was partly her inheritance; the whole family struggled psychologically. Jane's father and mother didn't help, but"—McCombs drops his voice—"that doomed love affair did most of the damage."

"They say she used to walk the grounds with a lantern late at night. That she sang naked on the upper balcony?"

McCoomb's face softens. "She probably did. She owned an old lantern. And she used to sing in the St. Dunstan's choir, but that was long before your day and before the day of that massive new priest, the congregation-in-one."

I chuckle but otherwise let that pass. "Would anyone be able to tell me about the lantern, the singing?"

"I don't know...Mildred"—he speaks without raising his voice though his tone changes—"since you are undoubtedly listening, do you know?"

His ancient intercom crackles. Mildred's voice answers. "Edna, her housekeeper. I think that nice Mr. Stroud hired her to do some light housework at the hall. She worked for Jane for a long time, up till near the end."

I met Edna the other day, the sciatica woman with the broom.

McCoomb shakes his head at himself. "Hell, I knew that. Yes—Edna.

Getting old tests your self-image. If you idolize yourself as a youngster, you're going to hate yourself as an oldster. Best not to get too attached to youth or to picture yourself only as young. Time will stomp on that."

I nod. "Thanks, Doc."

"I hear good things about your sister, Ford. Oh, and I hear she's taken up with that handsome Dr. Nettles."

I grin. Word travels like lightning in these towns.

"Good for her. That's a hell of a sister you have there."

"True," I say. I shake his hand, and Mildred shows me out.

MY EVENTUAL DESTINATION TODAY IS THE OPELIKA POLICE Department.

I want to know about what happened to Talbot. But I also know the OPD. It does not move quickly. So, I postpone that trip and head for the office. It's Saturday, so the office is closed, but I need a few minutes to myself.

I can't chase McCoomb's story about Jane's body from my head. And my anger about Talbot is returning.

I unlock the door and go inside, close the door, luxuriating for a moment in the cool dark of the office. It's not as hot as usual outside, but it is still hot. Talbot closed the blinds before he left the other day, and so there're only a few thin stripes of sunlight on the floor.

I huff to myself, trying to decide whether to open the blinds and chance someone taking the office to be open or sit in the dark. Neither option's attractive.

I consider not opening the door when I hear the knock. We're closed, but it could be important.

I open the door to Lake Thornton. I blink, both because I didn't expect him and because I hardly know him without his smile. He's not smiling. He looks over his shoulder and then back at me as I watch him.

"Do you have a minute, Ford? I can call you 'Ford,' right?" *Hell no.* I think of Bill Peppers's neighbor, but I nod my head.

He pushes past me into the office and then faces me. He's wearing a light-blue, short-sleeved polo shirt and dark-blue slacks pressed to perfection, the crease like a samurai blade, and a pair of brown loafers. Someone took the Hamptons, refashioned them as a human male, and tanned them, and now they stand before me in $600 loafers.

He's still not smiling. Odd. I didn't rate his smile as optional.

"Can we chat for a minute man-to-man?"

Oh goody. "Yes." I keep my answer very man-to-man à la John Wayne. Lake walks over and sits down in Talbot's chair. That pisses me off, but I try to ignore it.

"We need to talk about Rachel."

I raise an eyebrow but say nothing.

"She spent the night at your place last night, right?"

This is none of his business. I drop the eyebrow and just stare at him.

Something like pity slips into his voice. "I just want you to know, Ford, not to put too much into Rachel's...putting out. I can't count all the men she's slept with. I'd need my fingers and yours—and hers. I just don't want you to think you've been...well...*singled out* for any honor. At best, you get a participation trophy like all the others." Now the smile.

I'm tempted to get my gun and shoot him in that smile.

"Including you?" I finally ask.

He nods in showy indifference. "Yes, but I understand her; I don't expect faithfulness from Rachel Gunner. I know what I'm getting into. If she makes sure I'm satisfied, I don't care who else she satisfies or how she satisfies herself."

I may not fully self identify as a Southerner, but I do care about manners. Lake's conversation isn't just a breach of them; it's a damned overthrow.

"If you don't care, then why are you here?"

I'm puzzled he didn't anticipate that question because he clearly didn't. The smile falters for a moment.

"Because," he eventually offers, reasserting his smile, "*you* care. You don't know her, you see, and you won't like her when you do. You're going to regret last night, I'm afraid, joining the Not-as-Lucky-as-I-Thought Club."

I don't want to believe him. I don't believe him. His smile is now all the way back, an unadulterated smug.

"I can see you don't know whether to believe me. I'm sure Rachel's been pretending to be otherwise. Good. She's good at pretending. She's best at lies. I've never seen anyone better. Bail on her now, Ford, before she turns screwing you into screwing you over.

"I've seen her reduce better men to nothing, steal their hearts, steal their self-respect, and steal—"

"Get out, Lake," I say in a low voice as I stalk from the door where I'd been standing to the desk and start to circle it. "Get out before I provide you with free tuition on Southern manners."

He's in great shape, I know. But I'm taller, heavier, and I'm not going to give a damn about my face or teeth. I'm just going to beat the shit out of him. My anger from last night at what was done to Talbot rekindles and adds to the fire inside me. I don't believe Lake did that, but I don't care just now.

I'm a tower of flame.

Lake leaps from the chair and scoots to the far end of the desk.

"I'm here for your own good, Merrick," he mumbles as he heads for the door.

I follow him, but he's out before I can grab him. He hurries into the parking lot and then down the sidewalk to his parked car.

My hands are shaking. I'm not sure what I would've done if I'd grabbed him. I've never known myself this angry, this capable of violence, this willing to be violent.

I slam the office door and, facing it, lean on it with both hands, light-headed, my face burning, swallowed by a wave of nausea.

Rachel didn't sleep with me last night—not that way—but Lake thinks she did.

Rachel's past is hers. I don't know whether Lake is telling the truth or not, but even if he is, it's not his truth to tell.

Rachel wants to tell me her own stories. That's what I want; I want her to tell me her own stories. But she won't tell me if I don't trust her.

Lake accused Rachel of stealing, but he aimed at theft. He aimed to steal last night from Rachel and me—and Rachel's story from her.

I loathe Lake Thornton.

CHAPTER 18: *Dust*

I sit in the dark office as dust motes dance above the sunlight-striped floor.

Breath in, breath out. Lake in, Lake out. Breath in, breath out.

When I've calmed down enough to trust myself, I leave the office, lock up, and make the short drive to the Opelika Police Department.

THE OPD IS HOUSED IN A BIG BRICK BUILDING WITH A STEEPLE-LIKE turret on the top. I pass through the glass doors and into the main room. A large, high desk runs side to side with a narrow passage in the middle. Behind each half sits an officer. One, a woman, seems preoccupied, typing away on the computer in front of her. The other gives me an unwelcome glare and yells, "Captain Ziff! It's the town's dick."

The man who yelled is Tom Buford—not a fan of mine if you hadn't guessed. But he's a huge fan of dick jokes and has not, to my knowledge, ever tired of them, not since junior high. The man he yells to is Barry Ziff, the captain of police.

Barry was in my class in high school. He's done well as a policeman and is young to have been made captain. He's good at his job, but he's also the tortoise, not the hare. He plods. His officers plod. The department plods. I used to tell Helen that Barry always gets his man, but not until just before the statute of limitations has run out.

I'm betting he buys his meat from the Reduced Shelf at the Piggly Wiggly.

He and I are not and never have been enemies; he's not Certaine and was not one of Certaine's friends. But he finished behind me often and not just in every alphabetical roll call. I was a National Merit Scholar; he was a finalist. I was valedictorian; he was salutatorian. I was captain of the Brain Bowl Team; he was the first alternate. And so on.

When I became a detective, he seemed to believe I'd done it again: outpaced him and stolen his limelight. For some reason, he reckons being a detective more romantic, more glamorous than being police chief.

Barry walks out of his open office and frowns at me. "Hey, Merrick, it's been a while since you were in here, but I figured we'd see you today. How's Norton? I heard he went home?"

"Yes. I'm going to go by and see him. I stopped by, hoping you might know something about what happened?"

He walks to the desk and leans against it, resting on his elbows.

He's got white-blond hair, brown eyes, and very light skin. He's handsome but not charming. Tortoise, not hare.

He sighs and frowns at me again. "I hear you're dating that flashy blonde from Noble Hall, Stroud's niece. Rachel something. Is that right?"

An important note: he's crazy about Ruth Sutton, and he has been for years. He could've lived with finishing behind me in any other sweepstakes but that one, I suppose.

"Flashy?" The word brings back Lake and bile, and I repeat it in a sharp tone

Barry nods, stands, waves his hands. "Don't mean any offense. Never met her. She looks like a movie star."

He's stuck between excitement for himself and disappointment for

206

Ruth, between being pleased that I'm out of the picture and annoyed that I could prefer anyone else; each emotion takes a turn dictating his expression.

"Gunner. Rachel Gunner. She's great. So, what do you know about what happened last night?"

He doesn't seem happy that I'm not willing to say any more about Rachel, but he answers me. "Not much yet. The car was dark blue, large." He shifts position.

"We got a picture of it on the traffic cam downtown, but there was no plate, and we could not see the driver. There weren't any witnesses other than Kip Mott."

There's only one traffic cam in town, of course. "Make and model?"

"2018 Chrysler 300."

"No plate?" I ask. "You mean it didn't show in the cam photo?" I'm not sure how the cam could fail to show the driver but not show a plate.

"No, no plates. They'd been removed."

Understand a Friday night in downtown Opelika: it's busy down by the railroad tracks, the very center of downtown, but move just a couple of blocks away, especially if it's late as it was when Talbot and Kip were walking back from Wok and Roll, and it's like a ghost town. You expect Morricone music, tumbleweeds, and desert dust. The driver, whoever it was, picked a good spot or lucked into one.

Barry shakes his head. "Ten or so of those cars in the county. I have officers out now looking at any they can see. It had to leave some damage on the car; Norton was hit hard. Anything I need to know from you, Ford?"

I shake my head. He tilts his, gauging me. "Talbot's annoying— God knows, he was annoying in high school and ever since—but I can't imagine anyone *hating* him, feeling *threatened* by him. You sure there's nothing I need to know from you?"

"Nothing, but if I find anything, I'll let you know."

He nods, one skeptical nod, and frowns again. "Okay, I'll do the same." He pauses, starts to turn away, and then returns. "So, you're really dating the tall blonde?"

"Yes."

"And Ruth knows?"

I nod. As he turns, I see that he's no longer frowning.

I'M SURPRISED WHEN I REALIZE THAT EDNA, THE WOMAN WHO worked for Jane Pimberly, lives in the same apartment complex as Bill Peppers.

Her apartment is in a different building in the complex, but I drive by Peppers's place just to see if he's home. Slowing down, I roll down my passenger window. No truck.

I see his neighbor in her green robe, sitting in a fold-out lawn chair by her door. She has a small transistor on a plastic table beside her, turned up so loud that the tinny speaker distorts the music, but I recognize the song: Frankie Valli and the Four Seasons, "Big Girls Don't Cry."

A dirty house shoe dangles precariously from her air-tapping foot. She doesn't pay any attention as I go by. Her eyes are closed, and she's mouthing the words.

As I drive around to Edna's apartment—seventy-two—I see her neat little porch area and the hanging fern. Edna is in one of two chairs at the small matching table, a large book open before her.

I pull right up in front and get out. Edna turns and looks at me over her readers, a trace of both recognition and amusement in her face. "Well, if it ain't Doc Merrick's younger, *slower* brother."

I walk up onto the little porch. "You remember?"

She nods. "Jesus, son, I got sciatica, not dementia." She shakes her head as if I have yet again proven myself slower than Helen.

I point at the other chair. "May I sit down?"

She gestures for me to take a seat and shuts the book. I realize it is Shakespeare. I had expected the Bible.

I point to the book with the movement of one shoulder. "You're a fan?"

She raises an eyebrow, that long-resigned look returns to her face. "You think just 'cause I live in all this splendor, I cain't read Shakespeare?"

"No, no, I didn't mean that. I just wondered…" And then I realized I did think that, and I let my sentence expire.

She huffs in offended amusement and lifts one corner of her book. "This here, Mr. Merrick, is a *sweetener* of existence. My life hasn't offered me a lot of sweets, just a lot of bitterness, but a few pages of this here, and I remember I'm a human being and that a human being is *a piece of work*—and not just in a bad way."

She lifts her head; her voice changes, lilts. "'What a piece of work is man! How noble in reason, how infinite in faculty! In form and moving, how express and admirable! In action, how like an angel, in apprehension, how like a god! The beauty of the world. The paragon of animals.' When I read that, Mr. Merrick, I forget all this"—she makes a sweeping gesture around the apartment complex—"for a minute. For a minute, I know mine is a better part…"

I consider what she said. "But wasn't Hamlet scoffing?"

She reconsiders me for a moment. "Huh—maybe you ain't so slow. Yeah, but a man cain't scoff at what he don't believe to be truth."

Ouch. I've been schooled. I nod in acknowledgment of her point. We sit for a moment, and each of us looks around the complex then at each other.

"So, what can I do for you, Mr. Merrick?"

"Ford, please. I was told you worked for Jane Pimberly before her death."

She seems surprised but nods. "I did. I worked for her every Monday, Wednesday, and Friday for a couple of decades, I s'pose. Till she got too crazy and ran me off near the end."

"I'm a detective, and a case I'm working on has made me puzzled about Jane Pimberly. Could I ask you a question or two about her?"

She shrugs. "If you want. We weren't never friends, you know, so if you want her heart's secrets, you need to find somebody else."

"I just wondered about her…odd behavior."

"All Miss Pimberly's behavior was odd. What'd you have in mind?"

I pause for a moment. "I've heard she walked the grounds with a lantern. Is that true?"

"Yes," Edna says, nodding, "I used to have to try to darn singed spots in her nightgowns."

"What was she doing? What was she looking for?"

Edna stares at me and shakes her head. "Not what, Ford—*who*. That man who got her pregnant—what's his name?"

"Diamond?"

"Yeah, Diamond, him. She was a-looking for him. He told her he was coming back—promised—and she believed him. Some nights, when it was hot or when she'd gotten addled by something during the day, she'd get mixed up and start thinking he was due that night. She'd light the lantern and go out to meet him."

"Did she say that's what she was doing?"

"Say? No, not in so many words, I s'pose. She just muttered about him, about seeing him. Not his name, mind you, just *him*."

"And I heard she used to sing naked on the upper balcony?"

Edna's wrinkled face smooths a bit as she laughs kindly. "Naked as Eve beneath the apple. She'd stand up there and sing—old bluegrass songs, mostly."

"What was that all about?"

"Diamond too. Story is that, when they was young, he was working at the hall, and she'd taken a liking to him. Miss Pimberly was a handsome beauty when young, but her daddy never let nobody near her. But one night, no one else was around, and Miss Pimberly took advantage, took off her clothes, and sang to Diamond from upstairs, beckoning him. Kind of an R-rated, Southern, *Romeo and Juliet* scene, I s'pose.

"He went inside and climbed the steps right quick. And that was the beginning of things between them and the beginning of the end of Miss Pimberly…"

210

"What did she sing to him?"

"Don't rightly know. And I only pieced that story together from some things Miss Pimberly said on her bad nights."

"Bluegrass songs?"

"Yeah," Edna said, her eyes now focused on the past, "high and lonesome, you know. She loved them awful ones like 'Girl and the Dreadful Snake.' Bill Monroe. You know that one?"

"No, I've never been a fan." I've listened; I know some songs, but I'm not a fan. Hillbilly existentialism.

"Me, neither. There ain't no darker music. She liked that one, and 'Down in the Willow Garden,' and 'Long Black Veil' and 'Banks of the Ohio,' all them murder or death ballads." Edna wipes at her eyes; I hadn't seen her tear up. "Sorry, we weren't friends, but I pitied that poor soul. Money don't buy happiness, but it do surely cause misery."

For the first time in a while, it occurs to me that I have money. I need to talk to Helen.

"Did a man named Bill Peppers work at the hall?"

"Peppers?" Edna shudders. "Yeah, he did. 'Ventually, Miss Pimberly fired him. He was always creepin' around. He lives over there," she points in the direction of the building I passed earlier, "but Thank God, he don't drive 'round this way much. When he eyes you, it's like somebody digging your grave."

"Why'd Jane fire him?"

"I don't know. Stealing, maybe, but she didn't tell me. But they went way back, you know?"

I lean forward. "No, I didn't know."

"Well," she says, correcting herself, "she knew him for a long time. He was her son's best friend. He and Wade got in trouble together in high school. Nothing serious, I s'pose, but lots o' petty stuff, drinking and suchlike. Story is that Peppers daddy was one true sum-bitch and beat the boy like a cur. Bill sorta hid out at the hall."

"Are he and Wade still friends?"

She shrugs. "Don't know. Wade rarely came round the hall, and I don't remember him talking to Peppers when Peppers worked there."

"Okay," I say, mulling all this over. "I appreciate your time."

She looks up at me as I stand and smirks. "Say, 'Hi,' to your brighter sister, the Doc, for me."

I laugh. "I will. Take care of yourself."

Her expression slowly becomes serious. "I'll try, but there's only so much a body can do, Ford. We're all nothing but 'quintessence of dust,' you know, like Mr. Hamlet says. We're the *glory* of dust, yeah, but we're still dust."

I pass by Peppers's place again as I leave. He's not there, and his neighbor has taken her radio and gone inside too.

As I drive to Talbot's, I find some Bill Monroe on my phone and listen to it. I stop at Sheila C's Burger Barn and grab three burgers at the drive-through. The girl at the window makes a grim face when she hears my music: Monroe's curdling, dark yodel.

Olive greets me at the door. She looks tired, concerned, but not unhappy. "Ford, come in! Talbot's been expecting you. He's in the living room."

I walk in, and my anger returns. Talbot's been installed in the recliner. He's got a bandage on his head and more bandages on his arms and legs. I can see bruises and scrapes all over him. His face is marshmallowy.

But when he sees the hamburger bag, he grins, his grin puffy. "Ford, my man, and with medicine! Vitamin C's!"

He reaches eagerly for the bag then winces. I see red.

Talbot notices. "Man, it's okay. Really! It's just part of the job. If I'm going to be a detective, I have to roll with the punches."

"Tal, you look like a mummy. You need to learn to roll better, not roll up in bandages." I step closer and hand him the bag.

212

He grins. "I will, Ford."

Olive, of course, saw the bag in my hand. She comes in with paper plates and napkins. Sheila C's makes great burgers, but they're dripping messes.

Talbot takes a burger out for himself and one for me. He starts to get the third for his mom, but she gestures for him to stop.

"No, thank you. Thanks, Ford, but I already ate. I will save this one for Talbot. He'll need to keep up his strength and needs protein to heal." She leaves with the third burger in the bag.

Talbot carefully unwraps his. I do too. He puts his nose down to the burger, almost touching it, and inhales slowly and deeply. "The Hamburgler's wet, mayo dream!"

"God, Talbot," I say, annoyed and relieved to be annoyed; if he can annoy me, he must not be too miserable, "now I'm not sure I can eat mine."

"Pansy," Talbot mumbles through his first bite. I try to forget his words and take a bite of mine. Delicious, as always.

"So"—I rest my burger on the paper plate and rest the plate on the coffee table between us—"what the hell happened?"

Talbot finishes his second bite before he answers. "It was going great. Kip and I had this terrific meal. Shrimp Lo Mein and steamed dumplings and…"

"Talbot…"

He shakes his head. "Right. And so, we were walking home. And I was nervous, Ford, because dinner went well, and I hadn't said anything stupid or annoying, and we'd just talked and laughed. She's so much fun and so funny. Anyway, we were walking, and I was nervous. I wanted to hold her hand, but I thought she might not want to, and it might seem—I don't know—childish or something. But I reached out and took her hand, and she smiled at me, and the next thing I know, I'm airborne…"

"Did you see the car?"

"No, nothing. I remember Kip stooped over me and the paramedics, but I don't remember the car."

"Did you do anything else on the Briggs and Stratton case—anything I don't know about?"

Talbot glances away.

"Talbot…"

"I called Big Jim and told him I thought I was making progress."

"You did? You are?"

"No, but I told him so." He re-grins the puffy grin, mayo in the corners of his mouth. "Gotta keep up the client's faith, right?"

I would hit him if he hadn't just been hit-and-run over. "Talbot, did you talk to Big Jim?"

"No, I left a message with some guy in the office."

"Some guy? Who?"

Talbot shrugs then winces. "I didn't ask."

I sigh and take a bite of my burger. Olive is singing in the kitchen, and Talbot starts humming along as he chews.

I'M READY TO HEAD HOME, TO REST, BUT DECIDE THAT I CAN'T PUT off my expedition any longer. I need to equip myself, so I'll be ready to go when it gets dark.

I stop at the office. Inside, in the narrow closet behind Talbot's desk where he keeps the broom, I also keep various tools of the trade. I grab a good flashlight and a small, foldable military shovel I bought at a surplus store. I take them to the car and put them in the trunk.

As I shut the trunk, I hear Rachel's voice behind me. "Ford?"

I turn. She looks upset, hurriedly dressed. Her hair's combed but damp.

"Hey, Rachel." I try to keep Lake's visit from my mind. "What's up?"

"I was at the hall, Ford, swimming in the pond, and when I went back into the house, my room, I found this."

She brandishes a piece of paper then hands it to me. I look at it.

On it is a hurried-looking scribble.

Rachel,

I'm gone. Back to Cali.

I did you a favor before I left. I'll be waiting when your hayride ends.

See you soon,
Lake

I look up at Rachel. She's studying me closely—my reaction. I try to keep myself calm, and I hand it back to her.

She waits for me to say something, growing more agitated each moment I remain silent.

"So, is he gone?" I ask finally.

"Yes, he's gone."

"And you're...upset about that?" I know the question's stupid the moment I finish it.

Her blue eyes flash, a welder's flame. "No," she says slowly, distinctly, "I wanted him to go...*as I told you.* I want to know what *he* told *you.*"

"Me?" I don't want to have this conversation now, here on the sun-heated gravel of the parking lot.

"If he did me a *favor*"—her tone, not her hands, air-quotes that word—"then it involved *you.* What did he tell you, Ford?"

God, she's beautiful when she's angry. She's always beautiful. She is the *glory* of dust: *how like an angel.*

And then I hear Father Halsey in my head: *"One white-dressed rehearsal with a choir does not an angel make."*

"Ford?" She's still waiting for me to say something non-interrogative. Her eyes are melting me.

"Am I the hayride?"

She blows out a long breath. "Yes—from Lake's point of view, you're the hayride. Now, what did he tell you?"

I inhale. "He came to see me earlier. He wanted to do *me* a favor."
"What favor?"

"He thinks you and I slept together last night—you know, where 'slept' is an active verb, not so passive."

She grins but not in much amusement. "I told you once that I was not going to chase you all over the English language. So, he thought we slept together...*and...?*"

"*And* he wanted me to know that that was no *particular* honor, that I was just the latest...in a long, lonely line..." The nausea I felt when I chased Lake from the office returns. I hate saying this to her. Hate it.

Rachel stares at me. Her eyes cool, ice, and then that expression I can't name slowly overtakes them. "And you believed him." She asserts, doesn't ask.

"No, Rachel. I know so little about you, and I want to know more, everything, and you said you'd been a bad person, and...no, but..." I spiral at the worst time, always. It's a sure bet.

Rachel sighs. That unnamed expression leaves her eyes and leaves them sad. She shakes her head. "You really are soft boiled."

I'm still trying to understand that as she stomps to the Range Rover parked across the street. A moment later, she's gone.

No look back.

I stand bereft, unsure of what's happened—what I did or didn't do. I look down and realize I'm standing in one of the gravel-less ruts Talbot made when he slid and hit my car.

I kick at the dust. *Shit.*

CHAPTER 19: *Disinter*

Rachel's gone.

Damn me.

For a writer, words desert me too often.

Rachel said she wasn't going to chase me across the English language, but I couldn't master enough of it, muster enough courage to explain, to tell her what I need to tell her, namely that I love her and that Lake's assholery doesn't—didn't—change that.

It doesn't; it didn't. But it does make me worry about my love. *My love.* Yeah, I know, that's ambiguous. I'll just live with it, for now, live with it until I get myself sorted.

Until then, I have a case to work on. A plan, a suspicion. I focus on it.

I go back inside and extract my gun from my filing cabinet and my bullets from my desk, checking the gun and loading it carefully.

I return to the front office and the narrow closet one last time and grab my shoulder holster. After a quick check to make sure no one's watching, I carry the gun and holster stealthily to my car and put them into the glove compartment, locking it.

I sit with the car running, the AC pumping. My plan can't start until after dark.

After a moment's indecision, I drive to Ed's. It's something to do.

It's cool inside, and Ruth's at work. She's standing at the end of a booth, talking, iced tea pitcher in one hand. She waves at me with the other. I don't see that it's Barry Ziff she's talking to until I get to my booth. He nods at me unhappily when he sees me.

He didn't waste time. I sneak a glance or two at them as they talk. Ziff thinks he's Ruth's second choice—her red ribbon, I guess—but I'm not sure that's true. I'm not sure it's false, either. She's never talked to me much about him. She likes him, but I worry that he may rate that "liking" as romantic when it's not. I can't get much from her body language. They're talking about the Atlanta Braves, the recent losing streak.

After a moment, Ruth walks over to my booth. I see Ziff watching in the background.

"Hey, Ford, how's Talbot?"

News travels like lightning. "Hey, Ruth. He's doing okay. Home."

She smiles. "Good! Tell him I'm praying for him."

"Sure. Thanks. How's business?"

She smiles and shrugs. "Good enough. Saturdays are unpredictable in the summer."

I'm not sure whether that's a comment about Ziff showing up or about my recent hiatus—or both, or neither. Unsureness is the order of my day.

But I order a cup of coffee, and Ruth nods. "Be back with it in a minute."

She leaves, and I automatically pick up the menu on the table. I look at it and then realize I can't eat. Ruth comes back with my coffee. She puts it on the table; then she slides into the booth with me. Out of the corner of my eye, I see Ziff stiffen.

"Ford, can you come by the house tomorrow? Dad heard about Talbot, and he told me to tell you if I saw you: he'd like to talk to you."

"When?"

"Anytime in the afternoon should be okay."

"I'll be there—will you? I could use a buffer between Big Jim and myself."

She laughs. "I'll be there. Anything to eat?" She asks the question as she slides out of the booth.

"No, nothing. Stomach's bothering me."

She raises her eyebrows. "You? The Man with the Iron Stomach?"

"It's been touchy lately."

She nods, her eyes complicated: sympathetic, envious. She doesn't say anymore.

I sip at the coffee halfheartedly, taking my time.

The last two days have caught up with me. My hands feel shaky around the cup.

ZIFF LEAVES WITH A GOODBYE TO RUTH, AND THE DINNER CROWD grows. I've just taken the last cold sip of my coffee, and as I lower the cup, I see Father Halsey standing at my booth.

"Can I join you?"

"Sure, Father." He sits. He manages to move around quietly for such a large man. "What brings you to Opelika on a Saturday evening?" He's usually busy at St. Dunstan's on Saturdays.

"I came over to check on Talbot and Olive. They said you'd been by."

I nod. "Yeah, earlier in the afternoon."

He leans forward slightly and cocks his head. "You okay, Ford? You look…off."

"It's been a long couple of days."

He considers me for a moment more. "So, did the other high heel drop?"

"Huh?"

"Gunner. Something was bound to happen—the other shoe dropping. She's a beautiful woman, and beautiful women have baggage."

"Heels? Baggage? Aren't your metaphors getting mixed up?"

Father Halsey frowns. "Don't do your semantic soft-shoe, Ford. Talk straight to me. Does it involve her annoyingly present past boyfriend?"

I sigh. "Yes. He paid me a visit to…share some information."

He nods and leans back. "I see. Kind of him. You know better than to listen to him, right?"

Now I lean forward. "What do you mean, Father? Haven't *you* been warning me about her?"

He puts both of his large hands on the table just as Ruth makes it to us, points to my cup, and then to himself. She nods and looks at me. I put my hand over my cup—no more.

"Yeah, Ford, I have." He pauses. "My mistake. I watched her last night at the hospital, mulled over what I saw later. I watched her with Olive, with Helen, with Kip, with you. Mostly with you.

"Even when she was talking to someone else, she was watching over you, checking on you, keeping up with how you were doing. She has feelings for you. I'm sure of it. Whatever her ex had to say, just keep that in mind. She has real feelings for you."

This makes me feel worse, not better. I recollect the sadness in her eyes earlier, and I sigh again.

Father Halsey leans forward, laces his fingers, and rests his chin on them, his elbows on the table. Ruth brings his coffee, and he nods his thanks. He watches her leave without changing his posture.

"Lots of romantic mischance going around, eh?"

"I suppose." I take my empty cup in my hand, turn it, and watch the last drip of coffee in the bottom run curvy, side to side. "How should a person think about the past?"

"You are asking me that theologically?"

"Yeah, theologically."

He reflects for a moment, drinks some coffee. "You know me, Ford. I'm a *New Testament* guy. A rebirth guy. The Prodigal Son or daughter. No story's done until it's done." He pauses. "Life itself is a spiritual discipline—all of it—and there's no finishing early because the very ending can always surprise you, like the thief on the cross." He drains his cup and looks at me from under his brow.

I shake my head. "That's some dense, telegraphic theology, Father. I'm supposed to unpack all that now?"

He chuckles. "No, just bear it in mind. Let it *percolate* through you."

Ruth shows up at just that moment and refills his now-empty cup.

I shrug, yield, and push mine toward her too, gesturing to it.

Maybe I can drink another.

IN THE DARK, I DRIVE TOWARD NOBLE HALL.

Before I get there, I slow and pull into a gravel road that leads back to a green metal gate. The folks who keep their horses at the hall use the gate for loading and unloading horses and hay and so on.

I park with the nose of the Camry against the gate and turn off the lights. I sit for a little while and let the darkness thicken. Then I unlock the glove compartment, grab my holstered gun, stow my phone, get out of the car, and close the door quietly. I put the holster on, securing it in place. I open the trunk, quickly grab the flashlight and shovel, then shut the trunk. I pocket my keys. A car goes by, but I am parked too far from the road for their headlights to reach me.

I put the flashlight in my pocket and, shovel in hand, climb the fence. I walk through the grass toward the mansion, but it takes a few minutes before I can make it out ahead of me. Only one light, one upstairs, is on.

I climb the fence that runs alongside the driveway then crouch down when I've crossed it. The building is about a hundred feet from me. But Noble Hall itself is not my destination. My mind wanders to Rachel, but I'm not here to see her.

Keeping low, I move parallel to the fence. My intention is to pass by the hall and enter the woods using the path Rachel and I followed to the pond. As I near the house, I hear a door open. I look around but can't see any open door. But then I look up. The door to the second-floor balcony closes just after the light goes out.

I cross the driveway and get closer to the house, hiding behind a hedge. I look up but cannot see anyone. I'm panting a little and hear myself, so I try to calm down, slow my breathing. I listen.

I hear sobs. I look up and see Rachel. She's moved forward to the railing on the balcony, and she's standing against it, her arms around herself. For a moment, it looks like she's naked.

And for a moment, I'm David Diamond, and she's Jane Pimberly—Romeo and Juliet—and I half expect her to begin to sing. Instead, she sobs again.

A car goes by, and the headlight glow shows her enough to reveal that she has on a short, peach nightie. I am staring up at her when I realize the headlight glow revealed me to her. I hear her gasp.

"Ford? Ford, is that you?" Her voice is partly choked, thickened like the night.

I step forward in the dark, out from the hedge. "Yes, Rachel, it's me."

"What are you doing *here*? In the dark?" She wipes her eyes then tugs at the bottom of her nightie.

"Looking for someone," I say less than helpfully.

"Who? Me?"

"No, actually, not you, although I'm glad to find you, see you, and you look…great."

She pauses for a moment, looks down at herself, shakes her head as if to improve her bearings. "What are you carrying?"

I hold the shovel up, brandish it. "It's a shovel." I feel like I'm in a Monty Python skit but can't decide which one.

"Why are you beneath my balcony with a shovel, Ford?" A hint of mockery dances in her tone, in and around the sadness.

"Because I don't expect the person I'm looking for to answer my knock."

She stares down at me. I can feel her eyes in the dark—blue and demanding.

"Don't move. I'll throw on some clothes and shoes and be right down."

A few minutes later, Rachel comes outside. She doesn't turn on any light, but I hear the back door open and close and see her approaching me. She has on a dark top—she's still buttoning it—and jeans and sneakers.

She stops a few feet from me, and curiosity radiates from her—and anger and sadness. I had never imagined Rachel crying. It subtly changes my understanding of her, that elusive coolness that enters her eyes.

She's not crying now, but she was before, and I hardly know what to do or say.

But I'm not going to spiral again. No. I'm not going to let words fail me.

"So, what are you doing? Who are you looking for?" She sounds cautious, uncertain.

I look at her in the dark. "I'll get to that. Rachel, I'm sorry. I don't believe Lake—I didn't believe him. I just got overwhelmed for a bit. *I don't believe him.* But that's not what really matters. What matters is what I do believe: I do believe that I'm falling in love with you." *Fallen*—full disclosure—but I can't quite say that yet. "And nothing about your past, nothing you tell me about it—when you tell me about it—is going to stop that."

We stand facing each other but unable to clearly see the other's face. I begin to fear words have failed me again, even though I managed to speak words this time.

The moment seems to stretch on endlessly, eternal, but the darkness around us seems jumpy, restless.

And then Rachel's in my arms—or rather, I'm in hers. She's kissing me over and over. I can feel the tears on her cheeks. She pauses, laughs softly, wipes at them, and starts kissing me again. We hold each other tight.

Rachel steps back. She puts out her hand and cups my cheek.

"I'm sorry too. I was so afraid of what Lake might do and then so furious about what he did that I didn't really listen to you—not that what you said was crystalline. But I figured it out when I got here. And it wasn't fair for me to expect you to be wholly unaffected by what he told you. I *like* that you're soft boiled." She rubs my cheek. "But I worried that, between my tight lips and his loose ones, Lake and I had ruined everything, everything between you and me…"

I put my hand on her hand, pull her hand around to my lips, and kiss her palm.

"Love, huh?" She asks gently, carefully, as if she's walking on ice.

God help me. "Yeah."

AFTER MORE KISSES, MORE HUGS, RACHEL REACHES DOWN AND wraps her hand around my shovel. "So, explain this, please."

I decide I'm all in. "I have a case—not the one you fired me from, another one. I've been investigating the death of Jane Pimberly, the woman who used to own Noble Hall."

"Oh," Rachel says, nodding her head, taking that in. "But why are you here with a shovel?"

"Because I want to know something about her life."

I TAKE RACHEL'S HAND AND LEAD HER ACROSS THE DRIVEWAY AND down the road to the path.

"Are we going to the pond?"

I shake my head. "I don't think so. I take it no one is in the hall but you?"

"Right—Wylie's at the club, I think."

"Good." I nod and drop her hand, taking out my flashlight.

Rachel watches me. "God, Ford, between your shovel and your flashlight…"

I laugh softly. "And your peach nightie…"

"Good color vision. You liked that?"

224

"Dear God, yes."

I click on the flashlight and shine it up the path. Rachel takes my hand and gives it a squeeze. We walk as if we are going to the pond, but I train the flashlight mainly on the edges of the path, looking and watching. About a quarter of the distance to the pond, I see a smaller path leading away from the main one. We follow for a time until it dead-ends.

A breeze starts to blow, welcome for its coolness but unwelcome for the whispers with which it fills the woods—the rustling, moving leaves.

We retrace our steps, and at about halfway to the pond, we find another even smaller path, somewhat overgrown, leading away from the main one. As we walk, I quietly tell Rachel the story of Jane Pimberly and David Diamond, my hushed voice harmonizing with the rustling breeze.

Rachel stops and pulls me to her; I feel her shudder against me. "So, you mean we replayed what happened to them, sort of, just a few minutes ago? The balcony scene?"

"Yeah, guess so. Weird, huh? Some full circle."

"Definitely *weird*, Ford."

We walk a long way, and the path winds uphill. We almost lose it a couple of times but manage to refind it. Vines and leaves have obscured it; it's clear no one has walked it in a long time.

Eventually, it comes to an end in a small circle of ground. On one side of it is a log, cut as if for firewood. It's not part of any fallen tree. It was placed there. It's on its side and is worn almost smooth on top. I hand Rachel the flashlight and sit down on the log, as I imagine Jane did.

I sing these words softly:

She walks these hills in a long black veil.
She visits my grave when the night winds wail

Rachel shines the flashlight into my face. "Jesus, Ford, that's creepy."

"No," I say and feel the grimness of my smile, "that's Bill Monroe—his version of the song, anyway. Keep the flashlight on the ground for me, please."

I start digging with my shovel. I'm not sure how I realized this—what I'm doing, digging—but I did. The stories about Jane Pimberly and David Diamond, Jane's late-night lantern walks, Ruth's joke about her dad killing me and burying me in an unmarked grave, the Bill Monroe song—together they brought me here.

It takes a while, but I finally strike something hard. Kneeling, I start digging with my hands. Rachel leans closer. Bone is visible—at least I take it to be bone. In a moment, I know it is. A skull. One side of it is caved in badly. I hear Rachel inhale.

I look up at her. "We just found David Diamond."

RETRIEVING THE SHOVEL, I BEGIN TO DUMP DIRT BACK INTO THE shallow hole.

"What are you doing? Don't we need to...report this?" She sounds worried.

I keep shoveling, not looking up at her. She keeps the light on me. "Not yet. I'd like to talk first. I'd like to know some things about your uncle. I'm hoping you'll tell me. But it's your choice."

She's thinking so hard I can almost hear her. "About Uncle Wylie? Here? Now?"

"Yeah, about Uncle Wylie."

"Do we need to dig this up now? The past? My past."

I stop and shrug, holding a shovelful of dirt. "Seems like the night for it."

CHAPTER 20: *Disburden*

R achel stands silent as I toss dirt back on the bones of David
Diamond.

I'm not going to ask again about Uncle Wylie. I'm not
going to ask about her past. No doubt the two intertwine; that much
is obvious.

I shovel, but I'm tiring. The shovel's small; I did not uncover much of
Diamond, but it's like grave digging with a spork. Rachel's aiming the
flashlight at the grave, and nothing's in the light except the disturbed
dirt, my feet and lower legs, the shovel, and my hands and forearms.

It feels like that's all of me there is.

I finish, gently pat down the dirt, feel strange about that, and step
back out of the light. Rachel keeps the flashlight on the grave for a
moment longer—spotlight—then she clicks it off.

Everything's dark. Uncanny. The soft breeze still blows, and it
cools the sweat running down my back and off my brow. I wipe at
my forehead with the back of my wrist; my hands are dirty, and I
hear Rachel sigh.

She clears her throat softly. "So, Ford, to tell you about Uncle Wylie,
I have to tell you about me." She stops.

I put down the shovel, take the handkerchief I keep in my back pocket out and wipe my hands, then I walk around the grave to her and take her hand.

She takes that as her cue. "What I've told you about myself is *basically* true. My mom died of lupus." The sadness returns to her voice. "My dad moved us around constantly. I had no real friends in high school—maybe a few briefly in college and maybe a few since then. But I've omitted what I did with my dad—how I helped him with his work, what his work was. What I was.

"I have been a bad person. I have been fighting to change, not so successfully. But I guess I should just start at the beginning.

She pauses, looks around, starts again. "Can we go back to the hall? This is hard enough for me without feeling like I'm giving the eulogy at a stranger's long-overdue, graveside funeral."

"Okay, sure," I say softly.

I retrieve the shovel, and she clicks the flashlight on again. We turn, and she locates the path, hands me the flashlight, and I lead us away from the grave. The path's too narrow for us to walk side-by-side. We descend the hill and wind around. We've almost reached the path to the pond. The breeze has stopped. Nothing's moving but us.

Or that's true for a moment. We hear a crack in the distance ahead of us.

"Who—?" Rachel says as I tug her forward then drop her hand and begin running. I shut the flashlight off as I run; the larger path is only a few feet from me. I hear Rachel behind me, right behind me.

I reach the larger path and turn toward the hall, guessing about direction. We run on. As we reach the end of the path, I see the shadow of a runner well ahead of us, already at the mansion. I guessed right, but we're too far behind. By the time we reach the rear of Noble Hall, we can hear an engine moving away out on the road. We go around the hall, but the sound has receded by the time we get there. The driver has not turned on the headlights, so we cannot see anything—only hear.

I hope for another car to pass, but none comes. The engine becomes faint.

"Damn!" I curse between sucking breaths. Rachel's barely breathing hard, I realize.

"Who *was* that"

"I don't know. I wish I'd learned to tell engines by their sound."

Rachel makes a humming, thinking sound. "V6, five-speed."

I gape at her. "How—?"

She shrugs; I can feel the shrug more than see it. "Another thing I need to explain to you."

Rachel starts back around the hall. This time, I follow her.

I'm still trying to catch my breath as we enter the back door, and she clicks on the light.

I SIT DOWN AT THE SMALL TABLE IN THE KITCHEN AND PUT THE shovel on the floor beneath my chair. Rachel opens the refrigerator, takes out two bottles of beer, and hands me one. It's very cold. She finds an opener in a drawer and opens hers, then hands the opener to me.

She sits down as I open mine.

"Odd evening," I offer as if it were an idle comment on the weather.

Rachel laughs, that laugh I love. "And you said you were *boring*."

I laugh with her, and she takes a sip of her beer then narrows her eyes. "Who killed that man...*Diamond*? Do you know?"

"I don't *know*...but I've got a strong suspicion."

"You don't suspect Uncle Wylie, do you?"

"No, Rachel. Diamond's been dead a long time. But I do worry about whether your...uncle is somehow connected to it all."

She reflects for a minute.

"The man at the coliseum. I wondered why you never mentioned him to me again." She can do *detective* too; I need to remember that.

"Yes—no—maybe. That man, Bill Peppers, connects your uncle to the Pimberlys in a way that...worries me, a different way than the ownership of Noble Hall does. I don't believe Peppers killed Diamond, though."

I pause. "I'd like to hear what you were going to tell me."

Her gaze is troubled; she's shaking her head. "Uncle Wylie's not involved with Peppers. Not in the way that worries you. As I told you the night we swam in the pond…" She lights up unselfconsciously at the memory, troubled gaze gone momentarily. "I told you my parents split when I was little. They split because my mom couldn't stand—" She shakes her head.

"Let me back up a bit more. My dad was a con man. My mom met him when he was working at a traveling carnival, probably one of the last of its sort. He was all small cons—a carny at the time—and she…she believed she could change him." Rachel laughs softly. "The changes went the other way, though. Dad didn't want to change. He slowly pulled mom into his cons, charmed her. She was a beauty, smart except where Dad was concerned, and with her to help, his cons became steadily more ambitious: he started playing for bigger and bigger prizes.

They made money, easy money, and they lived fast. But, after a while, Mom got pregnant. She'd already begun to sour on the life they were living; she'd never managed to kill her conscience, just… outrun it for a while."

"They'd begun to fight months before I was born, and my birth made it worse. They loved each other, but Dad couldn't stop the cons, and Mom couldn't go back to them. So, she sent him packing, and I was in her arms, he told me years later, as she stood and watched him leave.

"My mother was a late-life baby, and her father had died before she met my dad, with her mom dying after Dad left. She inherited my grandmother's house, and we lived there for several years. But then Mom got sick and was unable to care for me. Although she hated it, she found Dad and told him that he would need to come get me. She somehow always seemed to know where he was. He agreed—he came and took me with him—but he could not give up the life, so *punch line*, he raised me in it."

"Wait," I extend my hand slowly, stopping her, "you're telling me that your *father* took you and included you in his cons? A young girl?"

She grimaces, nods. "I was nine. Mom lived on for a time, but she never got better, just slowly worse. Four years after I left home, she died. We went to the funeral, and Dad arranged to sell the house. Mom left it to him, and we were back on the road a few days later."

Rachel sips her beer again and picks at the label. I scoot my chair closer to her and take her other hand in mine.

She smiles sadly. "Dad knew how to use me. The first few years I was with him, I was his pig-tailed, blue-eyed blonde prop, mainly used to make people trust him since I looked so angelic." She smirks at me, but I can see a trace of bitterness in her eyes. "Later, as I got older, I became a more active part of the cons: playing small roles, distracting people, pretending to be sick or hurt so as to attract notice or sympathy or apology."

She tugs the label off her beer, but it does not come off cleanly. The gluey part remains attached to the bottle. I'm trying to decide what to say when she goes on.

"Even later, when I was older…more *developed*…I became a different kind of prop or a different kind of distraction. I played more active parts, lied and pretended…acted as a lure." She glances at me sideways and continues to pick at her bottle, now scratching determinedly at the gluey part of the label.

"I was good at it: my father's daughter. But it began to bother me: my mother's daughter. I had trouble sleeping. I lost weight. Dad had made a big score shortly after I graduated, so big that we settled—or as close to it as we ever managed—in California. North of San Francisco.

"I got into USC and went to LA for college in the fall. I had a hard time adjusting during the first term, but I did it. I got to know other students, even dated a few times. Nothing serious. But as much as I liked USC, I feared that it would all end, that I'd be found out, exposed as what I'd been, or that Dad would start conning again, demand that I rejoin him. He did start conning again, I found out, but he left me alone for a while; he was going to let me finish school.

She sips her beer again, the label now completely scraped off, the damp remains of the paper on the table.

"So, the second year, I relaxed, hoping that my life was becoming normal. But in the mid-year, just after the break, when I got back to campus, a man came to see me. He sat down unannounced at my table in the cafeteria, and he called me by my name..."

She inhales, and I'm puzzled. "He called you 'Rachel'?"

She purses her lips and takes her hand out of mine. "Ford, 'Rachel' is *not* my name. I mean, not my birth name."

"Oh." I don't know what else to say.

She drops her head a bit and studies me, that coolness showing in her eyes. It takes me a minute to realize she's worrying that I'm going to stand and leave. Instead, I take her hand back in mine.

"So," I say softly, "this guy calls you by name?"

"Yes, he called me by name, and then he showed me his ID. He was from the Central Intelligence Agency."

"The CIA?" I shake my head hard, not expecting that turn in the story. I let the question about her name pass.

She nods. "The CIA. You see, when I was about sixteen, Dad showed up one day at our hotel room with Lake Thornton." She pauses again, looks for a reaction, but I just nod.

"Anyway, Lake was three years older than I was, and he'd been conning for a while. Dad knew about him somehow and brought Lake in for a con he'd been planning. Lake worked with us for a while on that con, and then Dad used him regularly until I went to college.

"He'd been part of the big score that Dad made just after I finished high school. He...liked...me, I knew, but Dad was always careful to be with us, between us. At the time, that was fine with me. Lake left with his cut of that big score. I hadn't seen him since I started college."

She gets up and begins to pace. I don't think she quite realizes it. I'm outwardly calm, but inside I'm shocked. *The CIA? Lake?*

"The man told me that the CIA was interested in me, wanted to *recruit* me." Another pause. They'd *heard* about me. He asked me if I was interested." She sits back down and finishes her beer. She's visibly upset now, agitated.

"I should have said no, Ford. But I felt like my past had caught up with me, like my hope that I could outrun it was just mistaken. And although I liked school and was doing well, I had no idea what I would do when I finished; I worried I'd fall back into the life, that Dad would drag me in if I didn't go on my own. So, I told him I was interested.

"A few days later, I met with the Director of the CIA. Joan Miniver. We met at the airport in a meeting room there. She was between flights. When we started talking, I asked what the man had meant: 'the CIA had heard about me.' She was vague, intimating that my dad and I had worked with an agent without knowing it. We'd worked with a lot of other cons over the years like Lake—any good con, any big score, usually requires a team—but I couldn't figure out who it might have been.

"She told me about being an agent, about fieldwork. But mostly, she talked to me about patriotism, protecting the innocent—all this high-minded stuff, very 'Star-Spangled Banner.' At that moment, sitting there in the airport, it seemed like the perfect way to *transmute* my past, turn the gray-black stuff I'd done into red, white, and blue. Human alchemy. So, I said yes. I was slated to start at the end of school, the beginning of summer."

She stops again, sits, reaches for my beer, and looks at me; I nod. She takes a sip of it then sits back, holding it in two hands. "They sent me to the Farm. You've probably heard of it?"

"Yeah, although just on TV or in books."

"Well, it's not like that, or not much. One of the first things I realized, once I started and understood what I was doing, was that the other people in my class were mostly like me: people looking to hide, people with questionable pasts, few with any real sense of duty or honor. But I excelled and was at the top of my class."

That's one part of this that does not surprise me.

"My excellence clarified something. At the Farm, I hadn't left the con life behind. Spying was just the con life with a wardrobe change: a badge, a trench coat, and a gun. So, in the middle of my time there, disillusioned, I found I wanted out. I stopped trying in classes and created quite a stir. The instructors harangued me, and later Miniver came to the Farm to talk to me herself. But I was sure; I wanted out. She left, and a few hours later, Lake showed up."

"*Lake*?" I'm so caught up in the story that the name hits me without warning.

She looks uncertain, embarrassed. "It turned out he recommended me to Miniver. That's how she heard about me, decided to recruit me.

"Lake had blown through his money, his part of that big score, the last con he did with my dad and me, and he'd decided to join the CIA. He'd been in the CIA since around the time I started college. He told me all sorts of stories about how great it was being an agent, how Miniver would make us partners—glamorous stuff."

She hands my beer back to me. "I was tempted, but I still said no. Lake was *pissed*. He wanted me, and what I was doing made him look bad since he'd recommended me."

"So, you never became an agent?"

She shakes her head. "No. I never finished at the Farm. I used their rules against them, flunked out. A voluntary washout."

"Did you go back to USC?"

"No. That's what I should have done, but what happened at the Farm made me think I couldn't outrun my past. But I couldn't stop *trying* to outrun it. The only life I really knew was the con life. I worked a straight job for a while, but Dad called. He needed me. For the next couple of years, that's how it went. I'd quit Dad and start a job; he'd call and get me to come back—always one last con. Always."

"And then, in that cycle, Lake showed up again. He was still in the CIA—*is* still in the CIA—and he was working a long-term mission near me in California. He kept showing up, asking me out, and I finally said yes. He'd sneak away to come to see me when the mission allowed it. I thought we were getting serious even if it was a weird sort of long-distance relationship.

"But one day, I was off work, out for a drive, and I stopped at a little restaurant. Lake was there with a woman. He didn't see me, but I saw them. It was obvious that they were sleeping together the way they sat in orientation to one another—the touches, the glances. I had taken classes at the Farm, all about the psychology of influence and attraction. I knew what I was seeing." She frowns.

"You want another beer?" she asks. I've finished mine. I shake my head, and she sighs and starts again, watching me closely as I listen.

"I confronted Lake when he came to see me next, and he eventually told me the woman was his mark, that sleeping with her was a part of the CIA mission work—he actually called it that—and he told me that I just had to accept his job, his way of doing it. It meant nothing, he said. I tried to accept that, but I couldn't. Not the sort of relationship I wanted. Not close. Then I found out he was also sleeping with his female CIA partner. He couldn't call that work. It was all too much.

"I told him to get out of my life. But he kept showing up, returning, like Dad kept calling. Lake finally got the message, or I thought he had, but Dad kept calling." She breathes out, frustrated. "I couldn't *not* answer; he was my dad.

"But I finally did. I finally quit and *stayed quit* a year ago or so. Of course, Dad called from the East Coast—a big new score, the biggest—but I said no. I had a decent job and prospects that it would get better, a job in a fashion house. It was time for me to find the life I really wanted. Things were okay for a while: no Lake, no Dad, a job I liked, and people who liked me.

"And then one day a customer came into the fashion house—a woman who'd been Dad's mark in a con I'd helped with. I panicked. I hid from her in the warehouse, and then I quit, afraid she'd come back and see me or that someone else would."

She scoots closer and takes my hand again, stares right into my eyes. "'The wicked flee where none pursueth...'"

I nod my understanding.

"I was lost at that point, caught between a real life and the con life. I didn't want to be in the con life, but I couldn't seem to settle in a real life."

"And then your dad called again, and you came here." I cut to the relevant, next part.

She nods, deep worry in her eyes. Her shoulders sink. "Yes, Ford."

"And Dad is Uncle Wylie?"

She just nods, the worry in her eyes growing. "Yeah, it helps that I look like Mom."

No wonder Wylie plays a lousy uncle. He's a lousy dad. "And Lake showing up here—was Lake trying again?"

She frowns, anger flashing in her eyes. "Yes—I'm not sure how he found me, but he just showed up. I couldn't get rid of him because he said he'd expose us if I did. So I had to play along."

She stops. In the resulting silence, we hear a car arrive outside and park. I jump up and look out the back door. It's Wylie's Mercedes—Rachel's dad's Mercedes.

Rachel jumps up too, and I feel her look over my shoulder, feel her hand grab my shoulder, then tighten on it.

"Act like I haven't told you any of this, Ford, *please.*"

I look at her for a long moment, at her pleading eyes, then nod. We sit down at the table. I see that unnamable look flash cold in Rachel's eyes, and then her face is composed.

She smiles at "Uncle Wylie" as he comes smiling through the door.

CHAPTER 21:
Inextricable Difficulties

Wylie's smile is large—too large—and mobile. Sloppy. He stumbles when he raises his hand to wave at Rachel and me. The wave somehow misses us, and he sways. He's drunk, I realize—as he realizes I'm wearing my shoulder holster and gun. His eyes widen.

Rachel's face reddens; her eyes narrow. And she and Wylie speak at the same moment:

"Did you *drive* like that?"

"Why's he wearing a *gun?*"

For a moment, each of them waits for an answer.

Rachel's question gets answered first; a woman enters the door behind Wylie.

I know who she is, a mover and shaker at the club: Sherry Louden. Her wealthy husband died a few years ago. She's the most eligible widow in Lee County, willowy and elegant. She's got Wylie's car keys in her hand.

She smiles, her smile taut, brief, and embarrassed. "I drove him home. He's, um, tipsy. Too much whiskey."

Rachel gets up and goes to him. He's still staring at me—my gun—and hasn't stopped. Worry shows on his face, changing the character of his smile.

"Is he after someone?" He tries to point at me but sways and points at Rachel's empty chair.

"No, Wylie," Rachel says after a lightning-quick glance at me, "he's a *detective*, remember?"

The worry slides off his face slowly as if claimed by gravity and forgotten. "Oh, right. Ford-boy, dee-tec-teeve." He sings the comment, dancing wobbly. Then he stops, stabilizes himself by grabbing the back of a chair, and scans the kitchen, trying to assess the scene soberly, but he sways again, letting go of the chair.

Rachel and Sherry both reach out and steady him.

"Sorry about this, Sherry; I'll take him up to bed." Rachel offers, embarrassed.

Sherry's expression is complicated, a lot of thanks and a little disappointment lashed together. "Okay, Rachel. It was my fault. He was upset about something, and I tried to get him to talk about it but only managed to get him to drink."

"It was *good* whiskey." Wylie comments. "Good whiskey. Say, is there any whiskey here?"

Rachel's responding sigh is exasperated. "Yes, but you have reached your limit. Besides, it's a new bottle, and in your state, you'd never get it open."

"I'd figure it out. More than one way to skin a cat…"

That comment hits me funny. Funny *weird*, not funny *ha-ha*. Something clicks in my head. I stare transfixed at the tabletop.

Rachel notices. "It's okay, Ford; he'll be fine." She looks at me with curiosity and worry, troubled by my stare, I guess.

I give myself a shake and smile for her. "Do you need some help?"

She nods. Sherry slips to the side, and I stand and take her place.

"Thanks for getting him home, Sherry. Take his car. We'll work it out tomorrow."

Sherry smiles at Rachel. "Glad to help." Sherry shifts her attention to Wylie and becomes unsure. "I'll call you tomorrow?"

Wylie seems to forget me and Rachel for a minute then grins at Sherry, nods, and winks. On impulse, Sherry takes a step to him and pecks him on the lips. "Bye, Wylie."

Sherry leaves after a backward glance. The door closes, and Rachel turns her face to me. "Luckily, his bedroom's downstairs. C'mon, I'll show you."

We begin the trek to the bedroom, Wylie between us. He keeps looking question marks from me to my gun and then to Rachel. She avoids his eyes.

We get him to his room and onto the bed. He picks up his head, studies Rachel intently for a split second, and then smiles. His head drops onto the bed, and he snores once, sharply.

Rachel looks puzzled, steps back from the bed, and makes a face. She's standing on one side of it; I'm standing on the other. "I should undress him a little, make him more comfortable."

The fact of who he really is looms in the room, but neither of us seems up to facing it just now.

This has been as long a day as I have ever known, although it is now technically Sunday, no longer Saturday.

"It's okay. I'm done in." I meet her eyes. "I'll see you tomorrow."

She nods, scrutinizing my face, apprehensive. "Okay. You will, right, see me tomorrow?"

"Yes, I'll call. We'll go someplace private and finish our talk." My appointment to visit Big Jim Sutton crosses my mind. "I've got to go see Big Jim Sutton tomorrow. So, we won't be able to meet until after that."

She nods but continues to consider my face. Her eyes are soft but store secrets. "I want to finish it, tell you all, Ford."

Wylie suddenly lifts his head again. "Tell him what, Rachel?" He grins enormously into Rachel's penciled frown.

"Nothing, *Uncle Wylie*. Nothing. Go to sleep."

His head drops again. Rachel comes around the bed and takes my hand. Tension in her shoulders releases when I squeeze her hand in response. "Let me walk you out."

We retrace our steps to the kitchen. Our beer bottles and the peeled label are on the table. I pick up the shovel from the floor. "Look, keep your doors locked, okay. Given what you told me, I'm guessing you can take care of yourself, CIA and all."

"I can, Ford." She flips on the outside light.

We go outside, and I turn to her. "My car's down the road. So, all the cons, all those years—you and your dad, later, Lake too—you guys were half like Robin Hood, right?"

"Robin Hood? Half?"

"At least stealing from the rich—if not to give to the poor?"

Her face in the dim light shows too many things for me to read. "We stole for ourselves and from anyone we could con."

I sigh. "So, no *kind* cons?"

She gazes at me for a moment as if I'm some natural wonder. "There are no kind cons, Ford, only unkind ones."

With that, she kisses me quickly, stiffly, and walks back to the house. A moment later, the door closes, and the light goes off.

I WALK SLOWLY TO MY CAR. MY MIND FEELS WET AND SPONGY, MY heart too. I'm too tired to think; my feelings are boggy. I'll sort myself out after some sleep.

I get to my car, unlock it, take off my holster, and get inside. I unlock the glove compartment, take out my phone, and put the holster in.

On the phone is a message from Helen. She's at the house and wants to talk.

But she's undoubtedly asleep by now. I drive home, go inside, and fall into my bed without taking off my clothes or washing.

I'm dead as David Diamond. Almost.

Forgive me. Gallows humor is a sign that I've reached the end of my rope.

I WAKE THE NEXT MORNING LATE TO THE ENORMITY OF THE DAY before. My clothes have bound me during the night, and my forearms and pant legs are dirty. I stare into the ceiling for a time, hoping to shake answers from it by my upward gaze.

I'm reasonably sure about what Rachel—what *is* her name?—has left to tell me, but I'm not dwelling on it or making assumptions. Last night's story contained surprises enough to caution me against that. A con woman. I'm in love with a con woman. *A detective falls for a con woman.* I'd never write such a plot; it's stale. But living it, I don't find it stale. I feel like I've plunged into inextricable difficulties.

Rachel and Wylie—what *is* his name?—are both cons, father and daughter. Who are they conning? (Who am I kidding?)

David Diamond is in a disturbed, shallow grave up the hill from Noble Hall. Jane Pimberly is dead—murdered, I'm sure. Someone knows Rachel, and I discovered Diamond. Helen and I each have ten million dollars in the bank, and I've ignored all ten million of mine except the ones I promised Talbot for his raise. Someone hit Talbot and ran. Talbot has a girlfriend.

I'm confident I know who murdered Diamond and who murdered Jane Pimberly, but I feel like there's more to the story than I currently understand, moving currents and eddies that elude me. Of course, I have no proof of who murdered Diamond, and I am still working out the mechanics of Jane Pimberly's murder.

I stare upward for a long time despite my discomfort, ruminating, and it is almost midday when I hear Helen knocking softly on the door. "Ford? Are you up? Are you okay?"

"Come in, Helen; I'm up."

She opens the door. If she's surprised to find me in bed with my clothes on, she doesn't say so. She sits down in the chair near the edge of my bed. "Sorry I've been gone so much the last couple of days." She pauses. "Sam." She manages to make the single name a full explanation.

"I'm happy for you, Helen, really happy. He's a great guy."

Her eyes sparkle. "He is, Ford. And I am happy, holding-my-breath happy, worried it's all too good to be true."

I know my share of that sort of happiness. I look her in the eyes. "Is there something that worries you?"

She shakes her head. "No, not about *him*."

"About you?"

She bites her bottom lip for a moment. "Not so much *me* as the changes—all that money. I haven't told him about it."

"I haven't told anyone either, but hey, at least you know he's not after your money." I say the final words and feel a sting.

She laughs. "I hope he doesn't think I'm after his. His family's wealthy. Not on grandfather's scale, but they have money. And of course, he does too."

"So, what're we going to do, Helen, with the money?"

She shrugs. "I don't know about yours, but I've got charities to which I plan to donate. Big. I'm going to refurbish my office—but on a small scale—add another exam room, redecorate inside. Maybe bring a nurse practitioner on board. Beyond that, I don't know, really. It's not easy to spend that much money. What about you?"

"The sum total of my thoughts on it are that I'm going to give Talbot a raise."

She laughs again. "How is Talbot?"

"When I saw him yesterday, fine, or as fine as could be expected. It'll take some time for him to heal up, as you know better than I do."

She nods. "Yes, it will." Her face shows mischief. "And he has a girlfriend?"

I nod back at her. "So it seems."

"The end times are upon us, brother of mine. Has she seen *The Bikini Diary*?"

"No, and Talbot's promised to get rid of that, make it up to you."

She looks horrified. "Oh God. Who knows what that might mean?"

I make a placating gesture. "I honestly believe he's growing up—finally."

"Wow, whoever heard of a growth spurt at the end of your twenties?" Before I can respond, she shifts topics. "And what about you—what about Rachel?"

I'm not sure how to answer. I want to tell Helen what I know, but I'm worried about telling it before I know it all.

She notices my hesitation. "Well, at least you don't have to worry that she's after your money either. She has money of her own, right?"

She has money, but I have no idea whose it is—or was. Or how she plans—planned—to get more. (No idea?) "Right." I decide to keep all this to myself until I'm sure of it.

Helen seems to hear a wrong note in my "right." She gazes into my eyes for a second. I do my best to hold her gaze.

She stands. "You should get a shower, Ford. What were you doing last night? You stink of sweat."

"You wouldn't believe me if I told you," I reply as if I were joking.

She shakes her head and leaves my room. I make myself get up and take a shower.

I'M JUST ABOUT TO LEAVE FOR THE SUTTONS WHEN I GET A TEXT from Ruth.

Her dad's been called to the plant and wants to meet with me there. That doesn't make me happy. I'd been serious about wanting Ruth to run interference. A face-to-face with Big Jim is not what I'm in the mood for, particularly not in the furnace-like, industrial confines of Briggs and Stratton. But there's nothing to be done about it. I load myself in the hot-box Camry and head to the south end of Auburn, getting a head start on sweating.

Sundays are workdays at Briggs and Stratton, so I park among the employee cars. I look for Peppers's rusty truck but don't see it or Wade Pimberly's yellow Caddy.

I get out and go into the office. There's a large desk with "Briggs and Stratton" on the wall above it. Below the sign and behind the desk sits Ruth. "Hey, Ford!"

"Ruth, I didn't know you'd be here." I'm happy and relieved to see her.

"I wasn't going to throw you to that hammerhead dad of mine without any help. I'm just answering the phone until Rhoda gets back from the bathroom."

Rhoda—I take her to be Rhoda—walks in at just that moment. She's a middle-aged woman with a competent air. Ruth gets up, and Rhoda takes her seat and thanks her.

Ruth nods at Rhoda and smiles at me. "C'mon, Dad's on the factory floor."

We go through a wooden door and into a short hallway. At its end, we go through a heavy metal door. As soon as Ruth opens it, there's a hellish blast of heat and a concert blast of noise. The air-conditioned quiet of the office is obliterated.

The factory floor is a huge room with a high ceiling and smooth cement floor. Various machines stand in an obvious order, although I don't understand it. The assembly line. Ruth raises herself on her toes and looks around then waves. When she does, I see Big Jim near the far end of the building, talking to a man and a woman, both in coveralls. Big Jim's in a sweat-stained orange and blue Auburn polo.

Ruth leads me to him. I wipe at my forehead, sweat beading on my eyebrows and running down my back. I can see that Ruth's sweating too. "Glistening," I suppose, is the polite Southern term. As we move, the noise and heat decrease somewhat, and by the time we reach Big Jim, I believe we might be able to hear him when he speaks.

He's standing beside what looks like an industrial drill fitted with many different size bits. Some are needle-like. I'm not sure what part they play in small engine construction, but they look vaguely frightening. I begin to understand, as the conversation between Big Jim and the two employees finishes, that the machine is malfunctioning.

He shakes his head and leads us toward an exit. We step outside. It's hot outside but cooler than inside. The closing door all but eliminates the factory noise.

Big Jim fishes a handkerchief from his pocket and wipes his face. He offers it to me. I shake my head. "No, thanks, Mr. Sutton."

He shrugs and shoves it back in his pocket. "How's Norton?"

"He's doing okay, Mr. Sutton. He's skinned up and sore, but he's okay."

Big Jim's pleased. He smiles. He has a heavy face and a day's stubble. Ruth looks like her mom, but I realize her smile owes a lot to Big Jim's. She's listening to us.

"Good. I like that gremlin. Look, Merrick"—he says my name with distaste, but to his credit, he tries to disguise it. Ruth winces—"I'm worried that Bill Peppers might've been involved in what happened to Talbot. Talbot asked about him a few days ago, as you know, and on Friday, Rhoda—the woman at the front desk—said she stepped away for a few minutes, and when she came back, Bill Peppers was hanging up her phone. That area's off-limits to floor employees, so she mentioned it to me. I haven't said anything to him about it—he's off this weekend—but I wanted to tell you that."

"Why connect that to Talbot?"

Big Jim blinks. "Because Talbot's stayed in touch about this theft business. He said he would call me on Friday, but I never got a call."

"Oh, right."

Big Jim looks at his daughter. "Ruth, can you get me a cup of water?"

Ruth glances at me then back at her dad. "Um, sure. From the cooler inside?"

"Yeah, thanks, honey."

"You, Ford?"

"Please."

Ruth goes back inside with a trace of reluctance, and I face Big Jim alone. I swallow hard.

"Merrick, I hear you're dating Rachel Gunner."

"Yes, I am."

He stares at me and inflates. "So, you prefer her to Ruth?"

This isn't any of his business, and I know Ruth would hate him asking me the question, but I answer for her sake. "I wouldn't put it that way. I fell for one and not the other; I didn't *choose*. You must know how much I like and respect your daughter."

He shakes his head, exasperated, and deflates. "I do, and that makes it more annoying. It'd be one thing if I thought you didn't *see* Ruth, or one thing if I really believed you were the asshat I often accuse you of being, but I don't. I wonder, though, Merrick. You aren't a man who lives fast. But Gunner and that uncle of hers—they strike me as people who do. You really believe you can keep up with them?"

I pretend that question doesn't bother me. "My eyes are open."

He keeps shaking his head. "It's possible for them to be open and for you to still not notice what matters, Merrick."

Father Halsey's line about the people who are blind even though they see comes back to me. He was quoting scripture. I'd like to talk to him.

"That's true, sir, but I'm doing my best."

Ruth comes back outside, carrying two plastic cups of cold water. Big Jim takes one, and I do too. We both gulp them down. Ruth watches, trying to figure out what we've been saying.

"I've been looking for Peppers, sir, but haven't had any luck finding him at his apartment. Is there anywhere else I should look?"

Ruth's perplexed by the question, but Big Jim isn't. "He has a little cabin on the south end of West Point Lake."

"A cabin on the lake? Peppers?"

"Don't misunderstand. It isn't much. His father built it up there years ago, and Peppers inherited it. I was up there with him once, hunting with him. He even has an old AC jammed in a window. His dad had a buddy at the power company and strung line back to the place. It's well off the road in the woods beneath a bunch of tall trees. Better place to be on hot days than that Easy-Bake Oven apartment of his."

He tells me how to get there and then goes inside after giving Ruth a look.

"Did Dad drill you with questions?"

I shrug. "Not so bad. It could've been worse."

"Okay, I'm going to go back inside; he's my ride home. See you, Ford." She gives me a feathery kiss on my cheek, and returns to the building.

I stand there for a moment, ignoring the sun. I hear the muted, assembly-line noises from inside. I know how Jane Pimberly was murdered.

I SHOULD CALL RACHEL—SET UP A TIME TO SEE HER—BUT WHAT I now know makes me impatient to find Bill Peppers. I need him if I'm going to prove what I know.

I drive north toward Valley, a small town, and end up winding along county roads; the final two are unpaved gravel. I find the marker Big Jim told me to look for—an old pine with a red stripe low around the trunk—and I turn onto the pathway that leads from the road.

The Camry's not made for cart paths, and that's what this is, really. I'm jostled and tumbled as I slowly drive into the woods. I can see tracks in the ground; someone's been out here recently, maybe as recently as today.

Big Jim told me how far back the cabin is, and when I'm near, I find a spot where I can park the Camry off the path, leaving it against a stand of young pines and honeysuckle; I put on my holster as I walk.

In a few minutes, I see the cabin through the trees. I marvel that it could have electricity. I stop behind a bush and study the place. It's small, as Big Jim said, but it's in good repair. A porch, deep, runs along the entire front of the cabin. A few old trees stand near it, shading the cabin. Curtains, shut, are visible in the porch windows. The door's solid, covered in peeling red paint.

Heat hangs heavy in the hazy air. A low hum signals the presence of many insects. But as far as I can tell, the cabin's empty. I crouch down and stay as close to the high grass on the side of the path as I can. I risk the final open section to the porch and arrive on it with a small leap, landing carefully, bending my knees, and making no sound.

I still hear nothing nearby but insect sounds. In the distance, car wheels go by on the gravel road, but they pass, and the sound disappears. After a moment, I realize I don't hear only insects; I also hear an AC running. Its hum has mixed with that of the insects. I step carefully to a porch window and put my finger against it. It's cool to the touch. I listen again more keenly but still hear only the bugs and the AC.

I sidestep to the door and wrap my fingers around the knob. Holding my breath, I turn it. The door opens, and I step inside. I don't see anyone. The cool air feels heavenly.

The one interior room is kitchen, living room, and bedroom all at once but in different sections.

As I survey the interior, a cold gun barrel—colder than the AC—rests against my neck. Someone's on the other side of the door. "Hello, Ford! Nice to see you."

I know that voice, the hand that grips my shoulder.

CHAPTER 22: *Slow Show*

Here's the thing: sometimes you guess *wrong*.

Here's the thing, part two: it's incredible how fast mortifying thoughts can run with a gun resting against the back of your skull. I should not have been *wearing* my gun; I should have had it *out*. But I hadn't expected anyone to be here once I got close. Bill Peppers's rusty pickup is nowhere to be seen. I used the only space to park other than the empty one in front of the cabin.

Who else would know about this place?

I glance down at the hand on my shoulder. Yeah, wrong. Guessed wrong. Seriously wrong. But then again, I knew something was going on, something I still didn't understand. I should've paid more attention to that and less to what I do understand, I suppose.

I glance at the hand again. Glance: part two. Red fingernails. I peer down, partly in confirmation, partly to relieve the pressure of the barrel on my neck. Red toenails. I know what's—who's—between.

Patty Pimberly.

She pushes the gun barrel harder against my neck. "Walk to the end of the bed, Merrick."

Not "Melvin." I've been played—played by the *TFYWIF*. Funny how trophies have cropped up in the last few days. Lake mentioned one: a participation trophy. I suspect Patty's going to give me my *non*-participation trophy.

She pushes on me, and I do as she says. When I'm a step from the bed, she stops. I take the last step alone, turn, and sit.

Yeah, Patty Pimberly. She's in nothing but a bikini, and it's almost nothing. White with red polka dots. Polka dots must be her thing. The top and bottom are each so tiny that there's barely any background for the polka dots—any background other than Patty. Lots of Patty is showing, almost every tanned square inch. Her hair's up—a messy bun. Her tan looks darker than it did on my porch.

She has on her sunglasses indoors. She smiles beneath them, but the smile lacks the vacancy it sported when I saw it before.

"So, it's 'Merrick' now, not 'Melvin'?"

Her grin becomes alarmingly predatory. "It was never 'Melvin,' Ford. Not in my head." After mentioning her head, she shakes it. "I'm surprised but not unhappy to see you. I was getting bored out here. There's only so much a girl can do for herself. Only so many fingers and so many toes."

Toes? She's got the gun, so I don't ask. She smirks. "Bill left me out here to go and see about you and that trashy blonde. He had no idea you knew about this place."

Who's calling who trashy? But my next reaction is more fear than thought. *Rachel!*

"You and Peppers are *lovers?*"

She smiles, and it's like she's peeling her teeth. "We *screw*. I do what he wants in the bed; he does what I want out of it." She takes off her sunglasses and puts them down on a small table. Strangely, the removal does little to humanize her.

"What *you* want? What *do* you want?"

My mind races too fast through the corners. Tires screech.

I'm sure, despite my predicament, that Wade Pimberly used Bill

Peppers to kill his mother. I believe I know how Peppers did that. But how could Patty be involved in that and be *here* in Peppers's cabin, be doing what she's evidently been doing with Peppers?

"It'll be a while before Bill gets back, a good, *long* while..." She looks at me during her pause, and her eyes climb me from feet to head as if measuring me. They linger for a moment on my zipper.

The look in her eyes is cold, withdrawn, self-involved, and I understand at last the look I've seen in *Rachel's* eyes.

It was not a dissector's gaze; Patty's is that absolutely. No, it was not manipulative, not all about Rachel's advantage, not about what she wanted. Patty's is that completely. Rachel's was self-protective, an attempt to hide in plain sight. What I saw as contempt was instead shame, self-directed.

But I don't have time to work this out, not all the way. Patty continues. "...and he'll help me decide what to do with you—finally do with you." She shrugs as if this were some carefree beach moment, the two of us on a date.

But she shrugs with a gun in her hand, steadily aimed at me.

She lets her eyes sweep along me again—and again with the lingering delay in the middle. "But since we have free time, why don't you take off those clothes? I've wanted to see you naked since you came to the house. I'm curious about the caliber of the gun you're packing *under* the clothes."

For a moment, I just gawk at her. She giggles, a little-girl giggle, then her face hardens. "Not kidding, Ford. Start with the gun I *can* see, and be slow and careful with it—with everything. I wish I had some music to turn on. But I'm sure you'll do the *turning on.*"

This is my penalty for guessing wrong today, for being soft boiled every day. She waves the gun, motioning for me to begin. She's being careful. She's far enough from me to respond to any attempt I might make to take the gun, to rush her. She has me seated on a soft mattress. I've sunk a little, and that would slow any rush. All I can do is play for time. And that means doing what she wants.

And now, seeing her eyes for real, I don't doubt she'll kill me.

I slowly take off my shoulder holster, keeping my hands away from the gun. I drop it on the floor as she gestures for me to do. I'm wearing my regular detecting gear: T-shirt, jeans, sneakers. There's not a lot to come off. I should've dressed for deadly strip poker.

She gestures for me to continue. After she does, she readjusts herself in her chair.

She rests the gun on the arm of her chair, still carefully aimed at me, but then she slides her other hand up one of her long, dark thighs toward the small red polka dot between them. I must gawk again because her face fixes in what I can only describe as a cold leer. She sighs. "Go on; I'm ready now. And don't get any ideas. I'm very good at multitasking."

I try to stretch out the moment, delay. I am naturally modest. And I haven't been naked in front of a woman since college. I hoped that Rachel would be the first—and last. God, I do hope that, don't I?—the last. I'm in trouble, and not just in this cabin.

Patty sinks a little further in her chair, spreading her legs and angling herself so that I cannot fail to see her polka dot. She doesn't just want to watch me; she wants me to watch her watch.

My stomach turns. I understand that my humiliation will make this better for her, more exciting.

There's nothing for it. I take off my T-shirt. She lets out a small moan.

I've never considered myself a lady-killer. That should've made me more suspicious of Patty from the beginning. I'm tall, curly headed. I have a friendly, uncalculated smile. Neither brawny nor feeble, I'm lean and stronger than I look. But I keep my shirt on, habitually. Unlike—I'm guessing—Lake, I don't hunt opportunities to disrobe.

I don't want to do this. The stained, cheap furniture of the cabin, the drone of the air conditioner, the faint mildew smell, Patty's moan—it all makes this impossibly seedy.

I couldn't—I wouldn't—write this scene.

I sit for a moment, chest bare. Patty licks her lips, making a slow show of it. I decide to make my show slower, and then, insanely, that song by The National sounds in my head: "Slow Show."

I look down at my pants as Patty gestures toward them.

I put my hand on my belt, and Patty mews. I can't believe this is happening. The only advantage I have is that she *wants* me to go slow; she wants this to last.

It's repayment for turning her down on the porch.

I undo my buckle, and she wriggles in the chair, but the damn gun remains steady. I pull the belt through the buckle then let go of both the buckle and the belt. Her eyes narrow, but I'm going to try a different tactic. I'll try to get her to talk. She believes I'm at her mercy.

If Peppers is out after Rachel, it's got to be because we found David Diamond. And then I begin to suspect my mistake, the reason I guessed wrong.

"So, you and Peppers. You're not just sleeping together, are you?"

My brain's working like a detective's for the first time since Patty's barrel was pressed to my neck. It's moving fast but not racing. No screeching. "You're blackmailing your husband, *blackmailing* Wade..." I'm careful not to say more. A small smile lifts just the corners of her mouth. She sighs, willing for now to elongate my striptease. She likes having fooled me.

Her tone gloats. "Of course, we are. Wade's a bald piece of shit. Being married to him and living in his temple of tastelessness is about as bad as it gets. And that damn vanity plate he made me buy. *His* damn vanity. All I am to him is a poseable trophy, a screwable Barbie. But the damn prenup he made me sign—I'm stuck with him if I want access to his money and all the money he inherited from that mad bitch, his mother.

"So, when Peppers started coming around and started sniffing around me, I *cultivated* him, satisfied certain peculiar wishes, and got him to tell me about Wade, the past. All about Wade and his mother and father. We worked it out, worked out that Wade had killed Daddy Diamond. When we sent Wade the first note and he cashed-up, we knew we had him."

She doesn't know Wade killed Jane. Or that Peppers was involved. This is the opacity in things I couldn't make out. *Peppers.* He's double-dipping. (Sorry, gallows humor.) Peppers had been playing Patty against Wade, no doubt getting money both ways, from blackmailing Wade and from whatever payment he got for killing Jane. And he's been, well, screwing Patty. Peppers must reckon he's making out like a bandit. (Sorry again. Gallows humor plus punning cliché.) But hey, I'm in a fix here—a Chippendale life sentence.

I was right about one thing. Peppers is the key to all of this, my proof of all that's happened: Wade's patricide and matricide.

Patty continues, her hand now touching herself. She must find this storytelling stimulating. God! Her voice is getting husky. "So, we've been milking him and cuckolding him all at once. It's been *very* satisfying." She readjusts in her chair, wriggles, and trembles a little.

"Get back to work. I'm *ready* for the pants-drop." I try not to think about what that means. She can't really be planning *that* multitask.

"So, Peppers came to you?"

She leers at my wording but spares me the pun we both hear. "How could he not? I was bored and couldn't face a lifetime with Wade. Bill's a sick son of a bitch, too sick almost for me." She pauses then moves her hand from between her legs. Sits up a bit. Thinking.

"You know, Ford, I'd *much* prefer you to Peppers. You're out here, you've got your gun, you found Diamond"—*Bingo, I think*—"and you could just kill Bill and take his place. Bill already has holes dug in the woods for you and the blonde. Put him in yours." Her hand snakes up her thigh again and meets the polka dot. She sighs; the sigh is lengthy and moist. "I'd be happy to trade up."

Detectives have a bad reputation, a stereotype: not on the up-and-up, down with *whatever*. I blame books and movies. Too much noir. Too many detectives that seem to prefer the broad path. She really expects me to consider this. She makes sure I can see her still-moving hand, her fingers.

"So, you're proposing I kill Bill for you?"

She nods, mews a little. I pull my belt out of my pants very slowly. I give her a look, trying hard to pretend growing interest, even desire, although my stomach turns a second time.

I make myself look at her, mimicking her looks at me, sliding my eyes up and down the length of her, forcing my eyes to linger on her busy hand. I lift my shoulders, deciding to play to her stereotype and on her thin, tanned ego. *I'm sorry, Rachel.*

"Look, I see what's on offer, but frankly, if you know about the blonde, you must know that I'm satisfied, *curvy miles* from hard up. I'm not confident *I'd* be trading up."

She frowns; her hand stops.

"Oh, believe me, you'd be trading up. I can *do* things to you that you've never imagined, *expand* your horizons, *raise* your consciousness. With me, God's dead—*nothing's* forbidden."

The former beauty queen is a lot smarter than she led me to believe, whatever else is true.

She stands up, the gun still on me. She gestures for me to take off my pants. I do, again trying to look like I've begun to enjoy this slow, dumb show. She runs her hand over her breasts, licks her lips again, but not self-consciously. Her breathing's become ragged, fast—her green eyes deep, dilated.

I lift myself from my bed seat enough to slide my pants down. Slowly. Very slowly. She's now so invested in each movement that she's not paying attention to anything else. I've never used a woman's desire, twisted or not, against her before, and doing so adds to my disgust. But she's the one with the gun.

It's her show.

I decide to delay us once more with talk. "But wait"—I stop, my pants around my ankles. I hope she hasn't noticed that not all of me is on board with the desire I'm pretending. I need to distract her from that for a moment—"does Peppers have any proof that Wade killed Diamond?"

She grins. "Not exactly, but Wade's been paying, and Bill knows where Wade keeps proof. Bill's left it alone because he doesn't want Wade to suspect us. I know where it is too."

I need to know as well. I hadn't expected this bit of luck, and I don't deserve it, given the mess I've gotten myself into. I need to get out of it. But the only way to do that, it seems, is to convince Patty I want what she wants.

I reach down slowly to pull my pants off. She leans forward, eager, forgets that my gun's on the floor. When she stood, she decreased the distance between us, a mistake of anticipation. I need to take my pants off to move. I am careful to pull them over my shoes, using my hand away from my gun.

Many things happen almost at once. Patty shifts her eyes up to my boxers as my pants come off. I roll toward my gun, reaching to pull it from the holster. Outside, there's a crunch of gravel, the roar of an engine, the sound of a sliding stop.

Patty barks, "Shit," and looks toward the door as I roll forward, freeing my gun while shouldering her hard in the stomach. She falls backward, and her gun goes off, sending a bullet into the ceiling as she lands awkwardly on her chair then bounces off it, knocking over the table and sending her sunglasses airborne. She slams to the floor, and her sunglasses land beside her, upside down.

I have my gun on her, standing in my boxers and sneakers. Patty's gasping, and I'm gasping when the cabin door bursts open a moment later. Bill Peppers comes flying in, headlong, and crashes on the floor beside Patty. Rachel rushes through the door behind him, a pump shotgun in her hands.

I recall the water fight at Michelle's.

But then Rachel looks at me, shocked and angry. "What the hell, Ford?"

CHAPTER 23: *Twine Backward*

I glance down at myself, my snow-white boxers, and my now-sagging tube socks. I face Rachel and shrug, still with my gun in hand.

I glance down again to check that my boxers haven't gaped open. They haven't.

Rachel's shock and anger melt as she reconsiders the scene; she reorients, a hint of a smile in her eyes but not on her lips. Her shotgun's already pointed at Peppers and Patty, but now her eyes are too. Pointed.

"Ford," she says coolly, each word after my name stabbing, "find something to tie them with. If there's nothing else, take his"—she jabs the shotgun at Peppers, who's gathering himself on the floor—"boot laces. Be sure to tie that bastard *tight.*"

I nod, and I put my finger to my lips, a signal to Rachel to be careful what she says. Patty doesn't know her husband killed his mother. Peppers doesn't know what, if anything, Patty's told me. Rachel nods to me.

Patty sits up beside Peppers; Peppers is on all fours, facing the floor. Peppers coughs one word, "Bitch!" but his posture makes it hard to know whether he's addressed that to Rachel, Patty, or life itself.

Rachel's movements with the shotgun evince the baffling mix of precision and ease I've seen in all her movements. I cross to the kitchen, pull open a drawer. Kitchen gadgets. *Damn.* I pull open a second, a junk drawer, it seems. There's a stretch of heavy twine inside it, the kind often used in hay baling. Yes, I've done that in the brutal Alabama sun. Worst high school summer job ever. It makes me itch to remember it.

I grab the twine and then the two straight-backed chairs under the table in the kitchen corner. Patty's now watching me. The rage on her face disappears, and I bow mentally to her acting skill. She's all guile and beguile. I'm going to have to retool my view about femme fatales. Patty eyes Rachel.

"Your timing *sucks*. Ford here was just about to show me his *weapon* 'cause I promised to *clean it* for him. Spit shine."

Rachel takes two quick steps, like a dancer, toward Patty. The shotgun's single barrel stares into Patty's two eyes, Cyclops to Siren. Patty swallows, then looks away.

Rachel motions for Patty to get in one of the chairs I have put beside Patty and Peppers. She does. I glance at Rachel, and she motions for me to tie Patty to the chair. I do it quickly.

Patty smirks at me. "Second time today I've been tied up in here." I ignore her and turn around.

Peppers stares at me. I've never gotten a good long look at him although I've been hunting him for a while. His work boots are dusty; his jeans look like they could stand on their own, stiffened by dirt. He's got on a flannel shirt with the sleeves cut off, and on his wrist is a cheap, old, Timex digital watch. A pair of nice sunglasses are stuffed in his shirt pocket.

His eyes are small, hard, and dark—shiny in his head like they're stained-glass beads. There's something abysmal in his gaze, and I understand what both Ruth and Peppers's neighbor meant. His elongated, unshaven face is bruised, his lip split, blood on his sharp chin. His Adam's apple juts out as if he'd choked on a greedy bite of Adam's apple.

He carefully keeps his glass eyes off Rachel.

I'm eager to know the story of their arrival.

"Get in the other chair," Rachel says to him, not raising her voice but somehow raising her menace. Peppers feels it and clambers into the chair. I tie him to it, noticing the bruises that cover his arms and neck.

"Good, Ford"—Rachel nods—"now tip their chairs onto the floor. Make sure their tied hands aren't on the edges of the chairs." I'm not sure why she wants me to do that, but I tip them both backward, lowering each chair to the floor, leaving the two captives facing the ceiling. Not just the twine, but now gravity holds them. Rachel nods and points to the back door. I open it, and she quickly follows me outside.

I TURN AS SHE CLOSES THE BACK DOOR. SHE STANDS THE SHOTGUN against the back wall of the cabin and then springs into my arms, wrapping her arms and her legs around me and kissing my face over and over, brief comments between each warm, hard kiss.

"Ford, thank God! I was worried and sad. ... You didn't call. ... You said you'd call. ... Then *Peppers* sneaked into the hall with that shotgun, but he wasn't ready for me. ... I took it from him, and I was terrified he'd already *found* you. ... I might've *killed* him with it. ... I drove like a *crazy* woman, and then I heard that shot."

She squeezes me tighter but stops the kisses, her voice breaking. Her eyes are wet as she hears that shot echo in her mind. I kiss her this time, softly on the lips, allowing myself to linger for a moment. "I'm fine, Rachel. And Patty's lying to you."

"Of course she is, Ford. You know you're mine." Rachel's tone is proprietary, final, although she watches my face. "Who is she? Peppers wasn't talkative on the drive up, not with that shotgun in his ribs and being forced to shift the gears. Especially once we got on the gravel roads and started bouncing."

"She's Wade Pimberly's wife, Patty. The wife of the son of David Diamond and Jane Pimberly. We saw their house the day we followed Peppers."

Rachel remembers and nods. "So, did *they* kill Diamond? Patty and Peppers?"

I look around us. There's a clearing—not really a yard—behind the cabin. A fold-out lounge chair is in the sunshine, a sweating glass of iced tea—the ice all but gone—beside it on a fold-out stand. Beside the tea is a bottle of suntan lotion and a copy of one of my books, Logan Smythe's *Death, Where Is Thy Sting?* Not my best work although it sold well. Patty should've known better: Burney Lennox wouldn't have undressed for her either.

Jokes aside, the idea of Patty reading my books makes my flesh shift on my bones.

I make myself focus on what Rachel asked.

"No, Wade killed his father. Patty confirmed it. She and Peppers have been blackmailing him."

"I take it that's not all they've been doing?"

I shudder. "No, but I'll spare you those details, fingers, and toes."

Rachel looks nauseated for a moment. "God, with him, Peppers? That man's a bathless psychopath."

"They're a matched set. She was going to make me strip, then kill me if I didn't agree to take the place of Peppers."

"His place in all things?" She looks down at my boxers. I'd forgotten I was standing here nearly naked. "Well, at least she hasn't seen anything I haven't seen yet." Rachel raises an eyebrow as a late question mark after her sentence finishes.

I nod hard. "No. Scout's honor!" I give her the three-fingered Boy Scout salute.

She knows the salute and grins. "Of course you were a Boy Scout. Stay here; I'll get your clothes." She picks up the shotgun and goes back inside.

I WALK OVER TO THE FOLD-OUT TABLE AND PICK UP THE COPY OF my book. It was face-down on the table, open to the first chapter. Patty hadn't gotten far.

I'm looking through the book when Rachel comes outside, my clothes bunched under one arm. She pulls the door shut with her foot.

"So, Patty was reading a pulp detective novel while sunbathing?"

I feel oddly self-conscious. It must show; Rachel tilts her head, considering my reaction.

"Guess so."

Rachel looks at the cover: a man standing, shadowed, holding a gun above a woman, nearly naked, posed *just so* on the ground at his feet. I can never make my publisher stop using these lurid covers, even though there is no such scene in the novel. "Logan Smythe?" Rachel asks as she hands me my clothes. I put the book down and start quickly to dress. I sit in the fold-out chair to pull my jeans over my sneakers.

Rachel's still looking at the book. "You know, Diana at St. Dunstan's—she was reading a detective novel. I asked about it, and she told me, but she mentioned that Logan Smythe is her favorite. Odd, thinking of her reading a book that Patty would read."

As I stand and pull up my jeans, I confess: "That's my book."

Rachel looks at me. "How did Patty get your book?" There's a sharp edge in the question.

"No, it's not my *copy* of the book. It's my *book*; I wrote it."

"Wait, *you* are a writer?"

"Yes, but only Helen and Talbot know."

"I knew it!" Rachel says, her eyes shining. "Well, I mean, it just felt like it to me. So, you have an alias too?"

I hadn't thought of it that way. "I guess so. Say, Rachel, what is your name—your birth name?"

She pauses for a second and then answers. "Virginia, but I haven't used that name in a long time. Let's stick with 'Rachel.' I like the way you say it to me."

From inside, we hear a yell: Patty. "Hey, I have to pee!"

Before I can speak, Rachel does. "Then pee! Aim for a polka dot!"

Patty curses in a lowered voice. Pepper laughs. Patty curses him.

"Stop snickering, you sick puke."

Rachel shakes her head. "Quite a couple. But what're we going to do with them?"

I'm not sure. I apply myself to the question, listening to the insects and the AC. "I need your help to decide. But, before I do, I need to know about Wylie and Peppers."

Rachel's face changes. "Oh, that. Uncle Wylie"—she pauses and shakes her head—"*Dad* wanted you to see him having a mysterious conversation with someone. Peppers had come around the place a few times asking about handyman work or odd jobs. Dad needed a prop, thought of him, and hired him just to meet in the coliseum."

"So, that was *staged*?"

She nods reluctantly.

"And you were part of it?"

She nods again, more reluctantly.

"Because I'm your *mark*?"

"Mine? Yes and no." She stops, and I'm about to ask her to explain that contradiction when she continues. "But Peppers messed up. He was supposed to leave through the opposite exit, not the one we were watching from. Your following him wasn't planned, and we, Dad and I, had no notion that Peppers would go from there to Pimberly's place—that they were closely connected."

"Okay." I'll ask for more later. "Here's where things stand, I think. There have been two murders at Noble Hall. David Diamond—Wade Pimberly killed him years ago, acting on impulse, I believe, hatred, shame—and Jane Pimberly. Peppers killed her, but Wade hired him to do it. I'm guessing he had her killed because he feared his mother was going to reveal that Diamond was dead, reveal his body. Deliberately or accidentally.

"As she aged, Jane was slipping further and further into madness. She knew Wade killed Diamond all along but kept her son's secret. I suspect that initially unhinged her. I don't know when he figured out that she knew, but he did eventually, and I don't think he's rested well since then. He paid Peppers to kill her to protect that grave we found, only to end up being blackmailed by Peppers and Patty for it anyway.

She listens closely; I'm talking fast. "But, Ford, I don't understand Patty's role in all this."

I put my T-shirt on. "I didn't either, and that's how I ended up an involuntary stripper. She'd found out about Diamond from Peppers. I'm not exactly sure how Peppers knew, but I suspect he followed Jane on one of her 'black veil' vigils and worked it out. It was him in the woods with us the other night."

She smiles tightly for a second. "I worked that out already. One reason he failed to surprise me was that I recognized the engine in his truck when he pulled up—V6, five-speed. I was ready for him when he came in."

I kiss her quickly. "I *love* you!"

Her eyes widen, her jaw drops. I curse myself silently. *Damn! Too soon, jackass, too soon. Wrong place, wrong time.* But she rewards me with a smile like a holiday and kisses me back.

She doesn't say it back, but the smile was enough, more than enough. I make myself get back on topic. "Patty says that Wade kept something that proves he killed Jane and that she knows what it is, where it is. I need to know. I can ask Patty."

I take a step toward the door, but Rachel puts her hand on my chest. "*I'll* ask *Peppers*."

She goes inside, shotgun in hand. A moment later, Peppers screams, "Bitch!"—the single scream alive with misery and rage.

When she comes out a few minutes later, I look at her. She's flushed, and she shrugs, but not with real indifference.

"The Farm?" I ask.

She nods sharply, once. "*Interrogation* class. It was mostly a psychology and *physiology* class."

I don't ask a follow up.

264

"I know what it is, Ford, and where. It's the hammer Wade used to kill his father. He's kept it as a memento all these years. It's in the boathouse behind his place."

"So, let's go get it. These two will survive a few hours out here. They've got AC."

"Yeah," Rachel agrees, "but they're going to wish they had air fresheners if we don't hurry."

Chuckling, I kiss her cheek. "The Farm hard-boils its eggs."

She shakes her head, troubled by my words, staring at the shotgun. "They *try*. My whole life has tried. But I'm a few minutes short of hard too, Ford. Maybe closer to hard than you, but still, soft."

I grab her hand, and we hurry around the cabin. I stop and take the keys from Peppers's truck. Rachel nods her appreciation of my thought. We jog to the Camry and, once in it; we head out of the woods.

We drive along the Lake north toward Wade Pimberly's house. The subtropical Alabama scenery is resolutely green, resolutely thick. It crowds the asphalt edges of the county roads we travel.

The sky is slowly darkening. Another summer thunderstorm threatens.

Each of us is silent for a few minutes, then Rachel starts.

"So here's the story…" She looks away from me out the passenger side window. I sneak a look at her and only then notice she's wearing a dark T-shirt, jeans, and red, high-topped sneakers. I feel warm all over even as I brace for the story.

"…I told you Dad called me from out East. He was in Boston. He tried to run a con on your grandfather but pulled the plug on it. I don't know why, not exactly. He never explained. But I suspect it was because he'd decided to con you instead, a *long* con. He came to town and rented Noble Hall…"

"Rented?"

She turns to me.

"Dad's cash-flush due to some big scores lately, but he doesn't have the kind of money it would take to buy that place. He rented it through Pimberly's lawyer, then talked the lawyer into letting him claim that he bought it, paying extra for it. Then he started establishing himself here and learning about you. You were going to get an early, sizable inheritance from your grandfather." She looks out the passenger window again, her hand fidgeting in her lap. "I'm not sure how he found that out, but he did."

"Once he got established here, he started asking around about you, very casually, discreetly, irregularly, staying away from the folks closest to you but talking to other people who knew you. He even followed you around, but you never noticed. He ran into you once or twice but didn't try to…cultivate you. When he saw you had no one special in your life, he thought of me, of course. He called. I refused at first, but he kept at it."

"I should've just said, 'No,' but this time, when he said this was the last con, for some reason, I believed him. I still do. He's *different*. So, I came. He sent me to you, but what he told me about you, although factually accurate, was personally way off. He never said it, but he suggested you were…shady…mean. Hard-boiled. The con was for me to get you to start following him around, make you curious about what he was up to, and then for me to slowly work you from *curious observer* to *participant*. He was going to sell you on some investment scheme after I drew you in."

"So, he came at me…*backward*?"

She shrugs but doesn't look at me. "It's an old dodge in conning. You let the mark think he or she's discovered something, something that will make them a lot of money, something you don't seem to want them to know about at all, and that's how you set the hook. They don't suspect you; they're too busy congratulating themselves on how clever they are."

"So, you hired me to discover the scheme, a scheme designed to fleece me?"

"Yes, Ford. I'm sorry."

We drive, nearing Pimberly's house. "Why are you telling me this?"

"Because," she offers softly, "I knew Dad was wrong about you. I knew it the moment I saw that silly *Blade Runner* poster. And because I liked you. I liked you from the moment you admitted you were soft boiled.

"So, I started trying to work out what to do as I was simultaneously going through the motions of Dad's con and also falling for you. I kept forgetting the con, then remembering. I felt ashamed of myself and my dad, trapped between him and you. And then Lake showed up to complicate everything more…"

Pimberly's house comes into view, the old yellow Caddy in the driveway. The sun hides behind gray clouds. I drive past the house a short distance, park on the side of the road, and shut off the engine.

I take Rachel's hand in mine. She searches my eyes, holding her breath.

"Doesn't change anything, girlfriend." She exhales softly and treats me to that smile again.

We kiss, letting ourselves go for a moment, then both pull back. There's still work to do.

I check my gun as she reaches into the back seat and grabs the shotgun; then we get out of the car.

We do. And then it hits me. We're a team.

CHAPTER 24: *Trophies*

"Let's use the woods, stay in them past the house; then we'll have to break cover to cross to the boathouse," I whisper.

A wind's beginning to blow, damp, and turning the leaves so that their undersides show milky green.

The temperature's dropping, been dropping. It's cooler if not cool.

Rachel looks at me and nods resolutely. "Sounds good."

I reach out and stop her before she gets far into the underbrush. "Rachel, how did you find me at the cabin?" The question's been nagging at me.

She turns, crouches down, and I crouch with her. We're no longer visible from the road.

"When Peppers showed up at the hall, I disarmed him, fast and clean. I asked him about you. I was terrified he'd found you first." I see that on her face. "After the way I took his gun, he wasn't about to lie to me."

Her teeth show but not in a smile. "He hadn't found you although he'd looked for you first. You must've been hunting him while he was hunting you.

"I grabbed my phone and called Helen, but she didn't know where you were. She told me to call Father Halsey. He didn't know either. By that time, Peppers was panicking, my foot on his throat and his shotgun in his face as I made the calls. Father Halsey told me to call Ruth."

I see a flash of hurt pride on Rachel's face at that, at having to call Ruth to find out where I was.

"She was kind to me. She told me you'd talked to her dad. She asked him, and he told her he gave you directions to the cabin. Then I crammed Peppers in the truck…"

"You're *amazing*; do you know that?"

The hurt look disappears, and she starts moving again, but not before she whispers back: "You'll do too."

We sneak through the woods, skirting the house. We can see it. No one seems to be around. It's gotten overcast enough, dark enough, to seem like dusk although that's still an hour or two away. Despite the dark, there are no lights on in the house. But, after the mess at the cabin, I'm not making any more stupid moves. I'm assuming that Pimberly is in the house or the boathouse.

The woods next to Pimberly's house thin as we near the lake. Landscaping has pushed the edges back too to make for more yard, so as we near the water, staying in the woods takes us farther from the boathouse. I stop us at a point that seems far enough from the house without becoming too far from the boathouse.

As I turn to look at Rachel, I feel the cold, small shock of a raindrop, fat and heavy. Lightning flashes out over the lake, and its momentary flash shifts the colors of the woods. More drops follow. It's fixin' to be a downpour, a *frog strangler* as folks in the South say. I motion for Rachel to follow, and we dash together across the open yard. Sheeting rain begins all at once. We jump up onto the raised walkway that leads to the boathouse and run to the overhang at the door. I take my gun from my holster. Rachel presses herself against my back, warm and panting, as I turn the knob. It opens.

I don't know if that's a bad sign or a good one. It feels portentous.

THE BOATHOUSE HAS WALLS ON THREE SIDES: THE FRONT—THE
side facing Pimberly's house—and the two adjacent sides, left and
right. But there's no back wall. Instead, the roof extends out over the
water, and the floor stops beneath it, creating a sheltered pier.

A small motorboat, black and sleek, floats on the choppy water. The
wind has strengthened, and the water's surface moves.

Rachel leans against the door and shuts it with a soft click. I'm
studying the interior of the building.

Fishing gear is hooked on one wall, poles, nets. Beneath the gear
is a crude wooden table with a tackle box atop it. Reels and snarls of
fishing line and other bits spot the table around the box.

The opposite wall is covered with life preservers, life jackets, and
old buoys. Beneath them, on a green tarp, is a small boat engine.
It's cobwebbed and marooned in a black pool of its own oil, the oil
blacker against the green tarp. Heavy ropes, sloppily coiled, look like
fat snakes waiting for the engine to bleed its last.

The corners of the ceiling are all thickly cobwebbed. Pulleys hang
from the extended ceiling down above the motorboat, ropes hanging
from them.

No hammer's in view. But rain hammers on the boathouse's tin roof.

Rachel has moved beside me, and she's studying the interior too.
"Why would Pimberly keep the murder weapon all these years?"

I shrug. "I suspect he's as crazy as the rest of his family, that he's
just hidden it better over the years. High-functioning crazy, sort of
like Patty. And, of course, if we find the weapon, it may prove nothing.
But still…"

I return my gun to my holster and cross to the dusty tackle box;
it seems the likeliest hiding place. The box is metal, red but rusting,
and the latch broken. I open it, and the lid creaks. Inside the box is a
tray, divided, and in the tray are lures and line, hooks and sinkers, no
longer separated, if they ever were, but strewn together.

I remove the tray. It's jammed in the box, and I give it a sharp yank;

beneath it, wrinkled and dusty, is a black trash bag. It's got something in it. I take the bag out and put it on the table. When I investigate the now-empty tackle box, I realize it's bolted to the table.

Rachel is watching me intently. I unwind the bag—it's wrapped around its contents—then pull the top of it open. The bag exhales a stench. Rachel wrinkles her nose. "What is that?"

I take a breath and reach into the bag. "Ouch!"

I pull my hand out. A small, jagged cut runs across my palm. It's not deep, but it hurts.

"Ford!" Rachel says, but I put my hand in the bag again more cautiously. I feel around and remove an old, rusty hammer; one end of it still looks stained. I put it down as carefully as I can.

Rachel points at the stain. "Could that be…"

"Maybe…" I reach in again and this time remove a cat-food can, its lid still partially attached. The lid is what cut my palm, and the stench is coming from the food still in the can. I put it down beside the hammer, take the handkerchief from my pocket, and wrap it around my hand.

Rachel looks at me, lost. "A cat-food can?"

"A second murder weapon."

"Huh?"

"It's how Peppers murdered Jane."

"I don't understand."

I take a breath and tie off my handkerchief. "Peppers knew about Jane's heart condition. He'd been around the hall a few times. I suspect he spied on her, and he figured out something no one else seems to have noticed. No one noticed since, at the end, Jane was living alone; her housekeeper, Edna, was no longer coming regularly.

"Anyway, Peppers figured out that Jane, now almost completely mad, was living on cat food, eating with her cats. There was nothing else in her fridge, but no one thought about what that meant. Peppers used a very precise drill at Briggs and Stratton—I've seen it—to puncture that can, a tiny hole, and he injected a high dosage of potassium into it; that's my guess. Then he snuck into the house, put it on top of her pile of unopened cans, and waited for her to eat it. She did, and as he and Wade hoped, it caused a fatal arrhythmia, killing her. Killing her and a few of the old—I'm guessing tamer—cats who ate it with her. She fought off the other, more feral cats, made them wait. That'd been going on for a while. Crazy. So crazy no one imagined it, imagined that her lonely, cat-attended death could be foul play."

"No one except you." Rachel's voice is emphatic, admiring. "You have an unusual mind."

"No one except me and the person who sent Miller Solomon to me. Solomon's the one who hired me to dig into Jane's death, but he told me he was doing it for someone else."

We stand completely silent for a moment, and I'm again aware of the pelting rain.

"So," Rachel whispers, gesturing to the hammer and the can, "are those the son's mementos of his parents?"

"Yeah."

"And I'm going to add to my collection, looks like."

Rachel and I both spin. Wade Pimberly is standing inside the open door. He's soaked, a puddle forming around his feet; he has a gun in his hand and another tucked in his pants.

I've done it again. Another stupid move after all.

He points his gun at Rachel. "Put the shotgun down." His voice is high, excited. He peers more closely at Rachel for a moment. "I know you. I met you that day, the Briggs and Stratton lot; I was looking for Peppers. You were with Stroud, your uncle. But you're in the wrong place with the wrong man now."

One danger of being the sort of detective I am—the sort who also writes detective stories, who cares about stories—is that you can get lost in the story and lose track of other things. But Rachel got lost in the story too, I guess. Neither of us heard Pimberly come in although the rain pounding the roof helped him with that.

Rachel stares at Pimberly but deposits the shotgun on the floor. Pimberly turns his gun on me. "Now, put yours on the ground too."

I do, sliding it carefully from the holster. He walks forward, motioning for us to back up. He kicks our guns backward with his foot, one at a time, putting himself between us and them.

Pimberly motions to the table. "Put my mementos back in their bag. Although 'mementos' isn't the best term, I regard them as my *trophies*."

TFYWIF—right, right.

I turn and carefully return the hammer and can to the trash bag. I face Pimberly again after I've done it. He seems noticeably calmer. His voice sounds more normal. "Good, good."

"Trophies?" I ask, my tone neutral. Rachel looks at me; she likely wonders what I'm doing. "Trophies of your dad's murder, your mom's?"

Pimberly spits down into the puddle gathering around his feet.

"*Dad? Mom?* That bum, that feckless drifter? That crackpot tragedy, the damned cat lady? I deserved better parents, much better. I deserved better." His voice is cold, dry. "At least most people weren't sure Diamond was my father. I was stuck with lunatic Jane. And she couldn't quit that loser, Diamond, alive or dead. She pined for him for-goddamn-ever; then she found him where I hid him—followed me. I used to go every now and then to stomp on his grave. Pray his soul to hell. She was eventually going to tell someone about him, lead someone to him. She couldn't control herself or her mouth."

What a piece of work this man is. He's *not* the glory of dust. Patty can surely pick 'em. But she's a piece of work too. *"Man delights not me. No, nor woman neither."* I shake my head. No time for quotations to echo in my head. Ruth's right: words are going to do me in.

"Now, tell me how you found my trophies."

My hole card. I've been holding it and now I play it. I see Rachel tense subtly. I tell him the truth, waiting for a reaction. "Patty and Peppers, they told us the hammer was here. We found them together in his love nest. I don't think they knew about the can. I'm guessing Peppers 'ould be unhappy to know you kept that."

"Patty…*and* Peppers? Love nest?" He mouths "love nest" soundlessly a couple more times. Understanding dawns in Pimberly's eyes; they seem to catch flame. "That goddamned *whore*! She's mine!"

For a moment, Pimberly's focus is not on us. Peppers stole one of Pimberly's trophies.

Rachel moves before I can. She leaps forward, lands, then kicks the gun from Pimberly's hand. It all looks like one smooth motion, its analog continuity lost in my digital description. Pimberly's gun flies across the boathouse and lands on one of the coiled ropes.

Pimberly turns and runs out the open door, splashing into the rain. His hand moves to the gun tucked in his pants. It's out, and he aims it backward at us.

I've scooped up my gun. I aim it carefully. I have the handkerchief wrapped around my hand, so it makes my grip awkward. I fire. Lightning cracks just as I do.

Pimberly screams, the sound almost swallowed in the massive roll of the thunder. He grabs at his leg and falls in the wet grass. His gun splashes muddily into a puddle ahead of him.

I haven't wasted my time on those trips to the shooting range.

Rachel turns to me with a sharp nod. "See? You'll *do*. And you are *not* boring."

My hand hurts, and I holster my gun. Wade's writhing in the rain, grasping his calf. It starts raining harder.

Giving Rachel a weak smile, I start toward Pimberly. "Come on, let's make sure he doesn't bleed to death or crawl to that gun, and then call the police. We've got a lot to tell them."

I see my "we" register in her eyes. "Yes, we do."

"Don't worry; I can tell the story without bringing your dad into it."

She grabs my hand. "Thanks, Ford. He's going to be unhappy enough once he knows I told you about his con, once he knows it's over."

274

I face her, peering into her blue eyes, bright even in the gloomy boathouse. "Are you going to stay, Rachel?"

It's the question I've feared since I met her. I've dodged it and dodged it.

She nods her head. "I told you I'd stick, Ford."

WE BIND PIMBERLY'S LEG; HE'S NOT IN DANGER ALTHOUGH THE pain's obviously intense.

I phone Barry Ziff and explain things to him briefly, figuring he'll know who else to call. He does. After leaving me holding for a minute, he tells me an ambulance, a state trooper, and a country sheriff's unit is on the way and that he will follow soon too.

We're unable to leave Pimberly's house until deep in the night. By then, I'm sick of questions and explanations, sick of uniforms and titles, and sick of flashing lights, red and blue. The rain's stopped at least, but everything's soaked, and the flashing lights of the ambulance and the other cars are reflected and refracted by all the puddled water.

Ziff threatens to charge me with *something* for not reporting Diamond's body immediately, but he never tells me exactly what the charge will be, and later, he seems to have forgotten all about it.

The ambulance takes Pimberly away, followed by a phalanx of official cars. Eventually, it's only me, Rachel, and Barry Ziff. His car's parked behind Pimberly's yellow Caddy. He's mercifully turned off the flashing lights.

"So, Merrick, I haven't gotten a chance to tell you, but we found the car that hit Talbot."

"Where?"

"At a dump of a body shop near La Grange. The car was brought in by a woman in a tiny skirt, very tanned, in sunglasses. A man in a pickup drove her away after she dropped it off. I'm sure that was Patty Pimberly and that it was Peppers who picked her up. The car, the Chrysler, belonged to a friend of Patty's, some vacant socialite in

La Grange who was driving Patty's car. Evidently, Patty told her some story about needing to borrow the bigger car. It sounds like the friend took Patty to mean she needed a larger backseat..."

"So, Patty hit Talbot?"

"Either her or Peppers. I figure it was him."

I nod. "Now that you say it, I do too. Talbot wasn't chasing the Diamond murder; he was chasing the Pimberly murder. Talbot just didn't know it. Peppers probably did it with Patty's help. He probably told her Talbot was onto their blackmail scheme."

Ziff perks up. "What do you mean: Talbot was chasing the Pimberly murder?"

I sigh. My feet are soaked, and I can't think about anything except being stretched out with Rachel in a warm, dry bed. I don't want to think about anything else, but I need to explain this last thing.

"Patty didn't know about Jane. But Talbot was following up on some thefts at Briggs and Stratton. I believe those thefts were Pimberly's and that the only one that really mattered was the theft of a can of tuna."

"Tuna?" Ziff looks at me like I'm insane, but I see the inference tick over in Rachel's head.

"He practiced on the tuna can with the drill! At Briggs and Stratton," Rachel says softly, "then he stole the other things to conceal that."

"Yes, I'm guessing he got the idea there one night and was eager to start, but on the clock, and so found the tuna can. He took the other things as misdirection and because he wanted them—the clothes and other stuff—although I have a hard time imagining him reading *Harry Potter*."

I look at Ziff, who's still trying to catch up. "Peppers was punching out of his weight class. He's creepy, a creepy petty thief, and a creepy Peeping Tom. He'd have only been creepy and petty, but Wade and Patty—each in his or her own way—convinced him to dream bigger, darker dreams. By the way, Barry, Talbot wasn't paid to investigate the matter at Briggs and Stratton. Strictly amateur stuff, a friend-doing-a-friend-a-favor thing."

Barry shakes his head; he's tired too. "Whatever you say. I've got to go. The sheriff and the state patrol—I still need to sort this all out in terms of jurisdictions. A unit picked up Patty and Peppers at the cabin. The hammer and cat food can are on the way the lab. Still can't believe Pimberly kept them. Makes no damn sense."

"No," I agree, shrugging, "and yet it does. Trophies."

Ziff stares at me, still shaking his head. "Trophies? If you say so, Merrick."

RACHEL DRIVES US BACK TO NOBLE HALL.

On the way, I call Helen and give her the briefest explanation I can. Once Helen's sure that we're both okay, she lets me off the phone. The last thing she says is that she wants us at the house early for breakfast. We agree.

At the hall, Wylie's Mercedes is parked in the back. No lights are on. As far as we know, he has no idea what's happened, and we decide there's no reason to wake him. We tiptoe inside then up the stairs to Rachel's room.

We peel off our wet shoes and socks, our damp clothes. Rachel enters the bathroom; the shower starts. I lie down beneath the sheet and look around her room. The room's furnished with antiques. My guess is that the furniture was Jane Pimberly's, rented with the house. It hadn't occurred to me that Rachel would be living among Jane's things. It's strange to be in that room after what we've done today. I fold back the sheet, stand up, and walk out onto the balcony.

"Ford?" I turn. The shower's stopped; Rachel exits the bathroom. She's in the peach nightie I saw her wearing last night.

She pads to me, untellably lovely. I've never been in love before, never known its full resurrective power. Jane is gone, but Jane loved constantly, truly—if madly, tragically. From this balcony, she pined for David Diamond, sang to him, and wept for him. I open my arms, and Rachel walks into them. I turn, arms around her, and we both look out at a mute resonance of stars, heavenly fireflies.

We don't speak. We stand together, letting go of the day, holding on to each other.

After a while, we go to bed. I want desperately to make love to her, but once we're in bed together, and we're warm and dry and full of stars, all I manage is to hug her close before I drop into a deep and dreamless sleep.

CHAPTER 25: *Con Games*

Our life is an apprenticeship to the truth, that around every circle another can be drawn.

— Ralph Waldo Emerson

I wake up, and the bed is empty. Empty? Well, I'm in it.

At first, the *empty* fact doesn't register with me. I look outside. The sky outside Noble Hall is bottomless blue. The rain cleared off last night, and with it, the cooler temperatures. The balcony doors are open, and I can feel the Alabama heat seducing the bedroom already, even at 7:00 a.m. I throw back the sheet and prop myself up on my elbows.

Rachel's gone. It registers.

All that's left is her peach nightie, soft and creamy, on the end of the bed. And empty.

I stand and run my hand through my hair. I grab my jeans from the floor and put them on, then my T-shirt. I grab my socks and shoes and carry them out to the balcony. Noble Hall's long, manicured front lawn stretches in front of me, shrubberies and center path, Magnolia trees heavy with green leaves, and brown leathery ones scattered beneath them. Dew on the grass makes the green shiny. I can see horses in the distance, galloping in the field across the road.

I don't see Rachel.

One of the heavy, green steel chairs on the balcony, an odd seashell indentation in its back, allows me to sit and put on my socks, my shoes. I'm beginning to feel uneasy. I walk to the edge of the balcony and look straight down. No one's there.

Noble Hall stands silent.

Moving more quickly, I leave the balcony and enter the bathroom. I click on the light. Water's dripping in the shower, and the bathroom still feels damp, warm; the air's lightly scented a clean, floral scent. Rachel's.

I check myself in the mirror. I need a change of clothes and a shower. I wash my face and hands, dry them, run my fingers through my hair, attempting to make it less unruly, and I go down the stairs two at a time.

I expect to see Rachel in the kitchen, or at least Wylie. I still don't know his name. But neither one is there. My pulse ticks up, and then I see the note.

It's from Rachel, and it's on top of a copy of the *Opelika-Auburn News*. Above the fold, I see a headline.

Opelika Police Make Arrests for Two Murders

Ford,

I woke early, nervous about breakfast with Helen. The newspaper story mentions you and me, but it's sketchy on details. I went for a walk to the pond. Join me, please.

Rachel

I leave the newspaper for later.

Outside the house, I walk the road that leads back to the wood path.

Wylie's Mercedes is absent, but her Range Rover is present.

In a few minutes, I step from the dappled, dewy cool of the path into the sunlit warmth of the clearing. The smooth surface of the pond mirrors the sky so perfectly that the pond's shoreline seems to contain blue and clouds, not water.

I see Rachel's reflection in the water before I see her. She seems to walk among the clouds, hugging herself, pensive.

She looks up from the water and spots me. A hint of surprise accompanies her immediate smile, almost as if I am a surprise to her though she asked me to come. We walk to each other.

"Good morning." She seems almost shy.

"Morning, Rachel. It's beautiful out here morning and night, huh?"

She nods. "Yeah, it is." I notice for the first time how much her freckles have darkened. They add to her beauty.

"Are you ready to talk to Helen?"

She nods. "I am. I just needed to steel myself. I so want her to like me, to like me despite…everything."

"Would it be easier for you if we played at a neutral site?"

"What do you mean?"

I look at the water. "We could have her meet us at a coffee shop, say Well Red; I go there a lot. On a Monday morning in the summer, this early, no one will be around. We could sit outside on the rear deck."

Rachel considers that for a minute. "Yes, let's see if she's okay with that. Do you think she's already gone to some trouble, cooked?"

"No, I'm sure she's not up yet. If she is, she surely hasn't started cooking. She needs half a pot of coffee before she lights the stove."

Taking out my phone, I send Helen a text, requesting a change of plans, not surprised when she does not answer immediately. As I pocket my phone, Rachel takes my hand, and we walk out onto the pier, standing over the water and staring down. "So much has happened in so little time, Ford. So many things I hardly dared hope for."

"Yes."

"And you *love* me?"

Suspense sounds in her voice as if she needs to hear me repeat the word again. Maybe it wasn't too soon yesterday when I blurted it out, after all

I make myself face her, gently clear my throat. I don't want there to be any doubt. I take both her hands in mine. *No risk, no faith.* "I love you."

Her smile starts slowly but grows beyond bounds. Her eyes soften; she starts to respond then stops. She can't seem to say the words back to me.

Her smile falters a little, shrinking at the corners and the troubling look in her eyes returns, but now I understand that look. She is unhappy with herself. Turning, she leads me back off the pier.

She pauses as she heads to the path, gazes at me, her eyes apologetic but her tone resolved. "Okay, then I'm ready to face the day, the gauntlet your sister, then my dad. He's still asleep, I assume?"

"I didn't see him, but his car was gone."

She's puzzled. "He's gone? He was in bed when I came down; I checked. He's not an early riser. That's odd."

My phone buzzes and changes the subject. Helen's just woken up. She says she'll meet us in half an hour. I tell Rachel.

She takes a deep breath. "Okay, let's walk back."

Rachel decides she needs to change, and that takes a few minutes.

When she comes out of the hall, she overwhelms me. Her blouse is the blue of the sky, the blue that surrounded her in the mirroring pond. Beneath it, she has on white Capri pants and delicate white and blue interlaced sandals. With her sunny, blonde hair, she's the sky incarnate.

We take Rachel's Range Rover to Well Red. She drives, and her eyes are intent on the road though there's little traffic and the route to the shop is almost a straight line, less than three miles. I can tell

she's readying herself. I know how hard telling me about her past had been for her. Now she's going to tell Helen. And then she has to tell her father she revealed the con.

"What is your dad's name, Rachel?" I hope getting her to start talking may make talking to Helen easier.

"Roger, Roger Sitwell."

"So, you were born *Virginia Sitwell?*"

She nods. "I was. But Rachel Gunner is who I want to be. Dad paid for this legend; it's a good one, clean. It's going to stay that way."

We park behind Well Red. Helen's already sitting on the rear deck. She has three cups of coffee in front of her, and she's studying the newspaper. She puts it down long enough to wave to us as we get out. No one else is on the rear deck.

Helen's dressed casually, shorts and a large T-shirt, tennis shoes. Her hair's back in a ponytail. We sit down, and she gestures at the coffees. "Cinnamon rolls are on the way; they're being warmed."

Helen hands me the paper. "You two are famous, although that article's got less in it than you told me last night. Tell me about it again. How did Rachel end up involved?"

I relate to Helen what happened, starting with Solomon's visit to my office giving me the case. Helen sips her coffee, nodding, as I tell the initial parts of the story. Rachel's listening too; she hasn't heard all this herself. I sip my coffee as I talk. When I get to my nocturnal visit to Noble Hall, I let Rachel take over. She tells Helen about seeing me from the balcony, coming downstairs. About Jane Pimberly and David Diamond. I take over and narrate the exhumation of Diamond. When I get to my trip to Peppers's cabin, I omit certain details. But when I let Rachel take over the story again, she tells about Peppers sneaking into the hall, and at that point, she has to explain that she disarmed him, overpowered him, and forced him to take her to the cabin.

Helen stares at Rachel, a strange fascination on her face, but she asks no question.

Rachel then takes her time describing the scene she discovered at the cabin, lingering on details, careful to describe my snow-white boxers and tube socks, my gun in my hand. At first, Helen is shocked—deeply shocked—mortified, and outraged, and I feel vindicated, less silly. But then she and Rachel glance at each other, and the corners of their mouths twitch up, and I see each of them begin to smile. Soon they are rolling, laughing out loud.

Helen looks at me, breathless and teary-eyed, still laughing. "I know that must have been *awful*, Ford, but it turned out okay, and the thought of you in white and that cheap hussy in red polka dots, with just your gun between the two of you…"

I sit in red-faced silence. It wasn't funny at the time, but I admit I can see the *beginnings* of humor in it although it will never become an anecdote I voluntarily share.

As their laughter dies down, Helen finally asks the question. "How do you know how to do these things, Rachel? I mean, thank God you do; Ford's never been able to take care of himself, particularly around women, but…?"

Rachel inhales and settles her eyes on me. I nod to her and take her hand. "That's a long story, Helen…"

THE COFFEE'S DONE, AND THE CINNAMON ROLLS ARE EATEN BY the time Rachel finishes.

Helen's got her fork in her hand, and for the last few minutes, she's been moving a dollop of left-over icing around on her otherwise empty plate.

She stares at the plate but speaks to Rachel. "So, you and your dad, you knew Ford and I would inherit a lot of money?"

"Yes, we knew. Not the exact amount, but that it would be several million dollars each. We didn't have any designs on *your* money, Helen; the con wasn't going to involve you."

"And so, you were going to woo Ford, make him interested in

Wylie's—in Roger's—imaginary scheme, and take his money."

"In brief, yes."

"But you fell for Ford, and you told him about the con. And he believes you."

Rachel looks like she's hanging by a thread. Her voice is very soft. "Yes."

Helen finally lifts her head. She looks at me, not Rachel. "Do you believe her, Ford? We've both seen con movies, read books. It could be a con within a con. The larger, longer con could be getting you to think she's not conning you so that she *can* con you. She exposes her father to further cover herself, to confuse you…"

Rachel sighs and frowns but does not speak. She looks at me too and waits.

"I realize all that, Helen. There could always be a con within a con, another deception in each revelation, but I'm going to risk it." I hold Helen's eyes with my own. "She's worth whatever I risk. I believe her."

"You love her." Helen gives her verdict slowly.

I nod slowly. "I do."

"HELLO, FOLKS."

We've all three been so engrossed in our conversation that we didn't notice that Uncle Wylie—Roger—has come out of the shop and is standing behind us. I have no idea how long he's been standing there. That's three times in two days someone snuck up on me. I've got to do better.

Roger's got a large cup of coffee in his hand and a slight smile on his face.

Rachel jumps up. "Uncle Wylie!"

He pulls a chair to our table. Although a few patrons have gone by us, gone inside, we are still the only ones seated on the deck. Rachel's dad, Roger, must've gone in the front and found us out here.

I don't know how he found us.

He sits down and grins at Rachel. "Just call me 'Roger,' Rachel—everyone, call me 'Roger.' The jig's up."

Rachel stares at her dad. She suddenly looks small, young—someone's daughter. "Dad, I'm sorry...I couldn't do it. I just couldn't."

Roger's face hardens; his slight smile vanishes. "Why's that, *little girl?*"

Rachel blinks and winces at Roger's interrogator tone. "Because he's not—Ford's not—who you told me he was. He's a good man, the best I've ever known."

Roger leans toward his daughter. "But that's not *why*, is it, little girl?"

"Don't call me that, Dad." Her blue eyes flash. "Ford doesn't deserve what you had planned. You don't need what he has. You need to *stop*."

Roger's face becomes intense; he leans further forward. "But, *why*, little girl?"

"Because I love him!" Rachel balls her fists and glares at her dad. Then she looks at me; her eyes go wide. I smile; I can't possibly help it. I've never smiled with my whole body and soul before.

"I love you, Ford." She says the words to no one as if they were mere sounds, but then she repeats them meaningfully and says them to me. "I love you, Ford."

I take Rachel's hand in mine as Roger leans back. He sips his coffee then begins to laugh, his laugh growing in volume and in the amount of his body it involves. Soon, he is rolling as Rachel and Helen were rolling earlier.

The three of us look at each other, lost.

He winks at his daughter. "Con within a con, little girl. Don't you know, I knew who Ford was all along? I knew he was a good man. Don't forget that my only real talent is people, understanding them, reading between their lines, and I understood him the first time I saw him. He's all Boy Scout, all good guy. White hat."

He stops laughing and gives Rachel a serious, searching look. "And I can read *you*. Always could. I know what you want, have always wanted, and I know it's not conning, despite all my attempts to get you to want it. You're your mom's little girl. And I've always known the kind of man you could love.

"But you've loved me too much, and you've never been given a strong enough motive before, a motive to quit once and for all, quit for good. Quit me. It was never the *life* you couldn't quit; it was *me*. That made me a lucky man, but it was unlucky for you. Look, you'd have never come here, have never given Ford a chance if you thought *I thought* he was the man for you. So, I conned you from the beginning. I was never conning Ford, never going to con Ford. I just pretended to do what you expected so you'd think I was.

"I told you about him and told you all wrong because it was a *backward* con, little girl. I let you discover for yourself who and what Ford is, and you were so pleased by him you never suspected I wanted you to discover him."

Rachel's mouth has dropped open.

Helen's head is swiveling from Rachel to Roger to me and back to Rachel.

Rachel turns red. She jumps up from her chair and runs off the deck and down the ramp to the parking lot. I start to go after her, but Roger grabs my hand and shakes his head when I look at him.

Rachel stops running and just stands, her back to us, in the parking lot. Roger lets go of me and sips his coffee, his eyes on his daughter. I sit down, watching Rachel.

Rachel turns around slowly. "So, all this was about conning me, not Ford?"

"I wanted to deceive you into the truth, into the truth of what you've always wanted, little girl. The life you've secretly dreamed of." His use of "little girl" is sweet now, not challenging. "I'm tired of the con life too." He grins in self-congratulation. "And I believe Sherry Louden likes me. I like it here."

"But *Lake*, you brought him here? I worried you brought him here."

Roger shakes his head. "A good con knows how to turn any situation to his advantage. When Lake just showed up, I used him to motivate you two. He worried each of you about the other. All to the good. Although I admit, I thought he'd screwed everything up when he visited Ford.

"When he returned, he confessed to me his jealousy got in the way of my con. But he didn't know the direction of my con, and I couldn't risk him making things even worse, so I ran him off, sent the clotheshorse packing. I know things about him that he does not want anyone to know, including his current employer. I was so angry I went to the club and got drunk. But then I came home and found he hadn't ruined my con. You two were in the kitchen together and I decided that maybe Lake even helped it without his knowing it, without intending to do it."

Rachel folds her arms and tilts her head. She glares at her dad.

"You can be a real bastard. Making your own daughter your mark."

He laughs again. "Don't I know it?"

Rachel walks back up the ramp, assessing me carefully. I shake my head and reach for her hand. Giving it to me, she sits in my lap then kisses me hard and hugs me.

When she sits back, she laughs a little. "I guess there are some *kind* cons, Ford." She hugs me again and whispers the words into my ear, just for me, trembling as she does. "I love you."

I hug her to me as Roger laughs and Helen joins in.

It occurs to me, as I l hold the only woman I've ever loved, that the problem with my new Burney Lennox novel isn't that Burney needs a brush with a femme fatale, but rather that Burney needs a *partner*.

CHAPTER 26: *Intercession*

Four months later

I'm sitting quietly in St. Dunstan's. It's a Tuesday. Choir practice is tonight, our busy season. Decorations are up in preparation for the Nativity.

But I've stopped by to talk to Father Halsey this morning.

We've not had a chance to have a serious heart-to-heart lately. I've been busy, and so has he. He's been dating Olive Norton and watching a lot of *Andy* Griffith, all to the delight of their friends. It seems both so improbable and so fated. Add to that the fun of tormenting Talbot about having a *Father* father, and…well…it's been a hoot. Except maybe for Talbot, who, although he got onto better terms with Father Halsey during their fender-bending driving lessons, remains mostly terrified of him. "It's that collar," Talbot keeps telling me. "All white and holy. It weirds me out." But his mom's happy, and that's enough to make Talbot deal with the collar. And yes, Talbot now has a driver's license. God help us all.

Talbot's still dating Kip. She graduated and got hired as an assistant manager at the fancy Dixon Hotel and Conference Center just across from campus, but she still also volunteers at the Humane Society.

Talbot volunteers too, but ever since the details about Jane Pimberly became news, he's been finicky about cats. He only mixes with the dogs.

Despite his raise, Talbot quit working for me. Big Jim Sutton hired him to handle security at Briggs and Stratton, created the position for Talbot, even paid for Talbot to take a security guard training course. It all seems like overkill—the position and the training—since Talbot doesn't do much more than wear an unloaded gun, walk by the lockers now and then and walk the grounds. Mostly, he drinks coffee with the factory workers during their coffee breaks, helps Rhoda with the phones, and shows guests around. But he likes it; Big Jim pays him handsomely. Talbot bought himself a car, oddly enough a used Chrysler 300 (no, not *that* one). As he said, "If you can't beat 'em, buy 'em." Talbot's still a master of words as you can tell.

Kip has helped him in that regard, though. He now resorts less often to mere vocables. Except, Kip says, at certain moments between them. But telling you that will embarrass Talbot, and of course, that's why Kip delights in telling Rachel and me in front of him.

Talbot's changed enough that Helen now speaks to him. He even invited me over to watch him burn *The Bikini Diaries* on the backyard grill.

I still see Ruth regularly at Ed's. Rachel's almost always with me on those visits. Even though Ruth's dating Barry Ziff, and even though it seems to be growing serious, Rachel has never fully trusted Ruth around me. Ruth seems happy to me, though, and I know Barry is.

Lately, Ruth has been talking about going back to school and getting a teaching degree. I've encouraged her to do it. Good teachers are so important and so hard to find.

I don't see Certaine regularly, not at Ed's or anywhere else. He was working for Wade Pimberly, and for a time, he was listed as a person of interest in Jane Pimberly's murder. He wasn't involved it turns out. Wade had hired him to lean on me the one time, but that was all. Still, Certaine's name made it into the papers, and he's not been big on public appearances since. He's still working, still the competition, but at least I don't have to endure him or his entourage at Ed's anymore. Although, to tell the truth, the one time the entourage was there, Rachel was too, and when they started on me—even without Certaine there—Rachel gave them the same glare she gave Michelle's boys, and they shut up immediately. Michelle and Will and their boys are all fine. Rachel and I have babysat for them a couple of times in trades for favors from Michelle.

And besides, Rachel likes the boys. She calls it practice. I think I know what that means.

I should say that the reason Rachel is at Ed's with me is not primarily Ruth. It's that we work together. I asked her to be my partner at the agency, and she accepted. We renamed the agency; we're now Deep South Investigators. I bought the building from Miller. He moved his practice closer to the courthouse. He never told me who asked him to hire me.

Rachel sailed through the test to become an Alabama PI, and her Rachel Gunner legend held up—no worries about moral turpitude. We redid the offices so that there's now a small foyer and two adjoining larger offices: one for Rachel and one for me. Olive Norton works mornings for us as our receptionist and keeps us and our paperwork straight. She runs her dress shop now only in the afternoons.

Working with Rachel is great. It helps that we became a team before we formally became a team. We just fit together professionally; there's a natural division of professional labor. I like to say that I'm the brains and she's the brawn, but she always makes me pay for that, and the truth is that I suspect she's both the brains and the brawn and that I'm just along for the ride.

But I'll take it. I love her more than words can say.

We fit together personally too, and in all the best ways. In fact, that's a big reason I'm here, waiting to talk to Father Halsey. I have a ring in my pocket, and I need to talk to my friend about it.

I talked to Helen about it last night. She's all for it, all excited. I'm under strict orders to take Rachel to Helen's house later.

Oh, one other big change is that I moved out and bought a house of my own although it's just a couple of blocks from Helen. Rachel helped me pick it out. She loves the yard. I guess we both know what it meant when I asked her to help me house-shop and I bought the house she loved. Don't misunderstand; I love it too. It's an old Craftsman-style house with a great front porch and back porch, a deep, fenced-in yard overhung by a massive and beautiful silver maple tree. I've been in it for a couple of months, and Rachel's been helping me decorate it. Kip and Helen, now both close to Rachel, have helped too. The truth is that all I do is carry things and push things. As Rachel says: at home, I'm the brawn, and she's the brains. I love that she says "at home."

Rachel and Roger are still at Noble Hall although they'll be moving soon. Roger bought a newly built house in one of Auburn's upscale neighborhoods, and it'll be ready for them in a week or so. As far as Rachel and I can tell, Roger really has given up conning. He's been dating Sherry Louden, and he even told her about himself, his past. She knows his name is not really Wylie Stroud, although he's kept that name, and Rachel continues publicly as his niece, not his daughter. Sherry doesn't seem fazed by any of it. The two of them have a great time together. (At the moment, they're vacationing at her Florida home.) Roger keeps threatening to make me a member of the Lee County Country Club, but I've told him that I'm happy just as a visitor.

Helen gave away most of her money to charities, but she did make some improvements at her office, and she did take on a nurse practitioner. Helen's practice keeps growing. She's a terrific doctor. But Sam manages to get her to work a little less.

Together, we started a charity in our mom and dad's name to assist orphaned children. I talked Rachel into letting me use a chunk of my money to repay people she'd conned, the ones who weighed most on her mind. We found ways to get money anonymously to most of them. It quieted Rachel's mind and drew us closer. She complained about shifting debts from her victims to me, but I explained that I am her *voluntary* victim and that I regard her debts as mine. I think she knows what I meant. What I mean. What I'm planning.

I'm going to ask after choir practice.

I HEAR FOOTSTEPS AND LOOK UP. I'D BEEN STARING AT THE SHINING wooden floor as I thought. I look up, expecting to see Father Halsey, but it's Diana Wentworth.

"Hi, Ford," she says quietly, "I didn't know you were a praying man."

I missed her when I came in. She must've stepped out of the office. I grin but shake my head. "I'm not."

She lifts an eyebrow. "I don't know, meditating here, head down—do you have to intend to pray in order to pray?"

I don't know the answer to that. And I suppose, given what I'm planning, that I am in a prayerful mood, an asking mood.

She sits down in the pew in front of mine. "Say, Ford, any word about the new Burney Lennox novel?"

I nod. I've finished it, and it's with the publisher. "Yeah, the word is that it's going to be published in the spring."

"What'd you call it?"

"*Do I Not Bleed?*" I answer before I consider the question. I stop and look at her. "I mean, that's what I've heard the title is."

She smiles at me. "C'mon, Ford, I've known all along you write those books. No one could talk to you about them as I have and not know. Besides, you talk like a writer."

I stare at her. "You knew?"

She shrugs. "Yes." She narrows her eyes. "So, is Burney taking on a partner too?"

"Yes, he is."

"A beautiful blonde?"

"Yes."

"Art imitating life?"

I shrug. "I suppose. I hope."

She shifts in the pew, taking my meaning. "Tonight?"

"After practice."

"Good luck. You're both lucky, Ford."

"Thanks, Diana."

She stares at me for a moment. "Thanks to you, Ford, since we're trading secrets."

"Thanks for *what*?"

"For Jane Pimberly. For unearthing her true story, putting her to rest."

"It was you? You're the one who went to Miller?"

She looks around to see if anyone's listening then turns back to me. "Yes. She was the only one of the club girls who was ever nice to me when I was younger. And I never liked that boy of hers; there was always something wrong with him." She pauses. "I just had a hunch, like Burney or the other detectives in the books."

"But why not just ask me yourself?"

"Those young girls in the club set didn't like Jane being nice to me. They started some...rumors. They weren't true, and they died out, but those young girls are now *old* girls, and I worried that if I started making inquiries about Jane's death, they'd resurrect the old stories, reanimate them. One of the dangers of never marrying is that folks think there must be some story, one you're ashamed of, and they won't accept that the true story is that I never met the right man."

"I'm sorry you didn't, Diana."

She shakes her head. "You came along twenty years too late, Ford." She gives me a teasing grin. "But I don't begrudge you Rachel. I like her a lot." She winks at me. "I have it on good authority that she's going to say, 'Yes.' Have faith!"

Father Halsey walks up just as Diana finishes. "Hey, kid, what's up?"

Diana gets up and excuses herself. I watch her as she hurries away. She is an amazing woman; my life is blessed with amazing women.

Father Halsey sits down in Diana's spot, and the pew complains of the change. "Talking about Rachel?" One other good thing that's happened in the past few months is that he's gotten to know Rachel and Rachel to know him.

"Yes, among other things. Diana's something, you know it?"

Father Halsey nods. "I live in fear and trembling, Ford, fear and trembling… So, you wanted to see me?" I texted him last night.

"Yeah, I…um…You see…"

He grins. "Do you have the ring on you?"

My jaw drops. "How does everyone know what I'm doing?"

"You're an open book—for a detective."

I shake my head, but then I give Father Halsey a serious look. "What do you think, Father? Is it too early?"

"You love her; she loves you. Sounds like the perfect time to me."

"But you had serious doubts about her…" I'm not sure why I bring this up, but I do.

He nods. "I did. But there is something I never told you. I guess I can tell you now, given your plans. That day Talbot got hit, Wylie Stroud came to see me. Swearing me to secrecy, he told me what his plan was, explaining all about Rachel, her childhood, adulthood, what they had done, and her attempts to quit that life. He also told me what a wonder she was and that the two of you were perfect for each other. He asked me to help him along.

"I had mixed reactions to that request, to say the least. Priests don't normally get involved in cons. But what I told you later was true. I watched her that night at the hospital, and what I saw, I believed. I saw that she had feelings for you. So, when I told you that, I wasn't telling you to help the con, per se, but I was telling you the truth. And Roger…er…Wylie's right: you two are perfect for each other. If you're here looking for my blessing, Ford, you certainly have it. Personally and vocationally."

I'm leaning forward, head down and listening. He reaches to me and puts his large hand on my shoulder and squeezes it. He says a few words under his breath, his eyes closed. I can't make them out, but I know what he's doing.

I guess I've just prayed, and I'm sure I've been prayed for.

The ring feels warm and comfortable in my pocket. I'm eager for tonight.

I say goodbye to Father Halsey, zip my jacket, leave St. Dunstan's, and drive to the office. Rachel's Range Rover sits in the parking lot. It looks happy and homey there like it belongs.

I open the door. Rachel's coming out of her office, file in hand. Olive's laughing on the phone.

Rachel smiles at me, her holiday smile. Outside, I hear bells on trees. And I know that today will be a holiday.

The End

About THE AUTHOR

Photo by Wayne Bartsch

Kelly Dean Jolley is the Goodwin Philpott Endowed Chair in Religion and Professor of Philosophy at Auburn University. He lives in Auburn with his wife, Shanna, two dogs, too many typewriters, and looming stacks of books.

Made in the USA
Columbia, SC
25 September 2022

67905964R00178